'~ his fortune through *not*
~dike Rush of '98.
~ poured out

THE BODLEY HEAD

# JACK LONDON

VOLUME FOUR

# THE BODLEY HEAD

# JACK LONDON

## VOLUME IV

EDITED AND INTRODUCED BY
ARTHUR CALDER-MARSHALL

THE KLONDIKE DREAM

## THE BODLEY HEAD
LONDON · SYDNEY
TORONTO

Introduction © Arthur Calder-Marshall 1966
Printed and bound in Great Britain for
THE BODLEY HEAD LTD
9 Bow Street, London WC2
by William Clowes & Sons Ltd, Beccles
Set in Linotype Plantin
*First published in this edition 1966*

# CONTENTS

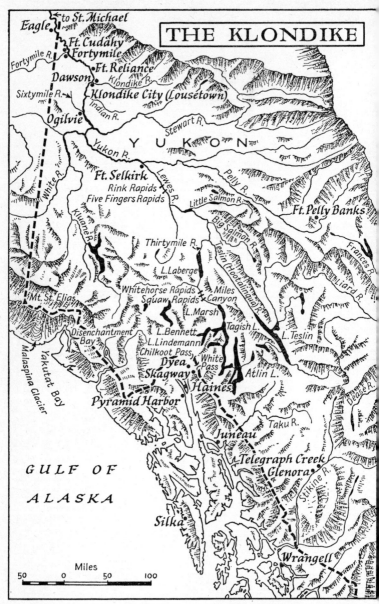

Redrawn by M. A. Verity from a map in *Klondike* by Pierre Berton.

# INTRODUCTION

THE FIRST volume of The Bodley Head Jack London was a
venture. What would be the response to the re-publication
of this author, vastly popular in his lifetime and consequently critically discounted even then, whose name though
still widely known is often confused with that of a con-
temporary prize-fighter? In secondhand bookshops even the
shoddily-bound and evilly-printed cheap editions of his
books were hard to come by. But would a new generation
respond to him? And if so to which of the many Jack
Londons: the sailor, the socialist, the tramp, the marine
burglar, the robber turned cop, the sealer, the gold-prospec-
tor, the wonder-boy, the circumnavigator, the blackbirder,
the alcoholic, the agrarian reformer, the champion of the
underdog, or the founder of a dynasty, meant to last a
thousand years, but which died with him?

That first volume illustrated many sides of that prodigally
gifted man. They would have been distributed more
methodically if the extent of the demand could have been
foreseen. Volume Four is concerned entirely with Jack London's vision of North-west America, the territory which he
first encountered during the Klondike Gold Rush in 1898
and he last saw as he sailed on the current down the Yukon
in the spring of the next year, crippled with scurvy. This
brief visit provided literary material which made his name
at the outset of his writing career and to which he continually returned.

Already printed in Volume One are many pieces which
are essential to the London vision of the North-west; *The
Call of the Wild*, which in the United States alone has sold
over 2,000,000 copies since he sold its copyright outright
for 2,000 dollars; and the short stories, *The White Silence*,
*The League of the Old Men*, and *To Build a Fire*.

7

In a way I am glad that these have already appeared, because even so I am embarrassed by the richness of what remains. I am glad also that this volume appears at the same time as Professor Franklin Walker's admirable study, *Jack London and the Klondike*, also under the Bodley Head imprint. Professor Walker with the assistance of the papers in the Huntingdon Library, San Marino, has traced more accurately than anyone previously what Jack London actually experienced in the North-west during the latter half of 1898 and the first half of 1899 and the use which he made of experience gained at first, second and later hand.

In compiling this volume, I have had the advantage of having read *Jack London and the Klondike* and I must acknowledge my indebtedness to Professor Walker, whose research I have at times plundered. But I have tried to do more than provide in full the principal stories from which Professor Walker quotes to illustrate his thesis. The stories, novels and articles which London wrote about the Yukon and Alaska from the time of his return up till his death in 1916, viewed biographically, seem like branches growing from the tree of his life. They sprouted haphazardly, stories about the Klondike and earlier Gold Rushes, stories about fur-traders in pre-Gold-Rush times, about Indians, Eskimos, Russians from the days before the United States acquired Alaska; stories about the unsullied tribe, about miscegenation, about the survival of the White Man as the fittest; about missionaries, traders, gamblers, belly-dancers, policemen, crooks, drunks, misfits and respectable women. There was no order about the writing of these stories; nor when London gathered them up for publication was there any care about their presentation. Reading his collections, one feels that he merely selected enough to make a book and sent them off to his publishers.

Yet gathering these stories of a lifetime together, I felt rather as if I held in my hand a pack of cards that could be unshuffled and rearranged to make a whole more significant than the sum of its parts. This I have tried to do.

It has not been easy. Their historical dating is often

vague. Sometimes their chronologies overlap. I have started
with Jack London's essay, *The Gold Hunters of the North*,
his completest summary of the history of the region. It contains the seeds of several of the later stories. They may have
appeared at the time of publication as tales of the Yukon or
Alaska, but they are more really historical fiction, em-
bellished by London's own experience. The reader will
notice the transition from fact to fiction. At the end of the
essay, for example, we read how Charley Anderson was sold
No. 29, Eldorado, for seven hundred and fifty dollars when
he was drunk. When forced to work it he earned over three-
quarters of a million dollars. The essay was written in 1902.
In *Too Much Gold*, published in *The Faith of Men* (1904),
not Charley Anderson, but Ans Handerson, in similar
circumstances buys No. 24, Eldorado, and makes half a
million.

I have arranged the stories themselves as nearly as possible
in historical sequence to show how the development of the
North-west appeared in Jack London's work. But of course
London was not, and did not pretend to be, a historian. He
was a saga writer to a nation of emotional frontiersmen, who
had reached the Pacific Ocean, only to find unemployment
as acute there as further east. The Alaskan Gold Rush
altered the cry 'Go West, young man!' to 'Go North-west';
London went and returned empty-handed. But he had
found in the land of the midnight sun the magic pot of gold
supposed to lie at the rainbow's end which had vanished
beyond the Pacific horizon when the frontiersmen reached
the Californian coast.

This dream of the frontiersmen was something more
varied than the fortunes in Bonanza and Eldorado. Of
course the lure of great riches won in a few weeks or months
was immensely attractive to everybody, not merely to the
men who staked everything in the hoping of finding it but
also to those who stayed behind to read about it, from the
hobo to the well-heeled businessman. Few people are without gambling fantasies. But the realities of gambling are
sordid and heart-breaking; and when the gamble involves

hard work, great hardship and the risk of limb and even life, most people prefer fantasy.

The popularity of the Norse and Icelandic sagas in the latter half of the nineteenth century owed much to discontentment with the dullness of urban life. The heroic values of Grettir the Strong seemed to have vanished from the earth until Jack London re-discovered them in the Yukon and Alaska. The age of heroes was not dead, but they had emigrated to the frozen north.

Jack London was influenced in his early stories by Kipling. The tiresome literary lucubrations which introduced such stories as *The Son of the Wolf* were deliberate imitations of Kipling which London later discarded when he found his own style of story-telling. The belief in the superiority of Anglo-Saxon man over lesser breeds without the law (together with an attraction towards and sympathy with those lesser breeds) he also shared with Kipling, but he never discarded it. Anglo-Saxon superiority he had accepted from his mother, who blamed dirty foreigners for what was in fact the consequence of her own improvidence.

Though Jack London considered himself to be a Marxist socialist, there is no evidence of this in his Klondike stories. The evolutionary principles enunciated by Charles Darwin in *The Origin of Species* and Thomas Huxley in his principle of The Survival of the Fittest had been taken over by Herbert Spencer to explain the evolution of human societies. Like many other self-taught writers of his time (such as Havelock Ellis and Olive Schreiner), Jack London accepted the analogy with little question. It provided him with the 'philosophy' he needed as a framework for his Klondike stories.

Why did he need a 'philosophy'?

Being very young and intellectually insecure, he needed a framework within which to work. Comparatively little of what he wrote about the North-west was based on first hand experience. Much more stemmed from anecdotes, heard in the Klondike, read later in books and newspapers or related to him in California. More again was dreamed up from casual contacts and observations made during his trip down the Yukon through Alaska, when he was sick with scurvy.*

Furthermore this 'philosophy' of Anglo-Saxon superiority and the survival of the fittest provided a common language between Jack London and his magazine public. Kipling and Spencer did not so much vulgarize, as eke out and sustain, his first-hand observation. He created an image of the Klondike rather in the way that R. D. Blackmore created the Doone Valley with *Lorna Doone*. *Lorna Doone* was a work largely of fiction which has established itself as historical fact. London's Klondike is a curious brew of fact and fiction.

I have referred above to the way in which Charley Anderson of No. 29, Eldorado, became Ans Handerson of No. 24, Eldorado. On his trip down the Yukon, London met a Jesuit priest in Alaska called Father Roubeau, who impressed him with his personality, wisdom and saintliness. In the stories printed in *The Son of the Wolf*, his first collection, Father Roubeau appears as a priest operating hundreds of miles up the river in the Canadian Yukon. To a British writer, dogged by fears of libel, this is fantastic. To give a real person's name in the description of a real incident is perilous enough. To introduce a real person's name into the description of an incident with which he had no connection is asking for trouble.

Yet London did this over and over again. In Dawson City, Jack London was befriended by a fat belly-dancer called Freda Moloof, whose act was too raw even for that tough city. She was run out and some years later Jack London met her in San Francisco. He presented her with an inscribed copy of his second collection of short stories, *The God of his Fathers*, wherein she featured in *The Scorn of Women* as a scandalous woman, with a heart of gold. Though she ap-

---

* An indication of how inaccurate he was is his reference to the 'Innuit' as a race distinct from the Eskimo, whereas 'Innuet', meaning people as opposed to animals, was the name the Eskimos gave themselves when they thought they were the only people on earth. A. C-M.

peared a figure of paste-board, like her respectable counter-part Mrs Eglington, Freda thought it was very nice.

I don't think that Jack London intentionally created a bogus Klondike in which his fictions took over from reality. He was a romantic. As a good clean writer of fiction he banished prostitution. Before Hollywood was thought of, he Hollywoodized fat Freda. He used her name, in gratitude perhaps for the solace of her bed, but also because he wanted to keep in mind the person of whom he was writing.

This happened over and over again—and not merely when he was writing about the Far North-west. A name was the stake which held fast the string on which he let up his imaginative balloons.

But it produced a very odd situation, especially as he became not just a famous, but a mythical, figure in his life-time. The real people, whose names he borrowed to authenticate his stories, borrowed his stories as part of their achievements. The actual Gold Rushes did not, when they occurred, seem to be like the Gold Rushes which Jack London described. They were less heroic and less colourful; as perhaps in earlier times the siege of Troy had been to its weary combatants. It needed Homer later to recognize the beauty of Helen and the valiance of Hector and Achilles. If they had lived to hear blind Homer sing, they might have been puzzled briefly before they came to accept that this indeed was how it had been throughout those ten protracted dreary years.

Jack London was a Homer of the Gold Rush who im-posed his romantic vision upon the participants themselves, sourdough and *chechaquo* alike. London perceived heroic qualities of which they had not been conscious at the time. If he wasn't right, it was at least heartening to believe that he was.

For every one who was in Dawson City that winter of 1898–9, there were hundreds who came later. When asked by friends and relatives outside, 'Did you meet Jack Lon-don?', they found it hard to say 'No'. (It would have been like going to Egypt and not seeing the Pyramids.) In consequence there were hundreds, if not thousands, of fantasists, claiming to have drunk with London in Dawson City saloons or to have met him for a yarn on Upper Island or encountered him on trail, who could vouch for the veracity of even the most far-fetched of London's stories.

Jack London's vision of the North-west Territories is rather like Robert J. Flaherty's vision of Eskimo life in the North-east territories revealed twenty years later in his classic film *Nanook of the North** (though Flaherty shifted interest from the almighty White man to the all-enduring Eskimo). The importance of both is less historical than imaginative, less in its truth to fact than in its appeal to the fancies of the public.

The primary purpose of this selection of London's stories about the Far North is to present as wide a range of subject as possible; and for that reason I have included a few stories which I would have rejected if my criteria had been purely literary. *The Scorn of Women* (which Jack London himself liked so much that he turned it into a play, which to his regret was never performed), preposterous though it is, gives an insight into his attempt to portray the conflict between respectability and disreputability in Dawson City within two years of its foundation.

The secondary purpose is to present London's best literary stories. I have deliberately not quoted from *A Daughter of the Snows* and from *Burning Daylight*. The first of these contains some fine descriptions, especially of the journey from Dyea to Dawson City. But it is vitiated as a novel by the heroine Frona Welse, the fantastic embodiment of London's dream of the New Woman. This same journey is described as well and more briefly in the two stories *The One Thousand Dozen* and *Like Argus of the Ancient Times*.

When London himself made the journey from Dyea over the Chilcot pass, he and his partners Sloper, Goodman and Thompson took on an old fellow from Santa Rosa named Tarwater who worked for them in return for food and pas-

---

* See *The Innocent Eye, the Life of Robert J. Flaherty*, Arthur Calder-Marshall, W. H. Allen, Ltd.

sage. The main character of *Like Argus of the Ancient Times* retains the name of Tarwater, Sloper becomes Anson, Goodman Big Bill Wilson, Thompson Charles Crayton, while London becomes Liverpool. The first half of the story, based on London's own experience, is a splendid example of London as what Professor Walker calls 'interpreter of things which are'. The second half betrays London's weakness when forced to fall back on invention.

The same weakness appears in the novel *Burning Daylight*. The part which is laid in the Klondike is fresh and compelling but when the action shifts one-third of the way through to the United States it becomes far-fetched.

Jack London was a shrewd judge of his limitations. His strength lay not in plot but in situation. If one takes a long story like *An Odyssey of the North* (which he had to cut to half its length before the Atlantic Monthly would accept it), the story can be summarized briefly. A man buys at a great price a bride who is taken from him by a white man. For years he pursues them to recapture her, but when he kills the man, his bride rejects him. All London's inventive power goes into the elaboration of details of the pursuit, none into the elaboration of the relations between the three people. His stories with complexities of plot tend to get out of hand, or else degenerate into anecdotes. He was happiest with a single person as in *To Build a Fire* (Vol. 1) or *The Love of Life*.

Professor Walker has an extremely interesting account of the origin and development of *The Love of Life* from an article *Lost in the Land of The Midnight Sun*, written by two journalists about the experience of a Canadian mining engineer, who sprained his ankle and wandered eight days before walking into an Indian encampment. London in his story eliminates the man's companion on the first page and then elaborates the situation by playing on a wide variety of food situations suggested by the original article. It is only when the man is rescued and faced with his fellow creatures that London's imagination fails. The situation cannot be sustained except by overstatement.

Professor Walker seems to me right in suggesting that the basic idea of *In a Far Country* was derived from Joseph Conrad's story *An Outpost of Progress* in *Tales of Unrest*. In translating the situation from an isolated post in the Congo to a lonely cabin between the Mackenzie and Yukon rivers Jack London gained the degree of imaginative liberty which he needed in order to inject his own experience (the mounting irritation of being cooped up in a log-cabin with Merritt Sloper) and make *In a Far Country* something quite different from Conrad's story.

But I do not agree with Professor Walker's verdict on *The Unexpected*. This story was published in August, 1906 in *McClure's Magazine*, with the footnote: 'Mr London's story is a real human document, based upon actual incidents. Michael Dennin was hanged at Latuya Bay by Mrs Nelson in 1900.' London read and clipped the story, which appeared in the Sunday section of the *San Francisco Examiner*, Oct. 14, 1900. The correspondent stated that Mrs Edith Nelson and her husband, Hans, had executed Michael Dennin by hanging for killing two other members of their party of five which had set out to seek gold in the Latuya Bay region. One morning, Dennin arrived late to breakfast with a shotgun in his hands, fatally wounded his two bunk-mates and would have succeeded in reloading and killing the Nelsons if Mrs Nelson had not sprung at his throat in the nick of time. Disarmed and tied up by the Nelsons, Dennin confessed that he intended to kill the whole of the party to secure the gold, which it had been agreed should be split five ways. His confession was written down and witnessed by the local Siwash Indians. The Nelsons hoisted a distress signal, but not being relieved by a passing boat, and being unable to bear more than ten days of standing guard night and day, they hanged him publicly before the Indians. Months later, returning to Skagway, they laid the matter before a United States court and were exonerated, Mrs Nelson being commended for bravery.

At this point I would like the reader to turn to *The Unexpected* and read the story for himself.

In Professor Walker's view London 'developed each of the characters in such a way as to make the action more plausible and fitting; he changed the season to midwinter so that he could accentuate the loneliness and strangeness of the environment and the helplessness of the Nelsons in getting outside aid; and he supplied the story with a generalizing theme ...' Professor Walker concludes: '*The Unexpected* is a competent metamorphosis of a real event. The trouble with the story, however, is that it once more illustrates the adage that truth is stranger, and less plausible, than fiction. The actual event remains quite incredible, even if it really took place, and the story based on it suffers in consequence.'

To me the news story is credible and most provoking to the imagination. But London's development is neither more plausible nor more fitting; and the generalizing theme distorts rather than promotes the drama. London has seized on one significant detail; that it was Edith Nelson, not Hans, who gripped Dennin by the throat. The heavy theorizing about Edith's conventional servant girl background and the racial nonsense about Hans's Teutonic Swedish slowness is unnecessary; though London is right to make Hans's slow reaction more lethal. But London's change of season and his lengthening of the wait before the execution betray the narrowness of his situation-sense. If he had only visualized the situation, what enormous possibilities the ten days of the news story could have held, even if he threw away a trump-card, such as that the Indians, having seen the gun in the hands of Hans, don't really know what has happened! London makes Dennin conveniently unconscious for hours while the Nelsons bury the dead. How much better, if he hadn't been! If he was trying to get free! And who fed him? And what happened when he wanted to go to the lavatory? And if he was Irish, hadn't he anything better to say than that story about his old mum? Couldn't he have tried to set the husband and wife against each other? Couldn't he, when one was sleeping and the other out seeing to the distress signal, have tried to bribe one of the Indians to set him free?

The mere physical difficulties of watching a man for ten days all round the clock bristle with plot-opportunities immediately the characters become people acting and reacting to one another. The original news-story could have been the basis for a magnificent short story, or for that matter novel, convincing at every stage of its inevitable progress. *The Unexpected* fails because Jack London had neither the intellectual nor the imaginative equipment to develop and explore the basic idea. By laying it in the winter, he was able to exploit, as he did on several other occasions, the physical difficulties of burying the dead in frozen ground. But in this story the dead are of secondary importance. The dramatic threat is the living murderer, who will murder again given the chance. By protracting the watching period, but never particularizing, London diminished his drama and his plausibility. The one touch that strikes true is Edith's laughter as the body dangles.

Jack London is popularly regarded as an 'action-writer'. But paradoxically he is at his best in describing inaction, especially the decline into death, the physical states of nature or of the human body, which cause the cessation of life and action. He was always much in love with death, like Hemingway, who also hunted the world wide to find the nobility of the frontier. Perhaps Professor Walker is right to suggest that, as a short story-writer, London was really an essayist, magnificent in his description of the rivers setting in autumn and in spring breaking into splendid chaos. But it is to me an astonishing phenomenon that Jack London had, and still has, such a grip, not merely in the United States, and English-speaking countries, but in translation throughout the world, especially with his Klondike stories.

The world has greatly changed since 1899, when Jack London landed at Dyea. The prospects of human nature being changed by revolution are less rosy to us than they were to him. The morality of Jack London's characters may have shocked his contemporaries; but after the atrocities of two world wars, we are inured. Our views of races, people and writing are infinitely more subtle and sophisticated. So what is the appeal of Jack London's vision of the North-west?

I suspect that it is the same old hankering after heroism. Rather than running for the bus to get to work on time, how much better to be racing behind a dog-sled to stake a claim or skimming across Lake Lindemann to avoid the freeze-up. Instead of wondering as we pull on a cigarette whether we will develop cancer of the lung, why not imagine what it would be like to be blown up with scurvy in 60 below? Why worry how to meet the instalment on the telly or the washing-machine, when we might strike Bonanza? And how re-assuring to read how likely it would be, if we did, that we would fall through the ice and freeze to death in a blizzard, the muskeg berries sticking to our lips! With Jack London, we can have it all ways. All-conquering Anglo-Saxons, we can carry off the beautiful daughter of the native chieftain and yet never have to smell the reek of blubber. We can die a thousand deaths and be ready for the next stampede to Squaw Creek or Eldorado. How palatable a battery broiler seems as we read of moccasin soup! And as the rime creeps up the cabin door, how snug it is to crouch over the gas-fire! Faced with atomic extinction at any moment in the future and the effort to keep up with the affluent society at every moment in the present, we turn nostalgically to the simple heroism of The Malemute Kid, Sitka Charley, even of the elegant Mrs Eglington and fat Freda Moloof.

A. CALDER-MARSHALL

# THE GOLD HUNTERS OF THE NORTH

'Where the Northern Lights come down o' nights to dance
on the houseless snow.'

'IVAN, I forbid you to go farther in this undertaking. Not
a word about this, or we are all undone. Let the Americans
and the English know that we have gold in these mountains, then we are ruined. They will rush in on us by
thousands, and crowd us to the wall—to the death.'

So spoke the old Russian governor, Baranov, at Sitka,
in 1804, to one of his Slavonian hunters, who had just
drawn from his pocket a handful of gold nuggets. Full well
Baranov, fur trader and autocrat, understood and feared
the coming of the sturdy, indomitable gold hunters of
Anglo-Saxon stock. And thus he suppressed the news, as
did the governors that followed him, so that when the
United States bought Alaska in 1867, she bought it for its
furs and fisheries, without a thought of its treasures under-
ground.

No sooner, however, had Alaska become American soil
than thousands of our adventurers were afoot and afloat
for the north. They were the men of 'the days of gold', the
men of California, Fraser, Cassiar, and Cariboo. With the
mysterious, infinite faith of the prospector, they believed
that the gold streak, which ran through the Americas from
Cape Horn to California, did not 'peter out' in British
Columbia. That it extended farther north, was their creed,
and 'Farther North!' became their cry. No time was lost,
and in the early seventies, leaving the Treadwell and the
Silver Bow Basin to be discovered by those who came after,
they went plunging on into the white unknown. North,
farther north, they struggled, till their picks rang in the
frozen beaches of the Arctic Ocean, and they shivered by
driftwood fires on the ruby sands of Nome.

But first, in order that this colossal adventure may be fully grasped, the recentness and the remoteness of Alaska must be emphasized. The interior of Alaska and the contiguous Canadian territory was a vast wilderness. Its hundreds of thousands of square miles were as dark and chartless as Darkest Africa. In 1847, when the first Hudson Bay Company agents crossed over the Rockies from the Mackenzie to poach on the preserves of the Russian Bear, they thought that the Yukon flowed north and emptied into the Arctic Ocean. Hundreds of miles below, however, were the outposts of the Russian traders. They, in turn, did not know where the Yukon had its source, and it was not till later that Russ and Saxon learned that it was the same mighty stream they were occupying. And a little over ten years later, Frederick Whymper voyaged up the Great Bend to Fort Yukon under the Arctic Circle.

From fort to fort, from York Factory on Hudson's Bay to Fort Yukon in Alaska, the English traders transported their goods—a round trip requiring from a year to a year and a half. It was one of their deserters, in 1867, escaping down the Yukon to Bering Sea, who was the first white man to make the North-west Passage by land from the Atlantic to the Pacific. It was at this time that the first accurate description of a fair portion of the Yukon was given by Dr W. H. Ball, of the Smithsonian Institution. But even he had never seen its source, and it was not given him to appreciate the marvel of that great natural highway.

No more remarkable river in this one particular is there in the world; taking its rise in Crater Lake, thirty miles from the ocean, the Yukon flows for twenty-five hundred miles, through the heart of the continent, ere it empties into the sea. A portage of thirty miles, and then a highway for traffic one tenth the girth of the earth!

As late as 1869, Frederick Whymper, fellow of the Royal Geographical Society, stated on hearsay that the Chilcat Indians were believed occasionally to make a short portage across the Coast Range from salt water to the head-reaches of the Yukon. But it remained for a gold hunter, questing north, ever north, to be first of all white men to cross the terrible Chilcoot Pass, and tap the Yukon at its head. This happened only the other day, but the man has become a dim legendary hero. Holt was his name, and already the mists of antiquity have wrapped about the time of his passage. 1872, 1874, and 1878 are the dates variously given— a confusion which time will never clear.

Holt penetrated as far as the Hootalinqua, and on his return to the coast reported coarse gold. The next recorded adventurer is one Edward Bean, who in 1880 headed a party of twenty-five miners from Sitka into the uncharted land. And in the same year, other parties (now forgotten, for who remembers or ever hears the wanderings of the gold hunters?) crossed the Pass, built boats out of the standing timber, and drifted down the Yukon and farther north.

And then, for a quarter of a century, the unknown and unsung heroes grappled with the frost and groped for the gold they were sure lay somewhere among the shadows of the Pole. In the struggle with the terrifying and pitiless natural forces, they returned to the primitive, garmenting themselves in the skins of wild beasts, and covering their feet with the walrus *mucluc* and the moose-hide moccasin. They forgot the world and its ways, as the world had forgotten them; killed their meat as they found it; feasted in plenty and starved in famine, and searched unceasingly for the yellow lure. They criss-crossed the land in every direction, threaded countless unmapped rivers in precarious birch-bark canoes, and with snowshoes and dogs broke trail through thousands of miles of silent white, where man had never been. They struggled on, under the aurora borealis or the midnight sun, through temperatures that ranged from one hundred degrees above zero to eighty degrees below, living, in the grim humour of the land, on 'rabbit tracks and salmon bellies'.

Today, a man may wander away from the trail for a hundred days, and just as he is congratulating himself that at last he is treading virgin soil, he will come upon some ancient and dilapidated cabin, and forget his disappointment in wonder at the man who reared the logs. Still, if one wanders from the trail far enough and deviously enough, he may chance upon a few thousand square miles which he may have all to himself. On the other hand, no matter how far and how deviously he may wander, the possibility always remains that he may stumble, not alone upon a deserted cabin, but upon an occupied one.

As an instance of this, and of the vastness of the land, no better case need be cited than that of Harry Maxwell. An able seaman, hailing from New Bedford, Massachusetts, his ship, the brig *Fannie E. Lee,* was pinched in the Arctic ice. Passing from whaleship to whaleship, he eventually turned up at Point Barrow in the summer of 1880. He was *north* of the Northland, and from this point of vantage he determined to pull south of the interior in search of gold. Across the mountains from Fort Macpherson, and a couple of hundred miles eastward from the Mackenzie, he built a cabin and established his headquarters. And here, for nineteen continuous years, he hunted his living and prospected. He ranged from the never opening ice to the north as far south as the Great Slave Lake. Here he met Warburton Pike, the author and explorer—an incident he now looks back upon as chief among the few incidents of his solitary life.

When this sailor-miner had accumulated $20,000 worth of dust he concluded that civilization was good enough for him, and proceeded 'to pull for the outside'. From the Mackenzie he went up the Little Peel to its headwaters, found a pass through the mountains, nearly starved to death on his way across to the Porcupine Hills, and eventually came out on the Yukon River, where he learned for the first time of the Yukon gold hunters and their discoveries. Yet for twenty years they had been working there, his next-door neighbours, virtually, in a land of such great spaces. At Victoria, British Columbia, previous to his going east over the Canadian Pacific (the existence of which he had just learned), he pregnantly remarked that he had faith in the Mackenzie watershed, and that he was going back after he had taken in the World's Fair and got a whiff or two of civilization.

Faith! It may or may not remove mountains, but it has certainly made the Northland. No Christian martyr ever possessed greater faith than did the pioneers of Alaska. They never doubted the bleak and barren land. Those who came remained, and more ever came. They could not leave. They 'knew' the gold was there, and they persisted. Somehow, the romance of the land and the quest entered into their blood, the spell of it gripped hold of them and would not let them go. Man after man of them, after the most terrible privation and suffering, shook the muck of the country from his moccasins and departed for good. But the following spring always found him drifting down the Yukon on the tail of the ice jams.

Jack McQuestion aptly vindicates the grip of the North. After a residence of thirty years he insists that the climate is delightful, and declares that whenever he makes a trip to the States he is afflicted with home-sickness. Needless to say, the North still has him and will keep tight hold of him until he dies. In fact, for him to die elsewhere would be inartistic and insincere. Of three of the 'pioneer' pioneers, Jack McQuestion alone survives. In 1871, from one to seven years before Holt ever went over Chilcoot, in the company of Al Mayo and Arthur Harper, McQuestion came into the Yukon from the North-west over the Hudson Bay Company route from the Mackenzie to Fort Yukon. The names of these three men, as their lives, are bound up in the history of the country, and so long as there be histories and charts, that long will the Mayo and McQuestion rivers and the Harper and Ladue town site of Dawson be remembered. As an agent of the Alaska Commercial Company, in 1873, McQuestion built Fort Reliance, six miles below the Klondike River. In 1898 the writer met Jack McQuestion at Minook, on the Lower Yukon. The old pioneer, though grizzled, was hale and hearty, and as optimistic as when he first journeyed into the land along the path of the Circle. And no man more beloved is there in all the North. There will be great sadness there when his soul goes questing on over the Last Divide—'farther north', perhaps—who can tell?

Frank Dinsmore is a fair sample of the men who made the Yukon country. A Yankee, born in Auburn, Maine, the *Wanderlust* early laid him by the heels, and at sixteen he was heading west on the trail that led 'farther north'. He prospected in the Black Hills, Montana, and in the Cœur d'Alene, then heard a whisper of the North, and went up to Juneau on the Alaskan Panhandle. But the North still whispered, and more insistently, and he could not rest till he went over Chilcoot, and down into the mysterious Silent Land. This was in 1882, and he went down the chain of lakes, down the Yukon, up the Pelly, and tried his luck on the bars of McMillan River. In the fall, a perambulating skeleton, he came back over the Pass in a blizzard, with a rag of shirt, tattered overalls, and a handful of raw flour.

But he was unafraid. That winter he worked for a grub-stake in Juneau, and the next spring found the heels of his moccasins turned towards salt water and his face toward Chilcoot. This was repeated the next spring, and the following spring, and the spring after that, until, in 1885, he went over the Pass for good. There was to be no return for him until he found the gold he sought.

The years came and went, but he remained true to his resolve. For eleven long years, with snow-shoe and canoe, pickaxe and gold-pan, he wrote out his life on the face of the land. Upper Yukon, Middle Yukon, Lower Yukon— he prospected faithfully and well. His bed was anywhere. Winter or summer he carried neither tent nor stove, and his six-pound sleeping-robe of Arctic hare was the warmest covering he was ever known to possess. Rabbit tracks and salmon bellies were his diet with a vengeance, for he depended largely on his rifle and fishing tackle. His endurance equalled his courage. On a wager he lifted thirteen fifty-pound sacks of flour and walked off with them. Wind-ing up a seven-hundred mile trip on the ice with a forty-mile run, he came into camp at six o'clock in the evening and found a 'squaw dance' under way. He should have been exhausted. Anyway, his *muclucs* were frozen stiff. But he kicked them off and danced all night in stocking-feet.

At the last fortune came to him. The quest was ended,

and he gathered up his gold and pulled for the outside. And his own end was as fitting as that of his quest. Illness came upon him down in San Francisco, and his splendid life ebbed slowly out as he sat in his big easy-chair, in the Commercial Hotel, the 'Yukoner's home'. The doctors came, discussed, consulted, the while he matured more plans of Northland adventure; for the North still gripped him and would not let him go. He grew weaker day by day, but each day he said, 'Tomorrow I'll be all right.' Other old-timers, 'out on furlough', came to see him. They wiped their eyes and swore under their breaths, then entered and talked largely and jovially about going in with him over the trail when spring came. But there in the big easy-chair it was that his Long Trail ended, and the life passed out of him still fixed on 'farther north'.

From the time of the first white man, famine loomed black and gloomy over the land. It was chronic with the Indians and Eskimos; it became chronic with the gold hunters. It was ever present, and so it came about that life was commonly expressed in terms of 'grub'—was measured by cups of flour. Each winter, eight months long, the heroes of the frost faced starvation. It became the custom, as fall drew on, for partners to cut the cards or draw straws to determine which should hit the hazardous trail for salt water, and which should remain and endure the hazardous darkness of the Arctic night.

There was never food enough to winter the whole population. The A. C. Company worked hard to freight up the grub, but the gold hunters came faster and dared more audaciously. When the A. C. Company added a new stern-wheeler to its fleet, men said, 'Now we shall have plenty'. But more gold hunters poured in over the passes to the south, more *voyageurs* and fur traders forced a way through the Rockies from the east, more sea hunters and coast adventurers poled up from Bering Sea on the west, more sailors deserted from the whale-ships to the north, and they all starved together in right brotherly fashion. More steamers were added, but the tide of prospectors welled always in advance. Then the N. A. T. & T. Company came upon the scene, and both companies added steadily to their fleets. But it was the same old story; famine would not depart. In fact, famine grew with the population, till, in the winter of 1897-1898, the United States government was forced to equip a reindeer relief expedition. As of old, that winter partners cut the cards and drew straws, and remained or pulled for salt water as chance decided. They were wise of old time, and had learned never to figure on relief expeditions. They had heard of such things, but no mortal man of them had ever laid eyes on one.

The hard luck of other mining countries pales into insignificance before the hard luck of the North. And as for the hardship, it cannot be conveyed by printed page or word of mouth. No man may know who has not undergone. And those who have undergone, out of their knowledge, claim that in the making of the world God grew tired, and when He came to the last barrowload, 'just dumped it, anyhow', and that was how Alaska happened to be. While no adequate conception of the life can be given to the stay-at-home, yet the men themselves sometimes give a clue to its rigours. One old Minook miner testified thus: 'Haven't you noticed the expression on the faces of us fellows? You can tell a new-comer the minute you see him; he looks alive, enthusiastic, perhaps jolly. We old miners are always grave, unless we're drinking.'

Another old-timer, out of the bitterness of a 'home-mood', imagined himself a Martian astronomer explaining to a friend, with the aid of a powerful telescope, the institutions of the earth. 'There are the continents', he indicated; 'and up there near the polar cap is a country, frigid and burning and lonely and apart, called Alaska. Now, in other countries and states there are great insane asylums, but, though crowded, they are insufficient; so there is Alaska given over to the worst cases. Now and then some poor insane creature comes to his senses in those awful solitudes, and, in wondering joy, escapes from the land and hastens back to his home. But most cases are incurable. They just suffer along, poor devils, forgetting their former life quite, or recalling it like a dream.'—Again the grip of the North, which will not let one go—for *'most cases are incurable'*.

For a quarter of a century the battle with frost and famine went on. The very severity of the struggle with Nature seemed to make the gold hunters kindly towards one another. The latch-string was always out, and the open hand was the order of the day. Distrust was unknown, and it was no hyperbole for a man to take the last shirt off his back for a comrade. Most significant of all, perhaps, in this connection, was the custom of the old days, that when August the first came around, the prospectors who had failed to locate "pay dirt" were permitted to go upon the ground of their more fortunate comrades and take out enough for the next year's grub-stake.

In 1885 rich bar-washing was done on the Stewart River, and in 1886 Cassiar Bar was struck just below the mouth of the Hootalinqua. It was at this time that the first moderate strike was made on Forty Mile Creek, so called because it was judged to be that distance below Fort Reliance of Jack McQuestion fame. A prospector named Williams started for the outside with dogs and Indians to carry the news, but suffered such hardship on the summit of Chilcoot that he was carried dying into the store of Captain John Healy at Dyea. But he had brought the news through—*coarse gold !* Within three months more than two hundred miners had passed in over Chilcoot, stampeding for Forty Mile. Find followed find—Sixty Mile, Miller, Glacier, Birch, Franklin, and the Koyokuk. But they were all moderate discoveries, and the miners still dreamed and searched for the fabled stream, 'Too Much Gold', where gold was so plentiful that gravel had to be shovelled into the sluice-boxes in order to wash it.

And all the time the Northland was preparing to play its own huge joke. It was a great joke, albeit an exceeding bitter one, and it has led the old-timers to believe that the land is left in darkness the better part of the year because God goes away and leaves it to itself. After all the risk and toil and faithful endeavour, it was destined that few of the heroes should be in at the finish when Too Much Gold turned its yellow treasure to the stars.

First, there was Robert Henderson—and this is true history. Henderson had faith in the Indian River district. For three years, by himself, depending mainly on his rifle, living on straight meat a large portion of the time, he prospected many of the Indian River tributaries, just missed finding the rich creeks, Sulphur and Dominion, and managed to make grub (poor grub) out of Quartz Creek and Australia Creek. Then he crossed the divide between Indian River and the Klondike, and on one of the 'feeders' of the latter found eight cents to the pan. This was considered excellent in those simple days. Naming the creek 'Gold Bottom', he recrossed the divide and got three men, Munson, Dalton, and Swanson, to return with him. The four took out $750. And be it emphasized, and emphasized again, *that this was the first Klondike gold ever shovelled in and washed out.* And be it also emphasized, *that Robert Henderson was the discoverer of Klondike, all lies and hearsay tales to the contrary.*

Running out of grub, Henderson again recrossed the divide, and went down the Indian River and up the Yukon to Sixty Mile. Here Joe Ladue ran the trading post, and here Joe Ladue had originally grub-staked Henderson. Henderson told his tale, and a dozen men (all it contained) deserted the Post for the scene of his find. Also, Henderson persuaded a party of prospectors, bound for Stewart River, to forgo their trip and go down and locate with him. He loaded his boat with supplies, drifted down the Yukon to the mouth of the Klondike, and towed and poled up the Klondike to Gold Bottom. But at the mouth of the Klondike he met George Carmack, and thereby hangs the tale.

Carmack was a squawman. He was familiarly known as 'Siwash' George—a derogatory term which had arisen out of his affinity for the Indians. At the time Henderson encountered him he was catching salmon with his Indian wife and relatives on the site of what was to become Dawson, the Golden City of the Snows. Henderson, bubbling over with good-will, open-handed, told Carmack of his discovery. But Carmack was satisfied where he was. He was possessed by no overwhelming desire for the strenuous life. Salmon were good enough for him. But Henderson urged him to come on and locate, until, when he yielded, he wanted to take the whole tribe along. Henderson refused to stand for this, said that he must give the preference over Siwashes to his old Sixty Mile friends, and, it is rumoured, said some things about Siwashes that were not nice.

The next morning Henderson went on alone up the Klondike to Gold Bottom. Carmack, by this time aroused, took a short cut afoot for the same place. Accompanied by his two Indian brothers-in-law, Skookum Jim and Tagish Charley, he went up Rabbit Creek (now Bonanza), crossed into Gold Bottom, and staked near Henderson's discovery. On the way up he had panned a few shovels on Rabbit Creek, and he showed Henderson 'colours' he had obtained. Henderson made him promise, if he found anything on the way back, that he would send up one of the Indians with the news. Henderson also agreed to pay for his services, for he seemed to feel that they were on the verge of something big, and he wanted to make sure.

Carmack returned down Rabbit Creek. While he was taking a sleep on the bank about half a mile below the mouth of what was to be known as Eldorado, Skookum Jim tried his luck, and from surface prospects got from ten cents to a dollar to the pan. Carmack and his brothers-in-law staked and hit 'the high places' for Forty Mile, where they filed on the claims before Captain Constantine, and renamed the creek Bonanza. And Henderson was forgotten. No word of it reached him. Carmack broke his promise.

Weeks afterwards, when Bonanza and Eldorado were staked from end to end and there was no more room, a party of late comers pushed over the divide and down to Gold Bottom, where they found Henderson still at work. When they told him they were from Bonanza, he was non-plussed. He had never heard of such a place. But when they described it, he recognized it as Rabbit Creek. Then they told him of its marvellous richness, and, as Tappan Adney relates, when Henderson realized what he had lost through

Carmack's treachery, 'he threw down his shovel and went and sat on the bank, so sick at heart that it was some time before he could speak.'

Then there were the rest of the old-timers, the men of Forty Mile and Circle City. At the time of the discovery, nearly all of them were over to the west at work in the old diggings or prospecting for new ones. As they said of themselves, they were the kind of men who are always caught out with forks when it rains soup. In the stampede that followed the news of Carmack's strike very few old miners took part. They were not there to take part. But the men who did go on the stampede were mainly the worthless ones, the new-comers, and the camp hangers-on. And while Bob Henderson plugged away to the east, and the heroes plugged away to the west, the greenhorns and rounders went up and staked Bonanza.

But the Northland was not yet done with its joke. When fall came on and the heroes returned to Forty Mile and to Circle City, they listened calmly to the up-river tales of Siwash discoveries and loafers' prospects, and shook their heads. They judged by the calibre of the men interested, and branded it a bunco game. But glowing reports continued to trickle down the Yukon, and a few old-timers went up to see. They looked over the ground—the unlikeliest place for gold in all their experience—and they went down the river again, 'leaving it to the Swedes'.

Again the Northland turned the tables. The Alaskan gold hunter is proverbial, not so much for his unveracity, as for his inability to tell the precise truth. In a country of exaggerations, he likewise is prone to hyperbolic description of things actual. But when it came to Klondike, he could not stretch the truth as fast as the truth itself stretched. Carmack first got a dollar pan. He lied when he said it was two dollars and a half. And when those who doubted him did get two-and-a-half pans, they said they were getting an ounce, and lo! ere the lie had fairly started on its way, they were getting, not one ounce, but five ounces. This they claimed was six ounces; but when they filled a pan of dirt to prove the lie, they washed out twelve ounces. And so it went. They continued valiantly to lie, but the truth continued to outrun them.

But the Northland's hyperborean laugh was not yet ended. When Bonanza was staked from mouth to source, those who had failed to 'get in', disgruntled and sore, went up the 'pups' and feeders. Eldorado was one of these feeders, and many men, after locating it, turned their backs upon their claims and never gave them a second thought. One man sold a half-interest in five hundred feet of it for a sack of flour. Other owners wandered around trying to bunco men into buying them out for a song. And then Eldorado 'showed up'. It was far, far richer than Bonanza, with an average value of a thousand dollars a foot to every foot of it.

A Swede named Charley Anderson had been at work on Miller Creek the year of the strike, and arrived in Dawson with a few hundred dollars. Two miners, who had staked No. 29 Eldorado, decided that he was the proper man upon whom to 'unload'. He was too canny to approach sober, so at considerable expense they got him drunk. Even then it was hard work, but they kept him befuddled for several days, and finally inveigled him into buying No. 29 for $750. When Anderson sobered up, he wept at his folly, and pleaded to have his money back. But the men who had duped him were hard-hearted. They laughed at him, and kicked themselves for not having tapped him for a couple of hundred more. Nothing remained for Anderson but to work the worthless ground. This he did, and out of it he took over three-quarters of a million of dollars.

It was not till Frank Dinsmore, who already had big holdings on Birch Creek, took a hand, that the old-timers developed faith in the new diggings. Dinsmore received a letter from a man on the spot, calling it 'the biggest thing in the world', and harnessed his dogs and went up to investigate. And when he sent a letter back, saying that he had never seen 'anything like it', Circle City for the first time believed, and at once was precipitated one of the wildest stampedes the country had ever seen or ever will see. Every dog was taken, many went without dogs, and even the women and children and weaklings hit the three hundred miles of ice through the long Arctic night for the biggest thing in the world. It is related that but twenty people, mostly cripples and unable to travel, were left in Circle City when the smoke of the last sled disappeared up the Yukon.

Since that time gold has been discovered in all manner of places, under the grass roots of the hill-side benches, in the bottom of Monte Cristo Island, and in the sands of the sea at Nome. And now the gold hunter who knows his business shuns the 'favourable looking' spots, confident in his hard-won knowledge that he will find the most gold in the least likely place. This is sometimes adduced to support the theory that the gold hunters, rather than the explorers, are the men who will ultimately win to the Pole. Who knows? It is in their blood, and they are capable of it.

# THE LAW OF LIFE

OLD KOSKOOSH listened greedily. Though his sight had long since faded, his hearing was still acute, and the slightest sound penetrated to the glimmering intelligence which yet abode behind the withered forehead, but which no longer gazed forth upon the things of the world. Ah! that was Sit-cum-to-ha, shrilly anathematizing the dogs as she cuffed and beat them into the harnesses. Sit-cum-to-ha was his daughter's daughter, but she was too busy to waste a thought upon her broken grandfather, sitting alone there in the snow, forlorn and helpless. Camp must be broken. The long trail waited while the short day refused to linger. Life called her, and the duties of life, not death. And he was very close to death now.

The thought made the old man panicky for the moment, and he stretched forth a palsied hand which wandered tremblingly over the small heap of dry wood beside him.

Reassured that it was indeed there, his hand returned to the shelter of his mangy furs, and he again fell to listening. The sulky crackling of half-frozen hides told him that the chief's moose-skin lodge had been struck, and even then was being rammed and jammed into portable compass. The chief was his son, stalwart and strong, head man of the tribesmen, and a mighty hunter. As the women toiled with the camp luggage, his voice rose, chiding them for their slowness. Old Koskoosh strained his ears. It was the last time he would hear that voice. There went Geehow's lodge! And Tusken's! Seven, eight, nine; only the shaman's could be still standing. There! They were at work upon it now. He could hear the shaman grunt as he piled it on the sled. A child whimpered, and a woman soothed it with soft, crooning gutturals. Little Koo-tee, the old man thought, a fretful child, and not overstrong. It would die soon, perhaps, and they would burn a hole through the frozen tundra and pile rocks above to keep the wolverines away. Well, what did it matter? A few years at best, and as many an empty belly as a full one. And in the end, Death waited, ever-hungry and hungriest of them all.

What was that? Oh, the men lashing the sleds and drawing tight the thongs. He listened, who would listen no more. The whip-lashes snarled and bit among the dogs. Hear them whine! How they hated the work and the trail! They were off! Sled after sled churned slowly away into the silence. They were gone. They had passed out of his life, and he faced the last bitter hour alone. No. The snow crunched beneath a moccasin; a man stood beside him; upon his head a hand rested gently. His son was good to do this thing. He remembered other old men whose sons had not waited after the tribe. But his son had. He wandered away into the past, till the young man's voice brought him back.

'Is it well with you?' he asked.

And the old man answered, 'It is well.'

'There be wood beside you,' the younger man continued, 'and the fire burns bright. The morning is grey, and the cold has broken. It will snow presently. Even now is it snowing.'

'Ay, even now is it snowing.'

'The tribesmen hurry. Their bales are heavy, and their bellies flat with lack of feasting. The trail is long and they travel fast. I go now. It is well?'

'It is well. I am as a last year's leaf, clinging lightly to the stem. The first breath that blows, and I fall. My voice is become like an old woman's. My eyes no longer show me the way of my feet, and my feet are heavy, and I am tired. It is well.'

He bowed his head in content till the last noise of the complaining snow had died away, and he knew his son was beyond recall. Then his hand crept out in haste to the wood. It alone stood between him and the eternity that yawned in upon him. At last the measure of his life was a handful of faggots. One by one they would go to feed the fire, and just so, step by step, death would creep upon him. When the last stick had surrendered up its heat, the frost would begin to gather strength. First his feet would yield, then his hands; and the numbness would travel, slowly, from the extremities to the body. His head would fall forward upon his knees, and he would rest. It was easy. All men must die.

He did not complain. It was the way of life, and it was just. He had been born close to the earth, close to the earth had he lived, and the law thereof was not new to him. It was the law of all flesh. Nature was not kindly to the flesh. She had no concern for that concrete thing called the individual. Her interest lay in the species, the race. This was the deepest abstraction old Koskoosh's barbaric mind was capable of, but he grasped it firmly. He saw it exemplified in all life. The rise of the sap, the bursting greenness of the willow bud, the fall of the yellow leaf—in this alone was told the whole history. But one task did Nature set the individual. Did he not perform it, he died. Did he perform it, it was all the same, he died. Nature did not care; there were plenty who were obedient, and it was only the obedience in this matter, not the obedient, which lived and lived always. The tribe of Koskoosh was very old. The old men he had known when a boy, had known old men before them. Therefore it was true that the tribe lived, that it stood for the obedience of all its members, way down into the forgotten past, whose very resting-places were unremembered. They did not count; they were episodes. They had passed away like clouds from a summer sky. He also was an episode, and would pass away. Nature did not care. To life she set one task, gave one law. To perpetuate was the task of life, its law was death. A maiden was a good creature to look upon, full-breasted and strong, with spring to her step and light in her eyes. But her task was yet before her. The light in her eyes brightened, her step quickened, she was now bold with the young men, now timid, and she gave them of her own unrest. And ever she grew fairer and yet fairer to look upon, till some hunter, able no longer to withhold himself, took her to his lodge to cook and toil for him and to become the mother of his children. And with the coming of her offspring her looks left her. Her limbs dragged and shuffled, her eyes dimmed and bleared, and only the little children found joy against the withered cheek of the old squaw by the fire. Her task was done. But a little while, on the first pinch of famine or the first long trail, and she would be left, even as he had been left, in the snow, with a little pile of wood. Such was the law.

He placed a stick carefully upon the fire and resumed his meditations. It was the same everywhere, with all things. The mosquitos vanished with the first frost. The little tree-squirrel crawled away to die. When age settled upon the rabbit it became slow and heavy, and could no longer out-foot its enemies. Even the big bald-face grew clumsy and blind and quarrelsome, in the end to be dragged down by a handful of yelping huskies. He remembered how he had abandoned his own father on an upper reach of the Klondike one winter, the winter before the missionary came with his talk-books and his box of medicines. Many a time had Koskoosh smacked his lips over the recollection of that box, though now his mouth refused to moisten. The 'painkiller' had been especially good. But the missionary was a bother after all, for he brought no meat into the camp, and he ate heartily, and the hunters grumbled. But he chilled his lungs on the divide by the Mayo, and the dogs afterwards nosed the stones away and fought over his bones.

Koskoosh placed another stick on the fire and harked back deeper into the past. There was the time of the Great Famine, when the old men crouched empty-bellied to the fire, and let fall from their lips dim traditions of the ancient day when the Yukon ran wide open for three winters, and then lay frozen for three summers. He had lost his mother in that famine. In the summer the salmon run had failed, and the tribe looked forward to the winter and the coming of the caribou. Then the winter came, but with it there were no caribou. Never had the like been known, not even in the lives of the old men. But the caribou did not come, and it was the seventh year, and the rabbits had not replenished, and the dogs were naught but bundles of bones. And through the long darkness the children wailed and died, and the women, and the old men; and not one in ten of the tribe lived to meet the sun when it came back in the spring. That *was* a famine!

But he had seen times of plenty, too, when the meat spoiled on their hands, and the dogs were fat and worthless with over-eating—times when they let the game go unkilled, and the women were fertile, and the lodges were cluttered with sprawling men-children and women-children. Then it was the men became high-stomached, and revived ancient quarrels, and crossed the divides to the south to kill the Pellys, and to the west that they might sit by the dead fires of the Tananas. He remembered, when a boy, during a time of plenty, when he saw a moose pulled down by the wolves. Zing-ha lay with him in the snow and watched—Zinga-ha, who later became the craftiest of hunters, and who, in the end, fell through an air-hole on the Yukon. They found him, a month afterward, just as he had crawled halfway out and frozen stiff to the ice.

But the moose. Zing-ha and he had gone out that day to play at hunting after the manner of their fathers. On the bed of the creek they struck the fresh track of a moose, and with it the tracks of many wolves. 'An old one,' Zing-ha, who was quicker at reading the sign, said—'an old one who cannot keep up with the herd. The wolves have cut him out from his brothers, and they will never leave him.' And it was so. It was their way. By day and by night, never resting, snarling on his heels, snapping at his nose, they would stay by him to the end. How Zing-ha and he felt the blood-lust quicken! The finish would be a sight to see!

Eager-footed, they took the trail, and even he, Kos-koosh, slow of sight and an unversed tracker, could have followed it blind, it was so wide. Hot were they on the heels of the chase, reading the grim tragedy, fresh-written, at every step. Now they came to where the moose had made a stand. Thrice the length of a grown man's body, in every direction, had the snow been stamped about and uptossed. In the midst were the deep impressions of the splay-hoofed game, and all about, everywhere, were the lighter footmarks of the wolves. Some, while their brothers harried the kill, had lain to one side and rested. The full-stretched impress of their bodies in the snow was as perfect as though made the moment before. One wolf had been caught in a wild lunge of the maddened victim and trampled to death. A few bones, well picked, bore witness.

Again, they ceased the uplift of their snow-shoes at a second stand. Here the great animal had fought desperately. Twice had he been dragged down, as the snow attested, and twice had he shaken his assailants clear and gained footing once more. He had done his task long since, but none the less was life dear to him. Zing-ha said it was a strange thing, a moose once down to get free again, but this one certainly had. The shaman would see signs and wonders in this when they told him.

And yet again, they came to where the moose had made to mount the bank and gain the timber. But his foes had laid on from behind, till he reared and fell back upon them, crushing two deep into the snow. It was plain the kill was at hand, for their brothers had left them untouched. Two more stands were hurried past, brief in time-length and very close together. The trail was red now, and the clean stride of the great beast had grown short and slovenly. Then they heard the first sounds of the battle—not the full-throated chorus of the chase, but the short, snappy bark which spoke of close quarters and teeth to flesh. Crawling up the wind, Zing-ha bellied it through the snow, and with him crept he, Koskoosh, who was to be chief of the tribesmen in the years to come. Together they shoved aside the under branches of a young spruce and peered forth. It was the end they saw.

The picture, like all of youth's impressions, was still strong with him, and his dim eyes watched the end played out as vividly as in that far-off time. Koskoosh marvelled at this, for in the days which followed, when he was a leader of men and a head of councillors, he had done great deeds and made his name a curse in the mouths of the Pellys, to say naught of the strange white man he had killed, knife to knife, in open fight.

For long he pondered on the days of his youth, till the fire died down and the frost bit deeper. He replenished it with two sticks this time, and gauged his grip on life by what remained. If Sit-cum-to-ha had only remembered her grandfather, and gathered a larger armful, his hours would have been longer. It would have been easy. But she was ever a careless child, and honoured not her ancestors from the time the Beaver, son of the son of Zing-ha, first cast eyes upon her. Well, what mattered it? Had he not done likewise in his own quick youth? For a while he listened to the silence. Perhaps the heart of his son might soften, and he would come back with the dogs to take his old father on with the tribe to where the caribou ran thick and the fat hung heavy upon them.

He strained his ears, his restless brain for the moment stilled. Not a stir, nothing. He alone took breath in the midst of the great silence. It was very lonely. Hark! What was that? A chill passed over his body. The familiar, long-drawn howl broke the void, and it was close at hand. Then on his darkened eyes was projected the vision of the moose —the old bull moose—the torn flanks and bloody sides, the riddled mane, and the great branching horns, down low and tossing to the last. He saw the flashing forms of grey, the gleaming eyes, the lolling tongues, the slavered fangs. And he saw the inexorable circle close in till it became a dark point in the midst of the stamped snow.

A cold muzzle thrust against his cheek, and at its touch his soul leaped back to the present. His hand shot into the fire and dragged out a burning faggot. Overcome for the nonce by his hereditary fear of man, the brute retreated, raising a prolonged call to his brothers; and greedily they answered, till a ring of crouching, jaw-slobbered grey was stretched round about. The old man listened to the drawing in of this circle. He waved his brand wildly, and sniffs turned to snarls; but the panting brutes refused to scatter. Now one wormed his chest forward, dragging his haunches after, now a second, now a third; but never a one drew back. Why should he cling to life? he asked, and dropped the blazing stick into the snow. It sizzled and went out. The circle grunted uneasily, but held its own. Again he saw the last stand of the old bull moose, and Koskoosh dropped his head wearily upon his knees. What did it matter after all? Was it not the law of life?

# THE STORY OF KEESH

KEESH LIVED long ago on the rim of the polar sea, was headman of his village through many and prosperous years, and died full of honours with his name on the lips of men. So long ago did he live that only the old men remember his name, his name and the tale, which they got from the old men before them, and which the old men to come will tell to their children and their children's children down to the end of time. And the winter darkness, when the north gales make their long sweep across the ice pack, and the air is filled with flying white, and no man may venture forth, is the chosen time for the telling of how Keesh, from the poorest igloo in the village, rose to power and place over them all.

He was a bright boy, so the tale runs, healthy and strong, and he had seen thirteen suns, in their way of reckoning time. For each winter the sun leaves the land in darkness, and the next year a new sun returns so that they may be warm again and look upon one another's faces. The father of Keesh had been a very brave man, but he had met his death in a time of famine, when he sought to save the lives of his people by taking the life of a great polar bear. In his eagerness he came to close grapples with the bear, and his bones were crushed; but the bear had much meat on him and the people were saved. Keesh was his only son, and after that Keesh lived alone with his mother. But the people are prone to forget, and they forgot the deed of his father; and he being but a boy, and his mother only a woman, they, too, were swiftly forgotten, and ere long came to live in the meanest of all the igloos.

It was at a council one night in the big igloo of Klosh-Kwan, the chief, that Keesh showed the blood that ran in his veins and the manhood that stiffened his back. With the dignity of an elder he rose to his feet and waited for silence amid the babble of voices.

'It is true that meat be apportioned me and mine,' he said. 'But it is ofttimes old and tough, this meat, and, moreover, it has an unusual quantity of bones.'

The hunters, grizzled and grey, and lusty and young, were aghast. The like had never been known before. A child that talked like a grown man and said harsh things to their very faces!

But steadily and with seriousness Keesh went on. 'For that I know my father, Bok, was a great hunter, I speak these words. It is said that Bok brought home more meat than any of the two best hunters, that with his own hands he attended to the division of it, that with his own eyes he saw to it that the least old woman and the last old man received fair share.'

'Na! Na!' the men cried. 'Put the child out!' 'Send him

off to bed!' 'He is no man that he should talk to men and greybeards!'

He waited calmly till the uproar died down.

'Thou hast a wife, Ugh-Gluk,' he said, 'and for her dost thou speak. And thou, too, Massuk, a mother also, and for them dost thou speak. My mother has no one save me; wherefore I speak. As I say, though Bok be dead because he hunted overkeenly, it is just that I, who am his son, and that Ikeega, who is my mother and was his wife, should have meat in plenty so long as there be meat in plenty in the tribe. I, Keesh, the son of Bok, have spoken.'

He sat down, his ears keenly alert to the flood of protest and indignation his words had created.

'That a boy should speak in council!' old Ugh-Gluk was mumbling.

'Shall the babes in arms tell us men the things we shall do?' Massuk demanded in a loud voice. 'Am I a man that I should be made a mock by every child that cries for meat?'

The anger boiled a white heat. They ordered him to bed, threatened that he should have no meat at all, and promised him sore beatings for his presumption. Keesh's eyes began to flash and the blood to pound darkly under his skin. In the midst of the abuse he sprang to his feet.

'Hear me, ye men!' he cried. 'Never shall I speak in the council again, never again till the men come to me and say, "It is well, Keesh, that thou shouldst speak, it is well and it is our wish." Take this now, ye men, for my last word. Bok, my father, was a great hunter. I, too, his son, shall go and hunt the meat that I eat. And be it known, now, that the division of that which I kill shall be fair. And no widow nor weak one shall cry in the night because there is no meat, when the strong men are groaning in great pain for that they have eaten overmuch. And in the days to come there shall be shame upon the strong men who have eaten overmuch. I, Keesh, have said it!'

Jeers and scornful laughter followed him out of the igloo, but his jaw was set and he went his way, looking neither to right nor left.

2*

The next day he went forth along the shore line where the ice and the land met together. Those who saw him go noted that he carried his bow, with a goodly supply of bone-barbed arrows, and that across his shoulder was his father's big hunting spear. And there was laughter, and much talk, at the event. It was an unprecedented occurrence. Never did boys of his tender age go forth to hunt, much less to hunt alone. Also were there shaking of heads and prophetic mutterings, and the women looked pityingly at Ikeega, and her face was grave and sad.

'He will be back ere long,' they said cheeringly.

'Let him go; it will teach him a lesson,' the hunters said. 'And he will come back shortly, and he will be meek and soft of speech in the days to follow.'

But a day passed, and a second, and on the third a wild gale blew, and there was no Keesh. Ikeega tore her hair and put soot of the seal oil on her face in token of her grief; and the women assailed the men with bitter words in that they had mistreated the boy and sent him to his death; and the men made no answer, preparing to go in search of the body when the storm abated.

Early next morning, however, Keesh strode into the village. But he came not shamefacedly. Across his shoulders he bore a burden of fresh-killed meat. And there was importance in his step and arrogance in his speech.

'Go, ye men, with the dogs and sledges, and take my trail for the better part of a day's travel,' he said. 'There is much meat on the ice—a she-bear and two half-grown cubs.'

Ikeega was overcome with joy, but he received her demonstrations in manlike fashion, saying: 'Come, Ikeega, let us eat. And after that I shall sleep, for I am weary.'

And he passed into their igloo and ate profoundly, and after that slept for twenty running hours.

There was much doubt at first, much doubt and discussion. The killing of a polar bear is very dangerous, but thrice dangerous is it, and three times thrice, to kill a mother bear with her cubs. The men could not bring themselves to believe that the boy Keesh, singlehanded, had accomplished so great a marvel. But the women spoke of the fresh-killed meat he had brought on his back, and this was an overwhelming argument against their unbelief. So they finally departed, grumbling gently that in all probability, if the thing were so, he had neglected to cut up the carcasses. Now in the North it is very necessary that this should be done as soon as a kill is made. If not, the meat freezes so solidly as to turn the edge of the sharpest knife, and a three-hundred-pound bear, frozen stiff, is no easy thing to put upon a sled and haul over the rough ice. But, arrived at the spot, they found not only the kill, which they had doubted, but that Keesh had quartered the beasts in true hunter fashion, and removed the entrails.

Thus began the mystery of Keesh, a mystery that deepened and deepened with the passing of the days. His very next trip he killed a young bear, nearly full-grown, and on the trip following, a large male bear and his mate. He was ordinarily gone from three to four days, though it was nothing unusual for him to stay away a week at a time on the ice field. Always he declined company on these expeditions, and the people marvelled. 'How does he do it?' they demanded of one another. 'Never does he take a dog with him, and dogs are of such great help, too.'

'Why doest thou hunt only bear?' Klosh-Kwan once ventured to ask him.

And Keesh made fitting answer. 'It is well known that there is more meat on the bear,' he said.

But there was also talk of witchcraft in the village. 'He hunts with evil spirits,' some of the people contended, 'wherefore his hunting is rewarded. How else can it be, save that he hunts with evil spirits?'

'Mayhap they be not evil, but good, these spirits,' others said. 'It is known that his father was a mighty hunter. May not his father hunt with him so that he may attain excellence and patience and understanding? Who knows?'

Nonetheless, his success continued, and the less skilful hunters were often kept busy hauling in his meat. And in the division of it he was just. As his father had done before him, he saw to it that the least old woman and the last old

man received a fair portion, keeping no more for himself
than his needs required. And because of this, and of his
merit as a hunter, he was looked upon with respect and
even awe; and there was talk of making him chief after old
Klosh-Kwan. Because of the things he had done they
looked for him to appear again in the council, but he never
came, and they were ashamed to ask.

'I am minded to build me an igloo,' he said one day to
Klosh-Kwan and a number of the hunters. 'It shall be a
large igloo, wherein Ikeega and I can dwell in comfort.'

'Aye.' They nodded gravely.

'But I have no time. My business is hunting, and it takes
all my time. So it is but just that the men and women of
the village who eat my meat should build me an igloo.'

And the igloo was built accordingly, on a generous scale
which exceeded even the dwelling of Klosh-Kwan. Keesh
and his mother moved into it, and it was the first prosperity
she had enjoyed since the death of Bok. Nor was material
prosperity alone hers, for, because of her wonderful son
and the position he had given her, she came to be looked
upon as the first woman in all the village; and the women
were given to visiting her, to asking her advice, and to
quoting her wisdom when arguments arose among themselves or with the men.

But it was the mystery of Keesh's marvellous hunting
that took chief place in all their minds. And one day Ugh-
Gluk taxed him with witchcraft to his face.

'It is charged,' Ugh-Gluk said ominously, 'that thou
dealest with evil spirits, wherefore thy hunting is rewarded.'

'Is not the meat good?' Keesh made answer. 'Has one in
the village yet to fall sick from the eating of it? How dost
thou know that witchcraft be concerned? Or dost thou
guess, in the dark, merely because of the envy that con-
sumes thee?'

And Ugh-Gluk withdrew, discomfited, the women laughing at him as he walked away. But in the council one night,
after long deliberation, it was determined to put spies on
his track when he went forth to hunt, so that his methods
might be learned. So on his next trip Bim and Bawn, two

young men, and of hunters the craftiest, followed after him, taking care not to be seen. After five days they returned, their eyes bulging and their tongues a-tremble to tell what they had seen. The council was hastily called in Klosh-Kwan's dwelling, and Bim took up the tale.

'Brothers! As commanded, we journeyed on the trail of Keesh, and cunningly we journeyed, so that he might not know. And midway of the first day he picked up with a great he-bear. It was a very great bear.'

'None greater,' Bawn corroborated, and went on himself. 'Yet was the bear not inclined to fight, for he turned away and made off slowly over the ice. This we saw from the rocks of the shore, and the bear came towards us, and after him came Keesh, very much unafraid. And he shouted harsh words after the bear, and waved his arms about, and made much noise. Then did the bear grow angry, and rise up on his hind legs, and growl. But Keesh walked right up to the bear.'

'Aye,' Bim continued the story. 'Right up to the bear Keesh walked. And the bear took after him, and Keesh ran away. But as he ran he dropped a little round ball on the ice. And the bear stopped and smelled of it, then swallowed it up. And Keesh continued to run away and drop little round balls, and the bear continued to swallow them up.'

Exclamations and cries of doubt were being made, and Ugh-Gluk expressed open unbelief.

'With our own eyes we saw it,' Bim affirmed.

And Bawn: 'Aye, with our own eyes. And this continued until the bear stood suddenly upright and cried aloud in pain, and thrashed his forepaws madly about. And Keesh continued to make off over the ice to a safe distance. But the bear gave him no notice, being occupied with the misfortune the little round balls had wrought within him.'

'Aye, within him,' Bim interrupted. 'For he did claw at himself, and leap about over the ice like a playful puppy, save for the way he growled and squealed it was plain it was not play but pain. Never did I see such a sight!'

'Nay, never was such a sight seen,' Bawn took up the strain. 'And furthermore, it was such a large bear.'

'Witchcraft,' Ugh-Gluk suggested.

'I know not,' Bawn replied. 'I tell only of what my eyes beheld. And after a while the bear grew weak and tired, for he was very heavy and he had jumped about with exceeding violence, and he went off along the shore ice, shaking his head slowly from side to side and sitting down ever and again to squeal and cry. And Keesh followed after the bear, and we followed after Keesh, and for that day and three days more we followed. The bear grew weak and never ceased crying from his pain.'

'It was a charm!' Ugh-Gluk exclaimed. 'Surely it was a charm!'

'It may well be.'

And Bim relieved Bawn. 'The bear wandered, now this way and now that, doubling back and forth and crossing his trail in circles, so that at the end he was near where Keesh had first come upon him. By this time he was quite sick, the bear, and could crawl no farther, so Keesh came up close and speared him to death.'

'And then?' Klosh-Kwan demanded.

'Then we left Keesh skinning the bear, and came running that the news of the killing might be told.'

And in the afternoon of that day the women hauled in the meat of the bear while the men sat in council assembled. When Keesh arrived a messenger was sent to him, bidding him come to the council. But he sent reply, saying that he was hungry and tired; also that his igloo was large and comfortable and could hold many men.

And curiosity was so strong on the men that the whole council, Klosh-Kwan to the fore, rose up and went to the igloo of Keesh. He was eating, but he received them with respect and seated them according to their rank. Ikeega was proud and embarrassed by turns, but Keesh was quite composed.

Klosh-Kwan recited the information brought by Bim and Bawn, and at its close said in a stern voice: 'So explanation is wanted, O Keesh, of thy manner of hunting. Is there witchcraft in it?'

Keesh looked up and smiled. 'Nay, O Klosh-Kwan. It is not for a boy to know aught of witches, and of witches I know nothing. I have but devised a means whereby I may kill the ice bear with ease, that is all. It be headcraft, not witchcraft.'

'And may any man?'

'Any man.'

There was a long silence. The men looked in one another's faces, and Keesh went on eating.

'And ... and ... and wilt thou tell us, O Keesh?' Klosh-Kwan finally asked in a tremulous voice.

'Yea, I will tell thee.' Keesh finished sucking a marrow-bone and rose to his feet. 'It is quite simple. Behold!'

He picked up a thin strip of whalebone and showed it to them. The ends were sharp as needle points. The strip he coiled carefully, till it disappeared in his hand. Then, suddenly releasing it, it sprang straight again. He picked up a piece of blubber.

'So,' he said, 'one takes a small chunk of blubber, thus, and thus makes it hollow. Then into the hollow goes the whalebone, so, tightly coiled, and another piece of blubber is fitted over the whalebone. After that it is put outside where it freezes into a little round ball. The bear swallows the little round ball, the blubber melts, the whalebone with its sharp ends stands out straight, the bear gets sick, and when the bear is very sick, why, you kill him with a spear. It is quite simple.'

And Ugh-Gluk said, 'Oh!' and Klosh-Kwan said 'Ah!' And each said something after his own manner, and all understood.

And this is the story of Keesh, who lived long ago on the rim of the polar sea. Because he exercised headcraft and not witchcraft, he rose from the meanest igloo to be headman of his village, and through all the years that he lived, it is related, his tribe was prosperous, and neither widow nor weak one cried aloud in the night because there was no meat.

# KEESH, THE SON OF KEESH

'THUS WILL I give six blankets, warm and double; six files, large and hard; six Hudson Bay knives, keen-edged and long; two canoes, the work of Mogum, The Maker of Things; ten dogs, heavy-shouldered and strong in the harness; and three guns—the trigger of one be broken, but it is a good gun and can doubtless be mended.'

Keesh paused and swept his eyes over the circle of intent faces. It was the time of the Great Fishing, and he was bidding to Gnob for Su-Su his daughter. The place was the St George Mission by the Yukon, and the tribes had gathered for many a hundred miles. From north, south, east, and west, they had come, even from Tozikakat, and far Tana-naw.

'And further, O Gnob, thou art the chief of the Tana-naw; and I, Keesh, the son of Keesh, am chief of the Thlunget. Wherefore, when my seed springs from the loins of thy daughter, there shall be a friendship between the tribes, a great friendship, and Tana-naw and Thlunget shall be brothers of the blood in the time to come. What I have said I will do, that will I do. And how is it with you, O Gnob, in this matter?'

Gnob nodded his head gravely, his gnarled and age-twisted face inscrutably masking the soul that dwelt behind. His narrow eyes burned like twin coals through their narrow slits, as he piped in a high-cracked voice, 'But that is not all.'

'What more?' Keesh demanded. 'Have I not offered full measure? Was there ever yet a Tana-naw maiden who fetched so great a price? Then name her!'

An open snicker passed round the circle, and Keesh knew that he stood in shame before these people.

'Nay, nay, good Keesh, thou dost not understand.' Gnob made a soft, stroking gesture. 'The price is fair. It is a good price. Nor do I question the broken trigger. But that is not all. What of the man?'

'Ay, what of the man?' the circle snarled.

'It is said,' Gnob's thrill voice piped, 'it is said that Keesh does not walk in the way of his fathers. It is said that he has wandered into the dark, after strange gods, and that he is become afraid.'

The face of Keesh went dark. 'It is a lie,' he thundered. 'Keesh is afraid of no man!'

'It is said,' old Gnob piped on, 'that he has harkened to the speech of the white man up at the Big House, and that he bends head to the white man's god, and, moreover, that blood is displeasing to the white man's god.'

Keesh dropped his eyes, and his hand clenched passionately. The savage circle laughed derisively, and in the ear of Gnob whispered Madwan, the shaman, high-priest of the tribe and maker of medicine.

The shaman poked among the shadows on the rim of the firelight and roused up a slender young boy, whom he brought face to face with Keesh; and in the hand of Keesh he thrust a knife.

Gnob leaned forward. 'Keesh! O Keesh! Darest thou to kill a man? Behold! This be Kitz-noo, a slave. Strike, O Keesh, strike with the strength of thy arm!'

The boy trembled and waited the stroke. Keesh looked at him, and thoughts of Mr Brown's higher morality floated through his mind, and strong upon him was a vision of the leaping flames of Mr Brown's particular brand of hell-fire. The knife fell to the ground, and the boy sighed and went out beyond the firelight with shaking knees. At the feet of Gnob sprawled a wolf-dog, which bared its gleaming teeth and prepared to spring after the boy. But the shaman ground his foot into the brute's body, and so doing, gave Gnob an idea.

'And then, O Keesh, what wouldst thou do, should a man do this thing to you?'—as he spoke, Gnob held a ribbon of salmon to White Fang, and when the animal attempted to take it, smote him sharply on the nose with a stick. 'And afterwards, O Keesh, wouldst thou do thus?'

—White Fang was cringing back on his belly and fawning to the hand of Gnob.

'Listen!'—leaning on the arm of Madwan, Gnob had risen to his feet. 'I am very old, and because I am very old I will tell thee things. Thy father, Keesh, was a mighty man. And he did love the song of the bowstring in battle, and these eyes have beheld him cast a spear till the head stood out beyond a man's body. But thou art unlike. Since thou left the Raven to worship the Wolf, thou art become afraid of blood, and thou makest thy people afraid. This is not good. For behold when I was a boy, even as Kitz-noo there, there was no white man in all the land. But they came, one by one, these white men, till now they are many. And they are a restless breed, never content to rest by the fire with a full belly and let the morrow bring its own meat. A curse was laid upon them, it would seem, and they must work it out in toil and hardship.'

Keesh was startled. A recollection of a hazy story told by Mr Brown of one Adam, of old time, came to him, and it seemed that Mr Brown had spoken true.

'So they lay hands upon all they behold, these white men, and they go everywhere and behold all things. And ever do more follow in their steps, so that if nothing be done they will come to possess all the land and there will be no room for the tribes of the Raven. Wherefore it is meet that we fight with them till none are left. Then will we hold the passes and the land, and perhaps our children and our children's children shall flourish and grow fat. There is a great struggle to come, when Wolf and Raven shall grapple; but Keesh will not fight, nor will he let his people fight. So it is not well that he should take to him my daughter. Thus have I spoken, I, Gnob, chief of the Tananaw.'

'But the white men are good and great,' Keesh made answer. 'The white men have taught us many things. The white men have given us blankets and knives and guns, such as we have never made and never could make. I remember in what manner we lived before they came. I was unborn then, but I have it from my father. When we went on the hunt we must creep so close to the moose that a spear-cast would cover the distance. To-day we use the white man's rifle, and farther away than can a child's cry be heard. We ate fish and meat and berries—there was nothing else to eat—and we ate without salt. How many be there among you who care to go back to the fish and meat without salt?'

It would have sunk home, had not Madwan leaped to his feet ere silence could come. 'And first a question to thee, Keesh. The white man up at the Big House tells you that it is wrong to kill. Yet do we not know that the white men kill? Have we forgotten the great fight on the Koyo-kuk? or the great fight at Nuklukyeto, where three white men killed twenty of the Tozikakats? Do you think we no longer remember the three men of the Tana-naw that the white man Macklewrath killed? Tell me, O Keesh, why does the Shaman Brown teach you that it is wrong to fight, when all his brothers fight?'

'Nay, nay, there is no need to answer,' Gnob piped, while Keesh struggled with the paradox. 'It is very simple. The Good Man Brown would hold the Raven tight whilst his brothers pluck the feathers.' He raised his voice. 'But so long as there is one Tana-naw to strike a blow, or one maiden to bear a man-child, the Raven shall not be plucked!'

Gnob turned to a husky young man across the fire. 'And what sayest thou, Makamuk, who are brother to Su-Su?'

Makamuk came to his feet. A long face-scar lifted his upper lip into a perpetual grin which belied the glowing ferocity of his eyes. 'This day,' he began with cunning irrelevance, 'I came by the Trader Macklewrath's cabin. And in the door I saw a child laughing at the sun. And the child looked at me with the Trader Macklewrath's eyes, and it was frightened. The mother ran to it and quieted it. The mother was Ziska, the Thlunget woman.'

A snarl of rage rose up and drowned his voice, which he stilled by turning dramatically upon Keesh with out-stretched arm and accusing finger.

'So? You give your women away, you Thlunget, and come to the Tana-naw for more? But we have need of our women, Keesh; for we must breed men, many men, against the day when the Raven grapples with the Wolf.'

Through the storm of applause, Gnob's voice shrilled clear. 'And thou, Nossabok, who art her favourite brother?'

The young fellow was slender and graceful, with the strong aquiline nose and high brows of his type; but from some nervous affliction the lid of one eye drooped at odd times in a suggestive wink. Even as he arose it so drooped and rested a moment against his cheek. But it was not greeted with the accustomed laughter. Every face was grave. 'I, too, passed by the Trader Macklewrath's cabin,' he rippled in soft girlish tones, wherein there was much of youth and much of his sister. 'And I saw Indians with the sweat running into their eyes and their knees shaking with weariness—I say, I saw Indians groaning under the logs for the store which the Trader Macklewrath is to build. And with my eyes I saw them chopping wood to keep the Shaman Brown's Big House warm through the frost of the long nights. This be squaw work. Never shall the Tana-naw do the like. We shall be blood brothers to men, not squaws; and the Thlunget be squaws.'

A deep silence fell, and all eyes centred on Keesh. He looked about him carefully, deliberately, full into the face of each grown man. 'So,' he said passionlessly. And 'So,' he repeated. Then turned on his heel without further word and passed out into the darkness.

Wading among sprawling babies and bristling wolf-dogs, he threaded the great camp, and on its outskirts came upon a woman at work by the light of a fire. With strings of bark stripped from the long roots of creeping vines, she was braiding rope for the Fishing. For some time, without speech, he watched her deft hands bringing law and order out of the unruly mass of curling fibres. She was good to look upon, swaying there to her task, strong-limbed, deep-chested, and with hips made for motherhood. And the bronze of her face was golden in the flickering light, her hair blue-black, her eyes jet.

'O Su-Su,' he spoke finally, 'thou hast looked upon me kindly in the days that have gone and in the days yet young——'

'I looked kindly upon thee for that thou wert chief of the Thlunget,' she answered quickly, 'and because thou wert big and strong.'

'Ay——'

'But that was in the old days of the Fishing,' she hastened to add, 'before the Shaman Brown came and taught thee ill things and led thy feet on strange trails.'

'But I would tell thee the——'

She held up one hand in a gesture which reminded him of her father. 'Nay, I know already the speech that stirs in thy throat, O Keesh, and I make answer now. It so happeneth that the fish of the water and the beasts of the forest bring forth after their kind. And this is good. Likewise it happeneth to women. It is for them to bring forth their kind, and even the maiden, while she is yet a maiden, feels the pang of the birth, and the pain of the breast, and the small hands at the neck. And when such feeling is strong, then does each maiden look about her with secret eyes for the man—for the man who shall be fit to father her kind. So have I felt. So did I feel when I looked upon thee and found thee big and strong, a hunter and fighter of beasts and men, well able to win meat when I should eat for two, well able to keep danger afar off when my helplessness drew nigh. But that was before the day the Shaman Brown came into the land and taught thee——'

'But it is not right, Su-Su. I have it on good word——'

'It is not right to kill. I know what thou wouldst say. Then breed thou after thy kind, the kind that does not kill; but come not on such quest among the Tana-naw. For it is said in the time to come, that the Raven shall grapple with the Wolf. I do not know, for this be the affair of men; but I do know that it is for me to bring forth men against that time.'

'Su-Su,' Keesh broke in, 'thou must hear me——'

'A *man* would beat me with a stick and make me hear,' she sneered. 'But thou . . . here!' She thrust a bunch of bark into his hand. 'I cannot give thee myself, but this, yes. It looks fittest in thy hands. It is squaw work, so braid away.'

He flung it from him, the angry blood pounding a muddy path under his bronze.

'One more thing,' she went on. 'There be an old custom which thy father and mine were not strangers to. When a man falls in battle, his scalp is carried away in token. Very good. But thou, who hast forsworn the Raven, must do more. Thou must bring me, not scalps, but heads, two heads, and then will I give thee, not bark, but a brave-beaded belt, and sheath, and long Russian knife. Then will I look kindly upon thee once again, and all will be well.'

'So,' the man pondered. 'So.' Then he turned and passed out through the light.

'Nay, O Keesh!' she called after him. 'Not two heads, but three at least!'

But Keesh remained true to his conversion, lived up-rightly, and made his tribespeople obey the gospel as pro-pounded by the Rev. Jackson Brown. Through all the time of the Fishing he gave no heed to the Tana-naw, nor took notice of the sly things which were said, nor of the laughter of the women of the many tribes. After the Fishing, Gnob and his people, with great store of salmon, sun-dried and smoke-cured, departed for the Hunting on the head reaches of the Tana-naw. Keesh watched them go, but did not fail in his attendance at Mission service, where he prayed regu-larly and led the singing with his deep bass voice.

The Rev. Jackson Brown delighted in that deep bass voice, and because of his sterling qualities deemed him the most promising convert. Macklewrath doubted this. He did not believe in the efficacy of the conversion of the heathen, and he was not slow in speaking his mind. But Mr Brown was a large man, in his way, and he argued it out with such convincingness, all of one long fall night, that the trader, driven from position after position, finally announced in desperation, 'Knock out my brains with apples, Brown, if I don't become a convert myself, if Keesh holds fast, true blue, for two years!' Mr Brown never lost an opportunity, so he clinched the matter on the spot with a virile hand-grip, and thenceforth the conduct of Keesh was to determine the ultimate abiding-place of Macklewrath's soul.

But there came news one day, after the winter's rime had settled down over the land sufficiently for travel. A Tana-naw man arrived at the St George Mission in quest of ammunition and bringing information that Su-Su had set eyes on Nee-Koo, a nervy young hunter who had bid brilliantly for her by old Gnob's fire. It was at about this time that the Rev. Jackson Brown came upon Keesh by the wood-trail which leads down to the river. Keesh had his best dogs in the harness, and shoved under shed-lashings was his largest and finest pair of snow-shoes.

'Where goest thou, O Keesh? Hunting?' Mr Brown asked, falling into the Indian manner.

Keesh looked him steadily in the eyes for a full minute, then started up his dogs. Then again, turning his deliberate gaze upon the missionary, he answered, 'No; I go to hell.'

In an open space, striving to burrow into the snow as though for shelter from the appalling desolateness, huddled three dreary lodges. Ringed all about, a dozen paces away, was the sombre forest. Overhead there was no keen, blue sky of naked space, but a vague, misty curtain, pregnant with snow, which had drawn between. There was no wind, no sound, nothing but the snow and silence. Nor was there even the general stir of life about the camp; for the hunting party had run upon the flank of the caribou herd and the kill had been large. Thus, after the period of fasting had come the plenitude of feasting, and thus, in broad daylight, they slept heavily under their roofs of moosehide.

By a fire, before one of the lodges, five pairs of snow-shoes stood on end in their element, and by the fire sat Su-Su. The hood of her squirrel-skin parka was about her hair, and well drawn up around her throat; but her hands were unmittened and nimbly at work with needle and sinew, completing the last fantastic design on a belt of leather faced with bright scarlet cloth. A dog, somewhere at the rear of one of the lodges, raised a short, sharp bark, then ceased as abruptly as it had begun. Once, her father, in the lodge at her back, gurgled and grunted in his sleep. 'Bad dreams,' she smiled to herself. 'He grows old, and that last joint was too much.'

She placed the last bead, knotted the sinew, and replenished the fire. Then, after gazing long into the flames, she lifted her head to the harsh *crunch-crunch* of a moccasined foot against the flinty snow granules. Keesh was at her side, bending slightly forward to a load which he bore upon his back. This was wrapped loosely in a soft-tanned moosehide, and he dropped it carelessly into the snow and sat down. They looked at each other long and without speech.

'It is a far fetch, O Keesh,' she said at last, 'a far fetch from St George Mission by the Yukon.'

'Ay,' he made answer, absently, his eyes fixed keenly upon the belt and taking note of its girth. 'But where is the knife?' he demanded.

'Here.' She drew it from inside her parka and flashed its naked length in the firelight. 'It is a good knife.'

'Give it me,' he commanded.

'Nay, O Keesh,' she laughed. 'It may be that thou wast not born to wear it.'

'Give it me!' he reiterated, without change of tone. 'I was so born.'

But her eyes, glancing coquettishly past him to the moosehide, saw the snow about it slowly reddening. 'It is blood, Keesh?' she asked.

'Ay, it is blood. But give me the belt and the long Russian knife.'

She felt suddenly afraid, but thrilled when he took the belt roughly from her, thrilled to the roughness. She looked at him softly, and was aware of a pain at the breast and of small hands clutching her throat.

'It was made for a smaller man,' he remarked grimly, drawing in his abdomen and clasping the buckle at the first hole.

Su-su smiled, and her eyes were yet softer. Again she

felt the soft hands at her throat. He was good to look upon, and the belt was indeed small, made for a smaller man; but what did it matter? She could make many belts.

'But the blood?' she asked, urged on by a hope new-born and growing. 'The blood, Keesh? Is it . . . are they . . . heads?'

'Ay.'

'They must be very fresh, else would the blood be frozen.'

'Ay, it is not cold, and they be fresh, quite fresh.'

'Oh, Keesh!' Her face was warm and bright. 'And for me?'

'Ay; for thee.'

He took hold of a corner of the hide, flirted it open, and rolled the heads out before her.

'Three,' he whispered savagely; 'nay, four at least.'

But she sat transfixed. There they lay—the soft-featured Nee-Koo; the gnarled old face of Gnob; Makamuk, grinning at her with his lifted upper lip; and lastly, Nossabok, his eyelid, up to its old trick, drooped on his girlish cheek in a suggestive wink. There they lay, the firelight flashing upon and playing over them, and from each of them a widening circle dyed the snow to scarlet.

Thawed by the fire, the white crust gave way beneath the head of Gnob, which rolled over like a thing alive, spun around, and came to rest at her feet. But she did not move. Keesh, too, sat motionless, his eyes unblinking, centred steadfastly upon her.

Once, in the forest, an overburdened pine dropped its load of snow, and the echoes reverberated hollowly down the gorge; but neither stirred. The short day had been waning fast, and darkness was wrapping round the camp when White Fang trotted up toward the fire. He paused to reconnoitre, but not being driven back, came closer. His nose shot swiftly to the side, nostrils a-tremble and bristles rising along the spine; and straight and true, he followed the sudden scent to his master's head. He sniffed it gingerly at first and licked the forehead with his red lolling tongue.

Then he sat abruptly down, pointed his nose up at the first faint star, and raised the long wolf-howl.

This brought Su-Su to herself. She glanced across at Keesh, who had unsheathed the Russian knife and was watching her intently. His face was firm and set, and in it she read the law. Slipping back the hood of her parka, she bared her neck and rose to her feet. There she paused and took a long look about her, at the rimming forest, at the faint stars in the sky, at the camp, at the snow-shoes in the snow—a last long comprehensive look at life. A light breeze stirred her hair from the side, and for the space of one deep breath she turned her head and followed it around until she met it full-faced.

Then she thought of her children, ever to be unborn, and she walked over to Keesh and said, 'I am ready'.

## NAM-BOK THE UNVERACIOUS

'A BIDARKA, is it not so? Look! a bidarka, and one man who drives clumsily with a paddle!'

Old Bask-Wah-Wan rose to her knees, trembling with weakness and eagerness, and gazed out over the sea.

'Nam-Bok was ever clumsy at the paddle,' she maundered reminiscently, shading the sun from her eyes and staring across the silver-spilled water. 'Nam-Bok was ever clumsy. I remember . . .'

But the women and children laughed loudly, and there was a gentle mockery in their laughter, and her voice dwindled till her lips moved without sound.

Koogah lifted his grizzled head from his bone-carving and followed the path of her eyes. Except when wide yaws took it off its course, a bidarka was heading in for the beach. Its occupant was paddling with more strength than dexterity, and made his approach along the zig-zag line of most resistance. Koogah's head dropped to his work again, and on the ivory tusk between his knees he scratched the dorsal fin of a fish the like of which never swam in the sea.

'It is doubtless the man from the next village,' he said finally, 'come to consult me about the markings of things on bone. And the man is a clumsy man. He will never know how.'

'It is Nam-Bok,' old Bask-Wah-Wan repeated. 'Should I not know my son?' she demanded shrilly. 'I say, and I say again, it is Nam-Bok.'

'And so thou hast said these many summers,' one of the women chided softly. 'Ever when the ice passed out of the sea hast thou sat and watched through the long day, saying at each chance canoe, "This is Nam-Bok". Nam-Bok is dead, O Bask-Wah-Wan, and the dead do not come back. It cannot be that the dead come back.'

'Nam-Bok!' the old woman cried, so loud and clear that the whole village was startled and looked at her.

She struggled to her feet and tottered down the sand. She stumbled over a baby lying in the sun, and the mother hushed its crying and hurled harsh words after the old woman, who took no notice. The children ran down the beach in advance of her, and as the man in the bidarka drew closer, nearly capsizing with one of his ill-directed strokes, the women followed. Koogah dropped his walrus tusk and went also, leaning heavily upon his staff, and after him loitered the men in twos and threes.

The bidarka turned broadside and the ripple of surf threatened to swamp it, only a naked boy ran into the water and pulled the bow high up on the sand. The man stood up and sent a questing glance along the line of villagers. A rainbow sweater, dirty and the worse for wear, clung loosely to his broad shoulders, and a red cotton handkerchief was knotted in sailor fashion about his throat. A fisherman's tam-o'-shanter on his close-clipped head, and dungaree trousers and heavy brogans, completed his outfit.

But he was none the less a striking personage to these simple fisherfolk of the great Yukon Delta, who, all their lives, had stared out on Bering Sea and in that time seen but two white men—the census enumerator and a lost Jesuit priest. They were a poor people, with neither gold in the ground nor valuable furs in hand, so the whites had passed them afar. Also, the Yukon, through the thousands of years, had shoaled that portion of the sea with the detritus of Alaska till vessels grounded out of sight of land. So the sodden coast, with its long inside reaches and huge mud-land archipelagoes, was avoided by the ships of men, and the fisherfolk knew not that such things were.

Koogah, the Bone-Scratcher, retreated backward in sudden haste, tripping over his staff and falling to the ground. 'Nam-Bok!' he cried, as he scrambled wildly for footing. 'Nam-Bok, who was blown off to sea, come back!'

The men and women shrank away, and the children scuttled off between their legs. Only Opee-Kwan was brave, as befitted the head man of the village. He strode forward and gazed long and earnestly at the newcomer.

'It *is* Nam-Bok,' he said at last, and at the conviction in his voice the women wailed apprehensively and drew farther away.

The lips of the stranger moved indecisively, and his brown throat writhed and wrestled with unspoken words.

'La la, it is Nam-Bok,' Bask-Wah-Wan croaked, peering up into his face. 'Ever did I say Nam-Bok would come back.'

'Ay, it is Nam-Bok come back.' This time it was Nam-Bok himself who spoke, putting a leg over the side of the bidarka and standing with one foot afloat and one ashore. Again his throat writhed and wrestled as he grappled after forgotten words. And when the words came forth they were strange of sound and a spluttering of the lips accompanied the gutturals. 'Greetings, O brothers,' he said, 'brothers of old time before I went away with the off-shore wind.'

He stepped out with both feet on the sand, and Opee-Kwan waved him back.

'Thou art dead, Nam-Bok,' he said.

Nam-Bok laughed. 'I am fat.'

'Dead man are not fat,' Opee-Kwan confessed. 'Thou hast fared well, but it is strange. No man may mate with the off-shore wind and come back on the heels of the years.'

'I have come back,' Nam-Bok answered simply.

'Mayhap thou art a shadow, then, a passing shadow of the Nam-Bok that was. Shadows come back.'

'I am hungry. Shadows do not eat.'

But Opee-Kwan doubted, and brushed his hand across his brow in sore puzzlement. Nam-Bok was likewise puzzled, and as he looked up and down the line found no welcome in the eyes of the fisherfolk. The men and women whispered together. The children stole timidly back among their elders, and bristling dogs fawned up to him and sniffed suspiciously.

'I bore thee, Nam-Bok, and I gave thee suck when thou wast little,' Bask-Wah-Wan whimpered, drawing closer; 'and shadow though thou be, or no shadow, I will give thee to eat now.'

Nam-Bok made to come to her, but a growl of fear and menace warned him back. He said something in a strange tongue which sounded like 'Goddam,' and added, 'No shadow am I, but a man.'

'Who may know concerning the things of mystery?' Opee-Kwan demanded, half of himself and half of his tribespeople. 'We are, and in a breath we are not. If the man may become shadow, may not the shadow become man? Nam-Bok was, but is not. This we know, but we do not know if this be Nam-Bok or the shadow of Nam-Bok.'

Nam-Bok cleared his throat and made answer. 'In the old time long ago, thy father's father, Opee-Kwan, went away and came back on the heels of the years. Nor was a place by the fire denied him. It is said . . .' He paused significantly, and they hung on his utterance. 'It is said,' he repeated, driving his point home with deliberation, 'that Sipsip, his *klooch*, bore him two sons after he came back.'

'But he had no doings with the off-shore wind,' Opee-Kwan retorted. 'He went away into the heart of the land, and it is in the nature of things that a man may go on and on into the land.'

'And likewise the sea. But that is neither here nor there. It is said . . . that thy father's father told strange tales of the things he saw.'

'Ay, strange tales he told.'

'I, too, have strange tales to tell,' Nam-Bok stated insidiously. And, as they wavered, 'And presents likewise.'

He pulled from the bidarka a shawl, marvellous of texture and colour, and flung it about his mother's shoulders. The women voiced a collective sigh of admiration, and old Bask-Wah-Wan ruffled the gay material and patted it and crooned in childish joy.

'He has tales to tell,' Koogah muttered. 'And presents,' a woman seconded.

And Opee-Kwan knew that his people were eager, and further, he was aware himself of an itching curiosity concerning those untold tales. 'The fishing has been good,' he said judiciously, 'and we have oil in plenty. So come, Nam-Bok, let us feast.'

Two of the men hoisted the bidarka on their shoulders and carried it up to the fire. Nam-Bok walked by the side of Opee-Kwan, and the villagers followed after, save those of the women who lingered a moment to lay caressing fingers on the shawl.

There was little talk while the feast went on, though many and curious were the glances stolen at the son of Bask-Wah-Wan. This embarrassed him—not because he was modest of spirit, however, but for the fact that the stench of the seal-oil had robbed him of his appetite, and that he keenly desired to conceal his feelings on the subject.

'Eat; thou art hungry,' Opee-Kwan commanded, and Nam-Bok shut both his eyes and shoved his fist into the big pot of putrid fish.

'La la, be not ashamed. The seal were many this year, and strong men are ever hungry.' And Bask-Wah-Wan sopped a particularly offensive chunk of salmon into the oil and passed it fondly and dripping to her son.

In despair, when premonitory symptoms warned him that his stomach was not so strong as of old, he filled his pipe and struck up a smoke. The people fed on noisily and watched. Few of them could boast of intimate acquaintance with the precious weed, though now and again small quantities and abominable qualities were obtained in trade from the Eskimos to the northward. Koogah, sitting next to him, indicated that he was not averse to taking a draw, and between two mouthfuls, with the oil thick on his lips, sucked away at the amber stem. And thereupon Nam-Bok held his stomach with a shaky hand and declined the proffered return. Koogah could keep the pipe, he said, for he had intended so to honour him from the first. And the people licked their fingers and approved of his liberality.

Opee-Kwan rose to his feet. 'And now, O Nam-Bok, the feast is ended, and we would listen concerning the strange things you have seen.'

The fisherfolk applauded with their hands and gathering about them their work, prepared to listen. The men were busy fashioning spears and carving on ivory, while the women scraped the fat from the hides of the hair seal and made them pliable or sewed muclucs with threads of sinew. Nam-Bok's eyes roved over the scene, but there was not the charm about it that his recollection had warranted him to expect. During the years of his wandering he had looked forward to just this scene, and now that it had come he was disappointed. It was a bare and meagre life, he deemed, and not to be compared to the one to which he had become used. Still, he would open their eyes a bit, and his own eyes sparkled at the thought.

'Brothers,' he began, with the smug complacency of a man about to relate the big things he has done, 'it was late summer of many summers back, with much such weather as this promises to be, when I went away. You all remember the day, when the gulls flew low, and the wind blew strong from the land, and I could not hold my bidarka against it. I tied the covering of the bidarka about me so that no water could get in, and all of the night I fought with the storm. And in the morning there was no land— only the sea—and the off-shore wind held me close in its arms and bore me along. Three such nights whitened into dawn and showed me no land, and the off-shore wind would not let me go.

'And when the fourth day came, I was as a madman. I could not dip my paddle for want of food; and my head went round and round, what of the thirst that was upon me. But the sea was no longer angry, and the soft south wind was blowing, and as I looked about me I saw a sight that made me think I was indeed mad.'

Nam-Bok paused to pick away a sliver of salmon lodged between his teeth, and the men and women, with idle hands and heads craned forward, waited.

'It was a canoe, a big canoe. If all the canoes I have ever seen were made into one canoe, it would not be so large.'

There were exclamations of doubt, and Koogah, whose years were many, shook his head.

'If each bidarka were as a grain of sand,' Nam-Bok defiantly continued, 'and if there were as many bidarkas as there be grains of sand in this beach, still would they not make so big a canoe as this I saw on the morning of the fourth day. It was a very big canoe, and it was called a *schooner*. I saw this thing of wonder, this great schooner, coming after me, and on it I saw men——'

'Hold, O Nam-Bok!' Opee-Kwan broke in. 'What manner of men were they?—big men?'

'Nay, mere men like you and me.'

'Did the big canoe come fast?'

'Ay.'

'The sides were tall, the men short.' Opee-Kwan stated the premises with conviction. 'And did these men dip with long paddles?'

Nam-Bok grinned. 'There were no paddles,' he said.

Mouths remained open, and a long silence dropped down. Opee-Kwan borrowed Koogah's pipe for a couple of contemplative sucks. One of the younger women giggled nervously and drew upon herself angry eyes.

'There were no paddles?' Opee-Kwan asked softly, returning the pipe.

'The south wind was behind,' Nam-Bok explained.

'But the wind-drift is slow.'

'The schooner had wings—thus.' He sketched a diagram of masts and sails in the sand, and the men crowded around and studied it. The wind was blowing briskly, and for more graphic elucidation he seized the corners of his

mother's shawl and spread them out till it bellied like a
sail. Bask-Wah-Wan scolded and struggled, but was blown
down the beach for a score of feet and left breathless and
stranded in a heap of driftwood. The men uttered sage
grunts of comprehension, but Koogah suddenly tossed back
his hoary head.

'Ho! Ho!' he laughed. 'A foolish thing, this big canoe!
A most foolish thing! The plaything of the wind! Where-
soever the wind goes, it goes too. No man who journeys
therein may name the landing beach, for always he goes
with the wind, and the wind goes everywhere, but no man
knows where.'

'It is so,' Opee-Kwan supplemented gravely. 'With the
wind the going is easy, but against the wind a man striveth
hard; and for that they had no paddles these men on the
big canoe did not strive at all.'

'Small need to strive,' Nam-Bok cried angrily. 'The
schooner went likewise against the wind.'

'And what said you made the sch—sch—schooner go?'
Koogah asked, tripping craftily over the strange word.

'The wind', was the impatient response.

'Then the wind made the sch—sch—schooner go against
the wind.' Old Koogah dropped an open leer to Opee-
Kwan, and, the laughter growing around him, continued:
'The wind blows from the south and blows the schooner
south. The wind blows against the wind. The wind blows
one way and the other at the same time. It is very simple.
We understand, Nam-Bok. We clearly understand.'

'Thou art a fool!'

'Truth falls from thy lips,' Koogah answered meekly. 'I
was over-long in understanding, and the thing was simple.'

But Nam-Bok's face was dark, and he said rapid words
which they had never heard before. Bone-scratching and
skin-scraping were resumed, but he shut his lips tightly on
the tongue that could not be believed.

'This sch—sch—schooner,' Koogah imperturbably
asked; 'it was made of a big tree?'

'It was made of many trees,' Nam-Bok snapped shortly.
'It was very big.'

He lapsed into sullen silence again, and Opee-Kwan nudged Koogah, who shook his head with slow amazement and murmured, 'It is very strange.'

Nam-Bok took the bait. 'That is nothing,' he said airily; 'you should see the *steamer*. As the grain of sand is to the bidarka, as the bidarka is to the schooner, so the schooner is to the steamer. Further, the steamer is made of iron. It is all iron.'

'Nay, nay, Nam-Bok,' cried the head man; 'how can that be? Always iron goes to the bottom. For behold, I received an iron knife in trade from the head man of the next village, and yesterday the iron knife slipped from my fingers and went down, down, into the sea. To all things there be law. Never was there one thing outside the law. This we know. And, moreover, we know that things of a kind have the one law, and that all iron has the one law. So unsay thy words, Nam-Bok, that we may yet honour thee.'

'It is so,' Nam-Bok persisted. 'The steamer is all iron and does not sink.'

'Nay, nay; this cannot be.'

'With my own eyes I saw it.'

'It is not in the nature of things.'

'But tell me, Nam-Bok,' Koogah interrupted, for fear the tale would go no farther, 'tell me the manner of these men in finding their way across the sea when there is no land by which to steer.'

'The sun points out the path.'

'But how?'

'At midday the head man of the schooner takes a thing through which his eye looks at the sun, and then he makes the sun climb down out of the sky to the edge of the earth.'

'Now this be evil medicine!' cried Opee-Kwan, aghast at the sacrilege. The men held up their hands in horror, and the women moaned. 'This be evil medicine. It is not good to misdirect the great sun which drives away the night and gives us the seal, the salmon, and warm weather.'

'What if it be evil medicine?' Nam-Bok demanded truculently. 'I, too, have looked through the thing at the sun and made the sun climb down out of the sky.'

Those who were nearest drew away from him hurriedly, and a woman covered the face of a child at her breast so that his eye might not fall upon it.

'But on the morning of the fourth day, O Nam-Bok,' Koogah suggested; 'on the morning of the fourth day when the sch—sch—schooner came after thee?'

'I had little strength left in me and could not run away. So I was taken on board and water was poured down my throat and good food given me. Twice, my brothers, you have seen a white man. These men were all white and as many as have I fingers and toes. And when I saw they were full of kindness, I took heart, and I resolved to bring away with me report of all that I saw. And they taught me the work they did, and gave me good food and a place to sleep.

'And day after day we went over the sea, and each day the head man drew the sun down out of the sky and made it tell where we were. And when the waves were kind, we hunted the fur seal and I marvelled much, for always did they fling the meat and the fat away and save only the skin.'

Opee-Kwan's mouth was twitching violently, and he was about to make denunciation of such waste when Koogah kicked him to be still.

'After a weary time, when the sun was gone and the bite of the frost come into the air, the head man pointed the nose of the schooner south. South and east we travelled for days upon days, with never the land in sight, and we were near to the village from which hailed the men——'

'How did they know they were near?' Opee-Kwan, unable to contain himself longer demanded. 'There was no land to see.'

Nam-Bok glowered on him wrathfully. 'Did I not say the head man brought the sun down out of the sky?'

Koogah interposed, and Nam-Bok went on.

'As I say, when we were near to that village a great storm blew up, and in the night we were helpless and knew not where we were——'

'Thou hast just said the head man knew——'

'Oh, peace, Opee-Kwan! Thou art a fool and cannot understand. As I say, we were helpless in the night, when

I heard, above the roar of the storm, the sound of the sea on the beach. And next we struck with a mighty crash and I was in the water, swimming. It was a rock-bound coast, with one patch of beach in many miles, and the law was that I should dig my hands into the sand and draw myself clear of the surf. The other men must have pounded against the rocks, for none of them came ashore but the head man, and him I knew only by the ring on his finger.

'When day came, there being nothing of the schooner, I turned my face to the land and journeyed into it that I might get food and look upon the faces of the people. And when I came to a house I was taken in and given to eat, for I had learned their speech, and the white men are ever kindly. And it was a house bigger than all the houses built by us and our fathers before us.'

'It was a mighty house,' Koogah said, masking his unbelief with wonder.

'And many trees went into the making of such a house,' Opee-Kwan added, taking the cue.

'That is nothing.' Nam-Bok shrugged his shoulders in belittling fashion. 'As our houses are to that house, so that house was to the houses I was yet to see.'

'And they are not big men?'

'Nay; mere men like you and me,' Nam-Bok answered. 'I had cut a stick that I might walk in comfort, and remembering that I was to bring report to you, my brothers, I cut a notch in the stick for each person who lived in that house. And I stayed there many days, and worked, for which they gave me *money*—a thing of which you know nothing, but which is very good.

'And one day I departed from that place to go farther into the land. And as I walked I met many people, and I cut smaller notches in the stick, that there might be room for all. Then I came upon a strange thing. On the ground before me was a bar of iron, as big in thickness as my arm, and a long step away was another bar of iron——'

'Then wert thou a rich man,' Opee-Kwan asserted; 'for iron be worth more than anything else in the world. It would have made many knives.'

'Nay, it was not mine.'

'It was a find, and a find be lawful.'

'Not so; the white men had placed it there. And further, these bars were so long that no man could carry them away —so long that as far as I could see there was no end to them.'

'Nam-Bok, that is very much iron,' Opee-Kwan cautioned.

'Ay, it was hard to believe with my own eyes upon it; but I could not gainsay my eyes. And as I looked I heard ...' He turned abruptly upon the head man. 'Opee-Kwan, thou hast heard the sea-lion bellow in his anger. Make it plain in thy mind of as many sea-lions as there be waves to the sea, and make it plain that all these sea-lions be made into one sea-lion, and as that one sea-lion would bellow so bellowed the thing I heard.'

The fisherfolk cried aloud in astonishment, and Opee-Kwan's jaw lowered and remained lowered.

'And in the distance I saw a monster like unto a thousand whales. It was one-eyed, and vomited smoke, and it snorted with exceeding loudness. I was afraid and ran with shaking legs along the path between the bars. But it came with the speed of the wind, this monster, and I leaped the iron bars with its breath hot on my face. . . .'

Opee-Kwan gained control of his jaw again. 'And—and then, O Nam-Bok?'

'Then it came by on the bars, and harmed me not; and when my legs could hold me up again it was gone from sight. And it is a very common thing in that country. Even the women and children are not afraid. Men make them to do work, these monsters.'

'As we make our dogs do work?' Koogah asked, with sceptic twinkle in his eye.

'Ay, as we make our dogs do work.'

'And how do they breed these—these things?' Opee-Kwan questioned.

'They breed not at all. Men fashion them cunningly of iron, and feed them with stone, and give them water to drink. The stone becomes fire, and the water becomes steam, and the steam of the water is the breath of their nostrils, and——'

'There, there, O Nam-Bok,' Opee-Kwan interrupted. 'Tell us of other wonders. We grow tired of this which we may not understand.'

'You do not understand?' Nam-Bok asked despairingly.

'Nay, we do not understand,' the men and women wailed back. 'We cannot understand.'

Nam-Bok thought of a combined harvester, and of the machines wherein visions of living men were to be seen, and of the machines from which came the voices of men, and he knew his people could never understand.

'Dare I say I rode this iron monster through the land?' he asked bitterly.

Opee-Kwan threw up his hands, palms outward, in open incredulity. 'Say on; say anything. We listen.'

'Then did I ride the iron monster, for which I gave money——'

'Thou saidst it was fed with stone.'

'And likewise, thou fool, I said money was a thing of which you know nothing. As I say, I rode the monster through the land, and through many villages, until I came to a big village on a salt arm of the sea. And the houses shoved their roofs among the stars in the sky, and the clouds drifted by them, and everywhere was much smoke. And the roar of that village was like the roar of the sea in storm, and the people were so many that I flung away my stick and no longer remembered the notches upon it.'

'Hadst thou made small notches,' Koogah reproved, 'thou mightst have brought report.'

Nam-Bok whirled upon him in anger. 'Had I made small notches! Listen, Koogah, thou scratcher of bone! If I had made small notches, neither the stick, nor twenty sticks, could have borne them—nay, not all the driftwood of all the beaches between this village and the next. And if all of you, the women and children as well, were twenty times as many, and if you had twenty hands each, and in each hand a stick and a knife, still the notches could not be cut for the people I saw, so many were they and so fast did they come and go.'

'There cannot be so many people in all the world,' Opee-Kwan objected, for he was stunned and his mind could not grasp such magnitude of numbers.

'What dost thou know of all the world and how large it is?' Nam-Bok demanded.

'But there cannot be so many people in one place.'

'Who art thou to say what can be and what cannot be?'

'It stands to reason there cannot be so many people in one place. Their canoes would clutter the sea till there was no room. And they could empty the sea each day of its fish, and they would not all be fed.'

'So it would seem,' Nam-Bok made final answer; 'yet it was so. With my own eyes I saw, and flung my stick away.' He yawned heavily and rose to his feet. 'I have paddled far. The day has been long, and I am tired. Now I will sleep, and to-morrow we will have further talk upon the things I have seen.'

Bask-Wah-Wan, hobbling fearfully in advance, proud indeed, yet awed by her wonderful son, led him to her igloo and stowed him away among the greasy, ill-smelling furs. But the men lingered by the fire, and a council was held wherein was there much whispering and low-voiced discussion.

An hour passed, and a second, and Nam-Bok slept, and the talk went on. The evening sun dipped toward the north-west, and at eleven at night was nearly due north. Then it was that the head man and the bone-scratcher separated themselves from the council and aroused Nam-Bok. He blinked up into their faces and turned on his side to sleep again. Opee-Kwan gripped him by the arm and kindly but firmly shook his senses back into him.

'Come, Nam-Bok, arise!' he commanded. 'It be time.'

'Another feast?' Nam-Bok cried. 'Nay, I am not hungry. Go on with the eating and let me sleep.'

'Time to be gone!' Koogah thundered.

But Opee-Kwan spoke more softly. 'Thou wast bidarka-mate with me when we were boys,' he said. 'Together we first chased the seal and drew the salmon from the traps. And thou didst drag me back to life, Nam-Bok, when the sea closed over me and I was sucked down to the black rocks. Together we hungered and bore the chill of the frost, and together we crawled beneath one fur and lay close to each other. And because of these things, and the kindness in which I stood to thee, it grieves me sore that thou shouldst return such a remarkable liar. We cannot understand, and our heads be dizzy with the things thou hast spoken. It is not good, and there has been much talk in the council. Wherefore we send thee away, that our heads may remain clear and strong and be not troubled by the unaccountable things.'

'These things thou speakest of be shadows,' Koogah took up the strain. 'From the shadow-world thou hast brought them, and to the shadow-world thou must return them. Thy bidarka be ready, and the tribespeople wait. They may not sleep until thou art gone.'

Nam-Bok was perplexed, but hearkened to the voice of the head man.

'If thou art Nam-Bok,' Opee-Kwan was saying, 'thou art a fearful and most wonderful liar; if thou art the shadow of Nam-Bok, then thou speakest of shadows, concerning which it is not good that living men have knowledge. This great village thou hast spoken of we deem the village of shadows. Therein flutter the souls of the dead; for the dead be many and the living few. The dead do not come back. Never have the dead come back—save thou with thy wonder-tales. It is not meet that the dead come back, and should we permit it, great trouble may be our portion.'

Nam-Bok knew his people well and was aware that the voice of the council was supreme. So he allowed himself to be led down to the water's edge, where he was put aboard his bidarka and a paddle thrust into his hand. A stray wildfowl honked somewhere to seaward, and the surf broke limply and hollowly on the sand. A dim twilight brooded over land and water, and in the north the sun smouldered, vague and troubled, and draped about with blood-red mists. The gulls were flying low. The offshore wind blew keen and chill, and the black-massed clouds behind it gave promise of bitter weather.

'Out of the sea thou camest,' Opee-Kwan chanted oracularly, 'and back into the sea thou goest. Thus is balance achieved and all things brought to law.'

Bask-Wah-Wan limped to the froth-mark and cried, 'I bless thee, Nam-Bok, for that thou remembered me.'

But Koogah, shoving Nam-Bok clear of the beach, tore the shawl from her shoulders and flung it into the bidarka.

'It is cold in the long nights,' she wailed; 'and the frost is prone to nip old bones.'

'The thing is a shadow,' the bone-scratcher answered, 'and shadows cannot keep thee warm.'

Nam-Bok stood up that his voice might carry. 'O Bask-Wah-Wan, mother that bore me!' he called. 'Listen to the words of Nam-Bok, thy son. There be room in his bidarka for two, and he would that thou camest with him. For his journey is to where there are fish and oil in plenty. There the frost comes not, and life is easy, and the things of iron do the work of men. Wilt thou come, O Bask-Wah-Wan?'

She debated a moment, while the bidarka drifted swiftly from her, then raised her voice to a quavering treble. 'I am old, Nam-Bok, and soon I shall pass down among the shadows. But I have no wish to go before my time. I am old, Nam-Bok, and I am afraid.'

A shaft of light shot across the dim-lit sea and wrapped boat and man in a splendour of red and gold. Then a hush fell upon the fisherfolk, and only was heard the moan of the off-shore wind and the cries of the gulls flying low in the air.

## LOST FACE

IT WAS the end. Subienkow had travelled a long trail of bitterness and horror, homing like a dove for the capitals of Europe, and here, farther away than ever, in Russian

3*

America, the trail ceased. He sat in the snow, arms tied behind him, waiting the torture. He stared curiously before him at a huge Cossack, prone in the snow, moaning in his pain. The men had finished handling the giant and turned him over to the women. That they had exceeded the fiendishness of the men the man's cries attested.

Subienkow looked on and shuddered. He was not afraid to die. He had carried his life too long in his hands, on that weary trail from Warsaw to Nulato, to shudder at mere dying. But he objected to the torture. It offended his soul. And this offence, in turn, was not due to the mere pain he must endure, but to the sorry spectacle the pain would make of him. He knew that he would pray, and beg, and entreat, even as Big Ivan and the others that had gone before. This would not be nice. To pass out bravely and cleanly, with a smile and a jest—ah, that would have been the way. But to lose control, to have his soul upset by the pangs of the flesh, to screech and gibber like an ape, to become the veriest beast—ah, that was what was so terrible.

There had been no chance to escape. From the beginning, when he dreamed the fiery dream of Poland's independence, he had become a puppet in the hands of fate. From the beginning, at Warsaw, at St Petersburg, in the Siberian mines, in Kamchatka, on the crazy boats of the fur thieves, fate had been driving him to this end. Without doubt, in the foundations of the world was graved this end for him—for him, who was so fine and sensitive, whose nerves scarcely sheltered under his skin, who was a dreamer and a poet and an artist. Before he was dreamed of, it had been determined that the quivering bundle of sensitiveness that constituted him should be doomed to live in raw and howling savagery, and to die in this far land of night, in this dark place beyond the last boundaries of the world.

He sighed. So that thing before him was Big Ivan—Big Ivan the giant, the man without nerves, the man of iron, the Cossack turned freebooter of the seas, who was as phlegmatic as an ox, with a nervous system so low that what was pain to ordinary men was scarcely a tickle to him. Well,

well, trust these Nulato Indians to find Big Ivan's nerves and trace them to the roots of his quivering soul. They were certainly doing it. It was inconceivable that a man could suffer so much and yet live. Big Ivan was paying for his low order of nerves. Already he had lasted twice as long as any of the others.

Subienkow felt that he could not stand the Cossack's sufferings much longer. Why didn't Ivan die? He would go mad if that screaming did not cease. But when it did cease, his turn would come. And there was Yakaga awaiting him, too, grinning at him even now in anticipation—Yakaga, whom only last week he had kicked out of the fort, and upon whose face he had laid the lash of his dog whip. Yakaga would attend to him. Doubtlessly Yakaga was saving for him more refined tortures, more exquisite nerve-racking. Ah! That must have been a good one, from the way Ivan screamed. The squaws bending over him stepped back with laughter and clapping of hands. Subienkow saw the monstrous thing that had been perpetrated, and began to laugh hysterically. The Indians looked at him in wonderment that he should laugh. But Subienkow could not stop.

This would never do. He controlled himself, the spasmodic twitchings slowly dying away. He strove to think of other things, and began reading back in his own life. He remembered his mother and his father, and the little spotted pony, and the French tutor who had taught him dancing and sneaked him an old worn copy of Voltaire. Once more he saw Paris, and dreary London, and gay Vienna, and Rome. And once more he saw that wild group of youths who had dreamed, even as he, the dream of an independent Poland with a king of Poland on the throne at Warsaw. Ah, there it was that the long trail began. Well, he had lasted longest. One by one, beginning with the two executed at St Petersburg, he took up the count of the passing of those brave spirits. Here one had been beaten to death by a jailer, and there, on that bloodstained highway of the exiles, where they had marched for endless months, beaten and maltreated by their Cossack guards, another had dropped by the way. Always it had been savagery—brutal, bestial savagery. They had died—of fever, in the mines, under the knout. The last two had died after the escape, in the battle with the Cossacks, and he alone had won to Kamchatka with the stolen papers and the money of a traveller he had left lying in the snow.

It had been nothing but savagery. All the years, with his heart in studios and theatres and courts, he had been hemmed in by savagery. He had purchased his life with blood. Everybody had killed. He had killed that traveller for his passports. He had proved that he was a man of parts by duelling with two Russian officers on a single day. He had had to prove himself in order to win a place among the fur thieves. He had had to win to that place. Behind him lay the thousand-years-long road across all Siberia and Russia. He could not escape that way. The only way was ahead, across the dark and icy sea of Bering to Alaska. The way had led from savagery to deeper savagery. On the scurvy-rotten ships of the fur thieves, out of food and out of water, buffeted by the interminable storms of that stormy sea, men had become animals. Thrice he had sailed east from Kamchatka. And thrice, after all manner of hardship and suffering, the survivors had come back to Kamchatka. There had been no outlet for escape, and he could not go back the way he had come, for the mines and the knout awaited him.

Again, the fourth and last time, he had sailed east. He had been with those who first found the fabled Seal Islands; but he had not returned with them to share the wealth of furs in the mad orgies of Kamchatka. He had sworn never to go back. He knew that to win to those dear capitals of Europe he must go on. So he had changed ships and remained in the dark new land. His comrades were Slavonian hunters and Russian adventurers, Mongols and Tatars and Siberian aborigines; and through the savages of the New World they had cut a path of blood. They had massacred whole villages that refused to furnish the fur tribute; and they in turn had been massacred by ships' companies. He, with one Finn, had been the sole survivors of such a company. They had spent a winter of solitude and starvation on a lonely Aleutian isle, and their rescue in the spring by another fur ship had been one chance in a thousand.

But always the terrible savagery had hemmed him in. Passing from ship to ship, and ever refusing to return, he had come to the ship that explored south. All down the Alaskan coast they had encountered nothing but hosts of savages. Every anchorage among the beetling islands or under the frowning cliffs of the mainland had meant a battle or a storm. Either the gales blew, threatening destruction, or the war canoes came off, manned by howling natives with the war paint on their faces, who came to learn the bloody virtues of the sea rovers' gunpowder. South, south they had coasted, clear to the myth land of California. Here, it was said, were Spanish adventurers who had fought their way up from Mexico. He had had hopes of those Spanish adventurers. Escaping to them, the rest would have been easy—a year or two, what did it matter more or less?—and he would win to Mexico, then a ship, and Europe would be his. But they had met no Spaniards. Only had they encountered the same impregnable wall of savagery. The denizens of the confines of the world, painted for war, had driven them back from the shores. At last, when one boat was cut off and every man killed, the commander had abandoned the quest and sailed back to the North.

The years had passed. He had served under Tebenkoff when Michaelovski Redoubt was built. He had spent two years in the Kuskokwim country. Two summers, in the month of June, he had managed to be at the head of Kotzebue Sound. Here, at this time, the tribes assembled for barter; here were to be found spotted deerskins from Siberia, ivory from the Diomedes, walrus skins from the shores of the Arctic, strange stone lamps, passing in trade from tribe to tribe, no one knew whence, and, once, a hunting knife of English make; and here, Subienkow knew, was the school in which to learn geography. For he met Eskimos from Norton Sound, from King Island and St

Lawrence Island, from Cape Prince of Wales, and Point Barrow. Such places had other names, and their distances were measured in days.

It was a vast region these trading savages came from, and a vaster region from which, by repeated trade, their stone lamps and that steel knife had come. Subienkow bullied and cajoled and bribed. Every far journeyer or strange tribesman was brought before him. Perils unaccountable and unthinkable were mentioned, as well as wild beasts, hostile tribes, impenetrable forests, and mighty mountain ranges; but always from beyond came the rumour and the tale of white-skinned men, blue of eye and fair of hair, who fought like devils and who sought always for furs. They were to the east—far, far to the east. No one had seen them. It was the word that had been passed along.

It was a hard school. One could not learn geography very well through the medium of strange dialects, from dark minds that mingled fact and fable and that measured distances by 'sleeps' that varied according to the difficulty of the going. But at last came the whisper that gave Subienkow courage. In the east lay a great river where were these blue-eyed men. The river was called the Yukon. South of Michaelovski Redoubt emptied another great river which the Russians knew as the Kwikpak. These two rivers were one, ran the whisper.

Subienkow returned to Michaelovski. For a year he urged an expedition up the Kwikpak. Then arose Malakoff, the Russian half-breed, to lead the wildest and most ferocious of the hell's broth of mongrel adventurers who had crossed from Kamchatka. Subienkow was his lieutenant. They threaded the mazes of the great delta of the Kwikpak, picked up the first low hills on the northern bank, and for half a thousand miles, in skin canoes loaded to the gunwales with trade goods and ammunition, fought their way against the five-knot current of a river that ran from two to ten miles wide in a channel many fathoms deep. Malakoff decided to build the fort at Nulato. Subienkow urged to go farther. But he quickly reconciled himself to Nulato. The long winter was coming on. It would be better to wait. Early the following summer, when the ice was gone, he would disappear up the Kwikpak and work his way to the Hudson's Bay Company's posts. Malakoff had never heard the whisper that the Kwikpak was the Yukon, and Subienkow did not tell him.

Came the building of the fort. It was enforced labour. The tiered walls of logs arose to the sighs and groans of the Nulato Indians. The lash was laid upon their backs, and it was the iron hand of the freebooters of the sea that laid on the lash. There were Indians that ran away, and when they were caught they were brought back and spread-eagled before the fort, where they and their tribe learned the efficacy of the knout. Two died under it; others were injured for life; and the rest took the lesson to heart and ran away no more. The snow was flying ere the fort was finished, and then it was the time for furs. A heavy tribute was laid upon the tribe. Blows and lashings continued, and that the tribute should be paid, the women and children were held as hostages and treated with the barbarity that only the fur thieves knew.

Well, it had been a sowing of blood, and now was come the harvest. The fort was gone. In the light of its burning, half the fur thieves had been cut down. The other half had passed under the torture. Only Subienkow remained, or Subienkow and Big Ivan, if that whimpering, moaning thing in the snow could be called Big Ivan. Subienkow caught Yakaga grinning at him. There was no gainsaying Yakago. The mark of the lash was still on his face. After all, Subienkow could not blame him, but he disliked the thought of what Yakaga would do to him. He thought of appealing to Makamuk, the head chief; but his judgment told him that such appeal was useless. Then, too, he thought of bursting his bonds and dying fighting. Such an end would be quick. But he could not break his bonds. Caribou thongs were stronger than he. Still devising, another thought came to him. He signed for Makamuk, and that an interpreter who knew the coast dialect should be brought.

'Oh, Makamuk,' he said. 'I am not minded to die. I am a great man, and it were foolishness for me to die. In truth, I shall not die. I am not like these other carrion.'

He looked at the moaning thing that had once been Big Ivan, and stirred it contemptuously with his toe.

'I am too wise to die. Behold, I have a great medicine. I alone know this medicine. Since I am not going to die, I shall exchange this medicine with you.'

'What is this medicine?' Makamuk demanded.

'It is a strange medicine.'

Subienkow debated with himself for a moment, as if loath to part with the secret.

'I will tell you. A little bit of this medicine rubbed on the skin makes the skin hard like a rock, hard like iron, so that no cutting weapon can cut it. The strongest blow of a cutting weapon is a vain thing against it. A bone knife becomes like a piece of mud; and it will turn the edge of the iron knives we have brought among you. What will you give me for the secret of the medicine?'

'I will give you your life,' Makamuk made answer through the interpreter.

Subienkow laughed scornfully.

'And you shall be a slave in my house until you die.'

The Pole laughed more scornfully.

'Untie my hands and feet and let us talk,' he said.

The chief made the sign; and when he was loosed Subienkow rolled a cigarette and lighted it.

'This is foolish talk,' said Makamuk. 'There is no such medicine. It cannot be. A cutting edge is stronger than any medicine.'

The chief was incredulous, and yet he wavered. He had seen too many devilries of fur thieves that worked. He could not wholly doubt.

'I will give you your life; but you shall not be a slave,' he announced.

'More than that.'

Subienkow played his game as coolly as if he were bartering for a fox skin.

'It is a very great medicine. It has saved my life many

times. I want a sled and dogs, and six of your hunters to travel with me down the river and give me safety to one day's sleep from Michaelovski Redoubt.'

'You must live here, and teach us all of your devilries,' was the reply.

Subienkow shrugged his shoulders and remained silent. He blew cigarette smoke out on the icy air, and curiously regarded what remained of the big Cossack.

'That scar!' Makamuk said suddenly, pointing to the Pole's neck, where a livid mark advertised the slash of a knife in a Kamchatkan brawl. 'The medicine is not good. The cutting edge was stronger than the medicine.'

'It was a strong man that drove the stroke.' (Subienkow considered.) 'Stronger than you, stronger than your strongest hunter, stronger than he.'

Again, with the toe of his moccasin, he touched the Cossack—a grisly spectacle, no longer conscious—yet in whose dismembered body the pain-racked life clung and was loath to go.

'Also the medicine was weak. For at that place where there were no berries of a certain kind, of which I see you have plenty in this country. The medicine here will be strong.'

'I will let you go downriver,' said Makamuk; 'and the sled and the dogs and the six hunters to give you safety shall be yours.'

'You are slow,' was the cool rejoinder. 'You have committed an offence against my medicine in that you did not at once accept my terms. Behold, I now demand more. I want one hundred beaver skins.' (Makamuk sneered.) 'I want one hundred pounds of dried fish.' (Makamuk nodded, for fish were plentiful and cheap.) 'I want two sleds—one for me and one for my furs and fish. And my rifle must be returned to me. If you do not like the price, in a little while the price will grow.'

Yakaga whispered to the chief.

'But how can I know your medicine is true medicine?' Makamuk asked.

'It is very easy. First, I shall go into the woods——'

Again Yakaga whispered to Makamuk, who made a suspicious dissent.

'You can send twenty hunters with me,' Subienkow went on. 'You see, I must get the berries and the roots with which to make the medicine. Then, when you have brought the two sleds and loaded on them the fish and the beaver skins and the rifle, and when you have told off the six hunters who will go with me—then, when all is ready, I will rub the medicine on my neck, so, and lay my neck there on that log. Then can your strongest hunter take the axe and strike three times on my neck. You yourself can strike the three times.'

Makamuk stood with gaping mouth, drinking in this latest and most wonderful magic of the fur thieves.

'But first,' the Pole added hastily, 'between each blow I must put on fresh medicine. The axe is heavy and sharp, and I want no mistakes.'

'All that you have asked shall be yours,' Makamuk cried in a rush of acceptance. 'Proceed to make your medicine.'

Subienkow concealed his elation. He was playing a desperate game, and there must be no slips. He spoke arrogantly.

'You have been slow. My medicine is offended. To make the offence clean you must give me your daughter.'

He pointed to the girl, an unwholesome creature, with a cast in one eye and a bristling wolf tooth. Makamuk was angry, but the Pole remained imperturbable, rolling and lighting another cigarette.

'Make haste,' he threatened. 'If you are not quick, I shall demand yet more.'

In the silence that followed, the dreary Northland scene faded from before him, and he saw once more his native land, and France, and once, as he glanced at the wolf-toothed girl, he remembered another girl, a singer and a dancer, whom he had known when first as a youth he came to Paris.

'What do you want with the girl?' Makamuk asked.

'To go down the river with me.' Subienkow glanced her over critically. 'She will make a good wife, and it is an honour worthy of my medicine to be married to your blood.'

Again he remembered the singer and dancer and hummed aloud a song she had taught him. He lived the old life over, but in a detached, impersonal sort of way, looking at the memory pictures of his own life as if they were pictures in a book of anybody's life. The chief's voice, abruptly breaking the silence, startled him.

'It shall be done,' said Makamuk. 'The girl shall go down the river with you. But be it understood that I myself strike the three blows with the axe on your neck.'

'But each time I shall put on the medicine,' Subienkow answered, with a show of ill-concealed anxiety.

'You shall put the medicine on between each blow. Here are the hunters who shall see you do not escape. Go into the forest and gather your medicine.'

Makamuk had been convinced of the worth of the medicine by the Pole's rapacity. Surely nothing less than the greatest of medicines could enable a man in the shadow of death to stand up and drive an old woman's bargain.

'Besides,' whispered Yakaga, when the Pole, with his guard, had disappeared among the spruce trees, 'when you have learned the medicine you can easily destroy him.'

'But how can I destroy him?' Makamuk argued. 'His medicine will not let me destroy him.'

'There will be some part where he has not rubbed the medicine,' was Yakaga's reply. 'We will destroy him through that part. It may be his ears. Very well; we will thrust a spear in one ear and out the other. Or it may be his eyes. Surely the medicine will be much too strong to rub on his eyes.'

The chief nodded. 'You are wise, Yakaga. If he possesses no other devil things, we will then destroy him.'

Subienkow did not waste time in gathering the ingredients for his medicine. He selected whatsoever came to hand such as spruce needles, the inner bark of the willow, a strip of birch bark, and a quantity of mossberries, which he made the hunters dig up for him from beneath the snow. A few frozen roots completed his supply, and he led the way back to camp.

Makamuk and Yakaga crouched beside him, noting the quantities and kinds of the ingredients he dropped into the pot of boiling water.

'You must be careful that the mossberries go in first,' he explained.

'And—oh, yes, one other thing—the finger of a man. Here, Yakaga, let me cut off your finger.'

But Yakaga put his hands behind him and scowled.

'Just a small finger,' Subienkow pleaded.

'Yakaga, give him your finger,' Makamuk commanded.

'There be plenty of fingers lying around,' Yakaga grunted, indicating the human wreckage in the snow of the score of persons who had been tortured to death.

'It must be the finger of a live man,' the Pole objected.

'Then shall you have the finger of a live man.' Yakaga strode over to the Cossack and sliced off a finger.

'He is not yet dead,' he announced, flinging the bloody trophy in the snow at the Pole's feet. 'Also, it is a good finger, because it is large.'

Subienkow dropped it into the fire under the pot and began to sing. It was a French love song that with great solemnity he sang into the brew.

'Without these words I utter into it the medicine is worthless,' he explained. 'The words are the chiefest strength of it. Behold, it is ready.'

'Name the words slowly, that I may know them,' Makamuk commanded.

'Not until after the test. When the axe flies back three times from my neck, then will I give you the secret of the words.'

'But if the medicine is not good medicine?' Makamuk queried anxiously.

Subienkow turned upon his wrathfully.

'My medicine is always good. However, if it is not good, then do by me as you have done to the others. Cut me up a bit at a time, even as you have cut him up.' He pointed to the Cossack. 'The medicine is now cool. Thus I rub it on my neck, saying this further medicine.'

With great gravity he slowly intoned a line of the 'Marseillaise,' at the same time rubbing the villainous brew thoroughly into his neck.

An outcry interrupted his play acting. The giant Cossack, with a last resurgence of his tremendous vitality, had arisen to his knees. Laughter and cries of surprise and applause arose from the Nulatos, as Big Ivan began flinging himself about in the snow with mighty spasms.

Subienkow was made sick by the sight, but he mastered his qualms and made believe to be angry.

'This will not do,' he said. 'Finish him, and then we will make the test. Here, you, Yakaga, see that his noise ceases.'

While this was being done, Subienkow turned to Makamuk.

'And remember, you are to strike hard. This is not baby work. Here, take the axe and strike the log, so that I can see you strike like a man.'

Makamuk obeyed, striking twice, precisely and with vigour, cutting out a large chip.

'It is well.' Subienkow looked about him at the circle of savage faces that somehow seemed to symbolize the wall of savagery that had hemmed him about ever since the Czar's police had first arrested him in Warsaw. 'Take your axe, Makamuk, and stand so. I shall lie down. When I raise my hand, strike, and strike with all your might. And be careful that no one stands behind you. The medicine is good, and the axe may bounce from off my neck and right out of your hands.'

He looked at the two sleds, with the dogs in harness, loaded with furs and fish. His rifle lay on top of the beaver skins. The six hunters who were to act as his guard stood by the sleds.

'Where is the girl?' the Pole demanded. 'Bring her up to the sleds before the test goes on.'

When this had been carried out, Subienkow lay down in the snow, resting his head on the log like a tired child about to sleep. He had lived so many dreary years that he was indeed tired.

'I laugh at you and your strength, O Makamuk,' he said. 'Strike, and strike hard.'

He lifted his hand. Makamuk swung the axe, a broadaxe for the squaring of logs. The bright steel flashed through the frosty air, poised for a perceptible instant above Makamuk's head, then descended upon Subienkow's bare neck. Clear through flesh and bone it cut its way, biting deeply into the log beneath. The amazed savages saw the head bounce a yard away from the blood-spouting trunk.

There was a great bewilderment and silence, while slowly it began to dawn in their minds that there had been no medicine. The fur thief had outwitted them. Alone, of all their prisoners, he had escaped the torture. That had been the stake for which he played. A great roar of laughter went up. Mamamuk bowed his head in shame. The fur thief had fooled him. He had lost face before all his people. Still they continued to roar out their laughter. Makamuk turned, and with bowed head stalked away. He knew that thenceforth he would be no longer known as Makamuk. He would be Lost Face; the record of his shame would be with him until he died; and whenever the tribes gathered in the spring for the salmon, or in the summer for the trading, the story would pass back and forth across the campfires of how the fur thief died peaceably, at a single stroke, by the hand of Lost Face.

'Who was Lost Face?' he could hear, in anticipation, some insolent young buck demand. 'Oh, Lost Face,' would be the answer, 'he who once was Makamuk in the days before he cut off the fur thief's head.'

## IN THE FORESTS OF THE NORTH

A WEARY journey beyond the last scrub timber and straggling copses, into the heart of the Barrens where the niggard North is supposed to deny the Earth, are to be found great sweeps of forest and stretches of smiling land. But this the world is just beginning to know. The world's explorers have known it, from time to time, but hitherto they have never returned to tell the world.

The Barrens—well, they are the Barrens, the bad lands of the Arctic, the deserts of the Circle, the bleak and bitter home of the musk-ox and the lean plains wolf. So Avery Van Brunt found them, treeless and cheerless, sparsely clothed with moss and lichens, and altogether uninviting. At least so he found them till he penetrated to the white blank spaces on the map, and came upon undreamed-of rich spruce forests and unrecorded Eskimo tribes. It had been his intention (and his bid for fame) to break up these white blank spaces and diversify them with the black markings of mountain-chains, sinks and basins, and sinuous river courses; and it was with added delight that he came to speculate upon the possibilities of timber belts and native villages.

Avery Van Brunt, or, in full distinction, Professor A. Van Brunt of the Geological Survey, was second in command of the expedition, and first in command of the sub-expedition which he had led on a side tour of some half a thousand miles up one of the branches of the Thelon and which he was now leading into one of his unrecorded villages. At his back plodded eight men, two of them French-Canadian *voyageurs,* and the remainder strapping Crees from Manitoba-way. He, alone, was full-blooded Saxon, and his blood was pounding fiercely through his veins to the traditions of his race. Clive and Hastings, Drake and Raleigh, Hengest and Horsa, walked with him. First of all men of his breed was he to enter this lone Northland village, and at the thought an exultancy came upon him, an exaltation, and his followers noted that his leg-weariness fell from him and that he insensibly quickened the pace.

The village emptied itself, and a motley crowd trooped out to meet him, men in the forefront, with bows and spears clutched menacingly, and women and children faltering timidly in the rear. Van Brunt lifted his right arm and made the universal peace sign, a sign which all peoples know, and the villagers answered in peace. But to his chagrin, a skin-clad man ran forward and thrust out his hand with a familiar 'Hello'. He was a bearded man, with cheeks and brow bronzed to copper-brown, and in him Van Brunt knew his kind.

'Who are you?' he asked, gripping the extended hand. 'Andrée?'

'Who's Andrée?' the man asked back.

Van Brunt looked at him more sharply. 'By George, you've been here some time.'

'Five years,' the man answered, a dim flicker of pride in his eyes. 'But come on, let's talk.'

'Let them camp alongside of me,' he answered Van Brunt's glance at his party. 'Old Tantlatch will take care of them. Come on.'

He swung off in a long stride, Van Brunt following at his heels through the village. In irregular fashion, wherever the ground favoured, the lodges of moose hide were pitched. Van Brunt ran his practised eye over them and calculated.

'Two hundred, not counting the young ones,' he summed up.

The man nodded. 'Pretty close to it. But here's where I live, out of the thick of it, you know—more privacy and all that. Sit down. I'll eat with you when your men get something cooked up. I've forgotten what tea tastes like... Five years and never a taste or smell.... Any tobacco? ... A-h, thanks, and a pipe? Good. Now for a fire-stick and we'll see if the weed has lost its cunning.'

He scratched the match with the painstaking care of the woodsman, cherished its young flame as though there were never another in all the world, and drew in the first mouthful of smoke. This he retained meditatively for a time, and blew out through his pursed lips slowly and caressingly. Then his face seemed to soften as he leaned back, and a soft blur to film his eyes. He sighed heavily, happily, with immeasurable content, and then said suddenly:

'God! But that tastes good!'

Van Brunt nodded sympathetically. 'Five years, you say?'

'Five years.' The man sighed again. 'And you, I presume, wish to know about it, being naturally curious, and this a sufficiently strange situation, and all that. But it's not much. I came in from Edmonton after musk-ox, and like Pike and the rest of them, had my mischances, only I lost my party and outfit. Starvation, hardship, the regular tale, you know, sole survivor and all that, till I crawled into Tantlatch's, here, on hand and knee.'

'Five years,' Van Brunt murmured retrospectively, as though turning things over in this mind.

'Five years on February last. I crossed the Great Slave early in May——'

'And you are . . . Fairfax?' Van Brunt interjected.

The man nodded.

'Let me see . . . John, I think it is, John Fairfax.'

'How did you know?' Fairfax queried lazily, half-absorbed in curling smoke-spirals upward in the quiet air.

'The papers were full of it at the time. Prevanche——'

'Prevanche!' Fairfax sat up, suddenly alert. 'He was lost in the Smoke Mountains.'

'Yes, but he pulled through and came out.'

Fairfax settled back again and resumed his smoke-spirals. 'I am glad to hear it,' he remarked reflectively. 'Prevanche was a bully fellow if he *did* have ideas about headstraps, the beggar. And he pulled through? Well, I'm glad.'

Five years . . . the phrase drifted recurrently through Van Brunt's thought, and somehow the face of Emily Southwaite seemed to rise up and take form before him. Five years . . . A wedge of wild-fowl honked low overhead and at sight of the encampment veered swiftly to the north into the smouldering sun. Van Brunt could not follow them. He pulled out his watch. It was an hour past midnight. The northward clouds flushed bloodily, and rays of sombre-red shot southward, firing the gloomy woods with a lurid radiance. The air was in breathless calm, not a needle quivered, and the least sounds of the camp were distinct and clear as trumpet calls. The Crees and *voyageurs* felt the spirit of it and mumbled in dreamy undertones, and the cook unconsciously subdued the clatter of pot and pan. Somewhere a child was crying, and from the depths of the forest, like a silver thread, rose a woman's voice in mournful chant: 'O-o-o-o-o-o-a-haa-ha-a-ha-aa-a-a, O-o-o-o-o-o-a-ha-a-ha-a.'

Van Brunt shivered and rubbed the backs of his hands briskly.

'And they gave me up for dead?' his companion asked slowly.

'Well, you never came back, so your friends——'

'Promptly forgot.' Fairfax laughed harshly, defiantly.

'Why didn't you come out?'

'Partly disinclination, I suppose, and partly because of circumstances over which I had no control. You see, Tantlatch, here, was down with a broken leg when I made his acquaintance—a nasty fracture—and I set it for him and got him into shape. I stayed some time, getting my strength back. I was the first white man he had seen, and of course I seemed very wise and showed his people no end of things. Coached them up in military tactics, among other things, so that they conquered the four other tribal villages (which you have not yet seen), and came to rule the land. And they naturally grew to think a good deal of me, so much so that when I was ready to go they wouldn't hear of it. Were most hospitable, in fact. Put a couple of guards over me and watched me day and night. And then Tantlatch offered me inducements—in a sense, inducements—so to say, and as it didn't matter much one way or the other, I reconciled myself to remaining.'

'I knew your brother at Freiburg. I am Van Brunt.'

Fairfax reached forward impulsively and shook his hand. 'You were Billy's friend, eh? Poor Billy! He spoke of you often.'

'Rum meeting place, though,' he added casting an embracing glance over the primordial landscape and listening for a moment to the woman's mournful notes. 'Her man was clawed by a bear, and she's taking it hard.'

'Beastly life!' Van Brunt grimaced his disgust. 'I suppose, after five years of it civilization will be sweet? What do you say?'

Fairfax's face took on a stolid expression. 'Oh, I don't know. At least they're honest folk and live according to their

lights. And then they are amazingly simple. No complexity
about them, no thousand and one subtle ramifications to
every single emotion they experience. They love, fear, hate,
are angered, or made happy, in common, ordinary and unmistakable terms. It may be a beastly life, but at least it is
easy to live. No philandering, no dallying. If a woman likes
you, she'll not be backward in telling you so. If she hates
you, she'll tell you so, and then, if you feel inclined, you
can beat her, but the thing is she knows precisely what
you mean, and you know precisely what she means. No
mistakes, no misunderstandings. It has its charm, after
civilization's fitful fever. Comprehend?'

'No, it's a pretty good life,' he continued, after a pause;
'good enough for me, and I intend to stay with it.'

Van Brunt lowered his head in a musing manner, and an
imperceptible smile played on his mouth. No philandering,
no dallying, no misunderstanding. Fairfax also was taking
it hard, he thought, just because Emily Southwaite had
been mistakenly clawed by a bear. And not a bad sort of
a bear, either, was Carlton Southwaite.

'But you are coming along with me,' Van Brunt said
deliberately.

'No, I'm not.'

'Yes, you are.'

'Life's too easy here, I tell you.' Fairfax spoke with decision. 'I understand everything, and I am understood. Summer and winter alternate like the sun flashing through the
palings of a fence, the seasons are a blur of light and shade,
and time slips by, and life slips by, and then . . . a wailing
in the forest, and the dark. Listen!'

He held up his hand, and the silver thread of the
woman's sorrow rose through the silence and the calm.
Fairfax joined in softly.

'O-o-o-o-o-a-haaa-ha-a-ha-aa-a-a, O-o-o-o-o-a-ha-a-ha-a,'
he sang. 'Can't you hear it? Can't you see it? The women
mourning? the funeral chant? my hair white-locked and
patriarchal? my skins wrapped in rude splendour about
me? my hunting-spear by my side? And who shall say it is
not well?'

Van Brunt looked at him coolly. 'Fairfax, you are a damned fool. Five years of this is enough to knock any man, and you are in an unhealthy, morbid condition. Further, Carlton Southwaite is dead.'

Van Brunt filled his pipe and lighted it, the while watching slyly and with almost professional interest. Fairfax's eyes flashed on the instant, his fists clenched, he half rose up, then his muscles relaxed and he seemed to brood. Michael, the cook, signalled that the meal was ready, but Van Brunt motioned back to delay. The silence hung heavy, and he fell to analysing the forest scents, the odours of mould and rotting vegetation, the resiny smells of pine cones and needles, the aromatic savours of many camp-smokes. Twice Fairfax looked up, but said nothing, and then:

'And ... Emily ... ?'

'Three years a widow, still a widow.'

Another long silence settled down, to be broken by Fairfax finally with a naïve smile. 'I guess you're right, Van Brunt. I'll go along.'

'I knew you would.' Van Brunt laid his hand on Fairfax's shoulder. 'Of course, one cannot know, but I imagine—for one in her position—she has had offers——'

'When do you start?' Fairfax interrupted.

'After the men have had some sleep. Which reminds me, Michael is getting angry, so come and eat.'

After supper, when the Crees and *voyageurs* had rolled into their blankets, snoring, the two men lingered by the dying fire. There was much to talk about—wars and politics and explorations, the doings of men and the happening of things, mutual friends, marriages, deaths—five years of history for which Fairfax clamoured.

'So the Spanish fleet was bottled up in Santiago,' Van Brunt was saying, when a young woman stepped lightly before him and stood by Fairfax's side. She looked swiftly into his face, then turned a troubled gaze upon Van Brunt.

'Chief Tantlatch's daughter, sort of princess,' Fairfax explained, with an honest flush. 'One of the inducements, in short, to make me stay. Thom, this is Van Brunt, friend of mine.'

Van Brunt held out his hand, but the woman maintained a rigid repose quite in keeping with her general appearance. Not a line of her face softened, not a feature unbent. She looked him straight in the eyes, her own piercing, questioning, searching.

'Precious lot she understands,' Fairfax laughed. 'Her first introduction, you know. But as you were saying, with the Spanish fleet bottled up in Santiago?'

Thom crouched down by her husband's side, motionless as a bronze statue, only her eyes flashing from face to face in ceaseless search. And Avery Van Brunt, as he talked on and on, felt a nervousness under the dumb gaze. In the midst of his most graphic battle descriptions he would become suddenly conscious of the black eyes burning into him, and would stumble and flounder till he could catch the gait and go again. Fairfax, hands clasped round knees, pipe out, absorbed, spurred him on when he lagged, and repictured the world he thought he had forgotten.

One hour passed, and two, and Fairfax rose reluctantly to his feet. 'And Cronje was cornered, eh? Well, just wait a moment till I run over to Tantlatch. He'll be expecting you, and I'll arrange for you to see him after breakfast. That will be all right, won't it?'

He went off between the pines, and Van Brunt found himself staring into Thom's warm eyes. Five years, he mused, and she can't be more than twenty now. A most remarkable creature. Being Eskimo, she should have a little flat excuse for a nose, and lo, it is neither broad nor flat, but aquiline, with nostrils delicately and sensitively formed as any fine lady's of a whiter breed—the Indian strain somewhere, be assured, Avery Van Brunt. And, Avery Van Brunt, don't be nervous, she won't eat you; she's only a woman, and not a bad-looking one at that. Oriental rather than aborigine. Eyes large and fairly wide apart, with just the faintest hint of Mongol obliquity. Thom, you're an anomaly. You're out of place here among the Eskimos, even if your father is one. Where did your mother come from? or your grandmother? And Thom, my dear, you're a beauty, a frigid, frozen little beauty with Alaskan lava in your blood, and please don't look at me that way.

He laughed and stood up. Her insistent stare disconcerted him. A dog was prowling among the grub-sacks. He would drive it away and place them into safely against Fairfax's return. But Thom stretched out a detaining hand and stood up, facing him.

'You?' she said, in the Arctic tongue which differs little from Greenland to Point Barrow. 'You?'

And the swift expression of her face demanded all for which 'you' stood, his reason for existence, his presence there, his relation to her husband—everything.

'Brother,' he answered in the same tongue, with a sweeping gesture to the south. 'Brothers we be, your man and I.'

She shook her head. 'It is not good that you be here.'

'After one sleep I go.'

'And my man?' she demanded, with tremulous eagerness.

Van Brunt shrugged his shoulders. He was aware of a certain secret shame, of an impersonal sort of shame, and an anger against Fairfax. And he felt the warm blood in his face as he regarded the young savage. She was just a woman. That was all—a woman. The whole sordid story over again, over and over again, as old as Eve and young as the last new love-light.

'My man! My man! My man!' she was reiterating vehemently, her face passionately dark, and the ruthless tenderness of the Eternal Woman, the Mate-Woman, looking out at him from her eyes.

'Thom,' he said gravely, in English, 'you were born in the Northland forest, and you have eaten fish and meat, and fought with frost and famine, and lived simply all the days of your life. And there are many things, indeed not simple, which you do not know and cannot come to understand. You do not know what it is to long for the flesh-pots afar, you cannot understand what it is to yearn for a fair woman's face. And the woman is fair, Thom, the woman is nobly fair. You have been woman to this man, and you have been your all, but your all is very little, very simple. Too little and too simple, and he is an alien man. Him you

have never known, you can never know. It is so ordained.
You held him in your arms, but you never held his heart,
this man with his blurring seasons and his dreams of a
barbaric end. Dreams and dream-dust, that is what he has
been to you. You clutched at form and gripped shadow,
gave yourself to a man and bedded with the wraith of a
man. In such manner, of old, did the daughters of men
whom the gods found fair. And, Thom, Thom, I should
not like to be John Fairfax in the night-watches of the years
to come, in the night-watches, when his eyes shall see, not
the sun-gloried hair of the woman by his side, but the dark
tresses of a mate forsaken in the forests of the North.'

Though she did not understand, she had listened with
intense attention, as though life hung on his speech. But
she caught at her husband's name and cried out in Eskimo:

'Yes! Yes! Fairfax! My man!'

'Poor little fool, how could he be your man?'

But she could not understand his English tongue, and
deemed that she was being trifled with. The dumb, insen-
sate anger of the Mate-Woman flamed in her face, and it
almost seemed to the man as though she crouched panther-
like for the spring.

He cursed softly to himself and watched the fire fade
from her face and the soft luminous glow of the appealing
woman spring up, of the appealing woman who forgoes
strength and panoplies herself wisely in her weakness.

'He is my man,' she said gently. 'Never have I known
other. It cannot be that I should ever know other. Nor can
it be that he should go from me.'

'Who has said he shall go from thee?' he demanded
sharply, half in exasperation, half in impotence.

'It is for thee to say he shall not go from me,' she
answered softly, a half-sob in her throat.

Van Brunt kicked the embers of the fire savagely and sat
down.

'It is for thee to say. He is my man. Before all women he
is my man. Thou art big, thou art strong, and behold, I am
very weak. See, I am at thy feet. It is for thee to deal with
me. It is for thee.'

'Get up!' He jerked her roughly erect and stood up himself. 'Thou art a woman. Wherefore the dirt is no place for thee, nor the feet of any man.'

'He is my man.'

'Then Jesus forgive all men!' Van Brunt cried out passionately.

'He is my man,' she repeated monotonously, beseechingly.

'He is my brother,' he answered.

'My father is Chief Tantlatch. He is a power over five villages. I will see that the five villages be searched for thy choice of all maidens, that thou mayest stay here by thy brother, and dwell in comfort.'

'After one sleep I go.'

'And my man?'

'Thy man comes now. Behold!'

From among the gloomy spruces came the light carolling of Fairfax's voice.

As the day is quenched by a sea of fog, so his song smote the light out of her face. 'It is the tongue of his own people,' she said, 'the tongue of his own people.'

She turned, with the free movement of a lithe young animal, and made off into the forest.

'It's all fixed,' Fairfax called as he came up. 'His regal highness will receive you after breakfast.'

'Have you told him?' Van Brunt asked.

'No. Nor shall I tell him till we're ready to pull out.'

Van Brunt looked with moody affection over the sleeping forms of his men.

'I shall be glad when we are a hundred leagues upon our way,' he said.


Thom raised the skin-flap of her father's lodge. Two men sat with him, and the three looked at her with swift interest. But her face betokened nothing as she entered and took seat quietly, without speech. Tantlatch drummed with his knuckles on a spear-haft across his knees, and gazed idly along the path of a sun-ray which pierced a lacing-hole and flung a glittering track across the murky atmosphere of the lodge. To his right, at his shoulder crouched Chugungatte, the shaman. Both were old men, and the weariness of many years brooded in their eyes. But opposite them sat Keen, a young man and chief favourite in the tribe. He was quick and alert of movement, and his black eyes flashed from face to face in ceaseless scrutiny and challenge.

Silence reigned in the place. Now and again camp noises penetrated, and from the distance, faint and far, like the shadows of voices, came the wrangling of boys in thin shrill tones. A dog thrust his head into the entrance and blinked wolfishly at them for a space, the slaver dripping from his ivory-white fangs. After a time he growled tentatively, and then, awed by the immobility of the human figures, lowered his head and grovelled away backward. Tantlatch glanced apathetically at his daughter.

'And thy man, how is it with him and thee?'

'He sings strange songs,' Thom made answer, 'and there is a new look on his face.'

'So? He hath spoken?'

'Nay, but there is a new look on his face, a new light in his eyes, and with the New-Comer he sits by the fire, and they talk and talk, and the talk is without end.'

Chugunatte whispered in his master's ear, and Keen leaned forward from his hips.

'There be something calling him from afar,' she went on, 'and he seems to sit and listen, and to answer, singing, in his own people's tongue.'

Again Chugungatte whispered and Keen leaned forward, and Thom held her speech till her father nodded his head that she might proceed.

'It be known to thee, O Tantlatch, that the wild goose and the swan and the little ringed duck be born here in the low-lying lands. It be known that they go away before the face of the frost to unknown places. And it be known, likewise, that always do they return when the sun is in the land and the waterways are free. Always do they return to where they were born, that new life may go forth. The land calls to them and they come. And now there is another land that calls, and it is calling to my man—the land where he was born—and he hath it in mind to answer the call. Yet is he my man. Before all women is he my man.'

'Is it well, Tantlatch? Is it well?' Chugunatte demanded, with the hint of menace in his voice.

'Ay, it is well!' Keen cried boldly. 'The land calls to its children, and all lands call their children home again. As the wild goose and the swan and the little ringed duck are called, so is called this Stranger Man who has lingered with us and who now must go. Also there be the call of kind. The goose mates with the goose, nor does the swan mate with the little ringed duck. It is not well that the swan should mate with the little ringed duck. Nor is it well that stranger men should mate with the women of our villages. Wherefore I say the man should go, to his own kind, in his own land.'

'He is my own man,' Thom answered, 'and he is a great man.'

'Ay, he is a great man.' Chugungatte lifted his head with a faint recrudescence of youthful vigour. 'He is a great man, and he put strength in thy arm, O Tantlatch, and gave thee power, and made thy name to be feared in the land, to be feared and to be respected. He is very wise, and there be much profit in his wisdom. To him we are beholden for many things—for the cunning in war and the secrets of the defence of a village and a rush in the forest, for the discussion in council and the undoing of enemies by word of mouth and hard-sworn promise, for the gathering of game and the making of traps and the preserving of food, for the curing of sickness and mending of hurts of trail and fight. Thou, Tantlatch, wert a lame old man this day, were it not that the Stranger Man came into our midst and attended on thee. And ever, when in doubt on strange questions, have we gone to him, that out of his wisdom he might make things clear, and ever has he made things clear. And there be questions yet to arise, and needs upon his wisdom yet to come, and we cannot bear to let him go. It is not well that we should let him go.'

Tantlatch continued to drum on the spear-haft, and gave

no sign that he had heard. Thom studied his face in vain, and Chugungatte seemed to shrink together and droop down as the weight of years descended upon him again.

'No man makes my kill.' Keen smote his breast a valorous blow. 'I make my own kill. I am glad to live when I make my own kill. When I creep through the snow upon the great moose, I am glad. And when I draw the bow so, with my full strength, and drive the arrow fierce and swift and to the heart, I am glad. And the meat of no man's kill tastes as sweet as the meat of my kill. I am glad to live, glad in my own cunning and strength, glad that I am a doer of things, a doer of things for myself. Of what other reason to live than that? Why should I live if I delight not in myself and the things I do? And it is because I delight and am glad that I go forth to hunt and fish, and it is because I go forth to hunt and fish that I grow cunning and strong. The man who stays in the lodge by the fire grows not cunning and strong. He is not made happy in the eating of my kill, nor is living to him a delight. He does not live. And so I say it is well this Stranger Man should go. His wisdom does not make us wise. If he be cunning, there is no need that we be cunning. If need arise, we go to him for his cunning. We eat the meat of his kill, and it tastes unsweet. We merit by his strength, and in it there is no delight. We do not live when he does our living for us. We grow fat and like women, and we are afraid to work, and we forget how to do things for ourselves. Let the man go, O Tantlatch, that we may be men! I am Keen, a man, and I make my own kill!'

Tantlatch turned a gaze upon him in which seemed the vacancy of eternity. Keen waited the decision expectantly; but the lips did not move, and the old chief turned toward his daughter.

'That which be given cannot be taken away,' she burst forth. 'I was but a girl when this Stranger Man, who is my man, came among us. And I knew not men, or the ways of men, and my heart was in the play of girls, when thou, Tantlatch, thou and none other, didst call me to thee and press me into the arms of the Stranger Man. Thou and none other, Tantlatch; and as thou didst give me to the man, so didst thou give the man to me. He is my man. In my arms has he slept, and from my arms he cannot be taken.'

'It were well, O Tantlatch,' Keen followed quickly, with a significant glance at Thom, 'it were well to remember that that which be given cannot be taken away.'

Chugungatte straightened up. 'Out of thy youth, Keen, come the words of thy mouth. As for ourselves, O Tantlatch, we be old men and we understand. We, too, have looked into the eyes of women and felt our blood go hot with strange desires. But the years have chilled us, and we have learned the wisdom of the council, the shrewdness of the cool head and hand, and we know that the warm heart be over-warm and prone to rashness. We know that Keen found favour in thy eyes. We know that Thom was promised him in the old days when she was yet a child. And we know that the new days came, and the Stranger Man, and that out of our wisdom and desire for welfare was Thom lost to Keen and the promise broken.'

The old shaman paused and looked directly at the young man.

'And be it known that I, Chugungatte, did advise that the promise be broken.'

'Nor have I taken other woman to my bed,' Keen broke in. 'And I have builded my own fire, and cooked my own food, and ground my teeth in loneliness.'

Chugungatte waved his hand that he had not finished. 'I am an old man and I speak from understanding. It be good to be strong and grasp for power. It be better to forgo power that good come out of it. In the old days I sat at thy shoulder, Tantlatch, and my voice was heard over all in the council, and my advice taken in affairs of moment. And I was strong and held power. Under Tantlatch I was the greatest man. Then came the Stranger Man, and I saw that he was cunning and wise and great. And in that he was wiser and greater than I, it was plain that greater profit should arise from him than from me. And I had thy ear, Tantlatch, and thou didst listen to my words, and the

Stranger Man was given power and place and thy daughter
Thom. And the tribe prospered under the new laws in the
new days, and so shall it continue to prosper with the
Stranger Man in our midst. We be old men, we two, O
Tantlatch, thou and I, and this be an affair of head, not
heart. Hear my words, Tantlatch! Hear my words! The
man remains!'

There was a long silence. The old chief pondered with
the massive certitude of God, and Chugungatte seemed to
wrap himself in the mists of a great antiquity. Keen looked
with yearning upon the woman, and she, unnoting, held
her eyes steadfastly upon her father's face. The wolf-dog
shoved the flap aside again, and plucking courage at the
quiet, wormed forward on his belly. He sniffed curiously
at Thom's listless hand, cocked ears challengingly at
Chugungatte, and hunched down upon his haunches before Tantlatch. The spear rattled to the ground, and the
dog, with a frightened yell, sprang sideways, snapping in
mid-air, and on the second leap cleared the entrance.

Tantlatch looked from face to face, pondering each one
long and carefully. Then he raised his head, with rude
royalty, and gave judgment in cold and even tones: 'The
man remains. Let the hunters be called together. Send a
runner to the next village with word to bring on the fighting men. I shall not see the New-Comer. Do thou, Chugungatte, have talk with him. Tell him he may go at once,
if he would go in peace. And if fight there be, kill, kill,
kill, to the last man; but let my word go forth that no harm
befall our man—the man whom my daughter hath wedded.
It is well.'

Chugungatte rose and tottered out; Thom followed; but
as Keen stooped to the entrance the voice of Tantlach
stopped him.

'Keen, it were well to hearken to my word. The man
remains. Let no harm befall him.'

Because of Fairfax's instructions in the art of war, the
tribesmen did not hurl themselves forward boldly and with
clamour. Instead, there was great restraint and self-control.

and they were content to advance silently, creeping and crawling from shelter to shelter. By the river bank, and partly protected by a narrow open space, crouched the Crees and *voyageurs*. Their eyes could see nothing, and only in vague ways did their ears hear, but they felt the thrill of life which ran through the forest, the indistinct, indefinable movement of an advancing host.

'Damn them,' Fairfax muttered. 'They've never faced powder, but I taught them the trick.'

Avery Van Brunt laughed, knocked the ashes out of his pipe, and put it carefully away with the pouch, and loosened the hunting-knife in its sheath at his hip.

'Wait,' he said. 'We'll wither the face of the charge and break their hearts.'

'They'll rush scattered if they remember my teaching.'

'Let them. Magazine rifles were made to pump. We'll— good! First blood! Extra tobacco, Loon!'

Loon, a Cree, had spotted an exposed shoulder, and with a stinging bullet apprised its owner of his discovery.

'If we can tease them into breaking forward,' Fairfax muttered—'if we can only tease them into breaking forward.'

Van Brunt saw a head peer from behind a distant tree, and with a quick shot sent the man sprawling to the ground in a death struggle. Michael potted a third, and Fairfax and the rest took a hand, firing at every exposure and into each clump of agitated brush. In crossing one little swale out of cover, five of the tribesmen remained on their faces, and to the left, where the covering was sparse, a dozen men were struck. But they took the punishment with sullen steadiness, coming on cautiously, deliberately, without haste and without lagging.

Ten minutes later, when they were quite close, all movement was suspended, the advance ceased abruptly, and the quietness that followed was portentous, threatening. Only could be seen the green and gold of the woods and undergrowth, shivering and trembling to the first faint puffs of the day-wind. The wan white morning sun mottled the earth with long shadows and streaks of light. A wounded man lifted his head and crawled painfully out of the swale, Michael following him with his rifle but forbearing to shoot. A whistle ran along the invisible line from left to right, and a flight of arrows arched through the air.

'Get ready,' Van Brunt commanded, a new metallic note in his voice. 'Now!'

They broke cover simultaneously. The forest heaved into sudden life. A great yell went up, and the rifles barked back sharp defiance. Tribesmen knew their death in mid-leap, and as they fell, their brothers surged over them in a roaring, irresistible wave. In the forefront of the rush, hair flying and arms swinging free, flashing past the tree-trunks, and leaping the obstructing logs, came Thom. Fairfax sighted on her and almost pulled trigger ere he knew her.

'The woman! Don't shoot!' he cried. 'See. She is un-armed!'

The Crees never heard, nor Michael and his brother *voyageur*, nor Van Brunt, who was keeping one shell continuously in the air. But Thom bore straight on, unharmed, at the heels of a skin-clad hunter who had veered in before her from the side. Fairfax emptied his magazine into the men to right and left of her, and swung his rifle to meet the big hunter. But the man, seeming to recognize him, swerved suddenly aside and plunged his spear into the body of Michael. On the moment Thom had one arm passed around her husband's neck, and twisting half about, with voice and gesture was splitting the mass of charging warriors. A score of men hurled past on either side, and Fairfax, for a brief instant's space, stood looking upon her and her bronze beauty thrilling, exulting, stirred to unknown deeps, visioning strange things, dreaming, immortally dreaming. Snatches and scraps of old-world philosophies and new-world ethics floated through his mind, and things wonderfully concrete and woefully incongruous—hunting scenes, stretches of sombre forest, vastnesses of silent snow, the glittering of ballroom lights, great galleries and lecture halls, a fleeting shimmer of glistening test-tubes, long rows of book-lined shelves, the throb of machinery and the roar of traffic, a fragment of forgotten song, faces of dead women and old chums, a lonely watercourse amid upstanding peaks, a shattered boat on a pebbly strand, quiet moonlit fields, fat vales, the smell of hay. . . .

A hunter, struck between the eyes with a rifle-ball, pitched forward lifeless, and with the momentum of his charge slid along the ground. Fairfax came back to himself. His comrades, those that lived, had been swept far back among the trees beyond. He could hear the fierce 'Hia! Hia!' of the hunters as they closed in and cut and thrust with their weapons of bone and ivory. The cries of the stricken men smote him like blows. He knew the fight was over, the cause was lost, but all his race traditions and race loyalty impelled him into the welter that he might die at least with his kind.

'My man! My man!' Thom cried. 'Thou art safe!'

He tried to struggle on, but her dead weight clogged his steps.

'There is no need! They are dead, and life be good!'

She held him close around the neck and twined her limbs about his till he tripped and stumbled, reeled violently to recover footing, tripped again, and fell backward to the ground. His head struck a jutting root, and he was half-stunned and could struggle but feebly. In the fall she had heard the feathered swish of an arrow darting past, and she covered his body with hers, as with a shield, her arms holding him tightly, her face and lips pressed upon his neck.

Then it was that Keen rose up from a tangled thicket a score of feet away. He looked about him with care. The fight had swept on and the cry of the last man was dying away. There was no one to see. He fitted an arrow to the string and glanced at the man and woman. Between her breast and arm the flesh of the man's side showed white. Keen bent the bow and drew back the arrow to its head. Twice he did so, calmly and for certainty, and then drove the bone-barbed missile straight home to the white flesh, gleaming yet more white in the dark-armed, dark-breasted embrace.

# AN ODYSSEY OF THE NORTH

## I

THE SLEDS were singing their eternal lament to the creaking of the harnesses and the tinkling bells of the leaders; but the men and dogs were tired and made no sound. The trail was heavy with new-fallen snow, and they had come far, and the runners, burdened with flintlike quarters of frozen moose, clung tenaciously to the unpacked surface and held back with a stubbornness almost human. Darkness was coming on, but there was no camp to pitch that night. The snow fell gently through the pulseless air, not in flakes, but in tiny frost crystals of delicate design. It was very warm—barely ten below zero—and the men did not mind. Meyers and Bettles had raised their ear flaps, while Malemute Kid had even taken off his mittens.

The dogs had been fagged out early in the afternoon, but they now began to show new vigour. Among the more astute there was a certain restlessness—an impatience at the restraint of the traces, an indecisive quickness of movement, a sniffing of snouts and pricking of ears. These became incensed at their more phlegmatic brothers, urging them on with numerous sly nips on their hind quarters. Those, thus chidden, also contracted and helped spread the contagion. At last the leader of the foremost sled uttered a sharp whine of satisfaction, crouching lower in the snow and throwing himself against the collar. The rest followed suit. There was an ingathering of back bands, a tightening of traces; the sleds leaped forward, and the men clung to the gee poles, violently accelerating the uplift of their feet that they might escape going under the runners. The weariness of the day fell from them, and they whooped encouragement to the dogs. The animals responded with joyous yelps. They were swinging through the gathering darkness at a rattling gallop.

4*

'Gee! Gee!' the men cried, each in turn, as their sleds abruptly left the main trail, heeling over on single runners like luggers on the wind.

Then came a hundred yards' dash to the lighted parchment window, which told its own story of the home cabin, the roaring Yukon stove, and the steaming pots of tea. But the home cabin had been invaded. Threescore huskies chorused defiance, and as many furry forms precipitated themselves upon the dogs which drew the first sled. The door was flung open, and a man, clad in the scarlet tunic of the Northwest Police, waded knee-deep among the furious brutes, calmly and impartially dispensing soothing justice with the butt end of a dog whip. After that the men shook hands; and in this wise was Malemute Kid welcomed to his own cabin by a stranger.

Stanley Prince, who should have welcomed him, and who was responsible for the Yukon stove and hot tea aforementioned, was busy with his guests. There were a dozen or so of them, as nondescript a crowd as ever served the Queen in the enforcement of her laws or the delivery of her mails. They were of many breeds, but their common life had formed of them a certain type—a lean and wiry type, with trail-hardened muscles, and sun-browned faces, and untroubled souls which gazed frankly forth, clear-eyed and steady. They drove the dogs of the Queen, wrought fear in the hearts of her enemies, ate of her meagre fare, and were happy. They had seen life, and done deeds, and lived romances; but they did not know it.

And they were very much at home. Two of them were sprawled upon Malemute Kid's bunk, singing chansons which their French forebears sang in the days when first they entered the Northwest land and mated with its Indian women. Bettles' bunk had suffered a similar invasion, and three or four lusty *voyageurs* worked their toes among its blankets as they listened to the tale of one who had served on the boat brigade with Wolseley when he fought his way to Khartoum. And when he tired, a cowboy told of courts and kings and lords and ladies he had seen when Buffalo Bill toured the capitals of Europe. In a corner two half-

breeds, ancient comrades in a lost campaign, mended harnesses and talked of the days when the Northwest flamed
with insurrection and Louis Riel was king.

Rough jests and rougher jokes went up and down, and
great hazards by trail and river were spoken of in the light
of commonplaces, only to be recalled by virtue of some
grain of humour or ludicrous happening. Prince was led
away by these uncrowned heroes who had seen history
made, who regarded the great and the romantic as but the
ordinary and incidental in the routine of life. He passed his
precious tobacco among them with lavish disregard, and
rusty chains of reminiscence were loosened, and forgotten
odysseys resurrected for his especial benefit.

When conversation dropped and the travellers filled the
last pipes and unlashed their tight-rolled sleeping furs,
Prince fell back upon his comrade for further information.

'Well, you now what the cowboy is,' Malemute Kid
answered, beginning to unlace his moccasins; 'and it's not
hard to guess the British blood in his bed partner. As for
the rest, they're all children of the *coureurs du bois*,
mingled with God knows how many other bloods. The two
turning in by the door are the regulation "breeds" or
*Boisbrûles*. That lad with the worsted breech scarf—notice
his eyebrows and the turn of his jaw—shows a Scotchman
wept in his mother's smoky tepee. And that handsome-
looking fellow putting the capote under his head is a French
half-breed—you heard him talking; he doesn't like the two
Indians turning in next to him. You see, when the "breeds"
rose under Riel the full-bloods kept the peace, and they've
not lost much love for one another since.'

'But I say, what's that glum-looking fellow by the stove?
I'll swear he can't talk English. He hasn't opened his mouth
all night.'

'You're wrong. He knows English well enough. Did you
follow his eyes when he listened? I did. But he's neither
kith nor kin to the others. When they talked their own
patois you could see he didn't understand. I've been wondering myself what he is. Let's find out.'

'Fire a couple of sticks into the stove!' Malemute Kid

commanded, raising his voice and looking squarely at the man in question.

He obeyed at once.

'Had discipline knocked into him somewhere,' Prince commented in a low tone.

Malemute Kid nodded, took off his socks, and picked his way among recumbent men to the stove. There he hung his damp footgear among a score or so of mates.

'When do you expect to get to Dawson?' he asked tentatively.

The man studied him a moment before replying. 'They say seventy-five mile. So? Maybe two days.'

The very slightest accent was perceptible, while there was no awkward hesitancy or groping for words.

'Been in the country before?'

'No.'

'Northwest Territory?'

'Yes.'

'Born there?'

'No.'

'Well, where the devil were you born? You're none of these.' Malemute Kid swept his hand over the dog drivers, even including the two policemen who had turned into Prince's bunk. 'Where did you come from? I've seen faces like yours before, though I can't remember just where.'

'I know you,' he irrelevantly replied, at once turning the drift of Malemute Kid's questions.

'Where? Ever see me?'

'No; your partner, him priest, Pastilik, long time ago. Him ask me if I see you, Malemute Kid. Him give me grub. I no stop long. You hear him speak 'bout me?'

'Oh! you're the fellow that traded the otter skins for the dogs?'

The man nodded, knocking out his pipe, and signified his disinclination for conversation by rolling up in his furs. Malemute Kid blew out the slush lamp and crawled under the blankets with Prince.

'Well, what is he?'

'Don't know—turned me off, somehow, and then shut

up like a clam. But he's a fellow to whet your curiosity. I've heard of him. All the coast wondered about him eight years ago. Sort of mysterious, you know. He came down out of the North, in the dead of winter, many a thousand miles from here, skirting Bering Sea and travelling as though the devil were after him. No one ever learned where he came from, but he must have come far. He was badly travel-worn when he got food from the Swedish missionary on Golovin Bay and asked the way south. We heard of this afterward. Then he abandoned the shore line, heading right across Norton Sound. Terrible weather, snowstorms and high winds, but he pulled through where a thousand other men would have died, missing St Michael's and making the land at Pastilik. He'd lost all but two dogs, and was nearly gone with starvation.

'He was so anxious to go on that Father Roubeau fitted him out with grub; but he couldn't let him have any dogs, for he was only waiting my arrival to go on a trip himself. Mr Ulysses knew too much to start on without animals, and fretted around for several days. He had on his sled a bunch of beautifully cured otter skins, sea otters, you know, worth their weight in gold. There was also at Pastilik an old Shylock of a Russian trader, who had dogs to kill. Well, they didn't dicker very long, but when the Strange One headed south again, it was in the rear of a spanking dog team. Mr Shylock, by the way, had the otter skins. I saw them, and they were magnificent. We figured it up and found the dogs brought him at least five hundred apiece. And it wasn't as if the Strange One didn't know the value of sea otter; he was an Indian of some sort, and what little he talked showed he'd been among white men.

'After the ice passed out of the sea, word came up from Nunivak Island that he'd gone in there for grub. Then he dropped from sight, and this is the first heard of him in eight years. Now where did he come from? and what was he doing there? and why did he come from there? He's Indian, he's been nobody knows where, and he's had discipline, which is unusual for an Indian. Another mystery of the North for you to solve, Prince.'

'Thanks awfully, but I've got too many on hand as it is,' he replied.

Malemute Kid was already breathing heavily; but the young mining engineer gazed straight up through the thick darkness, waiting for the strange orgasm which stirred his blood to die away. And when he did sleep his brain worked on, and for the nonce he, too, wandered through the white unknown, struggled with the dogs on endless trails, and saw men live, and toil, and die like men.

The next morning, hours before daylight, the dog drivers and policemen pulled out for Dawson. But the powers that saw to Her Majesty's interests and ruled the destinies of her lesser creatures gave the mailmen little rest, for a week later they appeared at Stuart River, heavily burdened with letters for Salt Water. However, their dogs had been replaced by fresh ones; but, then, they were dogs.

The men had expected some sort of a layover in which to rest up; besides, this Klondike was a new section of the Northland, and they had wished to see a little something of the Golden City where dust flowed like water and dance halls rang with never-ending revelry. But they dried their socks and smoked their evening pipes with much the same gusto as on their former visit, though one or two bold spirits speculated on desertion and the possibility of crossing the unexplored Rockies to the east, and thence, by the Mackenzie Valley, of gaining their old stamping grounds in the Chippewyan country. Two or three even decided to return to their homes by that route when their terms of service had expired, and they began to lay plans forthwith, looking forward to the hazardous undertaking in much the same way a city-bred man would to a day's holiday in the woods.

He of the Otter Skins seemed very restless, though he took little interest in the discussion, and at last he drew Malemute Kid to one side and talked for some time in low tones. Prince cast curious eyes in their direction, and the mystery deepened when they put on caps and mittens and went outside. When they returned, Malemute Kid placed his gold scales on the table, weighed out the matter of sixty ounces, and transferred them to the Strange One's sack. Then the chief of the dog drivers joined the conclave, and certain business was transacted with him. The next day the gang went on upriver, but He of the Otter Skins took several pounds of grub and turned his steps back toward Dawson.

'Didn't know what to make of it,' said Malemute Kid in response to Prince's queries; 'but the poor beggar wanted to be quit of the service for some reason or other—at least it seemed a most important one to him, though he wouldn't let on what. You see, it's just like the army: he signed for two years, and the only way to get free was to buy himself out. He couldn't desert and then stay here, and he was just wild to remain in the country. Made up his mind when he got to Dawson, he said; but no one knew him, hadn't a cent, and I was the only one he'd spoken two words with. So he talked it over with the lieutenant-governor, and made arrangements in case he could get the money from me—loan, you know. Said he'd pay back in the year, and, if I wanted, would put me on to something rich. Never'd seen it, but knew it was rich.

'And talk! why, when he got me outside he was ready to weep. Begged and pleaded; got down in the snow to me till I hauled him out of it. Palavered around like a crazy man. Swore he's worked to this very end for years and years, and couldn't bear to be disappointed now. Asked him what end, but he wouldn't say. Said they might keep him on the other half of the trail and he wouldn't get to Dawson in two years, and then it would be too late. Never saw a man take on so in my life. And when I said I'd let him have it, had to yank him out of the snow again. Told him to consider it in the light of a grubstake. Think he'd have it? No sir! Swore he'd give me all he found, make me rich beyond the dreams of avarice, and all such stuff. Now a man who puts his life and time against a grubstake ordinarily finds it hard enough to turn over half of what he finds. Something behind all this, Prince; just you make a note of it. We'll hear of him if he stays in the country——'

'And if he doesn't?'

'Then my good nature gets a shock, and I'm sixty some odd ounces out.'

The cold weather had come on with the long nights, and the sun had begun to play his ancient game of peekaboo along the southern snow line ere aught was heard of Malemute Kid's grubstake. And then, one bleak morning in early January, a heavily laden dog train pulled into his cabin below Stuart River. He of the Otter Skins was there, and with him walked a man such as the gods have almost forgotten how to fashion. Men never talked of luck and pluck and five-hundred-dollar dirt without bringing in the name of Axel Gunderson; nor could tales of nerve or strength or daring pass up and down the campfire without the summoning of his presence. And when the conversation flagged, it blazed anew at mention of the woman who shared his fortunes.

As has been noted, in the making of Axel Gunderson the gods had remembered their old-time cunning and cast him after the manner of men who were born when the world was young. Full seven feet he towered in his picturesque costume which marked a king of Eldorado. His chest, neck, and limbs were those of a giant. To bear his three hundred pounds of bone and muscle, his snowshoes were greater by a generous yard than those of other men. Rough-hewn, with rugged brow and massive jaw and unflinching eyes of palest blue, his face told the tale of one who knew but the law of might. Of the yellow of ripe corn silk, his frost-incrusted hair swept like day across the night and fell far down his coat of bearskin. A vague tradition of the sea seemed to cling about him as he swung down the narrow trail in advance of the dogs; and he brought the butt of his dog whip against Malemute Kid's door as a Norse sea rover, on southern foray, might thunder for admittance at the castle gate.

Prince bared his womanly arms and kneaded sour-dough bread, casting, as he did so, many a glance at the three guests—three guests the like of which might never come under a man's roof in a lifetime. The Strange One, whom Malemute Kid had surnamed Ulysses, still fascinated him; but his interest chiefly gravitated between Axel Gunderson and Axel Gunderson's wife. She felt the day's journey, for she had softened in comfortable cabins during the many days since her husband mastered the wealth of frozen pay streaks, and she was tired. She rested against his great breast like a slender flower against a wall, replying lazily to Malemute Kid's good-natured banter and stirring Prince's blood strangely with an occasional sweep of her deep, dark eyes. For Prince was a man, and healthy, and had seen few women in many months. And she was older than he, and an Indian besides. But she was different from all native wives he had met: she had travelled—had been in his country among others, he gathered from the conversation; and she knew most of the things the women of his own race knew, and much more that it was not in the nature of things for them to know. She could make a meal of sun-dried fish or a bed in the snow; yet she teased them with tantalizing details of many-course dinners, and caused strange internal dissensions to arise at the mention of various quondam dishes which they had well-nigh forgotten. She knew the ways of the moose, the bear, and the little blue fox, and of the wild amphibians of the Northern seas; she was skilled in the lore of the woods and the streams, and the tale writ by man and bird and beast upon the delicate snow crust was to her an open book; yet Prince caught the appreciative twinkle in her eye as she read the Rules of the Camp. These rules had been fathered by the Unquenchable Bettles at a time when his blood ran high, and were remarkable for the terse simplicity of their humour. Prince always turned them to the wall before the arrival of ladies; but who could suspect that this native wife——Well, it was too late now.

This, then, was the wife of Axel Gunderson, a woman whose name and fame had travelled with her husband's, hand in hand, through all the Northland. At table, Malemute Kid baited her with the assurance of an old friend, and Prince shook off the shyness of first acquaintance and joined in. But she held her own in the unequal contest, while her husband, slower in wit, ventured naught but applause. And he was very proud of her; his every look and action revealed the magnitude of the place she occupied in his life. He of the Otter Skins ate in silence, forgotten in the merry battle; and long ere the others were done he pushed back from the table and went out among the dogs. Yet all too soon his fellow travellers drew on their mittens and parkas and followed him.

There had been no snow for many days, and the sleds slipped along the hard-packed Yukon trail as easily as if it had been glare ice. Ulysses led the first sled; with the second came Prince and Axel Gunderson's wife; while Malemute Kid and the yellow-haired giant brought up the third.

'It's only a hunch, Kid,' he said, 'but I think it's straight. He's never been there, but he tells a good story, and shows a map I heard of when I was in the Kootenay country years ago. I'd like to have you go along; but he's a strange one, and swore point-blank to throw it up if anyone was brought in. But when I come back you'll get first tip, and I'll stake you next to me, and give you a half share in the town site besides.

'No! no!' he cried, as the other strove to interrupt. 'I'm running this, and before I'm done it'll need two heads. If it's all right, why, it'll be a second Cripple Creek, man; do you hear?—a second Cripple Creek! It's quartz, you know, not placer; and if we work it right we'll corral the whole thing—millions upon millions. I've heard of the place before, and so have you. We'll build a town—thousands of workmen—good waterways—steamship lines—big carrying trade—light-draught steamers for head reaches—survey a railroad, perhaps—sawmills—electric-light plant—do our own banking—commercial company—syndicate——Say! Just you hold your hush till I get back!'

The sleds came to a halt where the trail crossed the mouth of Stuart River. An unbroken sea of frost, its wide expanse stretched away into the unknown east. The snow-shoes were withdrawn from the lashings of the sleds. Axel

Gunderson shook hands and stepped to the fore, his great webbed shoes sinking a fair half yard into the feathery surface and packing the snow so the dogs should not wallow. His wife fell in behind the last sled, betraying long practice in the art of handling the awkward footgear. The stillness was broken with cheery farewells; the dogs whined; and He of the Otter Skins talked with his whip to a recalcitrant wheeler.

An hour later the train had taken on the likeness of a black pencil crawling in a long, straight line across a mighty sheet of foolscap.

II

One night, many weeks later, Malemute Kid and Prince fell to solving chess problems from the torn page of an ancient magazine. The Kid had just returned from his Bonanza properties and was resting up preparatory to a long moose hunt. Prince, too, had been on creek and trail nearly all winter, and had grown hungry for a blissful week of cabin life.

'Interpose the black knight, and force the king. No, that won't do. See, the next move——'

'Why advance the pawn two squares? Bound to take it in transit, and with the bishop out of the way——'

'But hold on! That leaves a hole, and——'

'No; it's protected. Go ahead! You'll see it works.'

It was very interesting. Somebody knocked at the door a second time before Malemute Kid said, 'Come in.' The door swung open. Something staggered in. Prince caught one square look and sprang to his feet. The horror in his eyes caused Malemute Kid to whirl about; and he, too, was startled, though he had seen bad things before. The thing tottered blindly towards them. Prince edged away till he reached the nail from which hung his Smith & Wesson.

'My God! what is it?' he whispered to Malemute Kid.

'Don't know. Looks like a case of freezing and no grub,' replied the Kid, sliding away in the opposite direction. 'Watch out! It may be mad,' he warned, coming back from closing the door.

The thing advanced to the table. The bright flame of the slush lamp caught its eye. It was amused, and gave voice to eldritch cackles which betokened mirth. Then, suddenly, he—for it was a man—swayed back, with a hitch to his skin trousers, and began to sing a chanty, such as men lift when they swing around the capstan circle and the sea snorts in their ears:

> 'Yan-kee ship come down de ri-ib-er,
>     Pull! my bully boys! Pull!
> D'yeh want—to know de captain ru-uns her?
>     Pull! my bully boys! Pull!
> Jon-a-than Jones ob South Caho-li-in-a,
>     Pull! my bully——'

He broke off abruptly, tottered with a wolfish snarl to the meat shelf, and before they could intercept was tearing with his teeth at a chunk of raw bacon. The struggle was fierce between him and Malemute Kid; but his mad strength left him as suddenly as it had come, and he weakly surrendered the spoil. Between them they got him upon a stool, where he sprawled with half his body across the table. A small dose of whisky strengthened him, so that he could dip a spoon into the sugar caddy which Malemute Kid placed before him. After his appetite had been some-what cloyed, Prince, shuddering as he did so, passed him a mug of weak beef tea.

The creature's eyes were alight with a sombre frenzy, which blazed and waned with every mouthful. There was very little skin to the face. The face, for that matter, sunken and emaciated, bore little likeness to human countenance. Frost after frost had bitten deeply, each depositing its stratum of scab upon the half-healed scar that went before. This dry, hard surface was of a bloody-black colour, ser-rated by grievous cracks wherein the raw red flesh peeped forth. His skin garments were dirty and in tatters, and the fur of one side was singed and burned away, showing where he had lain upon his fire.

Malemute Kid pointed to where the sun-tanned hide had been cut away, strip by strip—the grim signature of famine.

'Who—are—you?' slowly and distinctly enunciated the Kid.

The man paid no heed.

'Where do you come from?'

'Yan-kee ship come down de ri-ib-er,' was the quavering response.

'Don't doubt the beggar came down the river,' the Kid said, shaking him in an endeavour to start a more lucid flow of talk.

But the man shrieked at the contact, clapping a hand to his side in evident pain. He rose slowly to his feet, half leaning on the table.

'She laughed at me—so—with the hate in her eye; and she—would—not—come.'

His voice died away, and he was sinking back when Malemute Kid gripped him by the wrist and shouted, 'Who? Who would not come?'

'She, Unga. She laughed, and struck at me, so, and so. And then——'

'Yes?'

'And then——'

'And then what?'

'And then he lay very still in the snow a long time. He is—still in—the—snow.'

The two men looked at each other helplessly.

'Who is in the snow?'

'She, Unga. She looked at me with the hate in her eye, and then——'

'Yes, yes.'

'And then she took the knife, so; and once, twice—she was weak. I travelled very slow. And there is much gold in that place, very much gold.'

'Where is Unga?' For all Malemute Kid knew, she might be dying a mile away. He shook the man savagely, repeating again and again, 'Where is Unga? Who is Unga?'

'She—is—in—the—snow.'

'Go on!' The Kid was pressing his wrist cruelly.

'So—I—would—be—in—the snow—but—I—had—a—debt—to—pay. It—was—heavy—I—had—a—debt—to—

pay—a—debt—to—pay—I—had——' The faltering monosyllables ceased as he fumbled in his pouch and drew forth a buckskin sack. 'A debt—to—pay—five—pounds—of —gold—grub—stake—Mal—e—Mute—Kid—I——' The exhausted head dropped upon the table; nor could Malemute Kid rouse it again.

'It's Ulysses,' he said quietly, tossing the bag of dust on the table. 'Guess it's all day with Axel Gunderson and the woman. Come on, let's get him between the blankets. He's Indian; he'll pull through and tell a tale besides.'

As they cut his garments from him, near his right breast could be seen two unhealed, hard-lipped knife thrusts.

### III

'I will talk of the things which were in my own way; but you will understand. I will begin at the beginning, and tell of myself and the woman, and, after that, of the man.'

He of the Otter Skins drew over to the stove as do men who have been deprived of fire and are afraid the Promethean gift may vanish at any moment. Malemute Kid pricked up the slush lamp and placed it so its light might fall upon the face of the narrator. Prince slid his body over the edge of the bunk and joined them.

'I am Naass, a chief, and the son of a chief, born between a sunset and a rising, on the dark seas, in my father's oomiak. All of a night the men toiled at the paddles, and the women cast out the waves which threw in upon us, and we fought with the storm. The salt spray froze upon my mother's breast till her breath passed with the passing of the tide. But I—I raised my voice with the wind and the storm, and lived.

'We dwelt in Akatan——'

'Where?' asked Malemute Kid.

'Akatan, which is in the Aleutians; Akatan, beyond Chignik, beyond Kardalak, beyond Unimak. As I say, we dwelt in Akatan, which lies in the midst of the sea on the edge of the world. We farmed the salt seas for the fish, the seal, and the otter; and our homes shouldered about one another on the rocky strip between the rim of the forest and the yellow beach where our kayaks lay. We were not many, and the world was very small. There were strange lands to the east—islands like Akatan; so we thought all the world was islands and did not mind.

'I was different from my people. In the sands of the beach were the crooked timbers and wave-warped planks of a boat such as my people never built; and I remember on the point of the island which overlooked the ocean three ways there stood a pine tree which never grew there, smooth and straight and tall. It is said the two men came to that spot, turn about, through many days, and watched with the passing of the light. These two men came from out of the sea in the boat which lay in pieces on the beach. And they were white like you, and weak as the little children when the seal have gone away and the hunters come home empty. I know of these things from the old men and the old women, who got them from their fathers and mothers before them. These strange white men did not take kindly to our ways at first, but they grew strong, what of the fish and the oil, and fierce. And they built them each his own house, and took the pick of our women, and in time children came. Thus he was born who was to become the father of my father's father.

'As I said, I was different from my people, for I carried the strong, strange blood of this white man who came out of the sea. It is said we had other laws in the days before these men; but they were fierce and quarrelsome, and fought with our men till there were no more left who dared to fight. Then they made themselves chiefs, and took away our old laws and gave us new ones, insomuch that the man was the son of his father, and not his mother, as our way had been. They also ruled that the son, first-born, should have all things which were his father's before him, and that the brothers and sisters should shift for themselves. And they gave us other laws. They showed us new ways in the catching of fish and the killing of bear which were thick in the woods; and they taught us to lay by bigger stores for the time of famine. And these things were good.

'But when they had become chiefs, and there were no more men to face their anger, they fought, these strange white men, each with the other. And the one whose blood I carry drove his seal spear the length of an arm through the other's body. Their children took up the fight, and their children's children; and there was great hatred between them, and black doings, even to my time, so that in each family but one lived to pass down the blood of them that went before. Of my blood I was alone; of the other man's there was but a girl, Unga, who lived with her mother. Her father and my father did not come back from the fishing one night; but afterward they washed up to the beach on the big tides, and they held very close to each other.

'The people wondered, because of the hatred between the houses, and the old men shook their heads and said the fight would go on when children were born to her and children to me. They told me this as a boy, till I came to believe, and to look upon Unga as a foe, who was to be the mother of children which were to fight with mine. I thought of these things day by day, and when I grew to a stripling I came to ask why this should be so. And they answered, "We do not know, but that in such way your fathers did." And I marvelled that those which were to come should fight the battles of those that were gone, and in it I could see no right. But the people said it must be, and I was only a stripling.

'And they said I must hurry, that my blood might be the older and grow strong before hers. This was easy, for I was head man, and the people looked up to me because of the deeds and the laws of my fathers, and the wealth which was mine. Any maiden would come to me, but I found none to my liking. And the old men and the mothers of maidens told me to hurry, for even then were the hunters bidding high to the mother of Unga; and should her children grow strong before mine, mine would surely die.

'Nor did I find a maiden till one night coming back from the fishing. The sunlight was lying, so, low and full in the eyes, the wind free, and the kayaks racing with the white seas. Of a sudden the kayak of Unga came driving past me, and she looked upon me, so, with her black hair flying like a cloud of night and the spray wet on her cheek. As I say, the sunlight was full in the eyes, and I was a stripling; but somehow it was all clear, and I knew it to be the call of kind to kind. As she whipped ahead she looked back within the space of two strokes—looked as only the woman Unga could look—and again I knew it as the call of kind. The people shouted as we ripped past the lazy oomiaks and left them far behind. But she was quick at the paddle, and my heart was like the belly of a sail, and I did not gain. The wind freshened, the sea whitened, and, leaping like the seals on the windward breech, we roared down the golden pathway of the sun.'

Naass was crouched half out of his stool, in the attitude of one driving a paddle, as he ran the race anew. Somewhere across the stove he beheld the tossing kayak and the flying hair of Unga. The voice of the wind was in his ears, and its salt beat fresh upon his nostrils.

'But she made the shore, and ran up the sand, laughing, to the house of her mother. And a great thought came to me that night—a thought worthy of him that was chief over all the people of Akatan. So, when the moon was up, I went down to the house of her mother, and looked upon the goods of Yash-Noosh, which were piled by the door— the goods of Yash-Noosh, a strong hunter who had it in mind to be the father of the children of Unga. Other young men had piled their goods there and taken them away again, and each young man had made a pile greater than the one before.

'And I laughed to the moon and the stars, and went to my own house where my wealth was stored. And many trips I made, till my pile was greater by the fingers of one hand than the pile of Yash-Noosh. There were fish, dried in the sun and smoked; and forty hides of the hair seal, and half as many of the fur, and each hide was tied at the mouth and big bellied with oil; and ten skins of bear which I killed in the woods when they came out in the spring. And there were beads and blankets and scarlet cloths, such as I got in trade from the people who lived to the east, and who got them in trade from the people who lived still beyond in the east. And I looked upon the pile of Yash-Noosh and laughed, for I was head man in Akatan, and my wealth was greater than the wealth of all my young men, and my fathers had done deeds, and given laws, and put their names for all time in the mouths of the people.

'So, when the morning came, I went down to the beach, casting out of the corner of my eye at the house of the mother of Unga. My offer yet stood untouched. And the women smiled, and said sly things one to the other. I wondered, for never had such a price been offered; and that night I added more to the pile, and put beside it a kayak of well-tanned skins which never yet had swam in the sea. But in the day it was yet there, open to the laughter of all men. The mother of Unga was crafty, and I grew angry at the shame in which I stood before my people. So that night I added till it became a great pile, and I hauled up my oomiak, which was of the value of twenty kayaks. And in the morning there was no pile.

'Then made I preparation for the wedding, and the people that lived even to the east came for the food of the feast and the potlatch token. Unga was older than I by the age of four suns in the way we reckoned the years. I was only a stripling; but then I was a chief, and the son of a chief, and it did not matter.

'But a ship shoved her sails above the floor of the ocean, and grew larger with the breath of the wind. From her scuppers she ran clear water, and the men were in haste and worked hard at the pumps. On the bow stood a mighty man, watching the depth of the water and giving commands with a voice of thunder. His eyes were of the pale blue of the deep waters, and his head was maned like that of a sea lion. And his hair was yellow, like the straw of a southern harvest or the manila rope yarns which sailormen plait.

'Of late years we had seen ships from afar, but this was the first to come to the beach of Akatan. The feast was broken, and the women and children fled to the houses, while we men strung our bows and waited with spears in hand. But when the ship's forefoot smelled the beach the strange men took no notice of us, being busy with their own work. With the falling of the tide they careened the schooner and patched a great hole in her bottom. So the women crept back, and the feast went on.

'When the tide rose, the sea wanderers kedged the schooner to deep water and then came among us. They bore presents and were friendly; so I made room for them, and out of the largeness of my heart gave them tokens such as I gave all the guests, for it was my wedding day, and I was head man in Akatan. And he with the mane of the sea lion was there, so tall and strong that one looked to see the earth shake with the fall of his feet. He looked much and straight at Unga, with his arms folded, so, and stayed till the sun went away and the stars came out. Then he went down to his ship. After that I took Unga by the hand and led her to my own house. And there was singing and great laughter, and the women said sly things, after the manner of women at such times. But we did not care. Then the people left us alone and went home.

'The last noise had not died away when the chief of the sea wanderers came in by the door. And he had with him black bottles from which we drank and made merry. You see, I was only a stripling, and had lived all my days on the edge of the world. So my blood became as fire, and my heart as light as the froth that flies from the surf to the cliff. Unga sat silent among the skins in the corner, her eyes wide, for she seemed to fear. And he with the mane of the sea lion looked upon her straight and long. Then his men came in with bundles of goods, and he piled before me wealth such as was not in all Akatan. There were guns, both large and small, and powder and shot and shell, and bright axes and knives of steel, and cunning tools, and strange things the like of which I had never seen. When he showed me by sign that it was all mine, I thought him a great man to be so free; but he showed me also that Unga was to go away with him in his ship. Do you understand? —that Unga was to go away with him in his ship. The blood of my fathers flamed hot on the sudden, and I made

to drive him through with my spear. But the spirit of the
bottles had stolen the life from my arm, and he took me by
the neck, so, and knocked my head against the wall of the
house. And I was made weak like a newborn child, and my
legs would no more stand under me. Unga screamed, and
she laid hold of the things of the house with her hands, till
they fell all about us as he dragged her to the door. Then
he took her in his great arms, and when she tore at his
yellow hair laughed with a sound like that of the big bull
seal in the rut.

'I crawled to the beach and called upon my people, but
they were afraid. Only Yash-Noosh was a man, and they
struck him on the head with an oar, till he lay with his face
in the sand and did not move. And they raised the sails to
the sound of their songs, and the ship went away on the
wind.

'The people said it was good, for there would be no more
war of the bloods in Akatan; but I said never a word, waiting till the time of the full moon, when I put fish and oil in
my kayak and went away to the east. I saw many islands
and many people, and I, who had lived on the edge, saw
that the world was very large. I talked by signs; but they
had not seen a schooner nor a man with the mane of a sea
lion, and they pointed always to the east. And I slept in
queer places, and ate odd things, and met strange faces.
Many laughed, for they thought me light of head; but
sometimes old men turned my face to the light and blessed
me, and the eyes of the young women grew soft as they
asked me of the strange ship, and Unga, and the men of
the sea.

'And in this manner, through rough seas and great
storms, I came to Unalaska. There were two schooners
there, but neither was the one I sought. So I passed on to
the east, with the world growing ever larger, and in the
island of Unamok there was no word of the ship, nor in
Kadiak, nor in Atognak. And so I came one day to a rocky
land, where men dug great holes in the mountain. And
there was a schooner, but not my schooner, and men loaded
upon it the rocks which they dug. This I thought childish,

for all the world was made of rocks; but they gave me food and set me to work. When the schooner was deep in the water, the captain gave me money and told me to go; but I asked which way he went, and he pointed south. I made signs that I would go with him, and he laughed at first, but then, being short of men, took me to help work the ship. So I came to talk after their manner, and to heave on ropes, and to reef the stiff sails in sudden squalls, and to take my turn at the wheel. But it was not strange, for the blood of my fathers was the blood of the men of the sea.

'I had thought it an easy task to find him I sought, once I got among his own people; and when we raised the land one day, and passed between a gateway of the sea to a port, I looked for perhaps as many schooners as there were fingers to my hands. But the ships lay against the wharves for miles, packed like so many little fish; and when I went among them to ask for a man with the mane of a sea lion, they laughed, and answered me in the tongues of many peoples. And I found that they hailed from the uttermost parts of the earth.

'And I went into the city to look upon the face of every man. But they were like the cod when they run thick on the banks, and I could not count them. And the noise smote upon me till I could not hear and my head was dizzy with much movement. So I went on and on, through the lands which sang in the warm sunshine; where the harvests lay rich on the plains; and where great cities were fat with men that lived like women, with false words in their mouths and their hearts black with the lust of gold. And all the while my people of Akatan hunted and fished, and were happy in the thought that the world was small.

'But the look in the eyes of Unga coming home from the fishing was with me always, and I knew I would find her when the time was met. She walked down quiet lanes in the dusk of the evening, or led me chases across the thick fields wet with the morning dew, and there was a promise in her eyes such as only the woman Unga could give.

'So I wandered through a thousand cities. Some were gentle and gave me food, and others laughed, and still others cursed; but I kept my tongue between my teeth, and went strange ways and saw strange sights. Sometimes I, who was a chief and the son of a chief, toiled for men— men rough of speech and hard as iron, who wrung gold from the sweat and sorrow of their fellow men. Yet no word did I get of my quest till I came back to the sea like a homing seal to the rookeries. But this was at another port, in another country which lay to the north. And there I heard dim tales of the yellow-haired sea wanderer, and I learned that he was a hunter of seals, and that even then he was abroad on the ocean.

'So I shipped on a seal schooner with the lazy Siwashes, and followed his trackless trail to the north where the hunt was then warm. And we were away weary months, and spoke many of the fleet, and heard much of the wild doings of him I sought; but never once did we raise him above the sea. We went north, even to the Pribilofs, and killed the seals in herds on the beach, and brought their warm bodies aboard till our scuppers ran grease and blood and no man could stand upon the deck. Then we were chased by a ship of slow steam, which fired upon us with great guns. But we put on sail till the sea was over our decks and washed them clean, and lost ourselves in a fog.

'It is said, at this time, while we fled with fear at our hearts, that the yellow-haired sea wanderer put in to the Pribilofs, right to the factory, and while the part of his men held the servants of the company, the rest loaded ten thousand green skins from the salt houses. I say it is said, but I believe; for in the voyages I made on the coast with never a meeting the northern seas rang with his wildness and daring, till the three nations which have lands there sought him with their ships. And I heard of Unga, for the captains sang loud in her praise, and she was always with him. She had learned the ways of his people, they said, and was happy. But I knew better—knew that her heart harked back to her own people by the yellow beach of Akatan.

'So, after a long time, I went back to the port which is by a gateway of the sea, and there I learned that he had gone across the girth of the great ocean to hunt for the seal to the east of the warm land which runs south from the Russian Seas. And I, who was become a sailorman, shipped with men of his own race, and went after him in the hunt of the seal. And there were few ships off that new land; but we hung on the flank of the seal pack and harried it north through all the spring of the year. And when the cows were heavy with pup and crossed the Russian line, our men grumbled and were afraid. For there was much fog, and every day men were lost in the boats. They would not work, so the captain turned the ship back toward the way it came. But I knew the yellow-haired sea wanderer was unafraid, and would hang by the pack, even to the Russian Isles, where few men go. So I took a boat, in the black of night, when the lookout dozed on the fo'c'slehead, and went alone to the warm, long land. And I journeyed south to meet the men by Yeddo Bay, who are wild and unafraid. And the Yoshiwara girls were small, and bright like steel, and good to look upon; but I could not stop, for I knew that Unga rolled on the tossing floor by the rookeries of the north.

'The men by Yeddo Bay had met from the ends of the earth, and had neither gods nor homes, sailing under the flag of the Japanese. And with them I went to the rich beaches of Copper Island, where our salt piles became high with skins. And in that silent sea we saw no man till we were ready to come away. Then one day the fog lifted on the edge of a heavy wind, and there jammed down upon us a schooner, with close in her wake the cloudy funnels of a Russian man-of-war. We fled away on the beam of the wind, with the schooner jamming still closer and plunging ahead three feet to our two. And upon her poop was the man with the mane of the sea lion, pressing the rails under with the canvas and laughing in his strength of life. And Unga was there—I knew her on the moment—but he sent her below when the cannons began to talk across the sea. As I say, with three feet to our two, till we saw the rudder lift green at every jump—and I swinging on to the wheel and cursing, with my back to the Russian shot. For we knew he had it in mind to run before us, that he might get away while we were caught. And they knocked our masts out of us till we dragged into the wind like a wounded gull; but he went on over the edge of the sky line—he and Unga.

'What could we? The fresh hides spoke for themselves. So they took us to a Russian port, and after that to a lone country, where they set us to work in the mines to dig salt. And some died, and—and some did not die.'

Naass swept the blanket from his shoulders, disclosing the gnarled and twisted flesh, marked with the unmistakable striations of the knout. Prince hastily covered him, for it was not nice to look upon.

'We were there a weary time and sometimes men got away to the south, but they always came back. So, when we who hailed from Yeddo Bay rose in the night and took the guns from the guards, we went to the north. And the land was very large, with plains, soggy with water, and great forests. And the cold came, with much snow on the ground, and no man knew the way. Weary months we journeyed through the endless forest—I do not remember, now, for there was little food and often we lay down to die. But at last we came to the cold sea, and but three were left to look upon it. One had shipped from Yeddo as captain, and he knew in his head the lay of the great lands, and of the place where men may cross from one to the other on the ice. And he led us—I do not know, it was so long—till there were but two. When we came to that place we found five of the strange people which live in that country, and they had dogs and skins, and we were very poor. We fought in the snow till they died, and the captain died, and the dogs and skins were mine. Then I crossed on the ice, which was broken, and once I drifted till a gale from the west put me upon the shore. And after that, Golovin Bay, Pastilik, and the priest. Then south, south, to the warm sunlands where first I wandered.

'But the sea was no longer fruitful, and those who went upon it after the seal went to little profit and great risk. The fleets scattered, and the captains and the men had no word of those I sought. So I turned away from the ocean which never rests, and went among the lands, where the trees, the houses, and the mountains sit always in one place and do not move. I journeyed far, and came to learn many things, even to the way of reading and writing from books. It was well I should do this, for it came upon me that Unga must know these things, and that someday, when the time was met—we—you understand, when the time was met.

'So I drifted, like those little fish which raise a sail to the wind but cannot steer. But my eyes and my ears were open always, and I went among men who travelled so much, for I knew they had but to see those I sought to remember. At last there came a man, fresh from the mountains, with pieces of rock in which the free gold stood to the size of peas, and he had heard, he had met, he knew them. They were rich, he said, and lived in the place where they drew the gold from the ground.

'It was in a wild country, and very far away; but in time I came to the camp, hidden between the mountains, where men worked night and day, out of the sight of the sun. Yet the time was not come. I listened to the talk of the people. He had gone away—they had gone away—to England, it was said, in the matter of bringing men with much money together to form companies. I saw the house they had lived in; more like a palace, such as one sees in the old countries. In the night-time I crept in through a window that I might see in what manner he treated her. I went from room to room, and in such way thought kings and queens must live, it was all so very good. And they all said he treated her like a queen, and many marvelled as to what breed of woman she was for there was other blood in her veins, and she was different from the women of Akatan, and no one knew her for what she was. Aye, she was a queen; but I was a chief, and the son of a chief, and I had paid for her an untold price of skin and boat and bead.

'But why so many words? I was a sailorman, and knew the way of the ships on the seas. I followed to England, and then to other countries. Sometimes I heard of them by word of mouth, sometimes I read of them in the papers; yet never once could I come by them, for they had much money, and travelled fast, while I was a poor man. Then came trouble upon them, and their wealth slipped away one day like a curl of smoke. The papers were full of it at the time; but after that nothing was said, and I knew they had gone back where more gold could be got from the ground.

'They had dropped out of the world, being now poor, and so I wandered from camp to camp, even north to the Kootenay country, where I picked up the cold scent. They had come and gone, some said this way, and some that, and still others that they had gone to the country of the Yukon. And I went this way, and I went that, ever journeying from place to place, till it seemed I must grow weary of the world which was so large. But in the Kootenay I travelled a bad trail, and a long trail, with a breed of the Northwest, who saw fit to die when the famine pinched. He had been to the Yukon by an unknown way over the mountains, and when he knew his time was near gave me the map and the secret of a place where he swore by his gods there was much gold.

'After that all the world began to flock into the north. I was a poor man; I sold myself to be a driver of dogs. The rest you know. I met him and her in Dawson. She did not know me, for I was only a stripling, and her life had been large, so she had no time to remember the one who had paid for her an untold price.

'So? You bought me from my term of service. I went back to bring things about in my own way, for I had waited long, and now that I had my hand upon him was in no hurry. As I say, I had it in mind to do my own way, for I read back in my life, through all I had seen and suffered, and remembered the cold and hunger of the endless forest by the Russian Seas. As you know, I led him into the east —him and Unga—into the east where many have gone and few returned. I led them to the spot where the bones and the curses of men lie with the gold which they may not have.

'The way was long and the trail unpacked. Our dogs were many and ate much; nor could our sleds carry till the break of spring. We must come back before the river ran free. So here and there we cached grub, that our sleds might be lightened and there be no chance of famine on the back trip. At the McQuestion there were three men, and near them we built a cache, as also did we at the Mayo, where was a hunting camp of a dozen Pellys which had crossed the divide from the south. After that, as we went on into the east, we saw no men; only the sleeping river, the moveless forest, and the White Silence of the North. As I say, the way was long and the trail unpacked. Sometimes, in a day's toil, we made no more than eight miles, or ten, and at night we slept like dead men. And never once did they dream that I was Naass, head man of Atakan, the righter of wrongs.

'We now made smaller caches, and in the night-time it was a small matter to go back on the trail we had broken and change them in such way that one might deem the wolverines the thieves. Again there be places where there is a fall to the river, and the water is unruly, and the ice makes above and is eaten away beneath. In such a spot the sled I drove broke through, and the dogs; and to him and Unga it was ill luck, but no more. And there was much grub on that sled, and the dogs the strongest. But he laughed, for he was strong of life, and gave the dogs that were left little grub till we cut them from the harness one by one and fed them to their mates. We would go home light, he said, travelling and eating from cache to cache, with neither dogs nor sleds; which was true, for our grub was very short, and the last dog died in the traces the night we came to the gold and the bones and the curses of men.

'To reach that place—and the map spoke true—in the heart of the great mountains, we cut ice steps against the wall of a divide. One looked for a valley beyond, but there was no valley; the snow spread away, level as the great harvest plains, and here and there about us mighty mountains shoved their white heads among the stars. And midway on that strange plain which should have been a valley the earth and the snow fell away, straight down toward the heart of the world. Had we not been sailormen our heads would have swung round with the sight, but we stood on the dizzy edge that we might see a way to get down. And on one side, and one side only, the wall had fallen away till it was like the slope of the decks in a topsail breeze. I do not know why this thing should be so, but it was so. "It is the mouth of hell," he said; "let us go down." And we went down.

'And on the bottom there was a cabin, built by some man, of logs which he had cast down from above. It was a very old cabin, for men had died there alone at different times, and on pieces of birch bark which were there we read their last words and their curses. One had died of scurvy; another's partner had robbed him of his last grub and powder and stolen away; a third had been mauled by a bald-face grizzly; a fourth had hunted for game and starved—and so it went, and they had been loath to leave the gold, and had died by the side of it in one way or another. And the worthless gold they had gathered yellowed the floor of the cabin like in a dream.

'But his soul was steady, and his head clear, this man I had led thus far. "We have nothing to eat," he said, "and we will only look upon this gold, and see whence it comes and how much there be. Then we will go away quick, before it gets into our eyes and steals away our judgment. And in this way we may return in the end, with more grub, and possess it all." So we looked upon the great vein, which cut the wall of the pit as a true vein should, and we measured it, and traced it from above and below, and drove the stakes of the claims and blazed the trees in token of our rights. Then, our knees shaking with lack of food, and a sickness in our bellies, and our hearts chugging close to our mouths, we climbed the mighty wall for the last time and turned our faces to the back trip.

'The last stretch we dragged Unga between us, and we fell often, but in the end we made the cache. And lo, there was no grub. It was well done, for he thought it the wolverines, and damned them and his gods in the one breath. But Unga was brave, and smiled, and put her hand in his, till I turned away that I might hold myself. "We will rest by the fire," she said, "till morning, and we will gather strength from our moccasins." So we cut the tops of our moccasins in strips, and boiled them half the night, that we might chew them and swallow them. And in the morning we talked of our chance. The next cache was five days' journey; we could not make it. We must find game.

' "We will go forth and hunt," he said.

' "Yes," said I, "we will go forth and hunt."

'And he ruled that Unga stay by the fire and save her strength. And we went forth, he in quest of the moose and I to the cache I had changed. But I ate little, so they might not see in me much strength. And in the night he fell many times as he drew into camp. And I, too, made to suffer great weakness, stumbling over my snowshoes as though each step might be my last. And we gathered strength from our moccasins.

'He was a great man. His soul lifted his body to the last; nor did he cry aloud, save for the sake of Unga. On the second day I followed him, that I might not miss the end. And he lay down to rest often. That night he was near gone; but in the morning he swore weakly and went forth again. He was like a drunken man, and I looked many times for him to give up, but his was the strength of the strong, and his soul the soul of a giant, for he lifted his body through all the weary day. And he shot two ptarmigan, but would not eat them. He needed no fire; they meant life; but his thought was for Unga, and he turned toward camp. He no longer walked, but crawled on hand and knee through the snow. I came to him, and read death in his eyes. Even then it was not too late to eat of the ptarmigan. He cast away his rifle and carried the birds in his mouth like a dog. I walked by his side, upright. And he looked at me during the moments he rested, and wondered that I was so strong. I could see it, though he no longer spoke; and when his lips moved, they moved without sound. As I say, he was a great man, and my heart spoke for softness; but I read back in my life, and remembered the cold and hunger of the endless forest by the Russian Seas. Besides, Unga was mine, and I had paid for her an untold price of skin and boat and bead.

'And in this manner we came through the white forest,

with the silence heavy upon us like a damp sea mist. And the ghosts of the past were in the air and all about us; and I saw the yellow beach of Akatan, and the kayaks racing home from the fishing, and the houses on the rim of the forest. And the men who had made themselves chiefs were there, the lawgivers whose blood I bore and whose blood I had wedded in Unga. Aye, and Yash-Noosh walked with me, the wet sand in his hair, and his war spear, broken as he fell upon it, still in his hand. And I knew the time was met, and saw in the eyes of Unga the promise.

'As I say, we came thus through the forest, till the smell of the camp smoke was in our nostrils. And I bent above him, and tore the ptarmigan from his teeth. He turned on his side and rested, the wonder mounting in his eyes, and the hand which was under slipping slow toward the knife at his hip. But I took it from him, smiling close in his face. Even then he did not understand. So I make to drink from black bottles, and to build high upon the snow a pile of goods, and to live again the things which happened on the night of my marriage. I spoke no word, but he understood. Yet he was unafraid. There was a sneer to his lips, and cold anger, and he gathered new strength with the knowledge. It was not far, but the snow was deep, and he dragged himself very slow. Once he lay so long I turned him over and gazed into his eyes. And sometimes he looked forth, and sometimes death. And when I loosed him he struggled on again. In this way we came to the fire. Unga was at his side on the instant. His lips moved without sound, then he pointed at me, that Unga might understand. And after that he lay in the snow, very still, for a long while. Even now is he there in the snow.

'I said no word till I had cooked the ptarmigan. Then I spoke to her, in her own tongue, which she had not heard in many years. She straightened herself, so, and her eyes were wonder-wide, and she asked who I was, and where I had learned that speech.

' "I am Naass," I said.

' "You?" she said. "You?" And she crept close that she might look upon me.

' "Yes," I answered; "I am Naass, head man of Akatan, the last of the blood, as you are the last of the blood."

'And she laughed. By all the things I have seen and the deeds I have done may I never hear such a laugh again. It put the chill to my soul, sitting there in the White Silence, alone with death and this woman who laughed.

' "Come!" I said, for I thought she wandered. "Eat of the food and let us be gone. It is a far fetch from here to Akatan."

'But she shoved her face in his yellow mane, and laughed till it seemed the heavens must fall about our ears. I had thought she would be overjoyed at the sight of me, and eager to go back to the memory of old times, but this seemed a strange form to take.

' "Come!" I cried, taking her strong by the hand. "The way is long and dark. Let us hurry!"

' "Where?" she asked, sitting up, and ceasing from her strange mirth.

' "To Akatan," I answered, intent on the light to grow on her face at the thought. But it became like his, with a sneer to the lips, and cold anger.

' "Yes," she said; "we will go, hand in hand, to Akatan, you and I. And we will live in the dirty huts, and eat of the fish and oil, and bring forth a spawn—a spawn to be proud of all the days of our life. We will forget the world and be happy, very happy. It is good, most good. Come! Let us hurry. Let us go back to Akatan."

'And she ran her hand through his yellow hair, and smiled in a way which was not good. And there was no promise in her eyes.

'I sat silent, and marvelled at the strangeness of woman. I went back to the night when he dragged her from me and she screamed and tore at his hair—at his hair which now she played with and would not leave. Then I remembered the price and the long years of waiting; and I gripped her close, and dragged her away as he had done. And she held back, even as on that night, and fought like a she-cat for its whelp. And when the fire was between us and the man, I loosed her, and she sat and listened. And I told her of all that lay between, of all that had happened to me on strange seas, of all that I had done in strange lands; of my weary quest, and the hungry years, and the promise which had been mine from the first. Aye, I told all, even to what had passed that day between the man and me, and in the days yet young. And as I spoke I saw the promise grow in her eyes, full and large like the break of dawn. And I read pity there, the tenderness of woman, the love, the heart and the soul of Unga. And I was a stripling again, for the look was the look of Unga as she ran up the beach, laughing, to the home of her mother. The stern unrest was gone, and the hunger, and the weary waiting. The time was met. I felt the call of her breast, and it seemed there I must pillow my head and forget. She opened her arms to me, and I came against her. Then, sudden, the hate flamed in her eye, her hand was at my hip. And once, twice, she passed the knife.

' "Dog!" she sneered, as she flung me into the snow. "Swine!" And then she laughed till the silence cracked, and went back to her dead.

'As I say, once she passed the knife, and twice; but she was weak with hunger, and it was not meant that I should die. Yet I was minded to stay in that place, and to close my eyes in the last long sleep with those whose lives had crossed with mine and led my feet on unknown trails. But there lay a debt upon me which would not let me rest.

'And the way was long, the cold bitter, and there was little grub. The Pellys had found no moose, and had robbed my cache. And so had the three white men, but they lay thin and dead in their cabin as I passed. After that I do not remember, till I came here, and found food and fire—much fire.'

As he finished, he crouched closely, even jealously, over the stove. For a long while the slush-lamp played tragedies upon the wall.

'But Unga!' cried Prince, the vision still strong upon him.

'Unga? She would not eat of the ptarmigan. She lay with her arms about his neck, her face deep in his yellow hair. I drew the fire close, that she might not feel the frost, but she crept to the other side. And I built a fire there; yet it was little good, for she would not eat. And in this manner they still lie up there in the snow.'

'And you?' asked Malemute Kid.

'I do not know; but Akatan is small, and I have little wish to go back to live on the edge of the world. Yet is there small use in life. I can go to Constantine, and he will put irons upon me, and one day they will tie a piece of rope, so, and I will sleep good. Yet—no; I do not know.'

'But, Kid,' protested Prince, 'this is murder!'

'Hush!' commanded Malemute Kid. 'There be things greater than our wisdom, beyond our justice. The right and the wrong of this we cannot say, and it is not for us to judge.'

Naass drew yet closer to the fire. There was a great silence, and in each man's eyes many pictures came and went.

## THE WISDOM OF THE TRAIL

SITKA CHARLEY had achieved the impossible. Other Indians might have known as much of the wisdom of the trail as he did; but he alone knew the white man's wisdom, the honour of the trail, and the law. But these things had not come to him in a day. The aboriginal mind is slow to generalize, and many facts, repeated often, are required to compass an understanding. Sitka Charley, from boyhood, had been thrown continually with white men, and as a man he had elected to cast his fortunes with them, expatriating himself, once and for all, from his own people. Even then, respecting, almost venerating their power, and pondering over it, he had yet to divine its secret essence—the honour and the law. And it was only by the cumulative evidence of years that he had finally come to understand. Being an alien, when he did know, he knew it better than the white

5*

man himself; being an Indian, he had achieved the impossible.

And of these things had been bred a certain contempt for his own people—a contempt which he had made it a custom to conceal, but which now burst forth in a polygot whirlwind of curses upon the heads of Kah-Chucte and Gowhee. They cringed before him like a brace of snarling wolf dogs, too cowardly to spring, too wolfish to cover their fangs. They were not handsome creatures. Neither was Sitka Charley. All three were frightful-looking. There was no flesh to their faces; their cheekbones were massed with hideous scabs which had cracked and frozen alternately under the intense frost; while their eyes burned luridly with the light which is born of desperation and hunger. Men so situated, beyond the pale of the honour and the law, are not to be trusted. Sitka Charley knew this; and this was why he had forced them to abandon their rifles with the rest of the camp outfit ten days before. His rifle and Captain Eppingwell's were the only ones that remained.

'Come, get a fire started,' he commanded, drawing out the precious matchbox with its attendant strips of dry birchbark.

The two Indians fell sullenly to the task of gathering dead branches and underwood. They were weak and paused often, catching themselves, in the act of stooping, with giddy motions, or staggering to the centre of operations with their knees shaking like castanets. After each trip they rested for a moment, as though sick and deadly weary. At times their eyes took on the patient stoicism of dumb suffering; and again the ego seemed almost bursting forth with its wild cry, 'I, I, I want to exist!'—the dominant note of the whole living universe.

A light breath of air blew from the south, nipping the exposed portions of their bodies and driving the frost, in needles of fire, through fur and flesh to the bones. So, when the fire had grown lusty and thawed a damp circle in the snow about it, Sitka Charley forced his reluctant comrades to lend a hand in pitching a fly. It was a primitive affair, merely a blanket stretched parallel with the fire and to windward of it, at an angle of perhaps forty-five degrees. This shut out the chill wind and threw the heat backward and down upon those who were to huddle in its shelter. Then a layer of green spruce boughs was spread, that their bodies might not come in contact with the snow. When this task was completed, Kah-Chucte and Gowhee proceeded to take care of their feet. Their icebound moccasins were sadly worn by much travel, and the sharp ice of the river jams had cut them to rags. Their Siwash socks were similarly conditioned, and when these had been thawed and removed, the dead-white tips of the toes, in the various stages of mortification, told their simple tale of the trail.

Leaving the two to the drying of their footgear, Sitka Charley turned back over the course he had come. He, too, had a mighty longing to sit by the fire and tend his complaining flesh, but the honour and the law forbade. He toiled painfully over the frozen field, each step a protest, every muscle in revolt. Several times, where the open water between the jams had recently crusted, he was forced to miserably accelerate his movements as the fragile footing swayed and threatened beneath him. In such places death was quick and easy; but it was not his desire to endure no more.

His deepening anxiety vanished as two Indians dragged into view round a bend in the river. They staggered and panted like men under heavy burdens; yet the packs on their backs were a matter of but a few pounds. He questioned them eagerly, and their replies seemed to relieve him. He hurried on. Next came two white men, supporting between them a woman. They also behaved as though drunken, and their limbs shook with weakness. But the woman leaned lightly upon them, choosing to carry herself forward with her own strength. At the sight of her a flash of joy cast its fleeting light across Sitka Charley's face. He cherished a very great regard for Mrs Eppingwell. He had seen many white women, but this was the first to travel the trail with him. When Captain Eppingwell proposed the hazardous undertaking and made him an offer for his services, he had shaken his head gravely; for it was an un-

known journey through the dismal vastnesses of the Northland, and he knew it to be of the kind that try to the uttermost the souls of men. But when he learned that the captain's wife was to accompany them, he had refused flatly
to have anything further to do with it. Had it been a woman
of his own race he would have harboured no objections;
but these women of the Southland—no, no, they were too
soft, too tender, for such enterprises.

Sitka Charley did not know this kind of woman. Five
minutes before, he did not even dream of taking charge of
the expedition; but when she came to him with her wonderful smile and her straight clean English, and talked to
the point, without pleading or persuading, he had inconti-
nently yielded. Had there been a softness and appeal to
mercy in the eyes, a tremble to the voice, a taking advantage of sex, he would have stiffened to steel; instead her
clear-searching eyes and clear-ringing voice, her utter
frankness and tacit assumption of equality, had robbed him
of his reason. He felt, then, that this was a new breed of
woman; and ere they had been trail mates for many days
he knew why the sons of such women mastered the land
and the sea, and why the sons of his own womankind could
not prevail against them. *Tender and soft!* Day after day
he watched her, muscle-weary, exhausted, indomitable, and
the words beat in upon him in a perennial refrain. *Tender
and soft!* He knew her feet had been born to easy paths and
sunny lands, strangers to the moccasined pain of the North,
unkissed by the chill lips of the frost, and he watched and
marvelled at them twinkling ever through the weary day.

She had always a smile and a word of cheer, from which
not even the meanest packer was excluded. As the way
grew darker she seemed to stiffen and gather greater
strength, and when Kah-Chucte and Gowhee, who had
bragged that they knew every landmark of the way as a
child did the skin bails of the tepee, acknowledged that they
knew not where they were, it was she who raised a forgiving voice amid the curses of the men. She had sung to them
that night till they felt the weariness fall from them and
were ready to face the future with fresh hope. And when

the food failed and each scant stint was measured jealously, she it was who rebelled against the machinations of her husband and Sitka Charley, and demanded and received a share neither greater nor less than that of the others.

Sitka Charley was proud to know this woman. A new richness, a greater breadth, had come into his life with her presence. Hitherto he had been his own mentor, had turned to right or left at no man's beck; he had moulded himself according to his own dictates, nourished his manhood regardless of all save his own opinion. For the first time he had felt a call from without for the best that was in him. Just a glance of appreciation from the clear-searching eyes, a word of thanks from the clear-ringing voice, just a slight wreathing of the lips in the wonderful smile, and he walked with the gods for hours to come. It was a new stimulant to his manhood; for the first time he thrilled with a conscious pride in his wisdom of the trail; and between the twain they ever lifted the sinking hearts of their comrades.

The faces of the two men and the woman brightened as they saw him, for after all he was the staff they leaned upon. But Sitka Charley, rigid as was his wont, concealing pain and pleasure impartially beneath an iron exterior, asked them the welfare of the rest, told the distance to the fire, and continued on the back-trip. Next he met a single Indian, unburdened, limping, lips compressed, and eyes set with the pain of a foot in which the quick fought a losing battle with the dead. All possible care had been taken of him, but in the last extremity the weak and unfortunate must perish, and Sitka Charley deemed his days to be few. The man could not keep up for long, so he gave him rough cheering words. After that came two more Indians, to whom he had allotted the task of helping along Joe, the third white man of the party. They had deserted him. Sitka Charley saw at a glance the lurking spring in their bodies, and knew they had at last cast off his mastery. So he was not taken unawares when he ordered them back in quest of their abandoned charge, and saw the gleam of the hunting knives that they drew from the sheaths. A pitiful spectacle, three weak men lifting their puny strength in the face of the mighty vastness; but the two recoiled under the fierce rifle blows of the one and returned like beaten dogs to the leash. Two hours later, with Joe reeling between them and Sitka Charley bringing up the rear, they came to the fire, where the remainder of the expedition crouched in the shelter of the fly.

'A few words, my comrades, before we sleep,' Sitka Charley said after they had devoured their slim rations of unleavened bread. He was speaking to the Indians in their own tongue, having already given the import to the whites. 'A few words, my comrades, for your own good, that ye may yet perchance live. I shall give you the law; on his own head be the death of him that breaks it. We have passed the Hills of Silence, and we now travel the head reaches of the Stuart. It may be one sleep, it may be several, it may be many sleeps, but in time we shall come among the men of the Yukon, who have much grub. It were well that we look to the law. Today Kah-Chucte and Gowhee, whom I commanded to break trail, forgot they were men, and like frightened children ran away. True, they forgot; so let us forget. But hereafter let them remember. If it should happen they do not . . .' He touched his rifle carelessly, grimly. 'Tomorrow they shall carry the flour and see that the white man Joe lies not down by the trail. The cups of flour are counted; should so much as an ounce be wanting at nightfall . . . Do ye understand? Today there were others that forgot. Moose Head and Three Salmon left the white man Joe to lie in the snow. Let them forget no more. With the light of day shall they go forth and break trail. Ye have heard the law. Look well, lest ye break it.'

Sitka Charley found it beyond him to keep the line close up. From Moose Head and Three Salmon, who broke trail in advance, to Kah-Chucte, Gowhee, and Joe, it straggled out over a mile. Each staggered, fell or rested as he saw fit. The line of march was a progression through a chain of irregular halts. Each drew upon the last remnant of his strength and stumbled onward till it was expended, but in

some miraculous way there was always another last remnant. Each time a man fell it was with the firm belief that
he would rise no more; yet he did rise, and again, and
again. The flesh yielded, the will conquered; but each
triumph was a tragedy. The Indian with the frozen foot, no
longer erect, crawled forward on hand and knee. He rarely
rested, for he knew the penalty exacted by the frost. Even
Mrs Eppingwell's lips were at last set in a stony smile, and
her eyes, seeing, saw not. Often she stopped, pressing a
mittened hand to her heart, gasping and dizzy.

Joe, the white man, had passed beyond the stage of suffering. He no longer begged to be let alone, prayed to die;
but was soothed and content under the anodyne of
delirium. Kah-Chucte and Gowhee dragged him on
roughly, venting upon him many a savage glance or blow.
To them it was the acme of injustice. Their hearts were bitter with hate, heavy with fear. Why should they cumber
their strength with his weakness? To do so meant death;
not to do so—and they remembered the law of Sitka Charley, and the rifle.

Joe fell with greater frequency as the daylight waned,
and so hard was he to raise that they dropped farther and
farther behind. Sometimes all three pitched into the snow,
so weak had the Indians become. Yet on their backs was
life, and strength, and warmth. Within the flour sacks were
all the potentialities of existence. They could not but think
of this, and it was not strange, that which came to pass.
They had fallen by the side of a great timber jam where a
thousand cords of firewood waited the match. Near by was
an air hole through the ice. Kah-Chucte looked on the wood
and the water, as did Gowhee; then they looked on each
other. Never a word was spoken. Gowhee struck a fire;
Kah-Chucte filled a tin cup with water and heated it; Joe
babbled of things in another land, in a tongue they did not
understand. They mixed flour with the warm water till it
was a thin paste, and of this they drank many cups. They
did not offer any to Joe; but he did not mind. He did not
mind anything, not even his moccasins, which scorched and
smoked among the coals.

A crystal mist of snow fell about them, softly, caressingly, wrapping them in clinging robes of white. And their feet would have yet trod many trails had not destiny brushed the clouds aside and cleared the air. Nay, ten minutes' delay would have been salvation. Sitka Charley, looking back, saw the pillared smoke of their fire, and guessed. And he looked ahead at those who were faithful, and at Mrs Eppingwell.

'So, my good comrades, ye have again forgotten that you were men? Good! Very good. There will be fewer bellies to feed.'

Sitka Charley retied the flour as he spoke, strapping the pack to the one on his own back. He kicked Joe till the pain broke through the poor devil's bliss and brought him doddering to his feet. Then he shoved him out upon the trail and started him on his way. The two Indians attempted to slip off.

'Hold, Gowhee! And thou, too, Kah-Chucte! Hath the flour given such strength to thy legs that they may outrun the swift-winged lead? Think not to cheat the law. Be men for the last time, and be content that ye die full-stomached. Come, step up, back to the timber, shoulder to shoulder. Come!'

The two men obeyed, quietly, without fear; for it is the future which presses upon the man, not the present.

'Thou, Gowhee, hast a wife and children and a deerskin lodge in the Chipewyan. What is thy will in the matter?'

'Give thou her of the goods which are mine by the word of the captain—the blankets, the beads, the tobacco, the box which makes strange sounds after the manner of the white men. Say that I did die on the trail, but say not how.'

'And thou, Kah-Chucte, who hast nor wife nor child?'

'Mine is a sister, the wife of the factor at Koshim. He beats her, and she is not happy. Give thou her the goods which are mine by the contract, and tell her it were well she go back to her own people. Shouldst thou meet the man, and be so minded, it were a good deed that he should die. He beats her, and she is afraid.'

'Are ye content to die by the law?'

'We are.'

'Then good-bye, my good comrades. May ye sit by the well-filled pot, in warm lodges, ere the day is done.'

As he spoke he raised his rifle, and many echoes broke the silence. Hardly had they died away when other rifles spoke in the distance. Sitka Charley started. There had been more than one shot, yet there was but one other rifle in the party. He gave a fleeting glance at the men who lay so quietly, smiled viciously at the wisdom of the trail, and hurried on to meet the men of the Yukon.

## THE SON OF THE WOLF

MAN RARELY places a proper valuation upon his woman-kind, at least not until deprived of them. He has no conception of the subtle atmosphere exhaled by the sex feminine so long as he bathes in it; but let it be withdrawn, and an ever-growing void begins to manifest itself in his existence, and he becomes hungry, in a vague sort of way, for a something so indefinite that he cannot characterize it. If his comrades have no more experience than himself, they will shake their heads dubiously and dose him with strong physic. But the hunger will continue and become stronger; he will lose interest in the things of his every-day life and wax morbid; and one day, when the emptiness has become unbearable, a revelation will dawn upon him.

In the Yukon country, when this comes to pass, the man usually provisions a poling-boat, if it be summer, and if winter harnesses his dogs, and heads for the Southland. A few months later, supposing him to be possessed of a faith in the country, he returns with a wife to share with him in that faith, and incidentally in his hardships. This but serves to show the innate selfishness of man. It also brings us to the trouble of 'Scruff' Mackenzie, which occurred in the old days, before the country was stampeded and staked by a tidal-wave of *che-cha-quas,* and when the Klondike's only claim to notice was its salmon fisheries.

Scruff Mackenzie bore the ear-marks of a frontier birth and a frontier life. His face was stamped with twenty-five years of incessant struggle with Nature in her wildest moods—the last two, the wildest and hardest of all having been spent in groping for the gold which lies in the shadow of the Arctic Circle. When the yearning sickness came upon him he was not surprised, for he was a practical man, and had seen other men thus stricken. But he showed no sign of his malady, save that he worked harder. All summer he fought mosquitoes and washing the sure-thing bars of the Stuart River for a double grub-stake. Then he floated a raft of house-logs down the Yukon to Forty Mile, and put together as comfortable a cabin as any the camp could boast of. In fact, it showed such cosy promise that many men elected to be his partner, and to come and live with him. But he crushed their aspirations with rough speech, peculiar for its strength and brevity, and bought a double supply of grub from the trading-post.

As has been noted, Scruff Mackenzie was a practical man. If he wanted a thing he usually got it, but in doing so, went no farther out of his way than was necessary. Though a son of toil and hardship, he was averse to a journey of six hundred miles on the ice, a second of two thousand miles on the ocean, and still a third thousand miles or so to his last stamping-grounds—all in the mere quest of a wife. Life was too short. So he rounded up his dogs, lashed a curious freight to his sled, and faced across the divide whose westward slopes were drained by the head-reaches of the Tanana.

He was a sturdy traveller, and his wolf-dogs could work harder and travel farther on less grub than any other team in the Yukon. Three weeks later he strode into a hunting-camp of the Upper Tanana Sticks. They marvelled at his temerity; for they had a bad name, and had been known to kill white men for as trifling a thing as a sharp axe or a broken rifle. But he went among them single-handed, his bearing being a delicious composite of humility, familiarity, *sang-froid*, and insolence. It required a deft hand and deep knowledge of the barbaric mind effectually to handle such diverse weapons; but he was a past master in the art, knowing when to conciliate and when to threaten with Jove-like wrath.

He first made obeisance to the Chief Thling-Tinneh, presenting him with a couple of pounds of black tea and tobacco, and thereby winning his most cordial regard. Then he mingled with the men and maidens, and that night gave a *potlach*. The snow was beaten down in the form of an oblong, perhaps a hundred feet in length, and quarter as many across. Down the centre a long fire was built, while either side was carpeted with spruce boughs. The lodges were forsaken, and the fivescore or so members of the tribe gave tongue to their folk-chants in honour of their guest.

Scruff Mackenzie's two years had taught him the not many hundred words of their vocabulary, and he had likewise conquered their deep gutturals, their Japanese idioms, constructions, and honorific and agglutinative particles. So he made oration after their manner, satisfying their instinctive poetry-love with crude flights of eloquence and metaphorical contortions. After Thling-Tinneh and the Shaman had responded in kind, he made trifling presents to the menfolk, joined in their singing, and proved an expert in their fifty-two-stick gambling game.

And they smoked his tobacco and were pleased. But among the younger men there was a defiant attitude, a spirit of braggadocio, easily understood by the raw insinuations of the toothless squaws and the giggling of the maidens. They had known few white men, 'Sons of the Wolf', but from those few they had learned strange lessons.

Nor had Scruff Mackenzie, for all his seeming carelessness, failed to note these phenomena. In truth, rolled in his sleeping-furs, he thought it all over, thought seriously, and emptied many pipes in mapping out a campaign. One maiden only had caught his fancy—none other than Zarinska, daughter to the chief. In features, form, and poise, answering more nearly to the white man's type of beauty, she was almost an anomaly among her tribal sisters. He would possess her, make her his wife, and name her—ah, he would name her Gertrude! Having thus decided, he rolled over on his side and dropped off to sleep, a true son of his all-conquering race.

It was slow work and a stiff game; but Scruff Mackenzie manoeuvred cunningly, with an unconcern which served to puzzle the Sticks. He took great care to impress the men that he was a sure shot and a mighty hunter, and the camp rang with his plaudits when he brought down a moose at six hundred yards. Of a night he visited in Chief Thling-Tinneh's lodge of moose and caribou skins, talking big and dispensing tobacco with a lavish hand. Nor did he fail to likewise honour the Shaman; for he realized the medicine-man's influence with his people, and was anxious to make of him an ally. But that worthy was high and mighty, refused to be propitiated, and was unerringly marked down as a prospective enemy.

Though no opening presented for an interview with Zarinska, Mackenzie stole many a glance to her, giving fair warning of his intent. And well she knew, yet coquettishly surrounded herself with a ring of women whenever the men were away and he had a chance. But he was in no hurry; besides, he knew she could not help but think of him, and a few days of such thought would only better his suit.

At last, one night, when he deemed the time to be ripe, he abruptly left the chief's smoky dwelling and hastened to a neighbouring lodge. As usual, she sat with squaws and maidens about her, all engaged in sewing moccasins and beadwork. They laughed at his entrance, and badinage, which linked Zarinska to him, ran high. But one after the other they were unceremoniously bundled into the outer snow, whence they hurried to spread the tale through all the camp.

His cause was well pleaded, in her tongue, for she did not know his, and at the end of two hours he rose to go.

'So Zarinska will come to the White Man's Lodge? Good! I go now to have talk with thy father, for he may not be so minded. And I will give him many tokens; but he must not ask too much. If he say no? Good! Zarinska shall yet come to the White Man's lodge.'

He had already lifted the skin flap to depart, when a low exclamation brought him back to the girl's side. She brought herself to her knees on the bearskin mat, her face aglow with true Eve-light, and shyly unbuckled his heavy belt. He looked down, perplexed, suspicious, his ears alert for the slightest sound without. But her next move disarmed his doubt, and he smiled with pleasure. She took from her sewing-bag a moosehide sheath, brave with bright bead-work, fantastically designed. She drew his great hunting-knife, gazed reverently along the keen edge, half tempted to try it with her thumb, and shot it into place in its new home. Then she slipped the sheath along the belt to its customary resting-place, just above the hip.

For all the world, it was like a scene of olden time—a lady and her knight. Mackenzie drew her up full height and swept her red lips with his moustache—the, to her, foreign caress of the Wolf. It was a meeting of the stone age and the steel.

There was a thrill of excitement in the air as Scruff Mackenzie, a bulky bundle under his arm, threw open the flap of Thling-Tinneh's tent. Children were running about in the open, dragging dry wood to the scene of the *potlach*, a babble of women's voices was growing in intensity, the young men were consulting in sullen groups, while from the Shaman's lodge rose the eerie sounds of an incantation.

The chief was alone with his blear-eyed wife, but a glance sufficed to tell Mackenzie that the news was already old. So he plunged at once into the business, shifting the beaded sheath prominently to the fore as advertisement of the betrothal.

'O Thling-Tinneh, mighty chief of the Sticks and the land of the Tanana, ruler of the salmon and the bear, the moose and the caribou! The White Man is before thee with a great purpose. Many moons has his lodge been empty, and he is lonely. And his heart has eaten itself in silence, and grown hungry for a woman to sit beside him in his lodge, to meet him from the hunt with warm fire and good food. He has heard strange things, the patter of baby moccasins and the sound of children's voices. And one night a vision came upon him, and he beheld the Raven, who is thy father, the great Raven, who is the father of all the Sticks. And the Raven spake to the lonely White Man, saying: "Bind thou thy moccasins upon thee, and gird thy snowshoes on, and lash thy sled with food for many sleeps and fine tokens for the Chief Thling-Tinneh. For thou shalt turn thy face to where the midspring sun is wont to sink below the land, and journey to this great chief's hunting-grounds. There thou shalt make big presents, and Thling-Tinneh, who is my son, shall become to thee as a father. In his lodge there is a maiden into whom I breathed the breath of life for thee. This maiden shalt thou take to wife".

'O chief, thus spake the great Raven; thus do I lay my presents at thy feet; thus am I come to take thy daughter!'

The old man drew his furs about him with crude consciousness of royalty, but delayed reply while a youngster crept in, delivered a quick message to appear before the council, and was gone.

'O, White Man, whom we have named Moose-Killer, also known as the Wolf, and the Son of the Wolf! We know thou comest of a mighty race; we are proud to have thee our *potlach*-guest; but the king-salmon does not mate with the dog-salmon, nor the Raven with the Wolf.'

'Not so!' cried Mackenzie. 'The daughters of the Raven have I met in the camps of the Wolf—the squaw of Mortimer, the squaw of Tregidgo, the squaw of Barnaby, who came two ice-runs back, and I have heard of other squaws, though my eyes beheld them not.'

'Son, your words are true; but it were evil mating, like the water with the sand, like the snowflake with the sun. But met you one Mason and his squaw? No? He came ten ice-runs ago—the first of all the Wolves. And with him there was a mighty man, straight as a willow-shoot, and tall; strong as the bald-faced grizzly, with a heart like the full summer moon; his——'

'Oh!' interrupted Mackenzie, recognizing the well-known Northland figure—'Malemute Kid!'

'The same—a mighty man. But saw you aught of the squaw? She was full sister to Zarinska.'

'Nay, chief; but I have heard. Mason—far, far to the north, a spruce-tree, heavy with years, crushed out his life beneath. But his love was great, and he had much gold. With this, and her boy, she journeyed countless sleeps towards the winter's noonday sun, and there she yet lives—no biting frost, no snow, no summer's midnight sun, no winter's noonday night.'

A second messenger interrupted with imperative summons from the council. As Mackenzie threw him into the snow, he caught a glimpse of the swaying forms before the council-fire, heard the deep basses of the men in rhythmic chant, and knew the Shaman was fanning the anger of his people. Time pressed. He turned upon the chief.

'Come! I wish thy child. And now. See! here are tobacco, tea, many cups of sugar, warm blankets, handkerchiefs, both good and large; and here, a true rifle, with many bullets and much powder.'

'Nay,' replied the old man, struggling against the great wealth spread before him. 'Even now are my people come together. They will not have this marriage.'

'But thou art chief.'

'Yet do my young men rage because the Wolves have taken their maidens so that they may not marry.'

'Listen, O Thling-Tinneh! Ere the night has passed into the day, the Wolf shall face his dogs to the Mountains of the East, and fare forth to the Country of the Yukon. And Zarinska shall break trail for his dogs.'

'And ere the night has gained its middle, my young men may fling to the dogs the flesh of the Wolf, and his bones be scattered in the snow till the springtime lay them bare.'

It was threat and counter-threat. Mackenzie's bronzed face flushed darkly. He raised his voice. The old squaw, who till now had sat an impassive spectator, made to creep by him for the door. The song of the men broke suddenly, and there was a hubbub of many voices as he whirled the old woman roughly to her couch of skins.

'Again I cry—listen, O Thling-Tinneh! The Wolf dies with teeth fast-locked, and with him there shall sleep ten of thy strongest men—men who are needed, for the hunting is but begun, and the fishing is not many moons away. And again, of what profit should I die? I know the custom of thy people; thy share of my wealth shall be very small. Grant me thy child, and it shall all be thine. And yet again, my brothers will come, and they are many, and their maws are never filled; and the daughters of the Raven shall bear children in the lodges of the Wolf. My people are greater than thy people. It is destiny. Grant, and all this wealth is thine.'

Moccasins were crunching the snow without. Mackenzie threw his rifle to cock, and loosened the twin Colts in his belt.

'Grant, O chief!'

'And yet will my people say no.'

'Grant, and the wealth is thine. Then shall I deal with thy people after.'

'The Wolf will have it so. I will take his tokens—but I would warn him.'

Mackenzie passed over the goods, taking care to clog the rifle's ejector, and capping the bargain with a kaleidoscopic silk kerchief. The Shaman and half a dozen young braves entered, but he shouldered boldly among them and passed out.

'Pack!' was his laconic greeting to Zarinska as he passed her lodge and hurried to harness his dogs. A few minutes later he swept into the council at the head of his team, the woman by his side. He took his place at the upper end of the oblong, by the side of the chief. To his left, a step to the rear, he stationed Zarinska—her proper place. Besides, the time was ripe for mischief, and there was need to guard his back.

On either side, the men crouched to the fire, their voices lifted in a folk-chant out of the forgotten past. Full of strange, halting cadences and haunting recurrences, it was not beautiful. 'Fearful' may inadequately express it. At the lower end, under the eye of the Shaman, danced half a score of women. Stern were his reproofs to those who did not wholly abandon themselves to the ecstasy of the rite. Half hidden in their heavy masses of raven hair, all dishevelled and falling to their waists, they slowly swayed to and fro, their forms rippling to an ever-changing rhythm.

It was a weird scene; an anachronism. To the south, the nineteenth century was reeling off the few years of its last decade; here flourished man primeval, a shade removed from the prehistoric cave-dweller, a forgotten fragment of the Elder World. The tawny wolf-dogs sat between their skin-clad masters or fought for room, the fire-light cast backward from their red eyes and slavered fangs. The woods, in ghostly shroud, slept on unheeding. The White Silence, for the moment driven to the rimming forest, seemed ever crushing inward; the stars danced with great leaps, as is their wont in the time of the great Cold; while the Spirits of the Pole trailed their robes of glory athwart the heavens.

Scruff Mackenzie dimly realized the wild grandeur of the setting as his eyes ranged down the fur-fringed sides in quest of missing faces. They rested for a moment on a new-born babe, suckling at its mother's naked breast. It was forty below—seventy and odd degrees of frost. He thought of the tender women of his own race, and smiled grimly. Yet from the loins of some such tender woman had he sprung with a kingly inheritance—an inheritance which gave to him and his dominance over the land and sea, over the animals and the peoples of all the zones. Single-handed against fivescore, girt by the Arctic winter, far from his own, he felt the prompting of his heritage, the desire to possess the wild danger-love, the thrill of battle, the power to conquer or to die.

The singing and the dancing ceased, and the Shaman flared up in rude eloquence. Through the sinuosities of their vast mythology, he worked cunningly upon the credulity of his people. The case was strong. Opposing the creative principles as embodied in the Crow and the Raven, he stigmatized Mackenzie as the Wolf, the fighting and the destructive principle. Not only was the combat of these forces spiritual, but men fought, each to his totem. They were the children of Jelchs, the Raven, the Promethean fire-bringer; Mackenzie was the child of the Wolf, or, in other words, the Devil. For them to bring a truce to this perpetual warfare, to marry their daughters to the arch-enemy, were treason and blasphemy of the highest order. No phrase was harsh, nor figure vile enough in branding Mackenzie as a sneaking interloper and emissary of Satan. There was a subdued, savage roar in the deep chests of his listeners as he took the swing of his peroration.

'Ay, my brothers, Jelchs is all-powerful! Did he not bring heaven-born fire that we might be warm? Did he not draw the sun, moon, and stars from their holes that we might see? Did he not teach us that we might fight the spirits of famine and of frost? But now Jelchs is angry with his children, and they are grown to a handful, and he will not help. For they have forgotten him, and done evil things, and trod bad trails, and taken his enemies into their lodges to sit by their fires. And the Raven is sorrowful at the wickedness of his children; but when they shall rise up and show they have come back, he will come out of the darkness to aid them. O, brothers! the Fire-Bringer has whispered messages to thy Shaman; the same shall ye hear. Let the young men take the young women to their lodges; let them fly at the throat of the Wolf; let them be undying in their enmity! Then shall their women become fruitful, and they shall multiply into a mighty people! And the Raven shall lead great tribes of their fathers and their fathers' fathers from out of the North; and they shall beat back the Wolves till they are as last year's camp-fires; and they shall again come to rule over all the land! 'Tis the message of Jelchs, the Raven.'

This foreshadowing of the Messiah's coming brought a hoarse howl from the Sticks as they leaped to their feet. Mackenzie slipped the thumbs of his mittens, and waited. There was a clamour for the Fox, not to be stilled till one of the young men stepped forward to speak.

'Brothers! The Shaman has spoken wisely. The Wolves have taken our women, and our men are childless. We are grown to a handful. The Wolves have taken our warm furs, and given for them evil spirits which dwell in bottles, and clothes which come not from the beaver or the lynx, but are made from the grass. And they are not warm, and our men die of strange sicknesses. I, the Fox, have taken no woman to wife; and why? Twice have the maidens which pleased me gone to the camps of the Wolf. Even now have I laid by skins of the beaver, of the moose, of the caribou, that I might win favour in the eyes of Thling-Tinneh, that I might marry Zarinska, his daughter. Even now are her snowshoes bound to her feet, ready to break trail for the dogs of the Wolf. Nor do I speak for myself alone. As I have done, so has the Bear. He, too, had fain been the father of her children, and many skins has he cured thereto. I speak for all the young men who know not wives. The Wolves are ever hungry. Always do they take the choice meat at the killing. To the Ravens are left the leavings.

'There is Gugkla!' he cried, brutally pointing out one of the women, who was a cripple. 'Her legs are bent like the ribs of a birch canoe. She cannot gather wood nor carry the meat of the hunters. Did the Wolves choose her?'

'Ai! ai!' vociferated his tribesmen.

'There is Moyri, whose eyes are crossed by the Evil Spirit. Even the babes are affrighted when they gaze upon her, and it is said the bald-face gives her the trail. Was she chosen?'

Again the cruel applause rang out.

'And there sits Pischet. She does not hearken to my words. Never has she heard the cry of the chit-chat, the voice of her husband, the babble of her child. She lives in the White Silence. Cared the Wolves aught for her? No! Theirs is the choice of the kill; ours is the leavings.

'Brothers, it shall not be! No more shall the Wolves slink among our camp-fires. The time is come.'

A great streamer of fire, the aurora borealis, purple, green, and yellow, shot across the zenith, bridging horizon to horizon. With head thrown back and arms extended, he swayed to his climax.

'Behold! The spirits of our fathers have arisen, and great deeds are afoot this night!'

He stepped back, and another young man somewhat diffidently came forward, pushed on by his comrades. He towered a full head above them, his broad chest defiantly bared to the frost. He swung tentatively from one foot to the other. Words halted upon his tongue, and he was ill at ease. His face was horrible to look upon, for it had one time been half torn away by some terrific blow. At last he struck his breast with his clenched fist, drawing sound as from a drum, and his voice rumbled forth as the surf from an ocean cavern.

'I am the Bear—the Silver-Tip and the Son of the Silver-Tip! When my voice was yet as a girl's, I slew the lynx, the moose, and the caribou; when it whistled like the wolverines from under a cache, I crossed the Mountains of the South and slew three of the White Rivers; when it became as the roar of the Chinook, I met the bald-faced grizzly, but gave no trail.'

At this he paused, his hand significantly sweeping across the hideous scars.

'I am not as the Fox. My tongue is frozen like the river. I cannot make great talk. My words are few. The Fox says great deeds are afoot this night. Good! Talk flows from his tongue like the freshets of the spring, but he is chary of deeds. This night shall I do battle with the Wolf. I shall slay him, and Zarinska shall sit by my fire. The Bear has spoken.'

Though pandemonium raged about him, Scruff Mackenzie held his ground. Aware how useless was the rifle at close quarters, he slipped both holsters to the fore ready for action, and drew his mittens till his hands were barely shielded by the elbow gauntlets. He knew there was no hope in attack *en masse,* but true to his boast, was prepared to die with teeth fast locked. But the Bear restrained his comrades, beating back the more impetuous with his terrible fist. As the tumult began to die away, Mackenzie shot a glance in the direction of Zarinska. It was a superb picture. She was leaning forward on her snowshoes, lips apart and nostrils quivering, like a tigress about to spring. Her great black eyes were fixed upon her tribesmen in fear and in defiance. So extreme the tension, she had forgotten to breathe. With one hand pressed spasmodically against her breast and the other as tightly gripped about the dogwhip, she was as turned to stone. Even as he looked, relief came to her. Her muscles loosened; with a heavy sigh she settled back, giving him a look of more than love.

Thling-Tinneh was trying to speak, but his people drowned his voice. Then Mackenzie strode forward. The Fox opened mouth to a piercing yell, but so savagely did Mackenzie whirl upon him that he shrank back, his larynx all a-gurgle with suppressed sound. His discomfiture was greeted with roars of laughter, and served to soothe his fellows to a listening mood.

'Brothers! The White Man, whom ye have chosen to call the Wolf, came among you with fair words. He was not like the Innuit; he spoke not lies. He came as a friend, as one who would be a brother. But your men have had their say, and the time for soft words is past. First, I will tell you that the Shaman has an evil tongue, and is a false prophet, that the messages he spake are not those of the Fire-Bringer. His ears are locked to the voice of the Raven, and out of his own head he weaves cunning fancies, and he has made fools of you. He has no power. When the dogs were killed and eaten, and your stomachs were heavy with untanned hide and strips of moccasins; when the old men died, and the old women died, and the babes at the dry dugs of the mothers died; when the land was dark, and ye perished as do the salmon in the fall; ay, when the famine was upon you, did the Shaman bring reward to your hunters? did the Shaman put meat in your bellies? Again I say, the Shaman is without power. Thus! I spit upon his face!'

Though taken aback by the sacrilege, there was no uproar. Some of the women were even frightened, but among the men there was an uplifting, as though in preparation or anticipation of the miracle. All eyes were turned upon the two central figures. The priest realized the crucial moment, felt his power tottering, opened his mouth in denunciation, but fled backward before the truculent advance, upraised fist, and flashing eyes of Mackenzie. He sneered and resumed.

'Was I stricken dead? Did the lightning burn me? Did the stars fall from the sky and crush me? Pish! I have done with the dog. Now will I tell you of my people, who rule in all the lands. At first we hunt as I hunt, alone. After that we hunt in packs; and at last, like the caribou-run, we sweep across all the land. Those whom we take into our lodges live; those who will not come die. Zarinska is a comely maiden, full and strong, fit to become the mother of Wolves. Though I die, such shall she become; for my brothers are many, and they will follow the scent of my dogs. Listen to the law of the Wolf: *Whosoever taketh the life of one Wolf, the forfeit shall ten of his people pay.* In many lands has the price been paid; in many lands shall it yet be paid.

'Now will I deal with the Fox and the Bear. It seems they have cast eyes upon the maiden. So? Behold, I have bought her! Thling-Tinneh leans upon the rifle; the goods of purchase are by his fire. Yet will I be fair to the young men. To the Fox, whose tongue is dry with many words, will I give of tobacco five long plugs. Thus will his mouth be wetted that he may make much noise in the council. But to the Bear, of whom I am well proud, will I give of blankets two; of flour, twenty cups; of tobacco, double that of the Fox; and if he fare with me over the Mountains of the East, then will I give him a rifle, mate to Thling-Tinneh's. If not? Good! The Wolf is weary of speech. Yet once again will he say the law: *Whosoever taketh the life of one Wolf, the forfeit shall ten of his people pay.*'

Mackenzie smiled as he stepped back to his old position, but at heart he was full of trouble. The night was yet dark. The girl came to his side, and he listened closely as she told of the Bear's battle tricks with the knife.

The decision was for war. In a trice, scores of moccasins were widening the space of beaten snow by the fire. There was much chatter about the seeming defeat of the Shaman; some averred he had but withheld his power; while others conned past events and agreed with the Wolf. The Bear came to the centre of the battle-ground, a long naked hunting-knife of Russian make in his hand. The Fox called attention to Mackenzie's revolvers; so he stripped his belt, buckling it about Zarinska, into whose hands he also entrusted his rifle. She shook her head that she could not shoot—small chance had a woman to handle such precious things.

'Then, if danger come to my back, cry aloud, "My husband!" No; thus, "My husband!"'

He laughed as she repeated it, pinched her cheek, and re-entered the circle. Not only in reach and stature had the Bear the advantage of him, but his blade was longer by a good two inches. Scruff Mackenzie had looked into the eyes of men before, and he knew it was a man who stood against him; yet he quickened to the glint of light on the steel, to the dominant pulse of his race.

Time and again he was forced to the edge of the fire or the deep snow, and time and again, with the foot tactics of the pugilist, he worked back to the centre. Not a voice was lifted in encouragement, while his antagonist was heartened with applause, suggestions, and warnings. But his teeth only shut the tighter as the knives clashed together, and he thrust or eluded with a coolness born of conscious strength. At first he felt compassion for his enemy; but this fled before the primal instinct of life, which in turn gave way to the lust of slaughter. The ten thousand years of culture fell from him, and he was a cave-dweller, doing battle for his female.

Twice he pricked the Bear, getting away unscathed; but the third time caught, and to save himself, free hands closed on fighting hands, and they came together. Then did he realize the tremendous strength of his opponent. His muscles were knotted in painful lumps, and cords and tendons threatened to snap with the strain; yet nearer and nearer came the Russian steel. He tried to break away, but only weakened himself. The fur-clad circle closed in, certain of and anxious to see the final stroke. But with wrestler's trick, swinging partly to the side, he struck at his adversary with his head. Involuntarily the Bear leaned back, disturbing his centre of gravity. Simultaneous with this, Mackenzie tripped properly and threw his whole weight forward, hurling him clear through the circle into the deep snow. The Bear floundered out, and came back full tilt.

'Oh, my husband!' Zarinska's voice rang out, vibrant with danger.

To the twang of a bow-string, Mackenzie swept low to the ground, and a bone-barbed arrow passed over him into the breast of the Bear, whose momentum carried him over his crouching foe. The next instance Mackenzie was up and about. The Bear lay motionless, but across the fire was the Shaman, drawing a second arrow.

Mackenzie's knife leaped short in the air. He caught the heavy blade by the point. There was a flash of light as it spanned the fire. Then the Shaman, the hilt alone appearing without his throat, swayed a moment and pitched forward into the glowing embers.

Click! click!—The Fox had possessed himself of Thling-Tinneh's rifle, and was vainly trying to throw a shell into place. But he dropped it at the sound of Mackenzie's laughter.

'So the Fox has not learned the way of the plaything? He is yet a woman. Come! Bring it, that I may show thee!'

The Fox hesitated.

'Come, I say!'

He slouched forward like a beaten cur.

'Thus, and thus; so the thing is done.' A shell flew into place, and the trigger was at cock as Mackenzie brought it to shoulder.

'The Fox has said great deeds were afoot this night, and he spoke true. There have been great deeds, yet least among them were those of the Fox. Is he still intent to take Zarinska to his lodge? Is he minded to tread the trail already broken by the Shaman and the Bear? No? Good!'

Mackenzie turned contemptuously and drew his knife from the priest's throat.

'Are any of the young men so minded? If so, the Wolf will take them by two and three till none are left. No? Good! Thling-Tinneh, I now give thee this rifle a second time. If in the days to come thou shouldst journey to the country of the Yukon, know thou that there shall always be a place and much food by the fire of the Wolf. The night is now passing into the day. I go, but I may come again. And for the last time, remember the law of the Wolf!'

He was supernatural in their sight as he rejoined Zarinska. She took her place at the head of the team, and the dogs swung into motion. A few moments later they were swallowed up by the ghostly forest. Till now Mackenzie had waited; he slipped into his snowshoes to follow.

'Has the Wolf forgotten the five long plugs?'

Mackenzie turned upon the Fox angrily; then the humour of it struck him.

'I will give thee one short plug.'

'As the Wolf sees fit,' meekly responded the Fox, stretching out his hand.


## THE MEN OF FORTY MILE

WHEN Big Jim Belden ventured the apparently innocuous proposition that mush-ice was 'rather pecooliar', he little dreamed of what it would lead to. Neither did Lon McFane, when he affirmed that anchor-ice was even more so; nor did Bettles, as he instantly disagreed, declaring the very existence of such a form to be a bugaboo.

'An' ye'd be tellin' me this,' cried Lon, 'after the years ye've spint in the land! An' we atin' out the same pot this many's the day!'

'But the thing's agin reason,' insisted Bettles. 'Look you, water's warmer than ice——'

'An' little the difference, once ye break through.'

'Still it's warmer, because it ain't froze. An' you say it freezes on the bottom?'

'Only the anchor-ice, David, only the anchor-ice. An' have ye niver drifted along, the water clear as glass, whin suddin, belike a cloud over the sun, the mushy-ice comes bubblin' up an' up, till from bank to bank an' bind to bind it's drapin' the river like a first snowfall?'

'Unh, hunh! more'n once when I took a doze at the steering-oar. But it allus come out the nighest side-channel, an' not bubblin' up an' up.'

'But with niver a wink at the helm?'

'No; nor you. It's agin reason. I'll leave it to any man!'

Bettles appealed to the circle about the stove, but the fight was on between himself and Lon McFane.

'Reason or no reason, it's the truth I'm tellin' ye. Last fall, a year gone, 'twas Sitka Charley and meself saw the sight, droppin' down the riffle ye'll remember below Fort Reliance. An' regular fall weather it was—the glint o' the sun on the golden larch an' the quakin' aspens; an' the glister of light on ivery ripple; an' beyand, the winter an' the blue haze of the North comin' down hand in hand. It's well ye know the same, with a fringe to the river an' the ice formin' thick in the eddies—an' a snap an' sparkle to the air, an' ye a-feelin' it through all yer blood, a-takin' new lease of life with ivery suck of it. 'Tis then, me boy, the world grows small an' the wandther-lust lays ye by the heels.

'But it's meself as wandthers. As I was sayin', we a-pad-dlin', with niver a sign of ice, barrin' that by the eddies, when the Injin lifts his paddle an' sings out, "Lon McFane! Look ye below! So have I heard, but niver thought to see!" As ye know, Sitka Charley, like meself, niver drew first breath in the land; so the sight was new. Then we drifted, with a head over ayther side, peerin' down through the sparkly water. For the world like the days I spint with the pearlers, watchin' the coral banks a-growin' the same as so many gardens under the sea. There it was, the anchor-ice, clingin' an' clusterin' to ivery rock, after the manner of the white coral.

'But the best of the sight was to come. Just after clearin' the tail of the riffle, the water turns quick the colour of

milk, an' the top of it in wee circles, as when the graylin'
rise in the spring, or there's a splatter of wet from the
sky. 'Twas the anchor-ice comin' up. To the right, to the
lift, as far as iver a man cud see, the water was covered
with the same. An' like so much porridge it was, slickin'
along the bark of the canoe, stickin' like glue to the paddles. It's many's the time I shot the selfsame riffle before,
and it's many's the time after, but niver a wink of the
same have I seen. 'Twas the sight of a life-time.'

'Do tell!' dryly commented Bettles. 'D'ye think I'd
b'lieve such a yarn? I'd ruther say the glister of light'd
gone to your eyes, and the snap of the air to your tongue.'

' 'Twas me own eyes that beheld it, an' if Sitka Charley was here, he'd be the lad to back me.'

'But facts is facts, an' they ain't no gettin' round 'em.
It ain't in the nature of things for the water furtherest
away from the air to freeze first.'

'But me own eyes——'

'Don't git het up over it,' admonished Bettles, as the
quick Celtic anger began to mount.

'Then yer not after belavin' me?'

'Sence you're so blamed forehanded about it, no; I'd
b'lieve nature first, and facts.'

'Is it the lie ye'd be givin' me?' threatened Lon. 'Ye'd
beter be askin' that Siwash wife of yours. I'll lave it to
her, for the truth I spake.'

Bettles flared up in sudden wrath. The Irishman had
unwittingly wounded him; for his wife was the half-breed
daughter of a Russian fur-trader, married to him in the
Greek Mission of Nulato, a thousand miles or so down
the Yukon, thus being of much higher caste than the
common Siwash, or native, wife. It was a mere Northland
nuance, which none but the Northland adventurer may
understand.

'I reckon you kin take it that way,' was his deliberate
affirmation.

The next instant Lon McFane had stretched him on
the floor, the circle was broken up, and half a dozen men
had stepped between.

Bettles came to his feet, wiping the blood from his mouth. 'It hain't new, this takin' and payin' of blows, and don't you never think but that this will be squared.'

'An' niver in me life did I take the lie from mortal man,' was the retort courteous. 'An' it's an avil day I'll not be to hand, waitin' an' willin' to help ye lift yer debts, barrin' no manner of way.'

'Still got that 38-55?'

Lon nodded.

'But you'd better git a more likely calibre. Mine'll rip holes through you the size of walnuts.'

'Niver fear; it's me own slugs smell their way with soft noses, an' they'll spread like flapjacks against the coming out beyand. An' when'll I have the pleasure of waitin' on ye? The water-hole's a strikin' locality.'

' 'Tain't bad. Jest be there in an hour, and you won't set long on my coming.'

Both men mittened and left the Post, their ears closed to the remonstrances of their comrades. It was such a little thing; yet with such men, little things, nourished by quick tempers and stubborn natures, soon blossomed into big things. Besides, the art of burning to bed-rock still lay in the womb of the future, and the men of Forty-Mile, shut in by the long Arctic winter, grew high-stomached with over-eating and enforced idleness, and became as irritable as do the bees in the fall of the year when the hives are overstocked with honey.

There was no law in the land. The mounted police was also a thing of the future. Each man measured an offence, and meted out the punishment inasmuch as it affected himself. Rarely had combined action been necessary, and never in all the dreary history of the camp had the eighth article of the Decalogue been violated.

Big Jim Belden called an impromptu meeting. Scruff Mackenzie was placed as temporary chairman, and a messenger dispatched to solicit Father Roubeau's good offices. Their position was paradoxical, and they knew it. By the right of might could they interfere to prevent the duel; yet such action, while in direct line with their wishes, went counter to their opinions. While their rough-hewn, obsolete ethics recognized the individual prerogative of wiping out blow with blow, they could not bear to think of two good comrades, such as Bettles and McFane, meeting in deadly battle. Deeming the man who would not fight on provocation a dastard, when brought to the test it seemed wrong that he should fight.

But a scurry of moccasins and loud cries, rounded off with a pistol-shot, interrupted the discussion. Then the storm-doors opened and Malemute Kid entered, a smoking Colt's in his hand, and a merry light in his eye.

'I got him.' He replaced the empty shell, and added, 'Your dog, Scruff.'

'Yellow Fang?' Mackenzie asked.

'No; the lop-eared one.'

'The devil! Nothing the matter with him.'

'Come out and take a look.'

'That's all right after all. Guess he's got 'em, too. Yellow Fang came back this morning and took a chunk out of him, and came near to making a widower of me. Made a rush for Zarinska, but she whisked her skirts in his face and escaped with the loss of the same and a good roll in the snow. Then he took to the woods again. Hope he don't come back. Lost any yourself?'

'One—the best one of the pack—Shookum. Started amuck this morning, but didn't get very far. Ran foul of Sitka Charley's team, and they scattered him all over the street. And now two of them are loose, and raging mad; so you see he got his work in. The dog census will be small in the spring if we don't do something.'

'And the man census, too.'

'How's that? Who's in trouble now?'

'Oh, Bettles and Lon McFane had an argument, and they'll be down by the water-hole in a few minutes to settle it.'

The incident was repeated for his benefit, and Malemute Kid, accustomed to an obedience which his fellow men never failed to render, took charge of the affair. His quickly formulated plan was explained, and they promised to follow his lead implicitly.

'So you see,' he concluded, 'we do not actually take away their privilege of fighting; and yet I don't believe they'll fight when they see the beauty of the scheme. Life's a game and men the gamblers. They'll stake their whole pile on the one chance in a thousand. Take away that one chance, and—they won't play.'

He turned to the man in charge of the Post. 'Storekeeper, weight out three fathoms of your best half-inch manila.

'We'll establish a precedent which will last the men of Forty-Mile to the end of time,' he prophesied. Then he coiled the rope about his arm and led his followers out of doors, just in time to meet the principals.

'What danged right'd he to fetch my wife in?' thundered Bettles to the soothing overtures of a friend. ' 'Twa'n't called for,' he concluded decisively. ' 'Twa'n't called for,' he reiterated again and again, pacing up and down and waiting for Lon McFane.

And Lon McFane—his face was hot and tongue rapid as he flaunted insurrection in the face of the Church. 'Then, father,' he cried, 'it's with an aisy heart I'll roll in me flamy bankets, the broad of me back on a bed of coals. Niver shall it be said that Lon McFane took a lie 'twixt the teeth without iver liftin' a hand! An' I'll not ask a blessin'. The years have been wild, but it's the heart was in the right place.'

'But it's not the heart, Lon,' interposed Father Roubeau; 'It's pride that bids you forth to slay your fellow man.'

'Yer Frinch,' Lon replied. And then, turning to leave him, 'An' will ye say a mass if the luck is against me?'

But the priest smiled, thrust his moccasined feet to the fore, and went out upon the white breast of the silent river. A packed trail, the width of a sixteen-inch sled, led out to the water-hole. On either side lay the deep, soft snow. The men trod in single file, without conversation; and the black-stoled priest in their midst gave to the function the solemn aspect of a funeral. It was a warm winter's day for Forty-Mile—a day in which the sky, filled with heaviness, drew closer to the earth, and the mercury sought the unwonted level of twenty below. But there was no cheer in the warmth. There was little air in the upper strata, and the clouds hung motionless, giving sullen promise of an early snowfall. And the earth, unresponsive, made no preparation, content in its hibernation.

When the water-hole was reached, Bettles, having evidently reviewed the quarrel during the silent walk, burst out in a final ' 'Twa'n't called for,' while Lon McFane kept grim silence. Indignation so choked him that he could not speak.

Yet deep down, whenever their own wrongs were not uppermost, both men wondered at their comrades. They had expected opposition, and this tacit acquiescence hurt them. It seemed more was due them from the men they had been so close with, and they felt a vague sense of wrong, rebelling at the thought of so many of their brothers coming out, as on a gala occasion, without one word of protest, to see them shoot each other down. It appeared their worth had diminished in the eyes of the community. The proceedings puzzled them.

'Back to back, David. An' will it be fifty paces to the man, or double the quantity?'

'Fifty,' was the sanguinary reply, grunted out, yet sharply cut.

But the new manila, not prominently displayed, but casually coiled about Malemute Kid's arm, caught the quick eye of the Irishman, and thrilled him with a suspicious fear.

'An' what are ye doin' with the rope?'

'Hurry up!' Malemute Kid glanced at his watch. 'I've a batch of bread in the cabin, and I don't want it to fall. Besides, my feet are getting cold.'

The rest of the men manifested their impatience in various suggestive ways.

'But the rope, Kid? It's bran' new, an' sure yer bread's not that heavy it needs raisin' with the like of that?'

Bettles by this time had faced around. Father Roubeau,

the humour of the situation just dawning on him, hid a smile behind his mittened hand.

'No, Lon; this rope was made for a man.' Malemute Kid could be very impressive on occasion.

'What man?' Bettles was becoming aware of a personal interest.

'The other man.'

'An' which is the one ye'd mane by that?'

'Listen, Lon—and you, too, Bettles! We've been talking this little trouble of yours over, and we've come to one conclusion. We know we have no right to stop your fighting ——'

'True for ye, me lad!'

'And we're not going to. But this much we can do, and shall do—make this the only duel in the history of Forty-Mile, set an example for every *che-cha-qua* that comes up or down the Yukon. The man who escapes killing shall be hanged to the nearest tree. Now, go ahead!'

Lon smiled dubiously, then his face lighted up. 'Pace her off, David—fifty paces, wheel, an' niver a cease firin' till a lad's down for good. 'Tis their hearts'll niver let them do the deed, an' it's well ye should know it for a true Yankee bluff.'

He started off with a pleased grin on his face, but Malemute Kid halted him.

'Lon! It's a long while since you first knew me?'

'Many's the day.'

'And you, Bettles?'

'Five year next June high water.'

'And have you once, in all that time, known me to break my word? Or heard of me breaking it?'

Both men shook their heads, striving to fathom what lay beyond.

'Well, then, what do you think of a promise made by me?'

'As good as your bond,' from Bettles.

'The thing to safely sling yer hopes of heaven by,' promptly endorsed Lon McFane.

'Listen! I, Malemute Kid, give you my word—and you

know what that means—that the man who is not shot stretches rope within ten minutes after the shooting.' He stepped back as Pilate might have done after washing his hands.

A pause and a silence came over the men of Forty-Mile. The sky drew still closer, sending down a crystal flight of frost—little geometric designs, perfect, evanescent as a breath, yet destined to exist till the returning sun had covered half its northern journey. Both men had led forlorn hopes in their time—led, with a curse or a jest on their tongues, and in their souls an unswerving faith in the God of Chance. But that merciful deity had been shut out from the present deal. They studied the face of Malemute Kid, but they studied as one might the Sphinx. As the quiet minutes passed, a feeling that speech was incumbent on them began to grow. At last the howl of a wolf-dog cracked the silence from the direction of Forty-Mile. The weird sound swelled with all the pathos of a breaking heart, then died away in a long-drawn sob.

'Well I be danged!' Bettles turned up the collar of his mackinaw jacket and stared about him helplessly.

'It's a gloryus game yer running', Kid,' cried Lon McFane. 'All the percentage to the house an' niver a bit to the man that's buckin'. The Devil himself'd niver tackle such a cinch—and damned if I do.'

There were chuckles, throttled in gurgling throats, and winks brushed away with the frost which rimed the eye-lashes, as the men climbed the ice-notched bank and started across the street to the Post. But the long howl had drawn nearer, invested with a new note of menace. A woman screamed round the corner. There was a cry of, 'Here he comes!' Then an Indian boy, at the head of half a dozen frightened dogs, racing with death, dashed into the crowd. And behind came Yellow Fang, a bristle of hair and a flash of grey. Everybody but the Yankee fled. The Indian boy had tripped and fallen. Bettles stopped long enough to grip him by the slack of his furs, then headed for a pile of cord-wood already occupied by a number of his comrades. Yellow Fang, doubling after one of the dogs, came leaping back. The fleeing animal, free of the rabies, but crazed with fright, whipped Bettles off his feet and flashed on up the street. Malemute Kid took a flying shot at Yellow Fang. The mad dog whirled a half airspring, came down on his back, then, with a single leap, covered half the distance between himself and Bettles.

But the fatal spring was intercepted. Lon McFane leaped from the woodpile, countering him in midair. Over they rolled, Lon holding him by the throat at arm's length, blinking under the fetid slaver which sprayed his face. Then Bettles, revolver in hand and coolly waiting a chance, settled the combat.

' 'Twas a square game, Kid,' Lon remarked, rising to his feet and shaking the snow from out his sleeves; 'with a fair percentage to meself that bucked it.'

That night, while Lon McFane sought the forgiving arms of the Church in the direction of Father Roubeau's cabin, Malemute Kid talked long to little purpose.

'But would you,' persisted Mackenzie, 'supposing they had fought?'

'Have I ever broken my word?'

'No; but that isn't the point. Answer the question. Would you?'

Malemute Kid straightened up. 'Scruff, I've been asking myself that question ever since, and——'

'Well?'

'Well, as yet, I haven't found the answer.'

# TOO MUCH GOLD

THIS BEING a story—and a truer one than it may appear —of a mining country, it is quite to be expected that it will be a hard-luck story. But that depends on the point of view. Hard luck is a mild way of terming it so far as Kink Mitchell and Hootchinoo Bill are concerned; and that they have a decided opinion on the subject is a matter of common knowledge in the Yukon country.

It was in the fall of 1896 that the two partners came
down to the east bank of the Yukon, and drew a Peterborough canoe from a moss-covered cache. They were not
particularly pleasant-looking objects. A summer's prospecting, filled to repletion with hardship and rather empty of
grub, had left their clothes in tatters and themselves worn
and cadaverous. A nimbus of mosquitoes buzzed about
each man's head. Their faces were coated with blue clay.
Each carried a lump of this damp clay, and, whenever it
dried and fell from their faces, more was daubed on in its
place. There was a querulous plaint in their voices, an
irritability of movement and gesture, that told of broken
sleep and a losing struggle with the little winged pests.

'Them skeeters'll be the death of me yet,' Kink Mitchell
whimpered, as the canoe felt the current on her nose, and
leaped out from the bank.

'Cheer up, cheer up. We're about done,' Hootchinoo Bill
answered, with an attempted heartiness in his funereal
tones that was ghastly. 'We'll be in Forty Mile in forty
minutes, and then—cursed little devil!'

One hand left his paddle and landed on the back of his
neck with a sharp slap. He put a fresh daub of clay on the
injured part, swearing sulphurously the while. Kink Mitchell was not in the least amused. He merely improved the
opportunity by putting a thicker coating of clay on his own
neck.

They crossed the Yukon to its west bank, shot down-
stream with easy stroke, and at the end of forty minutes
swung in close to the left around the tail of an island. Forty
Mile spread itself suddenly before them. Both men
straightened their backs and gazed at the sight. They gazed
long and carefully, drifting with the current, in their faces
an expression of mingled surprise and consternation slowly
gathering. Not a thread of smoke was rising from the hundreds of log-cabins. There was no sound of axes biting
sharply into wood, of hammering and sawing. Neither dogs
nor men loitered before the big store. No steamboats lay
at the bank, no canoes, nor scows, nor poling-boats. The
river was as bare of craft as the town was of life.

'Kind of looks like Gabriel's tooted his little horn, and you an' me has turned up missing,' remarked Hootchinoo Bill.

His remark was casual, as though there was nothing unusual about the occurrence. Kink Mitchell's reply was just as casual as though he, too, were unaware of any strange perturbation of spirit.

'Looks as they was all Baptists, then, and took the boats to go by water,' was his contribution.

'My ol' dad was a Baptist,' Hootchinoo Bill supplemented. 'An' he always did hold it was forty thousand miles nearer that way.'

This was the end of their levity. They ran the canoe in and climbed the high earth bank. A feeling of awe descended upon them as they walked the deserted streets. The sunlight streamed placidly over the town. A gentle wind tapped the halyards against the flagpole before the closed doors of the Caledonia Dance Hall. Mosquitoes buzzed, robins sang, and moose birds tripped hungrily among the cabins; but there was no human life nor sign of human life.

'I'm just dyin' for a drink,' Hootchinoo Bill said, and unconsciously his voice sank to a hoarse whisper.

His partner nodded his head, loth to hear his own voice break the stillness. They trudged on in uneasy silence till surprised by an open door. Above this door, and stretching the width of the building, a rude sign announced the same as the 'Monte Carlo'. But beside the door, hat over eyes, chair tilted back, a man sat sunning himself. He was an old man. Beard and hair were long and white and patriarchal.

'If it ain't ol' Jim Cummings, turned up like us, too late for Resurrection!' said Kink Mitchell.

'Most like he didn't hear Gabriel tootin',' was Hootchinoo Bill's suggestion.

'Hello, Jim! Wake up!' he shouted.

The old man unlimbered lamely, blinking his eyes and murmuring automatically: 'What'll ye have, gents? What'll ye have?'

They followed him inside and ranged up against the long bar where of yore a half-dozen nimble barkeepers found little time to loaf. The great room, ordinarily aroar with life, was still and gloomy as a tomb. There was no rattling of chips, no whirring of ivory balls. Roulette and faro tables were like gravestones under their canvas covers. No women's voices drifted merrily from the dance-room behind. Ol' Jim Cummings wiped a glass with palsied hands, and Kink Mitchell scrawled his initials on the dust-covered bar.

'Where's the girls?' Hootchinoo Bill shouted, with affected geniality.

'Gone,' was the ancient bar-keeper's reply, in a voice thin and aged as himself, and as unsteady as his hand.

'Where's Bidwell and Barlow?'

'Gone.'

'And Sweetwater Charley?'

'Gone.'

'And his sister?'

'Gone too.'

'Your daughter Sally, then, and her little kid?'

'Gone, all gone.' The old man shook his head sadly, rummaging in an absent way among the dusty bottles.

'Great Sardanapolis! Where?' Kink Mitchell exploded, unable longer to restrain himself. 'You don't say you've had the plague?'

'Why, ain't you heerd?' The old man chuckled quietly. 'They-all's gone to Dawson.'

'What-like is that?' Bill demanded. 'A creek? or a bar? or a place?'

'Ain't never heerd of Dawson, eh?' The old man chuckled exasperatingly. 'Why, Dawson's a town, a city, bigger'n Forty Mile. Yes, sir, bigger'n Forty Mile.'

'I've ben in this land seven year,' Bill announced emphatically, 'an I make free to say I never heard tell of the burg before. Hold on! Let's have some more of that whisky. Your information's flabbergasted me, that it has. Now just whereabouts is this Dawson-place you was a-mentionin'?'

'On the big flat jest below the mouth of Klondike,' ol' Jim answered. 'But where has you-all ben this summer?'

'Never you mind where we-all's ben,' was Kink Mitchell's testy reply. 'We-all's ben where the skeeters is that thick you've got to throw a stick into the air so as to see the sun and tell the time of day. Ain't I right, Bill?'

'Right you are,' said Bill. 'But speakin' of this Dawson-place, how like did it happen to be, Jim?'

'Ounce to the pan on a creek caled Bonanza, an' they ain't got to bed-rock yet.'

'Who struck it?'

'Carmack.'

At mention of the discoverer's name the partners stared at each other disgustedly. Then they winked with great solemnity.

'Siwash George,' sniffed Hootchinoo Bill.

'That squaw-man,' sneered Kink Mitchell.

'I wouldn't put on my moccasins to stampede after anything he'd ever find,' said Bill.

'Same here,' announced his partner. 'A cuss that's too plumb lazy to fish his own salmon. That's why he took up with the Indians. S'pose that black brother-in-law of his, —lemme see, Skookum Jim, eh?—s'pose he's in on it?'

The old bar-keeper nodded. 'Sure, an' what's more, all Forty Mile, exceptin' me an' a few cripples.'

'And drunks,' added Kink Mitchell.

'No-sir-ee!' the old man shouted emphatically.

'I bet you the drinks Honkins ain't in on it!' Hootchinoo Bill cried with certitude.

Ol' Jim's face lighted up. 'I takes you, Bill, an' you loses.'

'However did that ol' soak budge out of Forty Mile?' Mitchell demanded.

'They ties him down an' throws him in the bottom of a polin'-boat,' ol' Jim explained. 'Come right in here, they did, an' takes him out of that there chair there in the corner, an' three more drunks they finds under the pianny. I tell you-alls the whole camp hits up the Yukon for Dawson jes' like Sam Scratch was after them—wimmen, children,

babes in arms, the whole shebang. Bidwell comes to me an'
sez, sez he, "Jim, I wants you to keep tab on the Monte
Carlo, I'm goin'."

' "Where's Barlow?" sez I. "Gone," sez he, "an' I'm a-
followin' with a load of whisky." An' with that, never
waitin' for me to decline, he makes a run for his boat an'
away he goes, polin' up river like mad. So here I be, an'
these is the first drinks I've passed out in three days.'

The partners looked at each other.

'Gosh darn my buttoms!' said Hootchinoo Bill. 'Seems
like you and me, Kink, is the kind of folks always caught
out with forks when it rains soup.'

'Wouldn't it take the saleratus out your dough, now?'
said Kink Mitchell. 'A stampede of tin-horns, drunks an'
loafers.'

'An' squaw-men,' added Bill. 'Not a genooine miner in
the whole caboodle.'

'Genooine miners like you an' me, Kink,' he went on
academically, 'is all out an' sweatin' hard over Birch Creek
way. Not a genooine miner in this whole crazy Dawson
outfit, and I say right here, not a step do I budge for any
Carmack strike. I've got to see the colour of the dust first.'

'Same here,' Mitchell agreed. 'Let's have another drink.'

Having wet this resolution, they beached the canoe,
transferred its contents to their cabin, and cooked dinner.
But as the afternoon wore along they grew restive. They
were men used to the silence of the great wilderness, but
this gravelike silence of a town worried them. They caught
themselves listening for familiar sounds—'waitin' for something to make a noise which ain't goin' to make a noise,' as
Bill put it. They strolled through the deserted streets to the
Monte Carlo for more drinks, and wandered along the river
bank to the steamer landing, where only water gurgled as
the eddy filled and emptied, and an occasional salmon leapt
flashing into the sun.

They sat down in the shade in front of the store and
talked with the consumptive storekeeper, whose liability to
haemorrhage accounted for his presence. Bill and Kink told
him how they intended loafing in their cabin and resting up

after the hard summer's work. They told him, with a certain insistence, that was half appeal for belief, half challenge for contradiction, how much they were going to enjoy their idleness. But the storekeeper was uninterested. He switched the conversation back to the strike on Klondike, and they could not keep him away from it. He could think of nothing else, talk of nothing else, till Hootchinoo Bill rose up in anger and disgust.

'Gosh darn Dawson, say I!' he cried.

'Same here,' said Kink Mitchell, with a brightening face. 'One'd think something was doin' up there, 'stead of bein' a mere stampede of greenhorns an' tinhorns.'

But a boat came into view from downstream. It was long and slim. It hugged the bank closely, and its three occupants, standing upright, propelled it against the stiff current by means of long poles.

'Circle City outfit,' said the storekeeper. 'I was lookin' for 'em along by afternoon. Forty Mile had the start of them by a hundred and seventy miles. But gee! they ain't losin' any time!'

'We'll just sit here quiet-like and watch 'em string by,' Bill said complacently.

As he spoke, another boat appeared in sight, followed after a brief interval by two others. By this time the first boat was abreast of the men on the bank. Its occupants did not cease poling while greetings were exchanged, and, though its progress was slow, a half-hour saw it out of sight up river.

Still they came from below, boat after boat, in endless procession. The uneasiness of Bill and Kink increased. They stole speculative, tentative glances at each other, and when their eyes met, looked away in embarrassment. Finally, however, their eyes met and neither looked away.

Kink opened his mouth to speak, but words failed him and his mouth remained open while he continued to gaze at his partner.

'Just what I was thinkin', Kink,' said Bill.

They grinned sheepishly at each other, and by tacit consent started to walk away. Their pace quickened, and by the time they arrived at their cabin they were on the run.

'Can't lose no time with all that multitude a-rushin' by,' Kink spluttered, as he jabbed the sour-dough can into the beanpot with one hand and with the other gathered in the frying-pan and coffee-pot.

'Should say not,' gasped Bill, his head and shoulders buried in a clothes-sack wherein were stored winter socks and underwear. 'I say, Kink, don't forget the saleratus on the corner shelf back of the stove.'

Half-an-hour later they were launching the canoe and loading up, while the storekeeper made jocular remarks about poor, weak mortals and the contagiousness of 'stampedin' fever'. But when Bill and Kink thrust their long poles to bottom and started the canoe against the current, he called after them:

'Well, so-long and good luck! And don't forget to blaze a stake or two for me!'

They nodded their heads vigorously and felt sorry for the poor wretch who remained perforce behind.

Kink and Bill were sweating hard. According to the revised Northland Scripture, the stampede is to the swift, the blazing of stakes to the strong, and the Crown, in royalties, gathers to itself the fullness thereof. Kink and Bill were both swift and strong. They took the soggy trail at a long, swinging gait that broke the hearts of a couple of tender-feet who tried to keep up with them. Behind, strung out between them and Dawson (where the boats were discarded and land travel began), was the vanguard of the Circle City outfit. In the race from Forty Mile the partners had passed every boat, winning from the leading boat by a length in the Dawson eddy, and leaving its occupants sadly behind the moment their feet struck the trail.

'Huh! couldn't see us for smoke,' Hootchinoo Bill chuckled, flirting the stinging sweat from his brow and glancing swiftly back along the way they had come.

Three men emerged from where the trail broke through

the trees. Two followed close at their heel, and then a man and a woman shot into view.

'Come on, you Kink! Hit her up! Hit her up!'

Bill quickened his pace. Mitchell glanced back in more leisurely fashion.

'I declare if they ain't lopin'!'

'And here's one that's loped himself out,' said Bill, pointing to the side of the trail.

A man was lying on his back, panting in the culminating stages of violent exhaustion. His face was ghastly, his eyes bloodshot and glazed, for all the world like a dying man.

'*Chechaquo!*' Kink Mitchell grunted, and it was the grunt of the old 'sour dough' for the green-horn, for the man who outfitted with 'self-risin'' flour and used baking-powder in his biscuits.

The partners, true to the old-timer custom, had intended to stake down-stream from the strike, but when they saw claim '81 BELOW' blazed on a tree—which meant fully eight miles below Discovery—they changed their minds. The eight miles were covered in less than two hours. It was a killing pace, over so rough trail, and they passed scores of exhausted men that had fallen by the wayside.

At Discovery little was to be learned of the upper creek. Carmack's Indian brother-in-law, Skookum Jim, had a hazy notion that the creek was staked as high as the '30's'; but when Kink and Bill looked at the corner-stakes of '79 ABOVE', they threw their stampeding packs off their backs and sat down to smoke. All their efforts had been vain. Bonanza was staked from mouth to source—'out of sight and across the next divide', Bill complained that night as they fried their bacon and boiled their coffee over Carmack's fire at Discovery.

'Try that pup,' Carmack suggested next morning.

'That pup' was a broad creek that flowed into Bonanza at '7 ABOVE'. The partners received his advice with the magnificent contempt of the sour dough for a squaw-man, and, instead, spent the day on Adam's Creek, another and more likely-looking tributary of Bonanza. But it was the old story over again—staked to the sky-line.

For three days Carmack repeated his advice, and for three days they received it contemptuously. But on the fourth day, there being nowhere else to go, they went up 'that pup'. They knew that it was practically unstaked, but they had no intention of staking. The trip was made more for the purpose of giving vent to their ill-humour than for anything else. They had become quite cynical, sceptical. They jeered and scoffed at everything, and insulted every *chechaquo* they met along the way.

At 'No. 23' the stakes ceased. The remainder of the creek was open for location.

'Moose pasture,' sneered Kink Mitchell.

But Bill gravely paced off five hundred feet up the creek and blazed the corner-stakes. He had picked up the bottom of a candle-box, and on the smooth side he wrote the notice for his centre-stake:

THIS MOOSE PASTURE IS RESERVED FOR THE
SWEDES AND CHECHAQUOS.
—BILL RADER.

Kink read it over with approval, saying:

'As them's my sentiments, I reckon I might as well subscribe.'

So the name of Charles Mitchell was added to the notice; and many an old sour dough's face relaxed that day at sight of the handiwork of a kindred spirit.

'How's the pup?' Carmack inquired when they strolled back into camp.

'To hell with pups!' was Hootchinoo Bill's reply. 'Me and Kink's goin' a-lookin' for Too Much Gold when we get rested up.'

Too Much Gold was the fabled creek of which all sour doughs dreamed, whereof it was said the gold was so thick that, in order to wash it, gravel must first be shovelled into the sluice-boxes. But the several days' rest, preliminary to the quest for Too Much Gold, brought a slight change in their plan, inasmuch as it brought one Ans Handerson, a Swede.

Ans Handerson had been working for wages all summer

at Miller Creek, over on the Sixty Mile, and, the summer
done, had strayed up Bonanza like many another waif helplessly adrift on the gold tides that swept willy-nilly across
the land. He was tall and lanky. His arms were long, like
prehistoric man's, and his hands were like soup-plates,
twisted and gnarled, and big-knuckled from toil. He was
slow of utterance and movement, and his eyes, pale blue as
his hair was pale yellow, seemed filled with an immortal
dreaming, the stuff of which no man knew, and himself
least of all. Perhaps this appearance of immortal dreaming
was due to a supreme and vacuous innocence. At any rate,
this was the valuation men of ordinary clay put upon him,
and there was nothing extraordinary about the composition
of Hootchinoo Bill and Kink Mitchell.

The partners had spent a day of visiting and gossip, and
in the evening met in the temporary quarters of the Monte
Carlo—a large tent where stampeders rested their weary
bones and bad whisky sold at a dollar a drink. Since the
only money in circulation was dust, and since the house
took the 'down-weight' on the scales, a drink cost something more than a dollar. Bill and Kink were not drinking,
principally for the reason that their one and common sack
was not strong enough to stand many excursions to the
scales.

'Say, Bill, I've got a *chechaquo* on the string for a sack
of flour,' Mitchell announced jubilantly.

Bill looked interested and pleased. Grub was scarce, and
they were not over-plentifully supplied for the quest after
Too Much Gold.

'Flour's worth a dollar a pound,' he answered. 'How like
do you calculate to get your finger on it?'

'Trade'm a half-interest in that claim of ourn,' Kink
answered.

'What claim?' Bill was surprised. Then he remembered
the reservation he had staken off for the Swedes, and said
'Oh!'

'I wouldn't be so clost about it, though,' he added. 'Give
'm the whole thing while you're about it, in a right free-
handed way.'

Bill shook his head. 'If I did, he'd get clean scairt and prance off. I'm lettin' on as how the ground is believed to be valuable, an' that we're lettin' go half just because we're monstrous short on grub. After the dicker we can make him a present of the whole shebang.'

'If somebody ain't disregarded our notice,' Bill objected, though he was plainly pleased at the prospect of exchanging the claim for a sack of flour.

'She ain't jumped,' Kink assured him. 'It's No. 24, and it stands. The *chechaquos* took it serious, and they begun stakin' where you left off. Staked clean over the divide, too. I was gassin' with one of them which has just got in with cramps in his legs.'

It was then, and for the first time, that they heard the slow and groping utterance of Ans Handerson.

'Ay like the looks,' he was saying to the barkeeper. 'Ay tank Ay gat a claim.'

The partners winked at each other, and a few minutes later a surprised and grateful Swede was drinking bad whisky with two hard-hearted strangers. But he was as hard-headed as they were hard-hearted. The sack made frequent journeys to the scales, followed solicitously each time by Kink Mitchell's eyes, and still Ans Handerson did not loosen up. In his pale blue eyes, as in summer seas, immortal dreams swam up and burned, but the swimming and the burning were due to the tales of gold and prospect pans he heard, rather than to the whisky he slid so easily down his throat.

The partners were in despair, though they appeared boisterous and jovial of speech and action.

'Don't mind me, my friend,' Hootchinoo Bill hiccoughed, his hand upon Ans Handerson's shoulder. 'Have another drink. We're just celebratin' Kink's birthday here. This is my pardner, Kink, Kink Mitchell. An' what might your name be?'

This learned, his hand descended resoundingly on Kink's back, and Kink simulated clumsy self-consciousness in that he was for the time being the centre of the rejoicing, while Ans Handerson looked pleased and asked them to have a drink with him. It was the first and last time he treated, until the play changed and his canny soul was roused to unwonted prodigality. But he paid for the liquor from a fairly healthy-looking sack. 'Not less 'n eight hundred in it,' calculated the lynx-eyed Kink; and on the strength of it he took the first opportunity of a privy conversation with Bidwell, proprietor of the bad whisky and the tent.

'Here's my sack, Bidwell,' Kink said, with the intimacy and surety of one old-timer to another. 'Just weigh fifty dollars into it for a day or so more or less, and we'll be yours truly, Bill an' me.'

Thereafter the journeys of the sack to the scales were more frequent, and the celebration of Kink's natal day waxed hilarious. He even essayed to sing the old-timer's classic, 'The Juice of the Forbidden Fruit', but broke down and drowned his embarrassment in another round of drinks. Even Bidwell honoured him with a round or two on the house; and he and Bill were decently drunk by the time Ans Handerson's eyelids began to droop and his tongue gave promise of loosening.

Bill grew affectionate, then confidential. He told his troubles and hard luck to the bar-keeper and the world in general, and to Ans Handerson in particular. He required no histrionic powers to act the part. The bad whisky attended to that. He worked himself into a great sorrow for himself and Bill, and his tears were sincere when he told how he and his partner were thinking of selling a half-interest in good ground just because they were short of grub. Even Kink listened and believed.

Ans Handerson's eyes were shining unholily as he asked, 'How much you tank you take?'

Bill and Kink did not hear him, and he was compelled to repeat the query. They appeared reluctant. He grew keener. And he swayed back and forward, holding on to the bar and listened with all his ears while they conferred together on one side, and wrangled as to whether they should or not, and disagreed in stage whispers over the price they should set.

'Two hundred and—hic!—fifty,' Bill finally announced, 'but we reckon as we won't sell.'

'Which is monstrous wise if I might chip in my little say,' seconded Bidwell.

'Yes, indeedy,' added Kink. 'We ain't in no charity business a-disgorgin' free an' generous to Swedes an' white men.'

'Ay tank we haf another drink,' hiccoughed Ans Handerson, craftily changing the subject against a more propitious time.

And thereafter, to bring about that propitious time, his own sack began to see-saw between his hip pocket and the scales. Bill and Kink were coy, but they finally yielded to his blandishments. Whereupon he grew shy and drew Bidwell to one side. He staggered exceedingly, and held on to Bidwell for support as he asked—

'They ban all right, them men, you tank so?'

'Sure,' Bidwell answered heartily. 'Known 'em for years. Old sour doughs. When they sell a claim, they sell a claim. They ain't no air-dealers.'

'Ay tank Ay buy,' Ans Handerson announced, tottering back to the two men.

But by now he was dreaming deeply, and he proclaimed he would have the whole claim or nothing. This was the cause of great pain to Hootchinoo Bill. He orated grandly against the 'hawgishness' of *chechaquos* and Swedes, albeit he dozed between periods, his voice dying away to a gurgle and his head sinking forward on his breast. But whenever roused by a nudge from Kink or Bidwell, he never failed to explode another volley of abuse and insult.

Ans Handerson was calm under it all. Each insult added to the value of the claim. Such unamiable reluctance to sell advertised but one thing to him, and he was aware of a great relief when Hootchinoo Bill sank snoring to the floor, and he was free to turn his attention to his less intractable partner.

Kink Mitchell was persuadable, though a poor mathematician. He wept dolefully, but was willing to sell a half-interest for two hundred and fifty dollars or the whole

claim for seven hundred and fifty. Ans Handerson and Bidwell laboured to clear away his erroneous ideas concerning
fractions, but their labour was vain. He spilled tears and
regrets all over the bar and on their shoulders, which tears,
however, did not wash away his opinion, that if one half
was worth two hundred and fifty, two halves were worth
three times as much.

In the end—and even Bidwell retained no more than
hazy recollections of how the night terminated—a bill of
sale was drawn up, wherein Bill Rader and Charles Mitchell
yielded up all right and title to the claim known as '24
ELDORADO', the same being the name the creek had received
from some optimistic *chechaquo*.

When Kink had signed, it took the united efforts of the
three to arouse Bill. Pen in hand, he swayed long over the
document; and, each time he rocked back and forth, in
Ans Handerson's eyes flashed and faded a wondrous golden
vision. When the precious signature was at last appended
and the dust paid over, he breathed a great sigh, and sank
to sleep under the table, where he dreamed immortally
until morning.

But the day was chill and grey. He felt bad. His first act,
unconscious and automatic, was to feel for his sack. Its
lightness startled him. Then, slowly, memories of the night
thronged into his brain. Rough voices disturbed him. He
opened his eyes and peered out from under the table. A
couple of early risers, or, rather, men who had been out on
trail all night, were vociferating their opinions concerning
the utter and loathsome worthlessness of Eldorado Creek.
He grew frightened, felt in his pocket, and found the deed
to '24 ELDORADO'.

Ten minutes later Hootchinoo Bill and Kink Mitchell
were roused from their blankets by a wild-eyed Swede that
strove to force upon them an ink-scrawled and very blotty
piece of paper.

'Ay tank Ay take my money back,' he gibbered. 'Ay tank
Ay take my money back.'

Tears were in his eyes and throat. They ran down his
cheeks as he knelt before them and pleaded and implored.

But Bill and Kink did not laugh. They might have been harder hearted.

'First time I ever heard a man squeal over a minin' deal,' Bill said. 'An' I make free to say 'tis too onusual for me to savvy.'

'Same here,' Kirk Mitchell remarked. 'Minin' deals is like horse-tradin'.'

They were honest in their wonderment. They could not conceive of themselves raising a wail over a business transaction, so they could not understand it in another man.

'The poor, ornery *chechaquo*,' murmured Hootchinoo Bill, as they watched the sorrowing Swede disappear up the trail.

'But this ain't Too Much Gold,' Kink Mitchell said cheerfully.

And ere the day was out they purchased flour and bacon at exorbitant prices with Ans Handerson's dust and crossed over the divide in the direction of the creeks that lie between Klondike and Indian River.

Three months later they came back over the divide in the midst of a snow-storm and dropped down the trail to '24 ELDORADO'. It merely chanced that the trail led them that way. They were not looking for the claim. Nor could they see much through the driving white till they set foot upon the claim itself. And then the air lightened, and they beheld a dump, capped by a windlass that a man was turning. They saw him draw a bucket of gravel from the hole and tilt it on the edge of the dump. Likewise they saw another man, strangely familiar, filling a pan with the fresh gravel. His hands were large; his hair was pale yellow. But before they reached him, he turned with the pan and fled towards a cabin. He wore no hat, and the snow falling down his neck accounted for his haste. Bill and Kink ran after him, and came upon him in the cabin, kneeling by the stove and washing the pan of gravel in a tub of water.

He was too deeply engaged to notice more than that somebody had entered the cabin. They stood at his shoulder and looked on. He imparted to the pan a deft circular motion, pausing once or twice to rake out the larger particles of gravel with his fingers. The water was muddy, and, with the pan buried in it, they could see nothing of its contents. Suddenly he lifted the pan clear and sent the water out of it with a flirt. A mass of yellow, like butter in a churn, showed across the bottom.

Hootchinoo Bill swallowed. Never in his life had he dreamed of so rich a test-pan.

'Kind of thick, my friend,' he said huskily. 'How much might you reckon that-all to be?'

Ans Handerson did not look up as he replied, 'Ay tank fafty ounces.'

'You must be scrumptious rich, then, eh?'

Still Ans Handerson kept his head down, absorbed in putting in the fine touches which wash out the last particles of dross, though he answered, 'Ay thank Ay wort' five hundred t'ousand dollar.'

'Gosh!' said Hootchinoo Bill, and he said it reverently.

'Yes, Bill, gosh!' said Kink Mitchell; and they went out softly and closed the door.


# IN A FAR COUNTRY

WHEN A man journeys into a far country, he must be pre-pared to forget many of the things he has learned, and to acquire such customs as are inherent with existence in the new land; he must abandon the old ideals and the old gods, and often-times he must reverse the very codes by which his conduct has hitherto been shaped. To those who have the protean faculty of adaptability, the novelty of such change may even be a source of pleasure; but to those who happen to be hardened to the ruts in which they were created, the pressure of the altered environment is unbear-able, and they chafe in body and in spirit under the new restrictions which they do not understand. This chafing is bound to act and react, producing divers evils and leading

to various misfortunes. It were better for the man who cannot fit himself to the new groove to return to his own
country; if he delays too long, he will surely die.

The man who turns his back upon the comforts of an
elder civilization, to face the savage youth, the primordial
simplicity of the North, may estimate success at an inverse
ratio to the quantity and quality of his hopelessly fixed
habits. He will soon discover, if he be a fit candidate, that
the material habits are the less important. The exchange of
such things as a dainty menu for rough fare, of the stiff
leather shoe for the soft, shapeless moccasin, of the feather
bed for a couch in the snow, is after all a very easy matter.
But his pinch will come in learning properly to shape his
mind's attitude toward all things, and especially toward
his fellow man. For the courtesies of ordinary life, he must
substitute unselfishness, forbearance, and tolerance. Thus,
and thus only, can he gain that pearl of great price—true
comradeship. He must not say 'Thank you'; he must mean
it without opening his mouth, and prove it by responding
in kind. In short, he must substitute the deed for the word,
the spirit for the letter.

When the world rang with the tale of Arctic gold, and
the lure of the North gripped the heartstrings of men,
Carter Weatherbee threw up his snug clerkship, turned
the half of his savings over to his wife, and with the remainder bought an outfit. There was no romance in his
nature—the bondage of commerce had crushed all that; he
was simply tired of the ceaseless grind, and wished to risk
great hazards in view of corresponding returns. Like many
another fool, disdaining the old trails used by the Northland pioneers for a score of years, he hurried to Edmonton
in the spring of the year; and there, unluckily for his soul's
welfare, he allied himself with a party of men.

There was nothing unusual about this party, except its
plans. Even its goal, like that of all other parties, was the
Klondike. But the route it had mapped out to attain the
goal took away the breath of the hardiest native, born and
bred to the vicissitudes of the north-west. Even Jacques
Baptiste, born of a Chippewa woman and a renegade

*voyageur* (having raised his first whimpers in a deerskin lodge north of the sixty-fifth parallel, and had the same hushed by blissful sucks of raw tallow), was surprised. Though he sold his services to them and agreed to travel even to the never-opening ice, he shook his head ominously whenever his advice was asked.

Percy Cuthfert's evil star must have been in the ascendant, for he, too, joined this company of argonauts. He was an ordinary man, with a bank account as deep as his culture, which is saying a good deal. He had no reason to embark on such a venture—no reason in the world, save that he suffered from an abnormal development of sentimentality. He mistook this for the true spirit of romance and adventure. Many another man has done the like, and made as fatal a mistake.

The first break-up of spring found the party following the ice-run of Elk River. It was an imposing fleet, for the outfit was large, and they were accompanied by a disreputable contingent of half-breed *voyageurs* with their women and children. Day in and day out, they laboured with the bateaux and canoes, fought mosquitoes and other kindred pests, or sweated and swore at the portages. Severe toil like this lays a man naked to the very roots of his soul, and ere Lake Athabasca was lost in the south, each member of the party had hoisted his true colours.

The two shirks and chronic grumblers were Carter Weatherbee and Percy Cuthfert. The whole party complained less of its aches and pains than did either of them. Not once did they volunteer for the thousand and one petty duties of the camp. A bucket of water to be brought, an extra armful of wood to be chopped, the dishes to be washed and wiped, a search to be made through the outfit for some suddenly indispensable article—and these two effete scions of civilization discovered sprains or blisters requiring instant attention. They were the first to turn in at night, with a score of tasks yet undone; the last to turn out in the morning, when the start should be in readiness before the breakfast was begun. They were the first to fall to at meal-time, the last to have a hand in the cooking; the

first to dive for a slim delicacy; the last to discover they had
added to their own another man's share. If they toiled at
the oars, they slyly cut the water at each stroke and allowed
the boat's momentum to float up the blade. They thought
nobody noticed; but their comrades swore under their
breaths, and grew to hate them, while Jacques Baptiste
sneered openly, and damned them from morning till night.
But Jacques Baptiste was no gentleman.

At the Great Slave, Hudson Bay dogs were purchased,
and the fleet sank to the guards with its added burden of
dried fish and pemmican. Then canoe and bateau answered
to the swift current of the Mackenzie, and they plunged
into the Great Barren Ground. Every likely-looking 'feeder'
was prospected, but the elusive 'pay-dirt' danced ever to
the north. At the Great Bear, overcome by the common
dread of the Unknown Lands, their *voyageurs* began to
desert, and Fort of Good Hope saw the last and bravest
bending to the tow-lines as they bucked the current down
which they had so treacherously glided. Jacques Baptiste
alone remained. Had he not sworn to travel even to the
never-opening ice?

The lying charts, compiled in main from hearsay, were
now constantly consulted. And they felt the need of hurry,
for the sun had already passed its northern solstice, and was
leading the winter south again. Skirting the shores of the
bay, where the Mackenzie disembogues into the Arctic
Ocean, they entered the mouth of the Little Peel River.
Then began the arduous up-stream toil, and the two Incapables fared worse than ever. Tow-line and pole, paddle
and tump-line, rapids and portages—such tortures served
to give the one a deep disgust for great hazards, and
printed for the other a fiery text on the true romance of
adventure. One day they waxed mutinous, and being vilely
cursed by Jacques Baptiste, turned, as worms sometimes
will. But the half-breed thrashed the twain, and sent them,
bruised and bleeding, about their work. It was the first
time either had been man-handled.

Abandoning their river craft at the headwaters of the
Little Peel, they consumed the rest of the summer in the

great portage over the Mackenzie watershed to the West
Rat. This little stream fed the Porcupine, which in turn
joined the Yukon where that mighty highway of the north
countermarches on the Arctic Circle. But they had lost in
the race with winter, and one day they tied their rafts to
the thick eddy-ice, and hurried their goods ashore. That
night the river jammed and broke several times; the following morning it had fallen asleep for good.

'We can't be more'n four hundred miles from the Yukon,'
concluded Sloper, multiplying his thumb nails by the scale
of the map. The council, in which the two Incapables had
whined to excellent disadvantage, was drawing to a close.

'Hudson Bay Post, long time ago. No use um now.'
Jacques Baptiste's father had made the trip for the Fur
Company in the old days, incidentally marking the trail
with a couple of frozen toes.

'Sufferin' cracky!' cried another of the party. 'No
whites?'

'Nary white,' Sloper sententiously affirmed; 'but it's only
five hundred more up the Yukon to Dawson. Call it a rough
thousand from here.'

Weatherbee and Cuthfert groaned in chorus. 'How
long'll that take, Baptiste?'

The half-breed figured for a moment. 'Workum like hell,
no man play out, ten—twenty-forty-fifty days. Um babies
come,' (designating the Incapables) 'no can tell. Mebbe
when hell freeze over; mebbe not then.'

The manufacture of snowshoes and moccasins ceased.
Somebody called the name of an absent member, who came
out of an ancient cabin at the edge of the camp-fire and
joined them. The cabin was one of the many mysteries
which lurk in the vast recesses of the north. Built when
and by whom, no man could tell. Two graves in the open,
piled high with stones, perhaps contained the secret of
those early wanderers. But whose hand had piled the
stones?

The moment had come. Jacques Baptiste paused in the
fitting of a harness, and pinned the struggling dog in the

snow. The cook made mute protest for delay, threw a handful of bacon into a noisy pot of beans, then came to attention. Sloper rose to his feet. His body was a ludicrous contrast to the healthy physiques of the Incapables. Yellow and weak, fleeing from a South American fever-hole, he had not broken his flight across the zones, and was still able to toil with men. His weight was probably ninety pounds, with the heavy hunting-knife thrown in, and his grizzled hair told of a prime which had ceased to be. The fresh young muscles of either Weatherbee or Cuthfert were equal to ten times the endeavour of his; yet he could walk them into the earth in a day's journey. And all this day he had whipped his stronger comrades into venturing a thousand miles of the stiffest hardship man can conceive. He was the incarnation of the unrest of his race, and the old Teutonic stubbornness, dashed with the quick grasp and action of the Yankee, held the flesh in the bondage of the spirit.

'All those in favour of going on with the dogs as soon as the ice sets, say ay.'

'Ay!' rang out eight voices—voices destined to string a trail of oaths along many a hundred miles of pain.

'Contrary minded?'

'No!' For the first time the Incapables were united without some compromise of personal interests.

'And what are you going to do about it?' Weatherbee added, belligerently.

'Majority rule! Majority rule!' clamoured the rest of the party.

'I know the expedition is liable to fall through if you don't come,' Sloper replied sweetly; 'but I guess, if we try real hard, we can manage to do without you. What do you say, boys?'

The sentiment was cheered to the echo.

'But I say, you know,' Cuthfert ventured apprehensively; 'what's a chap like me to do?'

'Ain't you coming with us?'

'No-o.'

'Then do as you damn well please. We won't have nothing to say.'

'Kind o' calkilate yuh might settle it with that canoodlin' pardner of yourn,' suggested a heavy-going Westerner from the Dakotas, at the same time pointing out Weatherbee. 'He'll be shore to ask yuh what yur a-goin' to do when it comes to cookin' an' gatherin' the wood.'

'Then we'll consider it all arranged,' concluded Sloper. 'We'll pull out tomorrow, if we camp within five miles— just to get everything in running order and remember if we've forgotten anything.'

The sleds groaned by on their steel-shod runners, and the dogs strained low in the harnesses in which they were born to die. Jacques Baptiste paused by the side of Sloper to get a last glimpse of the cabin. The smoke curled up pathetically from the Yukon stove-pipe. The two Incapables were watching them from the doorway.

Sloper laid his hand on the other's shoulder.

'Jacques Baptiste, did you ever hear of the Kilkenny cats?'

The half-breed shook his head.

'Well, my friend and good comrade, the Kilkenny cats fought till neither hide, nor hair, nor yowl, was left. You understand?—till nothing was left. Very good. Now, these two men don't like work. They won't work. We know that. They'll be all alone in that cabin all winter—a mighty long dark winter. Kilkenny cats—well?'

The Frenchman in Baptiste shrugged his shoulders, but the Indian in him was silent. Nevertheless, it was an eloquent shrug, pregnant with prophecy.

Things prospered in the little cabin at first. The rough badinage of their comrades had made Weatherbee and Cuthfert conscious of the mutual responsibility which had devolved upon them; besides, there was not so much work after all for two healthy men. And the removal of the cruel whip-hand, or in other words, the bulldozing half-breed, had brought with it a joyous reaction. At first, each strove to outdo the other, and they performed petty tasks with an unction which would have opened the eyes of their comrades who were now wearing out bodies and souls on the Long Trail.

All care was banished. The forest, which shouldered in upon them from three sides, was an inexhaustible wood-yard. A few yards from their door slept the Porcupine, and a hole through its winter robe formed a bubbling spring of water, crystal clear and painfully cold. But they soon grew to find fault with even that. The hole would persist in freezing up, and thus gave them many a miserable hour of ice-chopping. The unknown builders of the cabin had extended the side-logs so as to support a cache at the rear. In this was stored the bulk of the party's provisions. Food there was, without stint, for three times the men who were fated to live upon it. But the most of it was of the kind which built up brawn and sinew, but did not tickle the palate. True there was sugar in plenty for two ordinary men; but these two were little else than children. They early discovered the virtues of hot water judiciously saturated with sugar, and they prodigally swam their flapjacks and soaked their crusts in the rich, white syrup. Then coffee and tea, and especially the dried fruits, made disastrous inroads upon it. The first words they had were over the sugar question. And it is a really serious thing when two men, wholly dependent upon each other for company, begin to quarrel.

Weatherbee loved to discourse blatantly on politics, while Cuthfert, who had been prone to clip his coupons, and let the commonwealth jog on as best it might, either ignored the subject or delivered himself of startling epigrams. But the clerk was too obtuse to appreciate the clever shaping of thought, and this waste of ammunition irritated Cuthfert. He had been used to blinding people by his brilliancy, and it worked him quite a hardship, this loss of an audience. He felt personally aggrieved, and unconsciously held his mutton-head companion responsible for it.

Save existence, they had nothing in common—came in touch on no single point. Weatherbee was a clerk who had known naught but clerking all his life; Cuthfert was a master of arts, a dabbler in oils, and had written not a little. The one was a lower-class man, who considered himself a gentleman, and the other was a gentleman who knew himself to be such. From this it may be remarked that a man can be a gentleman without possessing the first instinct of true comradeship. The clerk was as sensuous as the other was æsthetic, and his love adventures, told at great length, and chiefly coined from his imagination, affected the super-sensitive master of arts in the same way as so many whiffs of sewer gas. He deemed the clerk a filthy, uncultured brute, whose place was in the muck with the swine, and told him so; and he was reciprocally informed that he was a milk-and-water cissy and a cad. Weatherbee could not have defined 'cad' for his life; but it satisfied its purpose, which after all seems the main point in life.

Weatherbee flatted every third note, and sang such songs as 'The Boston Burglar' and 'The Handsome Cabin Boy', for hours at a time, while Cuthfert wept with rage, till he could stand it no longer, and fled into the outer cold. But there was no escape. The intense frost could not be endured for long at a time, and the little cabin crowded them—beds, stove, table, and all—into a space of ten by twelve. The very presence of either became a personal affront to the other, and they lapsed into sullen silences which increased in length and strength as the days went by. Occasionally, the flash of an eye or the curl of a lip got the better of them, though they strove to wholly ignore each other during these mute periods. And a great wonder sprang up in the breast of each, as to how God had ever come to create the other.

With little to do, time became an intolerable burden to them. This naturally made them still lazier. They sank into a physical lethargy, which there was no escaping, and which made them rebel at the performance of the smallest chore. One morning when it was his turn to cook the common breakfast, Weatherbee rolled out of his blankets, and to the snoring of his companion, lighted first the slush-lamp and then the fire. The kettles were frozen hard, and there was no water in the cabin with which to wash. But he did not mind that. Waiting for it to thaw, he sliced the bacon and plunged into the hateful task of bread-making. Cuthfert had been slyly watching through his half-closed lids. Consequently there was a scene, in which they fervently blessed each other, and agreed, thenceforth, that each do his own cooking. A week later, Cuthfert neglected his morning ablutions, but none the less complacently ate the meal which he had cooked. Weatherbee grinned. After that the foolish custom of washing passed out of their lives.

As the sugar-pile and other luxuries dwindled, they began to be afraid they were not getting their proper shares, and in order that they might not be robbed, they fell to gorging themselves. The luxuries suffered in this gluttonous contest, as did also the men. In the absence of fresh vegetables and exercise, their blood became impoverished, and a loathsome, purplish rash crept over their bodies. Yet they refused to heed the warning. Next, their muscles and joints began to swell, the flesh turning black, while their mouths, gums and lips took on the colour of rich cream. Instead of being drawn together by their misery, each gloated over the other's symptoms as the scurvy took its course.

They lost all regard for personal appearance, and for that matter, common decency. The cabin became a pigpen, and never once were the beds made or fresh pine boughs laid underneath. Yet they could not keep to their blankets, as they would have wished; for the frost was inexorable, and the fire box consumed much fuel. The hair of their heads and faces grew long and shaggy, while their garments would have disgusted a ragpicker. But they did not care. They were sick, and there was no one to see; besides, it was very painful to move about.

To all this was added a new trouble—the Fear of the North. This Fear was the joint child of the Great Cold and the Great Silence, and was born in the darkness of December, when the sun dipped below the southern horizon for good. It affected them according to their natures. Weatherbee fell prey to the grosser superstitions, and did his best to resurrect the spirits which slept in the forgotten graves. It was a fascinating thing, and in his dreams they came to him from out of the cold, and snuggled into his blankets, and told him of their toils and troubles ere they died. He shrank away from their clammy contact as they drew closer and twined their frozen limbs about him, and when they whispered in his ear of things to come, the cabin rang with his frightened shrieks. Cuthfert did not understand—for they no longer spoke—and when thus awakened he invariably grabbed for his revolver. Then he would sit up in bed, shivering nervously, with the weapon trained on the unconscious dreamer. Cuthfert deemed the man going mad, and so came to fear for his life.

His own malady assumed a less concrete form. The mysterious artisan who had laid the cabin, log by log, had pegged a wind-vane to the ridge-pole. Cuthfert noticed it always pointed south, and one day, irritated by its steadfastness of purpose, he turned it towards the east. He watched eagerly, but never a breath came by to disturb it. Then he turned the vane to the north, swearing never again to touch it till the wind did blow. But the air frightened him with its unearthly calm, and he often rose in the middle of the night to see if the vane had veered—ten degrees would have satisfied him. But no, it poised above him as unchangeable as fate. His imagination ran riot, till it became to him a fetish. Sometimes he followed the path it pointed across the dismal dominions, and allowed his soul to become saturated with the Fear. He dwelt upon the unseen and the unknown till the burden of eternity appeared to be crushing him. Everything in the Northland had that crushing effect—the absence of life and motion; the darkness; the infinite peace of the brooding land; the ghastly silence, which made the echo of each heart-beat a sacrilege; the solemn forest which seemed to guard an awful, inexpressible something, which neither word nor thought could compass.

The world he had so recently left, with its busy nations and great enterprises, seemed very far away. Recollections occasionally obtruded—recollections of marts and galleries and crowded thoroughfares, of evening dress and social functions, of good men and dear women he had known—but they were dim memories of a life he had lived long centuries agone, on some other planet. This phantasm was the Reality. Standing beneath the wind-vane, his eyes fixed on the polar skies, he could not bring himself to realize that the Southland really existed, that at that very moment it was a-roar with life and action. There was no Southland, no men being born of women, no giving and taking in marriage. Beyond his bleak sky-line there stretched vast solitudes, and beyond these still vaster solitudes. There were no lands of sunshine, heavy with the perfume of flowers. Such things were only old dreams of paradise. The sun-lands of the West and the spicelands of the East, the smiling Arcadias and blissful Islands of the Blest—ha! ha! His laughter split the void, and shocked him with its unwonted sound. There was no sun. This was the Universe, dead and cold and dark, and he its only citizen. Weatherbee? At such moments Weatherbee did not count. He was a Caliban, a monstrous phantom, fettered to him for untold ages, the penalty of some forgotten crime.

He lived with Death among the dead, emasculated by the sense of his own insignificance, crushed by the passive mastery of the slumbering ages. The magnitude of all things appalled him. Everything partook of the superlative save himself—the perfect cessation of wind and motion, the immensity of the snow-covered wilderness, the height of the sky and the depth of the silence. That wind-vane—if it would only move. If a thunderbolt would fall, or the forest flare up in flame. The rolling up of the heavens as a scroll, the crash of Doom—anything, anything! But no, nothing moved; the Silence crowded in, and the Fear of the North laid icy fingers on his heart.

Once, like another Crusoe, by the edge of the river he came upon a track—the faint tracery of a snowshoe rabbit on the delicate snow-crust. It was a revelation. There was life in the Northland. He would follow it, look upon it, gloat over it. He forgot his swollen muscles, plunging through the deep snow in an ecstasy of anticipation. The forest swallowed him up, and the brief midday twilight vanished; but he pursued his quest till exhausted nature exerted itself and laid him helpless in the snow. There he groaned and cursed his folly, and knew the track to be the fancy of his brain; and late that night he dragged himself into the cabin on hands and knees, his cheeks frozen and a strange numbness about his feet. Weatherbee grinned malevolently, but made no offer to help him. He thrust needles into his toes and thawed them out by the stove. A week later mortification set in.

But the clerk had his own troubles. The dead men came out of their graves more frequently now, and rarely left him, waking or sleeping. He grew to wait and dread their coming, never passing the twin cairns without a shudder. One night they came to him in his sleep and led him forth to an appointed task. Frightened into inarticulate horror, he awoke between the heaps of stones, and fled wildly to the cabin. But he had lain there for some time, for his feet and cheeks were also frozen.

Sometimes he became frantic at their insistent presence, and danced about the cabin, cutting the empty air with an axe, and smashing everything within reach. During these ghostly encounters, Cuthfert huddled into his blankets and followed the madman about with a cocked revolver, ready to shoot him if he came too near. But, recovering from one of these spells, the clerk noticed the weapon trained upon him. His suspicions were aroused, and thenceforth, he, too, lived in fear of his life. They watched each other closely after that, and faced about in startled fright whenever either passed behind the other's back. This apprehensiveness became a mania which controlled them even in their sleep. Through mutual fear they tacitly let the slush-lamp burn all night, and saw to a plentiful supply of bacon-grease before retiring. The slightest movement on the part of one was sufficient to arouse the other, and many a still watch their gazes countered as they shook beneath their blankets with fingers on the trigger-guards.

What with the Fear of the North, the mental strain, and the ravages of the disease, they lost all semblance of humanity, taking on the appearance of wild beasts, hunted and desperate. Their cheeks and noses, as an aftermath of the freezing, had turned black. Their frozen toes had begun to drop away at the first and second joints. Every movement brought pain, but the fire-box was insatiable, wringing a ransom of torture from their miserable bodies. Day in, day out, it demanded its food—a veritable pound of flesh—and they dragged themselves into the forest to chop wood on their knees. Once, crawling thus in search of dry sticks, unknown to each other they entered a thicket from opposite sides. Suddenly, without warning, two peering death's-heads confronted each other. Suffering had so transformed them that recognition was impossible. They sprang to their feet, shrieking with terror, and dashed away on their mangled stumps; and falling at the cabin door, they clawed and scratched like demons till they discovered their mistake.

Occasionally they lapsed normal, and during one of these sane intervals, the chief bone of contention, the sugar, had been divided equally between them. They guarded their separate sacks, stored up in the cache, with jealous eyes; for there were but a few cupfuls left, and they were totally devoid of faith in each other. But one day Cuthfert made a mistake. Hardly able to move, sick with pain, with his head swimming and eyes blinded, he crept into the cache, sugar canister in hand, and mistook Weatherbee's sack for his own.

January had been born but a few days when this occurred. The sun had some time since passed its lowest southern declination, and at meridian now threw flaunting streaks of yellow light upon the northern sky. On the day following his mistake with the sugar-bag, Cuthfert found himself feeling better, both in body and spirit. As noontime drew near and the day brightened, he dragged himself outside to feast on the evanescent glow, which was to him an earnest of the sun's future intentions. Weatherbee was also feeling somewhat better, and crawled out beside him.

They propped themselves in the snow beneath the move-less wind-vane, and waited.

The stillness of death was about them. In other climes, when nature falls into such moods, there is a subdued air of expectancy, a waiting for some small voice to take up the broken strain. Not so in the north. The two men had lived seeming æons in this ghostly peace. They could re-member no song of the past; they could conjure no song of the future. This unearthly calm had always been—the tran-quil silence of eternity.

Their eyes were fixed upon the north. Unseen, behind their backs, behind the towering mountains to the south, the sun swept towards the zenith of another sky than theirs. Sole spectators of the mighty canvas, they watched the false dawn slowly grow. A faint flame began to glow and smoulder. It deepened in intensity, ringing the changes of reddish-yellow, purple, and saffron. So bright did it be-come that Cuthfert thought the sun must surely be behind it—a miracle, the sun rising in the north! Suddenly, with-out warning and without fading, the canvas was swept clean. There was no colour in the sky. The light had gone out of the day. They caught their breaths in half-sobs. But lo! the air was a-glint with particles of scintillating frost, and there, to the north, the wind-vane lay in vague outline on the snow. A shadow! A shadow! It was exactly mid-day. They jerked their heads hurriedly to the south. A golden rim peeped over the mountain's snowy shoulder, smiled upon them an instant, then dipped from sight again.

There were tears in their eyes as they sought each other. A strange softening came over them. They felt irresistibly drawn toward each other. The sun was coming back again. It would be with them to-morrow, and the next day, and the next. And it would stay longer every visit, and a time would come when it would ride their heaven day and night, never once dropping below the sky-line. There would be no night. The ice-locked winter would be broken; the winds would blow, and the forests answer; the land would bathe in the blessed sunshine, and life renew. Hand in hand, they would quit this horrid dream and journey back to the

Southland. They lurched blindly forward, and their hands met—their poor maimed hands, swollen and distorted beneath their mittens.

But the promise was destined to remain unfulfilled. The Northland is the Northland, and men work out their souls by strange rules, which other men, who have not journeyed into far countries, cannot come to understand.

An hour later, Cuthfert put a pan of bread into the oven, and fell to speculating on what the surgeons could do with his feet when he got back. Home did not seem so very far away now. Weatherbee was rummaging in the cache. Of a sudden, he raised a whirlwind of blasphemy, which in turn ceased with startling abruptness. The other man had robbed his sugar-sack. Still, things might have happened differently, had not the two dead men come out from under the stones and hushed the hot words in his throat. They led him quite gently from the cache, which he forgot to close. That consummation was reached; that something they had whispered to him in his dreams was about to happen. They guided him gently, very gently, to the woodpile, where they put the axe in his hands. Then they helped him shove open the cabin door, and he felt sure they shut it after him—at least he heard it slam and the latch fall sharply into place. And he knew they were waiting just without, waiting for him to do his task.

'Carter! I say, Carter!'

Percy Cuthfert was frightened at the look on the clerk's face, and he made haste to put the table between them.

Carter Weatherbee followed, without haste and without enthusiasm. There was neither pity nor passion in his face, but rather the patient, stolid look of one who has certain work to do and goes about it methodically.

'I say, what's the matter?'

The clerk dodged back, cutting off his retreat to the door, but never opening his mouth.

'I say, Carter, I say; let's talk. There's a good chap.'

The master of arts was thinking rapidly, now, shaping a skilful flank movement on the bed where his Smith and

7*

Wesson lay. Keeping his eyes on the madman, he rolled backward on the bunk, at the same time clutching the pistol.

'Carter!'

The powder flashed full in Weatherbee's face, but he swung his weapon and leaped forward. The axe bit deeply at the base of the spine, and Percy Cuthfert felt all consciousness of his lower limbs leave him. Then the clerk fell heavily upon him, clutching him by the throat with feeble fingers. The sharp bite of the axe had caused Cuthfert to drop the pistol, and as his lungs panted for release, he fumbled aimlessly for it among the blankets. Then he remembered. He slid a hand up the clerk's belt to the sheath-knife; and they drew very close to each other in that last clinch.

Percy Cuthfert felt his strength leave him. The lower portion of his body was useless. The inert weight of Weatherbee crushed him—crushed him and pinned him there like a bear under a trap. The cabin became filled with a familiar odour, and he knew the bread to be burning. Yet what did it matter? He would never need it. And there were all of six cupfuls of sugar in the cache—if he had foreseen this he would not have been so saving the last several days. Would the wind-vane ever move? It might even be veering now. Why not? Had he not seen the sun to-day? He would go and see. No; it was impossible to move. He had not thought the clerk so heavy a man.

How quickly the cabin cooled! The fire must be out. The cold was forcing in. It must be below zero already, and the ice creeping up the inside of the door. He could not see it, but his past experience enabled him to gauge its progress by the cabin's temperature. The lower hinge must be white ere now. Would the tale of this ever reach the world? How would his friends take it? They would read it over their coffee, most likely, and talk it over at the clubs. He could see them very clearly. 'Poor old Cuthfert,' they murmured; 'not such a bad sort of a chap, after all.' He smiled at the eulogies, and passed on in search of a Turkish bath. It was the same old crowd upon the streets. Strange, they did not notice his moosehide moccasins and tattered German socks. He would take a cab. And after the bath a shave would not be bad. No; he would eat first. Steak, and potatoes, and green things—how fresh it all was! And what was that? Squares of honey, streaming liquid amber! But why did they bring so much? Ha! ha! he could never eat it all. Shine! Why certainly. He put his foot on the box. The bootblack looked curiously up at him, and he remembered his moosehide moccasins, and went away hastily.

Hark! The wind-vane must be surely spinning. No; a mere singing in his ears. That was all—a mere singing. The ice must have passed the latch by now. More likely the upper hinge was covered. Between the moss-chinked roof-poles, little points of frost began to appear. How slowly they grew! No; not so slowly. There was a new one, and there another. Two—three—four; they were coming too fast to count. There were two growing together. And there, a third had joined them. Why, there were no more spots. They had run together and formed a sheet.

Well, he would have company. If Gabriel ever broke the silence of the north, they would stand together, hand in hand, before the great White Throne. And God would judge them, God would judge them!

Then Percy Cuthfert closed his eyes and dropped off to sleep.


## LIKE ARGUS
## OF THE ANCIENT TIMES

IT WAS the summer of 1897, and there was trouble in the Tarwater family. Grandfather Tarwater, after remaining properly subdued and crushed for a quiet decade, had broken out again. This time it was the Klondike fever. His first and one unvarying symptom of such attacks was song. One chant only he raised, though he remembered no more than the first stanza and but three lines of that. And the family knew his feet were itching and his brain was tingling with the old madness, when he lifted his hoarse-cracked voice, now falsetto-cracked, in:

> Like Argus of the ancient times,
>> We leave this modern Greece,
> Tum-tum, tum-tum, tum, tum, tum-tum,
>> To shear the Golden Fleece.

Ten years earlier he had lifted the chant, sung to the air of the 'Doxology', when afflicted with the fever to go gold-mining in Patagonia. The multitudinous family had sat upon him, but had had a hard time doing it. When all else had failed to shake his resolution, they had applied lawyers to him, with the threat of getting out guardianship papers and of confining him in the state asylum for the insane—which was reasonable for a man who had, a quarter of a century before, speculated away all but ten meagre acres of a California principality, and who had displayed no better business acumen ever since.

The application of lawyers to John Tarwater was like the application of a mustard plaster. For, in his judgment, they were the gentry, more than any other, who had skinned him out of the broad Tarwater acres. So, at the time of his Patagonian fever, the very thought of so drastic a remedy was sufficient to cure him. He quickly demonstrated he was not crazy by shaking the fever from him and agreeing not to go to Patagonia.

Next, he demonstrated how crazy he really was, by deeding over to his family, unsolicited, the ten acres on Tarwater Flat, the house, barn, outbuildings, and water-rights. Also did he turn over the eight hundred dollars in the bank that was the long-saved salvage of his wrecked fortune. But for this the family found no cause for committal to the asylum, since such committal would necessarily invalidate what he had done.

'Grandfather is sure peeved,' said Mary, his oldest daughter, herself a grandmother, when her father quit smoking.

All he had retained for himself was a span of old horses, a mountain buckboard, and his one room in the crowded house. Further, having affirmed that he would be beholden to none of them, he got the contract to carry the United States mail, twice a week, from Kelterville up over Tarwater Mountain to Old Almaden—which was a sporadically worked quicksilver mine in the upland cattle country. With his old horses it took all his time to make the two weekly round trips. And for ten years, rain or shine, he had never missed a trip. Nor had he failed once to pay his week's board into Mary's hand. This board he had insisted on, in the convalescence from his Patagonian fever, and he had paid it strictly, though he had given up tobacco in order to be able to do it.

'Huh!' he confided to the ruined water wheel of the old Tarwater Mill, which he had built from the standing timber and which had ground wheat for the first settlers. 'Huh! They'll never put me in the poor farm so long as I support myself. And without a penny to my name it ain't likely any lawyer fellows'll come snoopin' around after me.'

And yet, precisely because of these highly rational acts, it was held that John Tarwater was mildly crazy!

The first time he had lifted the chant of 'Like Argus of the Ancient times', had been in 1849, when, twenty-two years of age, violently attacked by the Californian fever, he had sold two hundred and forty Michigan acres, forty of it cleared, for the price of four yoke of oxen and a wagon, and had started across the Plains.

'And we turned off at Fort Hall, where the Oregon emigration went north'ard, and swung south for Californy,' was his way of concluding the narrative of that arduous journey. 'And Bill Ping and me used to rope grizzlies out of the underbrush of Cache Slough in the Sacramento Valley.'

Years of freighting and mining had followed, and, with a stake gleaned from the Merced placers, he satisfied the land-hunger of his race and time by settling in Sonoma County.

During the ten years of carrying the mail across Tar-water Township, up Tarwater Valley, and over Tarwater Mountain, most all of which land had once been his, he had spent his time dreaming of winning back that land before he died. And now, his huge gaunt form more erect than it had been for years, with a glinting of blue fires in his small and close-set eyes, he was lifting his ancient chant again.

'There he goes now—listen to him,' said William Tar-water.

'Nobody at home,' laughed Harris Topping, day labourer, husband of Annie Tarwater, and father of her nine children.

The kitchen door opened to admit the old man, return-ing from feeding his horses. The song had ceased from his lips; but Mary was irritable from a burnt hand and a grand-child whose stomach refused to digest properly diluted cows' milk.

'Now there ain't no use you carryin' on that way, father,' she tackled him. 'The time's past for you to cut and run for a place like the Klondike, and singing won't buy you nothing.'

'Just the same,' he answered quietly. 'I bet I could go to that Klondike place and pick up enough gold to buy back the Tarwater land.'

'Old fool!' Annie contributed.

'You couldn't buy them back for less'n three hundred thousand and then some,' was William's effort at squelch-ing him.

'Then I could pick up three hundred thousand, and then some, if I was only there,' the old man retorted placidly.

'Thank God you can't walk there, or you'd be startin', I know,' Mary cried. 'Ocean travel costs money.'

'I used to have money,' her father said humbly.

'Well, you ain't got any now—so forget it,' William advised. 'Them times is past, like roping bear with Bill Ping. There ain't no more bear.'

'Just the same——'

But Mary cut him off. Seizing the day's paper from the

kitchen table, she flourished it savagely under her aged progenitor's nose.

'What do those Klondikers say? There it is in cold print. Only the young and robust can stand the Klondike. It's worse than the north pole. And they've left their dead a-plenty there themselves. Look at their pictures. You're forty years older 'n the oldest of them.'

John Tarwater did look, but his eyes strayed to other photographs on the highly sensational front page.

'And look at the photys of them nuggets they brought down,' he said. 'I know gold. Didn't I gopher twenty thousand outa the Merced? And wouldn't it a-ben a hundred thousand if that cloudburst hadn't busted my wing-dam? Now if I was only in the Klondike——'

'Crazy as a loon,' William sneered in open aside to the rest.

'A nice way to talk to your father,' Old Man Tarwater censured mildly. 'My father'd have walloped the tar out of me with a single-tree if I'd spoke to him that way.'

'But you *are* crazy, father——' William began.

'Reckon you're right, son. And that's where my father wasn't crazy. He'd a-done it.'

'The old man's been reading some of them magazine articles about men who succeeded after forty,' Annie jibed.

'And why not, daughter?' he asked. 'And why can't a man succeed after he's seventy? I was only seventy this year. And mebbe I could succeed if only I could get to the Klondike——'

'Which you ain't going to get to,' Mary shut him off.

'Oh, well, then,' he sighed, 'seein's I ain't, I might just as well go to bed.'

He stood up, tall, gaunt, great-boned and gnarled, a splendid ruin of a man. His ragged hair and whiskers were not grey but snowy white, as were the tufts of hair that stood out on the backs of his huge bony fingers. He moved toward the door, opened it, sighed, and paused with a backward look.

'Just the same,' he murmured plaintively, 'the bottoms of my feet is itching something terrible.'

Long before the family stirred next morning, his horses fed and harnessed by lantern light, breakfast cooked and eaten by lamp light, Old Man Tarwater was off and away down Tarwater Valley on the road to Kelterville. Two things were unusual about this usual trip which he had made a thousand and forty times since taking the mail contract. He did not drive to Kelterville, but turned off on the main road south to Santa Rosa. Even more remarkable than this was the paper-wrapped parcel between his feet. It contained his one decent black suit, which Mary had been long reluctant to see him wear any more, not because it was shabby, but because, as he guessed what was at the back of her mind, it was decent enough to bury him in.

And at Santa Rosa, in a second-hand clothes shop, he sold the suit outright for two dollars and a half. From the same obliging shopman he received four dollars for the wedding ring of his long-dead wife. The span of horses and the wagon he disposed of for seventy-five dollars, although twenty-five was all he received down in cash. Chancing to meet Alton Granger on the street, to whom never before had he mentioned the ten dollars loaned him in '74, he reminded Alton Granger of the little affair, and was promptly paid. Also, of all unbelievable men to be in funds, he so found the town drunkard for whom he had bought many a drink in the old and palmy days. And from him John Tarwater borrowed a dollar. Finally, he took the afternoon train to San Francisco.

A dozen days later, carrying a half-empty canvas sack of blankets and old clothes, he landed on the beach of Dyea in the thick of the great Klondike Rush. The beach was screaming bedlam. Ten thousand tons of outfit lay heaped and scattered, and twice ten thousand men struggled with it and clamoured about it. Freight, by Indian-back, over Chilcoot to Lake Linderman, had jumped from sixteen to thirty cents a pound, which latter was a rate of six hundred dollars a ton. And the sub-arctic winter gloomed near at hand. All knew it, and all knew that of the twenty thousand of them very few would get across the passes, leaving the rest to winter and wait for the late spring thaw.

Such the beach old John Tarwater stepped upon; and straight across the beach and up the trail toward Chilcoot he headed, cackling his ancient chant, a very Grandfather Argus himself, with no outfit worry in the world, for he did not possess any outfit. That night he slept on the flats, five miles above Dyea, at the head of canoe navigation. Here the Dyea River became a rushing mountain torrent, plunging out of a dark canyon from the glaciers that fed it far above.

And here, early next morning, he beheld a little man weighing no more than a hundred, staggering along a foot-log under all of a hundred pounds of flour strapped on his back. Also, he beheld the little man stumble off the log and fall face-downward in a quiet eddy where the water was two feet deep and proceed quietly to drown. It was no desire of his to take death so easily, but the flour on his back weighed as much as he and would not let him up.

'Thank you, old man,' he said to Tarwater, when the latter had dragged him up into the air and ashore.

While he unlaced his shoes and ran the water out, they had further talk. Next, he fished out a ten-dollar gold-piece and offered it to his rescuer.

Old Tarwater shook his head and shivered, for the ice-water had wet him to his knees.

'But I reckon I wouldn't object to settin' down to a friendly meal with you.'

'Ain't had breakfast?' the little man, who was past forty and who had said his name was Anson, queried with a glance frankly curious.

'Nary bite,' John Tarwater answered.

'Where's your outfit? Ahead?'

'Nary outfit.'

'Expect to buy your grub on the Inside?'

'Nary a dollar to buy it with, friend. Which ain't so important as a warm bite of breakfast right now.'

In Anson's camp, a quarter of a mile on, Tarwater found a slender, red-whiskered young man of thirty cursing over

a fire of wet willow wood. Introduced as Charles, he transferred his scowl and wrath to Tarwater, who, genially
oblivious, devoted himself to the fire, took advantage of
the chill morning breeze to create a draught which the
other had left stupidly blocked by stones, and soon
developed less smoke and more flame. The third member
of the party, Bill Wilson, or Big Bill as they called him,
came in with a hundred-and-forty-pound pack; and what
Tarwater esteemed to be a very rotten breakfast was dished
out by Charles. The mush was half cooked and mostly
burnt, the bacon was charred carbon and the coffee was
unspeakable.

Immediately the meal was wolfed down, the three
partners took their empty pack straps and headed down
trail to where the remainder of their outfit lay at the last
camp a mile away. And old Tarwater became busy. He
washed the dishes, foraged dry wood, mended a broken
pack-strap, put an edge on the butcher-knife and camp-
axe, and repacked the picks and shovels into a more carry-
able parcel.

What had impressed him during the brief breakfast was
the sort of awe in which Anson and Big Bill stood of
Charles. Once, during the morning, while Anson took a
breathing spell after bringing in another hundred-pound
pack, Tarwater delicately hinted his impression.

'You see, it's this way,' Anson said. 'We've divided our
leadership. We've got specialities. Now I'm a carpenter.
When we get to Lake Linderman, and the trees are chopped
and whipsawed into planks, I'll boss the building of the
boat. Big Bill is a logger and miner. So he'll boss getting
out the logs and all mining operations. Most of our outfit's
ahead. We went broke paying the Indians to pack that
much of it to the top of Chilcoot. Our last partner is up
there with it, moving it along by himself down the other
side. His name's Liverpool, and he's a sailor. So, when the
boat's built, he's the boss of the outfit to navigate the lakes
and rapids to Klondike.'

'And Charles—this Mr Crayton—what might his
speciality be?' Tarwater asked.

'He's the business man. When it comes to business and organization he's boss.'

'Hum,' Tarwater pondered. 'Very lucky to get such a bunch of specialities into one outfit.'

'More than luck,' Anson agreed. 'It was all accident, too. Each of us started alone. We met on the steamer coming up from San Francisco, and formed the party.—Well, I got to be goin'. Charles is liable to get kicking because I ain't packin' my share. Just the same, you can't expect a hundred-pound man to pack as much as a hundred-and-sixty-pounder.'

'Stick around and cook us something for dinner,' Charles, on his next load in and noting the effects of the old man's handiness, told Tarwater.

And Tarwater cooked a dinner that was a dinner, washed the dishes, had real pork and beans for supper, and bread baked in a frying-pan that was so delectable that the three partners nearly foundered themselves on it. Supper dishes washed, he cut shavings and kindling for a quick and certain breakfast fire, showed Anson a trick with foot-gear that was invaluable to any hiker, sang his 'Like Argus of the Ancient Times', and told them of the great emigration across the Plains in Forty-nine.

'My goodness, the first cheerful and hearty-like camp since we hit the beach,' Big Bill remarked as he knocked out his pipe and began pulling off his shoes for bed.

'Kind of made things easy, boys, eh?' Tarwater queried genially.

All nodded. 'Well, then, I got a proposition, boys. You can take it or leave it, but just listen kindly to it. You're in a hurry to get in before the freeze-up. Half the time is wasted over the cooking by one of you that he might be puttin' in packin' outfit. If I do the cookin' for you, you all'll get on that much faster. Also, the cookin' 'll be better, and that'll make you pack better. And I can pack quite a bit myself in between times, quite a bit, yes, sir, quite a bit.'

Big Bill and Anson were just beginning to nod their heads in agreement, when Charles stopped them.

'What do you expect of us in return?' he demanded of the old man.

'Oh, I leave it up to the boys.'

'That ain't business,' Charles reprimanded sharply. 'You made the proposition. Now finish it.'

'Well, it's this way——'

'You expect us to feed you all winter, eh?' Charles interrupted.

'No, siree, I don't. All I reckon is a passage to Klondike in your boat would be mighty square of you.'

'You haven't an ounce of grub, old man. You'll starve to death when you get there.'

'I've been feedin' some long time pretty successful,' Old Tarwater replied, a whimsical light in his eyes. 'I'm seventy, and ain't starved to death never yet.'

'Will you sign a paper to the effect that you shift for yourself as soon as you get to Dawson?' the business one demanded.

'Oh, sure,' was the response.

Again Charles checked his two partners' expressions of satisfaction with the arrangements.

'One other thing, old man. We're a party of four, and we all have a vote on questions like this. Young Liverpool is ahead with the main outfit. He's got a say so, and he isn't here to say it.'

'What kind of a party might he be?' Tarwater inquired.

'He's a rough-neck sailor, and he's got a quick, bad temper.'

'Some turbulent,' Anson contributed.

'And the way he can cuss is simply God-awful,' Big Bill testified.

'But he's square,' Big Bill added.

Anson nodded heartily to this appraisal.

'Well, boys,' Tarwater summed up, 'I set out for California and I got there. And I'm going to get to Klondike. Ain't a thing can stop me, ain't a thing. I'm going to get three hundred thousand outa the ground, too. Ain't a thing can stop me, ain't a thing, because I just naturally need the money. I don't mind a bad temper so long's the boy is square. I'll take my chance, an' I'll work along with you till we catch up with him. Then, if he says no to the proposition, I reckon I'll lose. But somehow I just can't see 'm sayin' no, because that'd mean too close up to freeze-up and too late for me to find another chance like this. And, as I'm sure going to get to Klondike, it's just plumb impossible for him to say no.'

Old John Tarwater became a striking figure on a trail unusually replete with striking figures. With thousands of men, each back-tripping half a ton of outfit, retracing every mile of the trail twenty times, all came to know him and to hail him as 'Father Christmas'. And, as he worked, ever he raised his chant with his age-falsetto voice. None of the three men he had joined could complain about his work. True, his joints were stiff—he admitted to a trifle of rheumatism. He moved slowly, and seemed to creak and crackle when he moved; but he kept on moving. Last into the blankets at night; he was first out in the morning, so that the other three had hot coffee before their one before-breakfast pack. And, between breakfast and dinner and between dinner and supper, he always managed to back-trip for several packs himself. Sixty pounds was the limit of his burden, however. He could manage seventy-five, but he could not keep it up. Once, he tried ninety, but collapsed on the trail and was seriously shaky for a couple of days afterward.

Work! On the trail where hard-working men learned for the first time what work was, no man worked harder in proportion to his strength than Old Tarwater. Driven desperately on by the near-thrust of winter, and lured madly on by the dream of gold, they worked to their last ounce of strength and fell by the way. Others, when failure made certain, blew out their brains. Some went mad, and still others, under the irk of the man-destroying strain, broke partnerships and dissolved life-time friendships with fellows just as good as themselves and just as strained and mad.

Work! Old Tarwater could shame them all, despite his creaking and crackling and the nasty hacking cough he had developed. Early and late, on trail or in camp beside the trail, he was ever in evidence, ever busy at something, ever responsive to the hail of 'Father Christmas'. Weary back-trippers would rest their packs on a log or rock alongside of where he rested his, and would say: 'Sing us that song of yourn, dad, about Forty-Nine.' And, when he had wheezingly complied, they would arise under their loads, remark that it was real heartening, and hit the forward trail again.

'If ever a man worked his passage and earned it,' Big Bill confided to his two partners, 'that man's our old Skeezicks.'

'You bet,' Anson confirmed. 'He's a valuable addition to the party, and I, for one, ain't at all disagreeable to the notion of making him a regular partner——'

'None of that!' Charles Crayton cut in. 'When we get to Dawson we're quit of him—that's the agreement. We'd only have to bury him if we let him stay on with us. Besides, there's going to be a famine, and every ounce of grub'll count. Remember, we're feeding him out of our own supply all the way in. And if we run short in the pinch next year, you'll know the reason. Steamboats can't get grub to Dawson till the middle of June, and that's nine months away.'

'Well, you put as much money and outfit in as the rest of us,' Big Bill conceded, 'and you've a say according.'

'And I'm going to have my say,' Charles asserted with increasing irritability. 'And it's lucky for you with your fool sentiments that you've got somebody to think ahead for you, else you'd all starve to death. I tell you that famine's coming. I've been studying the situation. Flour will be two dollars a pound, or ten, and no sellers. You mark my words.'

Across the rubble-covered flats, up the dark canyon to Sheep Camp, past the overhanging and ever-threatening glaciers to the Scales, and from the Scales up the steep pitches of ice-scoured rock where packers climbed with hands and feet, Old Tarwater camp-cooked and packed and sang. He blew across Chilcoot Pass, above timber-line, in the first swirl of autumn snow. Those below, without firewood, on the bitter rim of Crater Lake, heard from the driving obscurity above them a weird voice chanting:

'Like Argus of the ancient times,
    We leave this modern Greece,
Tum-tum, tum-tum, tum, tum, tum-tum,
    To shear the Golden Fleece.'

And out of the snow flurries they saw appear a tall, gaunt form, with whiskers of flying white that blended with the storm, bending under a sixty-pound pack of camp dunnage.

'Father Christmas!' was the hail. And then: 'Three rousing cheers for Father Christmas!'

Two miles beyond Crater Lake lay Happy Camp—so named because here was found the uppermost fringe of the timber line, where men might warm themselves by fire again. Scarcely could it be called timber, for it was a dwarf rock-spruce that never raised its loftiest branches higher than a foot above the moss, and that twisted and grovelled like a pig-vegetable under the moss. Here, on the trail leading into Happy Camp, in the first sunshine of half a dozen days, Old Tarwater rested his pack against a huge boulder and caught his breath. Around this boulder the trail passed, laden men toiling slowly forward and men with empty pack-straps limping rapidly back for fresh loads. Twice Old Tarwater essayed to rise and go on, and each time, warned by his shakiness, sank back to recover more strength. From around the boulder he heard voices in greeting, recognized Charles Crayton's voice, and realized that at last they had met up with Young Liverpool. Quickly, Charles plunged into business, and Tarwater heard with great distinctness every word of Charles' unflattering description of him and of the proposition to give him passage to Dawson.

'A dam fool proposition,' was Liverpool's judgment, when Charles had concluded. 'An old granddad of seventy! If he's on his last legs, why in hell did you hook up with him? If there's going to be a famine, and it looks like it, we need every ounce of grub for ourselves. We only outfitted for four, not five.'

'It's all right,' Tarwater heard Charles assuring the other. 'Don't get excited. The old codger agreed to leave the final decision to you when we caught up with you. All you've got to do is put your foot down and say no.'

'You mean it's up to me to turn the old one down, after your encouraging him and taking advantage of his work clear from Dyea here?'

'It's a hard trail, Liverpool, and only the men that are hard will get through,' Charles strove to palliate.

'And I'm to do the dirty work?' Liverpool complained, while Tarwater's heart sank.

'That's just about the size of it,' Charles said. 'You've got the deciding.'

Then old Tarwater's heart uprose again as the air was rent by a cyclone of profanity, from the midst of which crackled sentences like: 'Dirty skunks! . . . See you in hell first! . . . My mind's made up! . . . Hell's fire and corruption! . . . The old codger goes down the Yukon with us, stack on that, my hearty! . . . Hard? You don't know what hard is unless I show you! . . . I'll bust the whole outfit to hell and gone if any of you try to side-track him! . . . Just try to side-track him, that's all, and you'll think the Day of Judgment and all God's blastingness has hit the camp in one chunk!'

Such was the invigoratingness of Liverpool's flow of speech that, quite without consciousness of effort, the old man arose easily under his load and strode on toward Happy Camp.

From Happy Camp to Long Lake, from Long Lake to Deep Lake, and from Deep Lake up over the enormous hog-back and  down to Linderman, the man-killing race against winter kept on. Men broke their hearts and backs and wept beside the trail in sheer exhaustion. But winter never faltered. The fall gales blew, and amid bitter soaking rains and ever-increasing snow flurries, Tarwater and the party to which he was attached piled the last of their outfit on the beach.

There was no rest. Across the lake, a mile above a roaring torrent, they located a patch of spruce and built their saw-pit. Here, by hand, with an inadequate whipsaw, they sawed the spruce-trunks into lumber. They worked night and day. Thrice, on the night shift, underneath in the saw-pit, Old Tarwater fainted. By day he cooked as well, and, in the betweenwhiles, helped Anson in the building of the boat beside the torrent as the green planks came down.

The days grew shorter. The wind shifted into the north and blew unending gales. In the mornings the weary men crawled from their blankets and in their socks thawed out their frozen shoes by the fire Tarwater always had burning for them. Ever arose the increasing tale of famine on the Inside. The last grub steamboats up from Bering Sea were stalled by low water at the beginning of the Yukon Flats hundreds of miles north of Dawson. In fact, they lay at the old Hudson Bay Company's post at Fort Yukon inside the Arctic Circle. Flour in Dawson was up to two dollars a pound, but no one would sell. Bonanza and Eldorado Kings, with money to burn, were leaving for the Outside because they could buy no grub. Miners' Committees were confiscating all grub and putting the population on strict rations. A man who held out an ounce of grub was shot like a dog. A score had been so executed already.

And, under a strain which had broken so many younger men, Old Tarwater began to break. His cough had become terrible, and had not his exhausted comrades slept like the dead, he would have kept them awake nights. Also, he began to take chills, so that he dressed up to go to bed. When he had finished so dressing, not a rag of garment remained in his clothes bag. All he possessed was on his back and swathed around his gaunt old form.

'Gee!' said Big Bill. 'If he puts all he's got on now, when it ain't lower than twenty above, what'll he do later on when it goes down to fifty and sixty below?'

They lined the rough-made boat down the mountain torrent, nearly losing it a dozen times, and rowed across the south end of Lake Linderman in the thick of a fall blizzard. Next morning they planned to load and start, squarely into the teeth of the north, on their perilous traverse of half a thousand miles of lakes and rapids and box canyons. But before he went to bed that night, Young Liverpool was out over the camp. He returned to find his whole party asleep. Rousing Tarwater, he talked with him in low tones.

'Listen, dad,' he said. 'You've got a passage in our boat, and if ever a man earned a passage you have. But you know yourself you're pretty well along in years, and your health right now ain't exciting. If you go on with us you'll croak surer'n hell.—Now wait till I finish, dad. The price for a passage has jumped to five hundred dollars. I've been throwing my feet and I've hustled a passenger. He's an official of the Alaska Commercial and just has to get in. He's bid up to six hundred to go with me in our boat. Now the passage is yours. You sell it to him, poke the six hundred into your jeans, and pull South for California while the goin's good. You can be in Dyea in two days, and in California in a week more. What d'ye say?'

Tarwater coughed and shivered for a space, ere he could get freedom of breath for speech.

'Son,' he said, 'I just want to tell you one thing. I drove my four yoke of oxen across the Plains in Forty-nine and lost nary a one. I drove them plumb to Californy, and I freighted with them afterward out of Sutter's Fort to American Bar. Now I'm going to Klondike. Ain't nothing can stop me, ain't nothing at all. I'm going to ride that boat, with you at the steering sweep, clean to Klondike, and I'm going to shake three hundred thousand out of the moss-roots. That being so, it's contrary to reason and common sense for me to sell out my passage. But I thank you kindly, son, I thank you kindly.'

The young sailor shot out his hand impulsively and gripped the old man's.

'By God, dad!' he cried. 'You're sure going to go then. You're the real stuff.' He looked with undisguised contempt across the sleepers to where Charles Crayton snored in his red beard. 'They don't seem to make your kind any more, dad.'

Into the north they fought their way, although old-timers, coming out, shook their heads and prophesied they would be frozen in on the lakes. That the freeze-up might come any day was patent, and delays of safety were no longer considered. For this reason, Liverpool decided to shoot the rapid stream connecting Linderman to Lake Bennett with the fully loaded boat. It was the custom to line the empty boats down and to portage the cargoes across. Even then, many empty boats had been wrecked. But the time was past for such precaution.

'Climb out, dad,' Liverpool commanded, as he prepared to swing from the bank and enter the rapids.

Old Tarwater shook his white head.

'I'm sticking to the outfit,' he declared. 'It's the only way to get through. You see, son, I'm going to Klondike. If I stick by the boat, then the boat just naturally goes to Klondike, too. If I get out, then most likely you'll lose the boat.'

'Well, there's no use in overloading,' Charles announced, springing abruptly out on the bank as the boat cast off.

'Next time you wait for my orders!' Liverpool shouted ashore as the current gripped the boat. 'And there won't be any more walking around rapids and losing time waiting to pick you up!'

What took them ten minutes by river, took Charles half an hour by land, and while they waited for him at the head of Lake Bennett they passed the time of day with several dilapidated old-timers on their way out. The famine news was graver than ever. The North-west Mounted Police, stationed at the foot of Lake Marsh where the gold-rushers entered Canadian territory, were refusing to let a man past who did not carry with him seven hundred pounds of grub. In Dawson City a thousand men, with dog-teams, were waiting the freeze-up to come out over the ice. The trading companies could not fill their grub-contracts, and partners were cutting the cards to see which should go and which should stay and work the claims.

'That settles it,' Charles announced, when he learned of the action of the mounted police on the boundary. 'Old Man, you might as well start back now.'

'Climb aboard!' Liverpool commanded. 'We're going to Klondike, and old dad is going along.'

A shift of gale to the south gave them a fair wind down Lake Bennett, before which they ran under a huge sail made by Liverpool. The heavy weight of outfit gave such ballast that he cracked on as a daring sailor should when moments counted. A shift of four points into the south-west, coming just at the right time as they entered Caribou Crossing, drove them down that connecting link to lakes Tagish and Marsh. In stormy sunset and twilight they made the dangerous crossing of Great Windy Arm, wherein they beheld two other boat-loads of gold-rushers capsize and drown.

Charles was for beaching for the night, but Liverpool held on, steering down Tagish by the sound of the surf on the shoals and by the occasional shore-fires that advertised wrecked or timid argonauts. At four in the morning, he aroused Charles. Old Tarwater, shiveringly awake, heard Liverpool order Crayton aft beside him at the steering-sweep, and also heard the one-sided conversation.

'Just listen, friend Charles, and keep your own mouth shut,' Liverpool began. 'I want you to get one thing into your head and keep it there: *old dad's going by the police. Understand? He's going by.* When they examine our outfit, old dad's got a fifth share in it, savvee? That'll put us all 'way under what we ought to have, but we can bluff it through. Now get this, and get it hard: *there ain't going to be any fall-down on this bluff——*'

'If you think I'd give away on the old codger——' Charles began indignantly.

'You thought that,' Liverpool checked him, 'because I never mentioned any such thing. Now—get me and get me hard: I don't care what you've been thinking. It's what you're going to think. We'll make the police post some time this afternoon, and we've got to get ready to pull the bluff without a hitch, and a word to the wise is plenty.'

'If you think I've got it in my mind——' Charles began again.

'Look here,' Liverpool shut him off. 'I don't know what's in your mind. I don't want to know. I want you to know what's in my mind. If there's any slip-up, if old dad gets turned back by the police, I'm going to pick out the first quiet bit of landscape and take you ashore on it. And then I'm going to beat you up to the Queen's taste. Get me, and get me hard. It ain't going to be any half-way beating, but a real, two-legged, two-fisted, he-man beating. I don't expect I'll kill you, but I'll come damn near to half-killing you.'

'But what can I do?' Charles almost whimpered.

'Just one thing,' was Liverpool's final word. 'You just pray. You pray so hard that old dad gets by the police that he does get by. That's all. Go back to your blankets.'

Before they gained Lake Le Barge, the land was sheeted with snow that would not melt for half a year. Nor could they lay their boat at will against the bank, for the rim-ice was already forming. Inside the mouth of the river, just ere it entered Lake Le Barge, they found a hundred storm-bound boats of the argonauts. Out of the north, across the full sweep of the great lake, blew an unending snow gale. Three mornings they put out and fought it and the cresting seas it drove that turned to ice as they fell in-board. While the others broke their hearts at the oars, Old Tarwater managed to keep up just sufficient circulation to survive by chopping ice and throwing it overboard.

Each day for three days, beaten to helplessness, they turned tail on the battle and ran back into the sheltering river. By the fourth day, the hundred boats had increased to three hundred, and the two thousand argonauts on board knew that the great gale heralded the freeze-up of Le Barge. Beyond, the rapid rivers would continue to run for days, but unless they got beyond, and immediately, they were doomed to be frozen in for six months to come.

'This day we go through,' Liverpool announced. 'We turn back for nothing. And those of us that dies at the oars will live again and go on pulling.'

And they went through, winning half the length of the lake by nightfall and pulling on through all the night hours as the wind went down, falling asleep at the oars and being rapped awake by Liverpool, toiling on through an age-long nightmare while the stars came out and the surface of the lake turned to the unruffledness of a sheet of paper and froze skin-ice that tinkled like broken glass as their oar-blades shattered it.

As day broke clear and cold, they entered the river, with behind them a sea of ice. Liverpool examined his aged passenger and found him helpless and almost gone. When he rounded the boat to against the rim-ice to build a fire and warm up Tarwater inside and out, Charles protested against such loss of time.

'This ain't business, so don't you come horning in,' Liverpool informed him. 'I'm running the boat trip. So you just climb out and chop firewood, and plenty of it. I'll take care of dad. You, Anson, make a fire on the bank. And you, Bill, set up the Yukon stove in the boat. Old dad ain't as young as the rest of us, and for the rest of this voyage he's going to have a fire on board to sit by.'

All of which came to pass; and the boat, in the grip of the current, like a river steamer with smoke rising from the two joints of stove-pipe, grounded on shoals, hung up on split currents, and charged rapids and canyons, as it drove deeper into the Northland winter. The Big and Little Salmon rivers were throwing mush-ice into the main river as they passed, and, below the riffles, anchor-ice arose from the river bottom and coated the surface with crystal scum. Night and day the rim-ice grew, till, in quiet places, it extended out a hundred yards from the shore. And Old Tarwater, with all his clothes on, sat by the stove and kept the fire going. Night and day, not daring to stop for fear of the imminent freeze-up, they dared to run, an increasing mushiness of ice running with them.

'What ho, old hearty?' Liverpool would call out at times.

'Cheer O,' Old Tarwater had learned to respond.

'What can I ever do for you, son, in payment?' Tarwater, stoking the fire, would sometimes ask Liverpool, beating now one released hand and now the other as he fought for circulation where he steered in the freezing stern-sheets.

'Just break out that regular song of yours, old Forty-Niner,' was the invariable reply.

And Tarwater would lift his voice in the cackling chant, as he lifted it at the end, when the boat swung in through driving cake-ice and moored to the Dawson City bank, and all waterfront Dawson pricked its ears to the triumphant pæan:

> Like Argus of the ancient times,
>   We leave this modern Greece,
> Tum-tum, tum-tum, tum, tum, tum-tum,
>   To shear the Golden Fleece.

Charles did it, but he did it so discreetly that none of his party, least of all the sailor, ever learned of it. He saw two great open barges being filled up with men, and, on inquiry, learned that these were grubless ones being rounded up and sent down the Yukon by the Committee of Safety. The barges were to be towed by the last little steamboat in Dawson, and the hope was that Fort Yukon, where lay the stranded steamboats, would be gained before the river froze. At any rate, no matter what happened to them, Dawson would be relieved of their grub-consuming presence. So to the Committee of Safety Charles went, privily to drop a flea in its ear concerning Tarwater's grubless, moneyless, and aged condition. Tarwater was one of the last gathered in, and when Young Liverpool returned to the boat, from the bank he saw the barges in a run of cake-ice, disappearing around the bend below Moose-hide Mountain.

Running in cake-ice all the way, and several times escaping jams in the Yukon Flats, the barges made their hundreds of miles of progress farther into the north and froze up cheek by jowl with the grub-fleet. Here, inside the Arctic Circle, Old Tarwater settled down to pass the long winter. Several hours' work a day, chopping firewood for the steamboat companies, sufficed to keep him in food. For the rest of the time there was nothing to do but hibernate in his log cabin.

Warmth, rest, and plenty to eat, cured his hacking cough

and put him in as good physical condition as was possible for his advanced years. But, even before Christmas, the lack of fresh vegetables caused scurvy to break out, and disappointed adventurer after disappointed adventurer took to his bunk in abject surrender to this culminating misfortune. No so Tarwater. Even before the first symptoms appeared on him, he was putting into practice his one prescription, namely, exercise. From the junk of the old trading post he resurrected a number of rusty traps, and from one of the steamboat captains he borrowed a rifle.

Thus equipped, he ceased from wood-chopping, and began to make more than a mere living. Nor was he downhearted when the scurvy broke out on his own body. Ever he ran his trap-lines and sang his ancient chant. Nor could the pessimist shake his surety of the three hundred thousand of Alaskan gold he was going to shake out of the moss-roots.

'But this ain't gold-country,' they told him.

'Gold is where you find it, son, as I should know who was mining before you was born, 'way back in Forty-Nine,' was his reply. 'What was Bonanza Creek but a moose-pasture? No miner'd look at it; yet they washed five-hundred-dollar pans and took out fifty million dollars. Eldorado was just as bad. For all you know, right under this here cabin, or right over the next hill, is millions just waiting for a lucky one like me to come and shake it out.'

At the end of January came his disaster. Some powerful animal that he decided was a bob-cat, managing to get caught in one of his smaller traps, dragged it away. A heavy snow-fall put a stop mid-way to his pursuit, losing the trail for him and losing himself. There were but several hours of daylight each day between the twenty hours of intervening darkness, and his efforts in the grey light and continually falling snow succeeded only in losing him more thoroughly. Fortunately, when winter snow falls in the Northland the thermometer invariably rises; so, instead of the customary forty and fifty and even sixty degrees below zero, the temperature remained fifteen below. Also, he was warmly clad and had a full matchbox. Further to mitigate his predicament, on the fifth day he killed a wounded moose that weighed over half a ton. Making his camp beside it on a spruce-bottom, he was prepared to last out the winter, unless a searching party found him or his scurvy grew worse.

But at the end of two weeks there had been no sign of search, while his scurvy had undeniably grown worse. Against his fire, banked from outer cold by a shelter-wall of spruce-boughs, he crouched long hours in sleep and long hours in waking. But the waking hours grew less, becoming semi-waking or half-dreaming hours as the processes of hibernation worked their way with him. Slowly the sparkle point of consciousness and identity that was John Tarwater sank, deeper and deeper, into the profounds of his being that had been compounded ere man was man, and while he was becoming man, when he, first of all animals, regarded himself with an introspective eye and laid the beginnings of morality in foundations of nightmare peopled by the monsters of his own ethic-thwarted desires.

Like a man in fever, waking to intervals of consciousness, so Old Tarwater awoke, cooked his moose-meat, and fed the fire; but more and more time he spent in his torpor, unaware of what was day-dream and what was sleep-dream in the content of his unconsciousness. And here, in the unforgettable crypts of man's unwritten history, unthinkable and unrealizable, like passages of nightmare or impossible adventures of lunacy, he encountered the monsters created of man's first morality that ever since have vexed him into the spinning of fantasies to elude them or do battle with them.

In short, weighted by his seventy years, in the vast and silent loneliness of the North, Old Tarwater, as in the delirium of drug or anæsthetic, recovered, within himself, the infantile mind of the child-man of the early world. It was in the dusk of Death's fluttery wings that Tarwater thus crouched, and, like his remote forebear, the child-man, went to myth-making, and sun-heroizing, himself hero-maker and the hero in quest of the immemorable treasure difficult of attainment.

Either must he attain the treasure—for so ran the inexorable logic of the shadowland of the unconscious—or else sink into the all-devouring sea, the blackness eater of the light that swallowed to extinction the sun each night ... the sun that arose ever in rebirth next morning in the east, and that had become to man man's first symbol of immortality through rebirth. All this, in the deeps of his unconsciousness (the shadowy western land of descending light), was the near dusk of Death down into which he slowly ebbed.

But how to escape this monster of the dark that from within him slowly swallowed him? Too deep-sunk was he to dream of escape or feel the prod of desire to escape. For him reality had ceased. Nor from within the darkened chamber of himself could reality recrudesce. His years were too heavy upon him, the debility of disease and the lethargy and torpor of the silence and the cold were too profound. Only from without could reality impact upon him and re-awake within him an awareness of reality. Otherwise he would ooze down through the shadow-realm of the unconscious into the all-darkness of extinction.

But it came, the smash of reality from without, crashing upon his ear drums in a loud, explosive snort. For twenty days, in a temperature that had never risen above fifty below, no breath of wind had blown movement, no slightest sound had broken the silence. Like the smoker on the opium couch refocusing his eyes from the spacious walls of dream to the narrow confines of the mean little room, so Old Tarwater stared vague-eyed before him across his dying fire, at a huge moose that stared at him in startlement, dragging a wounded leg, manifesting all signs of extreme exhaustion; it, too, had been straying blindly in the shadow-land, and had wakened to reality only just ere it stepped into Tarwater's fire.

He feebly slipped the large fur mitten lined with thickness of wool from his right hand. Upon trial he found the trigger finger too numb for movement. Carefully, slowly, through long minutes, he worked the bare hand inside his blankets, up under his fur *parka*, through the chest openings of his shirts, and into the slightly warm hollow of his left arm-pit. Long minutes passed ere the finger could move, when, with equal slowness of caution, he gathered his rifle to his shoulder and drew bead upon the great animal across the fire.

At the shot, of the two shadow-wanderers, the one reeled downward to the dark and the other reeled upward to the light, swaying drunkenly on his scurvy-ravaged legs, shivering with nervousness and cold, rubbing swimming eyes with shaking fingers, and staring at the real world all about him that had returned to him with such sickening suddenness. He shook himself together, and realized that for long, how long he did not know, he had bedded in the arms of Death. He spat, with definite intention, heard the spittle crackle in the frost, and judged it must be below and far below sixty below. In truth, that day at Fort Yukon, the spirit thermometer registered seventy-five degrees below zero, which, since freezing-point is thirty-two above, was equivalent to one hundred and seven degrees of frost.

Slowly Tarwater's brain reasoned to action. Here, in the vast alone, dwelt Death. Here had come two wounded moose. With the clearing of the sky after the great cold came on, he had located his bearings, and he knew that both wounded moose had trailed to him from the east. Therefore, in the east, were men—whites or Indians he could not tell, but at any rate men who might stand by him in his need and help moor him to reality above the sea of dark.

He moved slowly, but he moved in reality, girding himself with rifle, ammunition, matches, and a pack of twenty pounds of moose-meat. Then, an Argus rejuvenated, albeit lame of both legs and tottery, he turned his back on the perilous west and limped into the sun-arising, re-birthing east. . . .

Days later—how many days later he was never to know —dreaming dreams and seeing visions, cackling his old gold-chant of Forty-Nine, like one drowning and swimming feebly to keep his consciousness above the engulfing dark, he came out upon the snow-slope to a canyon and saw below smoke rising and men who ceased from work to gaze at him. He tottered down the hill to them, still singing; and when he ceased from lack of breath they called him variously: Santa Claus, Old Christmas, Whiskers, the Last of the Mohicans, and Father Christmas. And when he stood among them he stood very still, without speech, while great tears welled out of his eyes. He cried silently, a long time, till, as if suddenly bethinking himself, he sat down with much creaking and crackling of his joints, and from this low vantage point toppled sidewise and fainted calmly and easily away.

In less than a week Old Tarwater was up and limping about the housework of the cabin, cooking and dish-washing for the five men of the creek. Genuine sourdoughs (pioneers) they were, tough and hard-bitten, who had been buried so deeply inside the Circle that they did not know there was a Klondike Strike. The news he brought them was their first word of it. They lived on an almost straight-meat diet of moose, caribou, and smoked salmon, eked out with wild berries and somewhat succulent wild roots they had stocked up with in the summer. They had forgotten the taste of coffee, made fire with a burning glass, carried live fire-sticks with them wherever they travelled, and in their pipes smoked dry leaves that bit the tongue and were pungent to the nostrils.

Three years before, they had prospected from the head-reaches of the Koyokuk northward and clear across to the mouth of the Mackenzie on the Arctic Ocean. Here, on the whaleships, they had beheld their last white men and equipped themselves with the last white man's grub, consisting principally of salt and smoking tobacco. Striking south and west on the long traverse, to the junction of the Yukon and Porcupine at Fort Yukon, they had found gold on this creek and remained over to work the ground.

They hailed the advent of Tarwater with joy, never tired of listening to his tales of Forty-Nine, and rechristened him Old Hero. Also, with tea made from spruce needles, with concoctions brewed from the inner willow bark, and with sour and bitter roots and bulbs from the ground, they dosed his scurvy out of him, so that he ceased limping and began to lay on flesh over his bony framework. Further, they saw no reason at all why he should not gather a rich treasure of gold from the ground.

'Don't know about all of three hundred thousand,' they told him one morning, at breakfast, ere they departed to their work, 'but how'd a hundred thousand do, Old Hero? That's what we figure a claim is worth, the ground being badly spotted, and we've already staked your location notices.'

'Well, boys,' Old Tarwater answered, 'and thanking you kindly, all I can say is that a hundred thousand will do nicely, and very nicely, for a starter. Of course, I ain't goin' to stop till I get the full three hundred thousand. That's what I come into the country for.'

They laughed and applauded his ambition and reckoned they'd have to hunt a richer creek for him. And Old Hero reckoned that as the spring came on and he grew spryer, he'd have to get out and do a little snooping around himself.

'For all anybody knows,' he said, pointing to a hillside across the creek bottom, 'the moss under the snow there may be plumb rooted in nugget gold.'

He said no more, but as the sun rose higher and the days grew longer and warmer, he gazed often across the creek at the definite bench-formation half-way up the hill. And, one day, when the thaw was in full swing, he crossed the stream and climbed to the bench. Exposed patches of ground had already thawed an inch deep. On one such patch he stopped, gathered a bunch of moss in his big gnarled hands, and ripped it out by the roots. The sun smouldered on dully glistening yellow. He shook the handful of moss, and coarse nuggets, like gravel, fell to the ground. It was the Golden Fleece ready for the shearing.

Not entirely unremembered in Alaskan annals is the summer stampede of 1898 from Fort Yukon to the bench diggings of Tarwater Hill. And when Tarwater sold his holdings to the Bowdie interests for a sheer half-million and faced for California, he rode a mule over a new-cut trail, with convenient road houses along the way, clear to the steamboat landing at Fort Yukon.

At the first meal on the ocean-going steamship out of St Michaels, a waiter, greyish-haired, pain-ravaged of face, scurvy-twisted of body, served him. Old Tarwater was compelled to look him over twice in order to make certain he was Charles Crayton.

'Got it bad, eh, son?' Tarwater queried.

'Just my luck,' the other complained, after recognition and greeting. 'Only one of the party that the scurvy attacked. I've been through hell. The other three are all at work and healthy, getting grub-stake to prospect up White River this winter. Anson's earning twenty-five a day at carpentering, Liverpool's getting twenty logging for the saw-mill, and Big Bill's getting forty a day as chief sawyer. I tried my best, and if it hadn't been for scurvy . . .'

'Sure, son, you done your best, which ain't much, you being naturally irritable and hard from too much business. Now I'll tell you what. You ain't fit to work crippled up this way. I'll pay your passage with the captain in kind remembrance of the voyage you gave me, and you can lay up and take it easy for the rest of the trip. And what are your circumstances when you land at San Francisco?'

Charles Crayton shrugged his shoulders.

'Tell you what,' Tarwater continued. 'There's work on the ranch for you till you can start business again.'

'I could manage your business for you——' Charles began eagerly.

'No, siree,' Tarwater declared emphatically. 'But there's always post-holes to dig, and cordwood to chop, and the climate's fine. . . .'

Tarwater arrived home a true prodigal grandfather for whom the fatted calf was killed and ready. But first, ere he sat down at table, he must stroll out and around. And sons and daughters of his flesh and of the law needs must go with him, fulsomely eating out of the gnarled old hand that had half a million to disburse. He led the way, and no opinion he slyly uttered was preposterous or impossible enough to draw dissent from his following. Pausing by the ruined water wheel which he had built from the standing timber, his face beamed as he gazed across the stretches of Tarwater Valley, and on and up the far heights to the summit of Tarwater Mountain—now all his again.

A thought came to him that made him avert his face and blow his nose in order to hide the twinkle in his eyes. Still attended by the entire family, he strolled on to the dilapidated barn. He picked up an age-weathered single-tree from the ground.

'William,' he said. 'Remember that little conversation we had just before I started to Klondike? Sure, William, you remember. You told me I was crazy. And I said my father'd have walloped the tar out of me with a single-tree if I'd spoke to him that way.'

'Aw, but that was only foolin',' William temporized.

William was a grizzled man of forty-five, and his wife and grown sons stood in the group, curiously watching Grandfather Tarwater take off his coat and hand it to Mary to hold.

'William—come here,' he commanded imperatively.

No matter how reluctantly, William came.

'Just a taste, William, son, of what my father give me often enough,' Old Tarwater crooned, as he laid on his son's back and shoulders with the single-tree. 'Observe, I ain't hitting you on the head. My father had a gosh-wollickin' temper and never drew the line at heads when he went after tar.—Don't jerk your elbows back that way! You're likely to get a crack on one by accident. And just tell me one thing, William, son: is there nary notion in your head that I'm crazy?'

'No!' William yelped out in pain, as he danced about. 'You ain't crazy, father! Of course you ain't crazy!'

'You said it,' Old Tarwater remarked sententiously, tossing the single-tree aside and starting to struggle into his coat. 'Now let's all go in and eat.'

## THE ONE THOUSAND DOZEN

DAVID RASMUNSEN was a hustler, and, like many a greater man, a man of the one idea. Wherefore, when the clarion call of the North rang on his ear, he conceived an adventure in eggs and bent all his energy to its achievement. He figured briefly and to the point, and the adventure became iridescent-hued, splendid. That eggs would sell at Dawson for five dollars a dozen was a safe working premise. Whence it was incontrovertible that one thousand dozen would bring, in the Golden Metropolis, five thousand dollars.

On the other hand, expense was to be considered, and he considered it well, for he was a careful man, keenly practical, with a hard head and a heart that imagination never warmed. At fifteen cents a dozen, the inital cost of his thousand dozen would be one hundred and fifty dollars, a mere bagatelle in face of the enormous profit. And suppose, just suppose, to be wildly extravagant for once, that transportation for himself and eggs should run up eight hundred and fifty more; he would still have four thousand clear cash and clean when the last egg was disposed of and the last dust had rippled into his sack.

'You see, Alma'—he figured it over with his wife, the cosy dining-room submerged in a sea of maps, government surveys, guide-books, and Alaskan itineraries—'you see, expenses don't really begin till you make Dyea—fifty dollars 'll cover it with a first-class passage thrown in. Now from Dyea to Lake Linderman, Indian packers take your goods over for twelve cents a pound, twelve dollars a hundred, or one hundred and twenty dollars a thousand. Say I have fifteen hundred pounds, it'll cost one hundred and eighty dollars—call it two hundred and be safe. I am creditably informed by a Klondiker just come out that I can buy a boat for three hundred. But the same man says I'm sure to get a couple of passengers for one hundred and fifty each, which will give me the boat for nothing, and, further, they can help me manage it. And . . . that's all; I put my eggs ashore from the boat at Dawson. Now let me see how much is that?'

'Fifty dollars from San Francisco to Dyea, two hundred from Dyea to Linderman, passengers pay for the boat—two hundred and fifty all told,' she summed up swiftly.

'And a hundred for my clothes and personal outfit,' he went on happily; 'that leaves a margin of five hundred for emergencies. And what possible emergencies can arise?'

Alma shrugged her shoulders and elevated her brows. If that vast Northland was capable of swallowing up a man and a thousand dozen eggs, surely there was room and to spare for whatever else he might happen to possess. So she thought, but she said nothing. She knew David Rasmunsen too well to say anything.

'Doubling the time because of chance delays, I should make the trip in two months. Think of it, Alma! Four thousand in two months! Beats the paltry hundred a month I'm getting now. Why, we'll build further out where we'll have more space, gas in every room, and a view, and the rent of the cottage 'll pay taxes, insurance, and water, and leave something over. And then there's always the chance of my striking it and coming out a millionaire. Now tell me, Alma, don't you think I'm very moderate?'

And Alma could hardly think otherwise. Besides, had not her own cousin—though a remote and distant one to be sure, the black sheep, the harum-scarum, the ne'er-do-well—had not he come down out of that weird North country with a hundred thousand in yellow dust, to say nothing of a half-ownership in the hole from which it came?

David Rasmunsen's grocer was surprised when he found him weighing eggs in the scales at the end of the counter, and Rasmunsen himself was more surprised when he found that a dozen eggs weighed a pound and a half—fifteen hundred pounds for his thousand dozen! There would be no weight left for his clothes, blankets, and cooking utensils, to say nothing of the grub he must necessarily consume

8*

by the way. His calculations were all thrown out, and he was just proceeding to recast them when he hit upon the idea of weighing small eggs. 'For whether they be large or small, a dozen eggs is a dozen eggs,' he observed sagely to himself; and a dozen small ones he found to weigh but a pound and a quarter. Thereat the city of San Francisco was overrun by anxious-eyed emissaries, and commission houses and dairy associations were startled by a sudden demand for eggs running not more than twenty ounces to the dozen.

Rasmunsen mortgaged the little cottage for a thousand dollars, arranged for his wife to make a prolonged stay among her own people, threw up his job, and started North. To keep within his schedule, he compromised on a second-class passage, which, because of the rush, was worse than steerage; and in the late summer, a pale and wobbly man, he disembarked with his eggs on the Dyea beach. But it did not take him long to recover his land legs and appetite. His first interview with the Chilkoot packers straightened him up and stiffened his backbone. Forty cents a pound they demanded for the twenty-eight-mile portage, and while he caught his breath and swallowed, the price went up to forty-three. Fifteen husky Indians put the straps on his packs at forty-five, but took them off at an offer of forty-seven from a Skaguay Crœsus in dirty shirt and ragged overalls who had lost his horses on the White Pass trail and was now making a last desperate drive at the country by way of Chilkoot.

But Rasmunsen was clean grit, and at fifty cents found takers, who, two days later, set his eggs down intact at Linderman. But fifty cents a pound is a thousand dollars a ton, and his fifteen hundred pounds had exhausted his emergency fund and left him stranded at the Tantalus point where each day he saw the fresh whipsawed boats departing for Dawson. Further, a great anxiety brooded over the camp where the boats were built. Men worked frantically, early and late, at the height of their endurance, caulking, nailing, and pitching in a frenzy of haste for which adequate explanation was not far to seek. Each day the snow-line crept farther down the bleak, rock-shouldered peaks, and gale followed gale, with sleet and slush and snow, and in the eddies and quiet places young ice formed and thickened through the fleeting hours. And each morn, toil-stiffened men turned wan faces across the lake to see if the freeze-up had come. For the freeze-up heralded the death of their hope—the hope that they would be floating down the swift river ere navigation closed on the chain of lakes.

To harrow Rasmunsen's soul further, he discovered three competitors in the egg business. It was true that one, a little German, had gone broke and was himself forlornly back-tripping the last pack of the portage; but the other two had boats nearly completed, and were daily supplicating the god of merchants and traders to stay the iron hand of winter for just another day. But the iron hand closed down over the land. Men were being frozen in the blizzard which swept Chilkoot, and Rasmunsen frosted his toes ere he was aware. He found a chance to go passenger with his freight in a boat just shoving off through the rubble, but two hundred hard cash was required, and he had no money.

'Ay tank you yust wait one leedle w'ile,' said the Swedish boat-builder, who had struck his Klondike right there and was wise enough to know it—'one leedle w'ile und I make you a tam fine skiff boat, sure Pete.'

With this unpledged word to go on, Rasmunsen hit the back trail to Crater Lake, where he fell in with two press correspondents whose tangled baggage was strewn from Stone House, over across the Pass, and as far as Happy Camp.

'Yes,' he said with consequence. 'I've a thousand dozen eggs at Linderman, and my boat's just about got the last seam caulked. Consider myself in luck to get it. Boats are at a premium, you know, and none to be had.'

Whereupon and almost with bodily violence, the correspondents clamoured to go with him, fluttered greenbacks before his eyes, and spilled yellow twenties from hand to hand. He could not hear of it, but they over-persuaded him, and he reluctantly consented to take them at three hundred apiece. Also they pressed upon him the passage money in advance. And while they wrote to their respective journals concerning the Good Samaritan with the thousand dozen eggs, the Good Samaritan was hurrying back to the Swede at Linderman.

'Here, you! Gimme that boat!' was his salutation, his hand jingling the correspondents' gold pieces and his eyes hungrily bent upon the finished craft.

The Swede regarded him stolidly and shook his head.

'How much is the other fellow paying? Three hundred? Well, here's four. Take it.'

He tried to press it upon him, but the man backed away.

'Ay tank not. Ay say him get der skiff boat. You yust wait——'

'Here's six hundred. Last call. Take it or leave it. Tell 'm it's a mistake.'

The Swede wavered. 'Ay tank yes,' he finally said, and the last Rasmunsen saw of him his vocabulary was going to wreck in a vain effort to explain the mistake to the other fellows.

The German slipped and broke his ankle on the steep hog-back above Deep Lake, sold out his stock for a dollar a dozen, and with the proceeds hired Indian packers to carry him back to Dyea. But on the morning Rasmunsen shoved off with his correspondents, his two rivals followed suit.

'How many you got?' one of them, a lean little New Englander, called out.

'One thousand dozen,' Rasmunsen answered proudly.

'Huh! I'll go you even stakes I beat you in with my eight hundred.'

The correspondents offered to lend him the money; but Rasmunsen declined, and the Yankee closed with the remaining rival, a brawny son of the sea and a sailor of ships and things, who promised to show them all a wrinkle or two when it came to cracking on. And crack on he did, with a large tarpaulin square sail which pressed the bow half under at every jump. He was the first to run out of Linderman, but, disdaining the portage, piled his loaded boat on the rocks in the boiling rapids. Rasmunsen and the Yankee, who likewise had two passengers, portaged across on their backs and then lined their empty boats down through the bad water to Bennett.

Bennett was a twenty-five-mile lake, narrow and deep, a funnel between the mountains through which storms ever romped. Rasmunsen camped on the sand-pit at its head, where were many men and boats bound north in the teeth of the Arctic winter. He awoke in the morning to find a piping gale from the south, which caught the chill from the whited peaks and glacial valleys and blew as cold as north wind ever blew. But it was fair, and he also found the Yankee staggering past the first bold headland with all sail set. Boat after boat was getting under way, and the correspondents fell to with enthusiasm.

'We'll catch him before Caribou Crossing,' they assured Rasmunsen, as they ran up the sail and the *Alma* took the first icy spray over her bow.

Now Rasmunsen all his life had been prone to cowardice on water, but he clung to the kicking steering-oar with set face and determined jaw. His thousand dozen were there in the boat before his eyes, safely secured beneath the correspondents' baggage, and somehow, before his eyes were the little cottage and the mortgage for a thousand dollars.

It was bitter cold. Now and again he hauled in the steering-sweep and put out a fresh one while his passengers chopped the ice from the blade. Wherever the spray struck, it turned instantly to frost, and the dipping boom of the spritsail was quickly fringed with icicles. The *Alma* strained and hammered through the big seas till the seams and butts began to spread, but in lieu of bailing the correspondents chopped ice and flung it overboard. There was no let-up. The mad race with winter was on, and the boats tore along in a desperate string.

'W-w-we can't stop to save our souls!' one of the correspondents chattered, from cold, not fright.

'That's right! Keep her down the middle, old man!' the other encouraged.

Rasmunsen replied with an idiotic grin. The iron-bound shores were in a lather of foam, and even down the middle the only hope was to keep running away from the big seas. To lower sail was to be overtaken and swamped. Time and again they passed boats pounding among the rocks, and once they saw one on the edge of the breakers about to strike. A little craft behind them, with two men, jibed over and turned bottom up.

'W-w-watch out, old man,' cried he of the chattering teeth.

Rasmunsen grinned and tightened his aching grip on the sweep. Scores of times had the send of the sea caught the big square stern of the *Alma* and thrown her off from dead before it till the after leach of the spritsail fluttered hollowly, and each time, and only with all his strength, had he forced her back. His grin by then had become fixed, and it disturbed the correspondents to look at him.

They roared down past an isolated rock a hundred yards from shore. From its wave-drenched top a man shrieked wildly, for the instant cutting the storm with his voice. But the next instant the *Alma* was by, and the rock growing a black speck in the troubled froth.

'That settles the Yankee! Where's the sailor?' shouted one of his passengers.

Rasmunsen shot a glance over his shoulder at a black square-sail. He had seen it leap up out of the grey to windward, and for an hour, off and on, had been watching it grow. The sailor had evidently repaired damages and was making up for lost time.

'Look at him come!'

Both passengers stopped chopping ice to watch. Twenty miles of Bennett were behind them—room and to spare for the sea to toss up its mountains toward the sky. Sinking and soaring like a storm-god, the sailor drove by them. The huge sail seemed to grip the boat from the crests of the waves, to tear it bodily out of the water, and fling it crashing and smothering down into the yawning troughs.

'The sea'll never catch him!'

'But he'll r-r-run her nose under!'

Even as they spoke, the black tarpaulin swooped from sight behind a big comber. The next wave rolled over the spot, and the next, but the boat did not reappear. The *Alma* rushed by the place. A little riffraff of oars and boxes was seen. An arm thrust up and a shaggy head broke surface a score of yards away.

For a time there was silence. As the end of the lake came in sight, the waves began to leap aboard with such steady recurrence that the correspondents no longer chopped ice but flung the water out with buckets. Even this would not do, and, after a shouted conference with Rasmunsen, they attacked the baggage. Flour, bacon, beans, blankets, cooking-stove, ropes, odds and ends, everything they could get hands on, flew overboard. The boat acknowledged it at once, taking less water and rising more buoyantly.

'That'll do!' Rasmunsen called sternly, as they applied themselves to the top layer of eggs.

'The h-hell it will!' answered the shivering one, savagely. With the exception of their notes, films, and cameras, they had sacrificed their outfit. He bent over, laid hold of an egg-box, and began to worry it out from under the lashing.

'Drop it! Drop it, I say!'

Rasmunsen had managed to draw his revolver, and with the crook of his arm over the sweep head was taking aim. The correspondent stood up on the thwart, balancing back and forth, his face twisted with menace and speechless anger.

'My God!'

So cried his brother correspondent, hurling himself, face downward, into the bottom of the boat. The *Alma*, under the divided attention of Rasmunsen, had been caught by a great mass of water and whirled around. The after leach hollowed, the sail emptied and jibed, and the boom, sweeping with terrific force across the boat, carried the angry correspondent overboard with a broken back. Mast and sail had gone over the side as well. A drenching sea followed, as the boat lost headway, and Rasmunsen sprang to the bailing bucket.

Several boats hurtled past them in the next half-hour— small boats, boats of their own size, boats afraid, unable to do aught but run madly on. Then a ten-ton barge, at imminent risk of destruction, lowered sail to windward and lumbered down upon them.

'Keep off! Keep off!' Rasmunsen screamed.

But his low gunwale ground against the heavy craft, and the remaining correspondent clambered aboard. Rasmunsen was over the eggs like a cat and in the bow of the *Alma*, striving with numb fingers to bend the hauling-lines together.

'Come on!' a red-whiskered man yelled at him.

'I've a thousand dozen eggs here,' he shouted back. 'Gimme a tow. I'll pay you!'

'Come on!' they howled in chorus.

A big whitecap broke just beyond, washing over the barge and leaving the *Alma* half swamped. The men cast off, cursing him as they ran up their sail. Rasmunsen cursed back and fell to bailing. The mast and sail, like a sea anchor, still fast by the halyards, held the boat head on to wind and sea and gave him a chance to fight the water out.

Three hours later, numbed, exhausted, blathering like a lunatic, but still bailing, he went ashore on an ice-strewn beach near Caribou Crossing. Two men, a government courier and a half-breed voyageur, dragged him out of the surf, saved his cargo, and beached the *Alma*. They were paddling out of the country in a Peterborough, and gave him shelter for the night in their storm-bound camp. Next morning they departed, but he elected to stay by his eggs. And thereafter the name and fame of the man with the thousand dozen eggs began to spread through the land. Gold-seekers who made in before the freeze-up carried the news of his coming. Grizzled old-timers of Forty Mile and Circle City, sour doughs with leathern jaws and bean-calloused stomachs, called up dream memories of chickens and green things at mention of his name. Dyea and Skaguay took an interest in his being, and questioned his progress from every man who came over the passes, while Dawson—golden, omeletless Dawson—fretted and worried, and waylaid every chance arrival for word of him.

But of this Rasmunsen knew nothing. The day after the wreck he patched up the *Alma* and pulled out. A cruel east wind blew in his teeth from Tagish, but he got the oars over the side and bucked manfully into it, though half the time he was drifting backward and chopping ice from the blades. According to the custom of the country, he was driven ashore at Windy Arm; three times on Tagish saw him swamped and beached; and Lake Marsh held him at the freeze-up. The *Alma* was crushed in the jamming of the floes, but the eggs were intact. These he back-tripped two miles across the ice to the shore, where he built a cache, which stood for years after and was pointed out by men who knew.

Half a thousand miles stretched between him and Dawson, and the waterway was closed. But Rasmunsen, with a peculiar tense look in his face, struck back up the lakes on foot. What he suffered on that lone trip, with nought but a single blanket, an axe, and a handful of beans, is not given to ordinary mortals to know. Only the Arctic adventurer may understand. Suffice that he was caught in a blizzard on Chilkoot and left two of his toes with the surgeon at Sheep Camp. Yet he stood on his feet and washed dishes in the scullery of the *Pawona* to the Puget Sound, and from there passed coal on a P.S. boat to San Francisco.

It was a haggard, unkempt man who limped across the shining office floor to raise a second mortgage from the bank people. His hollow cheeks betrayed themselves through the scraggy beard, and his eyes seemed to have retired into deep caverns where they burned with cold fires. His hands were grained from exposure and hard work, and the nails were rimmed with tight-packed dirt and coal-dust. He spoke vaguely of eggs and ice-packs, winds and tides; but when they declined to let him have more than a second thousand, his talk became incoherent, concerning itself chiefly with the price of dogs and dog-food, and such things as snowshoes and moccasins and winter trails. They let him have fifteen hundred, which was more than the cottage warranted, and breathed easier when he scrawled his signature and passed out the door.

Two weeks later he went over Chilkoot with three dog sleds of five dogs each. One team he drove, the two Indians with him driving the others. At Lake Marsh they broke out the cache and loaded up. But there was no trail. He was the first in over the ice, and to him fell the task of packing the snow and hammering away through the rough river jams. Behind him he often observed a camp-fire smoke trickling thinly up through the quiet air, and he wondered why the people did not overtake him. For he was a stranger to the land and did not understand. Nor could he understand his Indians when they tried to explain. This they conceived to be a hardship, but when they balked and refused to break camp of mornings, he drove them to their work at pistol point.

When he slipped through an ice bridge near the White Horse and froze his foot, tender yet and over-sensitive from the previous freezing, the Indians looked for him to lie up. But he sacrificed a blanket, and, with his foot encased in an enormous moccasin, big as a water-bucket, continued to take his regular turn with the front sled. Here was the cruellest work, and they respected him, though on the side they rapped their foreheads with their knuckles and significantly shook their heads. One night they tried to run away, but the zip-zip of his bullets in the snow brought them back, snarling but convinced. Whereupon, being only savage Chilkat men, they put their heads together to kill him; but he slept like a cat, and, waking or sleeping, the chance never came. Often they tried to tell him the import of the smoke wreath in the rear, but he could not comprehend and grew suspicious of them. And when they sulked or shirked, he was quick to let drive at them between the eyes, and quick to cool their heated souls with sight of his ready revolver.

And so it went—with mutinous men, wild dogs, and a trail that broke the heart. He fought the men to stay with him, fought the dogs to keep them away from the eggs, fought the ice, the cold, and the pain of his foot, which would not heal. As fast as the young tissue renewed, it was bitten and seared by the frost, so that a running sore developed, into which he could almost shove his fist. In the mornings, when he first put weight upon it, his head went dizzy, and he was near to fainting with the pain; but later on in the day it usually grew numb, to recommence when he crawled into his blankets and tried to sleep. Yet he, who had been a clerk and sat at a desk all his days, toiled till the Indians were exhausted, and even out-worked the dogs. How hard he worked, how much he suffered, he did not know. Being a man of the one idea, now that the idea had come, it mastered him. In the foreground of his consciousness was Dawson, in the background his thousand dozen eggs, and midway between the two his ego fluttered, striving always to draw them together to a glittering golden point. This golden point was the five thousand dollars, the consummation of the idea and the point of departure for whatever new idea might present itself. For the rest, he was a mere automaton. He was unaware of other things, seeing them as through a glass darkly, and giving them no thought. The work of his hands he did with machine-like wisdom; likewise the work of his head. So the look on his face grew very tense, till even the Indians were afraid of it, and marvelled at the strange white man who had made them slaves and forced them to toil with such foolishness.

Then came a snap on Lake Le Barge, when the cold of outer space smote the tip of the planet, and the force ranged sixty and odd degrees below zero. Here, labouring with open mouth that he might breathe more freely, he chilled his lungs, and for the rest of the trip he was troubled with a dry, hacking cough, especially irritable in smoke of camp or under stress of undue exertion. On the Thirty Mile river he found much open water, spanned by precarious ice bridges and fringed with narrow rim ice, tricky and uncertain. The rim ice was impossible to reckon on, and he dared it without reckoning, falling back on his revolver when his drivers demurred. But on the ice bridges, covered with snow though they were, precautions could be taken. These they crossed on their snowshoes, with long poles, held crosswise in their hands, to which to cling in case of accident. Once over, the dogs were called to follow. And on such a bridge, where the absence of the centre ice was masked by the snow, one of the Indians met his end.

He went through as quickly and neatly as a knife through thin cream, and the current swept him from view down under the stream ice.

That night his mate fled away through the pale moonlight, Rasmunsen futilely puncturing the silence with his revolver—a thing that he handled with more celerity than cleverness. Thirty-six hours later the Indian made a police camp on the Big Salmon.

'Um—um—um funny mans—what you call?—top um head all loose,' the interpreter explained to the puzzled captain. 'Eh? Yep, clazy, much clazy mans. Eggs, eggs, all a time eggs—savvy? Come bime-by.'

It was several days before Rasmunsen arrived, the three sleds lashed together, and all the dogs in a single team. It was awkward, and where the going was bad he was compelled to back-trip it sled by sled, though he managed most of the time, through herculean efforts, to bring all along on the one haul. He did not seem moved when the captain of police told him his name was hitting the high places for Dawson, and was by that time, probably, half-way between Selkirk and Stewart. Nor did he appear interested when informed that the police had broken the trail as far as Pelly; for he had attained to a fatalistic acceptance of all natural dispensations, good or ill. But when they told him that Dawson was in the bitter clutch of famine, he smiled, threw the harness on his dogs, and pulled out.

But it was at his next halt that the mystery of the smoke was explained. With the word at Big Salmon that the trail was broken to Pelly, there was no longer any need for the smoke wreath to linger in his wake; and Rasmunsen, crouching over his lonely fire, saw a motley string of sleds go by. First came the courier and the half-breed who had hauled him out from Bennett; then mail-carriers for Circle City, two sleds of them, and a mixed following of ingoing Klondikers. Dogs and men were fresh and fat, while Rasmunsen and his brutes were jaded and worn down to the skin and bone. They of the smoke wreath had travelled one day in three, resting and reserving their strength for the dash to come when broken trail was met with; while each day he had plunged and floundered forward, breaking the spirit of his dogs and robbing them of their mettle.

As for himself, he was unbreakable. They thanked him kindly for his efforts in their behalf, those fat, fresh men—thanked him kindly, with broad grins and ribald laughter; and now, when he understood, he made no answer. Nor did he cherish silent bitterness. It was immaterial. The idea—the fact behind the idea—was not changed. Here he was and his thousand dozen; there was Dawson; the problem was unaltered.

At the Little Salmon, being short of dog food, the dogs got into his grub, and from there to Selkirk he lived on beans—coarse brown beans, big beans, grossly nutritive, which griped his stomach and doubled him up at two-hour intervals. But the Factor at Selkirk had a notice on the door of the Post to the effect that no steamer had been up the Yukon for two years, and in consequence grub was beyond price. He offered to swap flour, however, at the rate of a cupful of each egg, but Rasmunsen shook his head and hit the trail. Below the Post he managed to buy frozen horse hide for the dogs, the horses having been slain by the Chilkat cattle men, and the scraps and offal preserved by the Indians. He tackled the hide himself, but the hair worked into the bean sores of his mouth, and was beyond endurance.

Here at Selkirk he met the forerunners of the hungry exodus of Dawson, and from there on they crept over the trail, a dismal throng. 'No grub!' was the song they sang. 'No grub, and had to go.' Everybody holding candles for a rise in the spring.' 'Flour dollar 'n a half a pound, and no sellers.'

'Eggs?' one of them answered. 'Dollar apiece, but there ain't none.'

Rasmunsen made a rapid calculation. 'Twelve thousand dollars,' he said aloud.

'Hey?' the man asked.

'Nothing,' he answered, and *mushed* the dogs along.

When he arrived at Stewart River, seventy miles from

Dawson, five of his dogs were gone, and the remainder were falling in the traces. He, also, was in the traces, hauling with what little strength was in him. Even then he was barely crawling along ten miles a day. His cheek-bones and nose, frost-bitten again and again, were turned bloody-black and hideous. The thumb, which was separated from the fingers by the gee-pole, had likewise been nipped and gave him great pain. The monstrous moccasin still encased his foot, and strange pains were beginning to rack the leg. At Sixty Mile, the last beans, which he had been rationing for some time, were finished; yet he steadfastly refused to touch the eggs. He could not reconcile his mind to the legitimacy of it, and staggered and fell along the way to Indian River. Here a fresh-killed moose and an open-handed old-timer gave him and his dogs new strength, and at Ainslie's he felt repaid for it all when a stampede, ripe from Dawson in five hours, was sure he could get a dollar and a quarter for every egg he possessed.

He came up the steep bank by the Dawson barracks with fluttering heart and shaking knees. The dogs were so weak that he was forced to rest them, and, waiting, he leaned limply against the gee-pole. A man, an eminently decorous-looking man, came sauntering by in a great bearskin coat. He glanced at Rasmunsen curiously, then stopped and ran a speculative eye over the dogs and the three lashed sleds.

'What you got?' he asked.

'Eggs,' Rasmunsen answered huskily, hardly able to pitch his voice above a whisper.

'Eggs! Whoopee! Whoopee!' He sprang up into the air, gyrated madly, and finished with half-a-dozen war steps. 'You don't say—all of 'em?'

'All of 'em.'

'Say, you must be the Egg Man.' He walked around and viewed Rasmunsen from the other side. 'Come, now, ain't you the Egg Man?'

Rasmunsen didn't know, but supposed he was, and the man sobered down a bit.

'What d'ye expect to get for 'em?' he asked cautiously.

Rasmunsen became audacious. 'Dollar 'n a half,' he said. 'Done!' the man came back promptly. 'Gimme a dozen.'

'I—I mean a dollar 'n a half apiece,' Rasmunsen hesitatingly explained.

'Sure. I heard you. Make it two dozen. Here's the dust.'

The man pulled out a healthy gold sack the size of a small sausage and knocked it negligently against the gee-pole. Rasmunsen felt a strange trembling in the pit of his stomach, a tickling of the nostrils, and an almost overwhelming desire to sit down and cry. But a curious, wide-eyed crowd was beginning to collect, and man after man was calling out for eggs. He was without scales, but the man with the bearskin coat fetched a pair and obligingly weighed in the dust while Rasmunsen passed out the goods. Soon there was a pushing and shoving and shouldering, and a great clamour. Everybody wanted to buy and to be served first. And as the excitement grew, Rasmunsen cooled down. This would never do. There must be something behind the fact of their buying so eagerly. It would be wiser if he rested first and sized up the market. Perhaps eggs were worth two dollars apiece. Anyway, whenever he wished to sell, he was sure of a dollar and a half. 'Stop!' he cried, when a couple of hundred had been sold. 'No more now. I'm played out. I've got to get a cabin, and then you can come and see me.'

A groan went up at this, but the man with the bearskin coat approved. Twenty-four of the frozen eggs went rattling in his capacious pockets, and he didn't care whether the rest of the town ate or not. Besides, he could see Rasmunsen was on his last legs.

'There's a cabin right around the second corner from the Monte Carlo,' he told him—'the one with the sody-bottle window. It ain't mine, but I've got charge of it. Rents for ten a day and cheap for the money. You move right in, and I'll see you later. Don't forget the sody-bottle window.'

'Tra-la-loo!' he called back a moment later. 'I'm goin' up the hill to eat eggs and dream of home.'

On his way to the cabin, Rasmunsen recollected he was

hungry and bought a small supply of provisions at the N. A. T. & T. store—also a beefsteak at the butcher shop and dried salmon for the dogs. He found the cabin without difficulty, and left the dogs in the harness while he started the fire and got the coffee under way.

'A dollar 'n a half apiece—one thousand dozen—eighteen thousand dollars!' he kept muttering it to himself, over and over, as he went about his work.

As he flopped the steak into the frying-pan the door opened. He turned. It was the man with the bearskin coat. He seemed to come in with determination, as though bound on some explicit errand, but as he looked at Rasmunsen an expression of perplexity came into his face.

'I say—now I say——' he began, then halted.

Rasmunsen wondered if he wanted the rent.

'I say, damn it, you know, them eggs is bad.'

Rasmunsen staggered. He felt as though someone had struck him an astounding blow between the eyes. The walls of the cabin reeled and tilted up. He put out his hand to steady himself and rested it on the stove. The sharp pain and the smell of the burning flesh brought him back to himself.

'I see,' he said slowly, fumbling in his pocket for the sack. 'You want your money back.'

'It ain't the money,' the man said, 'but hain't you got any eggs—good?'

Rasmunsen shook his head. 'You'd better take the money.'

But the man refused and backed away. 'I'll come back,' he said, 'when you've taken stock, and get what's comin'.'

Rasmunsen rolled the chopping-block into the cabin and carried in the eggs. He went about it quite calmly. He took up the hand-axe, and, one by one, chopped the eggs in half. These halves he examined carefully and let fall to the floor. At first he sampled from the different cases, then deliberately emptied one case at a time. The heap on the floor grew larger. The coffee boiled over and the smoke of the burning beefsteak filled the cabin. He chopped steadfastly and monotonously till the last case was finished.

Somebody knocked at the door, knocked again, and let himself in.

'What a mess!' he remarked, as he paused and surveyed the scene.

The severed eggs were beginning to thaw in the heat of the stove, and a miserable odour was growing stronger.

'Must a-happened on the steamer,' he suggested.

Rasmunsen looked at him long and blankly.

'I'm Murray, Big Jim Murray, everybody knows me,' the man volunteered. 'I'm just hearin' your eggs is rotten, and I'm offerin' you two hundred for the batch. They ain't good as salmon, but still they're fair scoffin's for dogs.'

Rasmunsen seemed turned to stone. He did not move. 'You go to hell,' he said passionlessly.

'Now just consider. I pride myself it's a decent price for a mess like that, and it's better 'n nothin'. Two hundred. What you say?'

'You go to hell,' Rasmunsen repeated softly, 'and get out of here.'

Murray gaped with a great awe, then went out carefully, backward, with his eyes fixed on the other's face.

Rasmunsen followed him out and turned the dogs loose. He threw them all the salmon he had bought, and coiled a sled-lashing up in his hand. Then he re-entered the cabin and drew the latch in after him. The smoke from the cindered steak made his eyes smart. He stood on the bunk, passed the lashing over the ridge-pole, and measured the swing-off with his eye. It did not seem to satisfy, for he put the stool on the bunk and climbed upon the stool. He drove a noose in the end of the lashing and slipped his head through. The other end he made fast. Then he kicked the stool out from under.

# THE RACE FOR NUMBER ONE

## I

'HUH! GET on to the glad rags!'

Shorty surveyed his partner with simulated disapproval, and Smoke, vainly attempting to rub the wrinkles out of the pair of trousers he had just put on, was irritated.

'They sure fit you close for a second-hand buy,' Shorty went on. 'What was the tax?'

'One hundred and fifty for the suit,' Smoke answered. 'The man was nearly my own size. I thought it was remarkable reasonable. What are you kicking about?'

'Who? Me? Oh, nothin'. I was just thinkin' it was goin' some for a meat-eater that hit Dawson in an ice-jam, with no grub, one suit of underclothes, a pair of mangy moccasins, an' overalls that looked like they'd ben through the wreck of the *Hesperus*. Pretty gay front, pardner. Pretty gay front. Say——?'

'What do you want now?' Smoke demanded testily.

'What's her name?'

'There isn't any her, my friend. I'm to have dinner at Colonel Bowie's, if you want to know. The trouble with you, Shorty, is you're envious because I'm going into high society and you're not invited.'

'Ain't you some late?' Shorty queried with concern.

'What do you mean?'

'For dinner. They'll be eatin' supper when you get there.'

Smoke was about to explain with elaborate sarcasm when he caught the twinkle in the other's eyes. He went on dressing, with fingers that had lost their deftness, tying a Windsor tie in a bow-knot at the throat of the soft cotton shirt.

'Wish I hadn't sent all my starched shirts to the laundry,' Shorty murmured sympathetically. 'I might a-fitted you out.'

By this time Smoke was straining at a pair of shoes. The thick woollen socks were too thick to go into them. He looked appealingly at Shorty, who shook his head.

'Nope. If I had thin ones I wouldn't lend 'em to you. Back to the moccasins, pardner. You'd sure freeze your toes in skimpy-fangled gear like that.'

'I paid fifteen dollars for them, second-hand,' Smoke lamented.

'I reckon they won't be a man not in moccasins.'

'But there are to be women, Shorty. I'm going to sit down and eat with real live women—Mrs Bowie, and several others, so the Colonel told me.'

'Well, moccasins won't spoil their appetite none,' was Shorty's comment. 'Wonder what the Colonel wants with you?'

'I don't know, unless he's heard about my finding Surprise Lake. It will take a fortune to drain it, and the Guggenheims are out for investment.'

'Reckon that's it. That's right, stick to the moccasins. Gee! That coat is sure wrinkled, an' it fits you a mite too swift. Just peck around at your vittles. If you eat hearty you'll bust through. And if them womenfolks gets to droppin' handkerchiefs, just let 'em lay. Don't do any pickin' up. Whatever you do, don't.'

II

As became a high-salaried expert and the representative of the great house of Guggenheim, Colonel Bowie lived in one of the most magnificent cabins in Dawson. Of squared logs, hand-hewn, it was two stories high, and of such extravagant proportions that it boasted a big living room that was used for a living room and for nothing else.

Here were big bear-skins on the rough board floor, and on the walls horns of moose and caribou. Here roared an open fireplace and a big wood-burning stove. And here Smoke met the social elect of Dawson—not the mere pick-handle millionaires, but the ultra-cream of a mining city whose population had been recruited from all the world—

men like Warburton Jones, the explorer and writer, Captain Consadine of the Mounted Police, Haskell, Gold Commissioner of the North-West Territory, and Baron von Schroeder, an emperor's favourite with an international duelling reputation.

And here, dazzling in evening gown, he met Joy Gastell, whom hitherto he had encountered only on trail, befurred and moccasined. At dinner he found himself beside her.

'I feel like a fish out of water,' he confessed. 'All you folks are so real grand, you know. Besides I never dreamed such Oriental luxury existed in the Klondike. Look at Von Schroeder there. He's actually got a dinner jacket, and Consadine's got a starched shirt. I noticed he wore moccasins just the same. How do you like *my* outfit?'

He moved his shoulders about as if preening himself for Joy's approval.

'It looks as if you'd grown stout since you came over the Pass,' she laughed.

'Wrong. Guess again.'

'It's somebody else's.'

'You win. I bought it for a price from one of the clerks at the A. C. Company.'

'It's a shame clerks are so narrow-shouldered,' she sympathized. 'And you haven't told me what you think of *my* outfit.'

'I can't,' he said. 'I'm out of breath. I've been living on trail too long. This sort of thing comes to me with a shock, you know. I'd quite forgotten that women have arms and shoulders. Tomorrow morning, like my friend Shorty, I'll wake up and know it's all a dream. Now, the last time I saw you on Squaw Creek——'

'I was just a squaw,' she broke in.

'I hadn't intended to say that. I was remembering that it was on Squaw Creek that I discovered you had feet.'

'And I can never forget that you saved them for me,' she said. 'I've been wanting to see you ever since to thank you——' (He shrugged his shoulders deprecatingly.) 'And that's why you are here to-night——'

'You asked the Colonel to invite me?'

'No! Mrs Bowie. And I asked her to let me have you at table. And here's my chance. Everybody's talking. Listen, and don't interrupt. You know Mono Creek?'

'Yes.'

'It has turned out rich—dreadfully rich. They estimate the claims as worth a million or more apiece. It was only located the other day.'

'I remember the stampede.'

'Well, the whole creek was staked to the sky-line, and all the feeders, too. And yet, right now, on the main creek, Number Three below Discovery is unrecorded. The creek was so far away from Dawson that the Commissioner allowed sixty days for recording after location. Every claim was recorded except Number Three Below. It was staked by Cyrus Johnson. And that was all. Cyrus Johnson has disappeared. Whether he died, whether he went down river or up, nobody knows. Anyway, in six days, the time for recording will be up. Then the man who stakes it, and reaches Dawson first and records it, gets it.'

'A million dollars,' Smoke murmured.

'Gilchrist, who has the next claim below, has got six hundred dollars in a single pan off bedrock. He's burned one hole down, and the claim on the other side is even richer. I know.'

'But why doesn't everybody know?' Smoke queried sceptically.

'They're beginning to know. They kept it secret for a long time, and it is only now that it's coming out. Good dog-teams will be at a premium in another twenty-four hours. Now, you've got to get away as decently as you can as soon as dinner is over. I've arranged it. An Indian will come with a message for you. You read it, let on that you're very much put out, make your excuses, and get away.'

'I—er—I fail to follow.'

'Ninny!' she exclaimed in a half-whisper. 'What you must do is to get out to-night and hustle dog-teams. I know of two. There's Hanson's team, seven big Hudson Bay dogs —he's holding them at four hundred each. That's top price to-night, but it won't be to-morrow. And Sitka Charley has eight Malemutes he's asking thirty-five hundred for. To-morrow he'll laugh at an offer of five thousand. Then you've got your own team of dogs. And you'll have to buy several more teams. That's your work to-night. Get the best. It's dogs as well as men that will win this race. It's a hundred and ten miles, and you'll have to relay as frequently as you can.'

'Oh, I see, you want me to go in for it,' Smoke drawled.

'If you haven't the money for dogs, I'll——'

She faltered, but before she could continue Smoke was speaking.

'I can buy the dogs. But—er—aren't you afraid this is gambling?'

'After your exploits at roulette in the Elkhorn,' she retorted, 'I'm not afraid that you're afraid. It's a sporting proposition, if that's what you mean. A race for a million, and with some of the stiffest dog-mushers and travellers in the country entered against you. They haven't entered yet, but by this time to-morrow they will, and dogs will be worth what the richest man can afford to pay. Big Olaf is in town. He came up from Circle City last month. He is one of the most terrible dog-mushers in the country, and if he enters he will be your most dangerous man. Arizona Bill is another. He's been a professional freighter and mail-carrier for years. If he goes in, interest will be centred on him and Big Olaf.'

'And you intend me to come along as a sort of dark horse.'

'Exactly. And it will have its advantages. You will not be supposed to stand a show. After all, you know, you are still classed as a *chechaquo*. You haven't seen the four seasons go around. Nobody will take notice of you until you come into the home stretch in the lead.'

'It's on the home stretch the dark horse is to show up its classy form, eh?'

She nodded, and continued earnestly.

'Remember, I shall never forgive myself for the trick I played on the Squaw Creek Stampede until you win this

Mono Claim. And if any man can win this race against the old-timers, it's you.'

It was the way she said it. He felt warm all over, and in his heart and head. He gave her a quick searching look, involuntary and serious, and for the moment that her eyes met his steadily, ere they fell, it seemed to him that he read something of vaster import than the claim Cyrus Johnson had failed to record.

'I'll do it,' he said. 'I'll win it.'

The glad light in her eyes seemed to promise a greater need than all the gold in the Mono claim. He was aware of a movement of her hand in her lap next to his. Under the screen of the tablecloth he thrust his own hand across and met a firm grip of woman's fingers that sent another wave of warmth through him.

'What will Shorty say?' was the thought that flashed whimsically through his mind as he withdrew his hand. He glanced almost jealously at the faces of Von Schroeder and Jones, and wondered if they had not divined the remarkableness and deliciousness of this woman who sat beside him.

He was aroused by her voice, and realized that she had been speaking for some moments.

'So you see, Arizona Bill is a white Indian,' she was saying. 'And Big Olaf is—a bear wrestler, a king of the snows, a mighty savage. He can out-travel and out-endure an Indian, and he's never known any other life but that of the wild and the frost.'

'Who's that?' Captain Consadine broke in from across the table.

'Big Olaf,' she answered. 'I was just telling Mr Bellew what a traveller he is.'

'You're right,' the Captain's voice boomed. 'Big Olaf is the greatest traveller in the Yukon. I'd back him against Old Nick himself for snow-bucking and ice-travel. He brought in the government despatches in 1895, and he did it after two couriers were frozen on Chilcoot and the third drowned in the open water of Thirty Mile.'

## III

Smoke had travelled in a leisurely fashion up to Mono Creek, fearing to tire his dogs before the big race. Also, he had familiarized himself with every mile of the trail and located his relay camps. So many men had entered the race, that the hundred and ten miles of its course was almost a continuous village. Relay camps were everywhere along the trail. Von Schroeder, who had gone in purely for the sport, had no less than eleven dog teams—a fresh one for every ten miles. Arizona Bill had been forced to content himself with eight teams. Big Olaf had seven, which was the complement of Smoke. In addition, over two-score of other men were in the running. Not every day, even in the golden north, was a million dollars the prize for a dog race. The country had been swept of dogs. No animal of speed and endurance escaped the fine-tooth comb that had raked the creeks and camps, and the prices of dogs had doubled and quadrupled in the course of the frantic speculation.

Number Three Below Discovery was ten miles up Mono Creek from its mouth. The remaining hundred miles was to be run on the frozen breast of the Yukon. On Number Three itself were fifty tents and over three hundred dogs. The old stakes, blazed and scrawled sixty days before by Cyrus Johnson, still stood, and every man had gone over the boundaries of the claim again and again, for the race with the dogs was to be preceded by a foot and obstacle race. Each man had to re-locate the claim for himself, and this meant that he must place two centre-stakes and four corner-stakes and cross the creek twice, before he could start for Dawson with his dogs.

Furthermore, there were to be no 'sooners'. Not until the stroke of midnight of Friday night was the claim open for re-location, and not until the stroke of midnight could a man plant a stake. This was the ruling of the Gold Commissioner at Dawson, and Captain Consadine had sent up a squad of mounted police to enforce it. Discussion had arisen about the difference between sun-time and police-time, but Consadine had sent forth his fiat that police time went, and, further, that it was the watch of Lieutenant Pollock that went.

The Mono trail ran along the level creek-bed, and, less than two feet in width, was like a groove, walled on either side by the snow-fall of months. The problem of how forty-odd sleds and three hundred dogs were to start in so narrow a course was in everybody's mind.

'Huh!' said Shorty. 'It's goin' to be the gosh-dangdest mix-up that ever was. I can't see no way out, Smoke, except main strength an' sweat an' plough through. If the whole creek was glare-ice they ain't room for a dozen teams abreast. I got a hunch right now they's goin' to be a heap of scrappin' before they get strung out. An' if any of it comes our way you got to let me do the punchin'.'

Smoke squared his shoulders and laughed non-committally.

'No, you don't!' his partner cried in alarm. 'No matter what happens, you don't dast hit. You can't handle dogs a hundred miles with a busted knuckle, an' that's what'll happen if you land on somebody's jaw.'

Smoke nodded his head.

'You're right, Shorty. I couldn't risk the chance.'

'An' just remember,' Shorty went on, 'that I got to do all the shovin' for them first ten miles an' you got to take it easy as you can. I'll sure jerk you through to the Yukon. After that it's up to you an' the dogs. Say—what d'ye think Schroeder's scheme is? He's got his first team a quarter of a mile down the creek an' he'll know it by a green lantern. But we got him skinned. Me for the red flare every time.'

## IV

The day had been clear and cold, but a blanket of cloud formed across the face of the sky and the night came on warm and dark, with the hint of snow impending. The thermometer registered fifteen below zero, and in the Klondike winter fifteen below is esteemed very warm.

At a few minutes before midnight, leaving Shorty with the dogs five hundred yards down the creek, Smoke joined the racers on Number Three. There were forty-five of them waiting the start for the thousand-thousand dollars Cyrus Johnson had left lying in the frozen gravel. Each man carried six stakes and a heavy wooden mallet, and was clad in a smock-like *parka* of heavy cotton drill.

Lieutenant Pollock, in a big bearskin coat, looked at his watch by the light of a fire. It lacked a minute of midnight.

'Make ready,' he said, as he raised a revolver in his right hand and watched the second hand tick around.

Forty-five hoods were thrown back from the *parkas*. Forty-five pairs of hands unmittened, and forty-five pairs of moccasins pressed tensely into the packed snow. Also, forty-five stakes were thrust into the snow, and the same number of mallets lifted in the air.

The shots ran out, and the mallets fell. Cyrus Johnson's right to the million had expired. To prevent confusion, Lieutenant Pollock had insisted that the lower centre-stake be driven first, next the south-eastern; and so on around the four sides, including the upper centre-stake on the way.

Smoke drove in his stake and was away with the leading dozen. Fires had been lighted at the corners, and by each fire stood a policeman, list in hand checking off the names of the runners. A man was supposed to call out his name and show his face. There was to be no staking by proxy while the real racer was off and away down the creek.

At the first corner, beside Smoke's stake, Von Schroeder placed his. The mallets struck at the same instant. As they hammered, more arrived from behind and with such impetuosity as to get in one another's way and cause jostling and shoving. Squirming through the press and calling his name to the policeman, Smoke saw the Baron, struck in collision by one of the rushers, hurled clean off his feet into the snow. But Smoke did not wait. Others were still ahead of him. By the light of the vanishing fire he was certain that he saw the back, hugely looming, of Big Olaf, and at the south-western corner Big Olaf and he drove their stakes side by side.

It was no light work, this preliminary obstacle race. The boundaries of the claim totalled nearly a mile, and most of it was over the uneven surface of a snow-covered, nigger-head flat. All about Smoke men tripped and fell, and several times he pitched forward himself, jarringly, on hands and knees. Once, Big Olaf fell so immediately in front of him as to bring him down on top.

The upper centre-stake was driven by the edge of the bank, and down the bank the racers plunged, across the frozen creek-bed, and up the other side. Here, as Smoke clambered, a hand gripped his ankle and jerked him back. In the flickering light of a distant fire, it was impossible to see who had played the trick. But Arizona Bill, who had been treated similarly, rose to his feet and drove his fist into the offender's face. Smoke saw and heard as he was scrambling to his feet, but before he could make another lunge for the bank a fist dropped him half-stunned into the snow. He staggered up, located the man, half-swung a hook for his jaw, then remembered Shorty's warning and refrained. The next moment, struck below the knees by a hurtling body, he went down again.

It was a foretaste of what would happen when the men reached their sleds. Men were pouring over the other bank and piling into the jam. They swarmed up the bank in bunches, and in bunches were dragged back by their impatient fellows. More blows were struck, curses rose from the panting chests of those who still had wind to spare, and Smoke, curiously visioning the face of Joy Gastell, hoped that the mallets would not be brought into play. Overthrown, trod upon, groping in the snow for his lost stakes, he at last crawled out of the crush and attacked the bank farther along. Others were doing this, and it was his luck to have many men in advance of him in the race for the north-western corner.

Down to the fourth corner, he tripped midway and in the long sprawling fall lost his remaining stake. For five minutes he groped in the darkness before he found it, and all the time the panting runners were passing him. From the last corner to the creek he began overtaking men for whom the mile-run had been too much. In the creek itself Bedlam had broken loose. A dozen sleds were piled up and overturned, and nearly a hundred dogs were locked in combat. Among them men struggled, tearing the tangled animals apart, or beating them apart with clubs. In the fleeting glimpse he caught of it, Smoke wondered if he had ever seen a Doré grotesquery to compare.

Leaping down the bank beyond the glutted passage, he gained the hard-footing of the sled-trail and made better time. Here, in packed harbours beside the narrow trail, sleds and men waited for runners that were still behind. From the rear came the whine and rush of dogs, and Smoke had barely time to leap aside into the deep snow. A sled tore past, and he made out the man, kneeling and shouting madly. Scarcely was it by when it stopped with a crash of battle. The excited dogs of a harboured sled, resenting the passing animals, had got out of hand and sprung upon them.

Smoke plunged around and by. He could see the green lantern of Von Schroeder, and, just below it, the red flare that marked his own team. Two men were guarding Schroeder's dogs, with short clubs interposed between them and the trail.

'Come on, you Smoke! Come on, you Smoke!' he could hear Shorty calling anxiously.

'Coming!' he gasped.

By the red flare he could see the snow torn up and trampled, and from the way his partner breathed he knew a battle had been fought. He staggered to the sled, and in a moment he was falling on it. Shorty's whip snapped as he yelled:

'Mush! you devils! Mush!'

The dogs sprang into the breast-bands, and the sled jerked abruptly ahead. They were big animals—Hanson's prize team of Hudson Bays—and Smoke had selected them for the first stage, which included the ten miles of Mono, the heavy-going of the cut-off across the flat at the mouth, and the first ten miles of the Yukon stretch.

'How many are ahead? he asked.

'You shut up an' save your wind,' Shorty answered. 'Hi! you brutes! Hit her up! Hit her up!'

He was running behind the sled, towing on a short rope. Smoke could not see him; nor could he see the sled on which he lay at full length. The fires had been left in the rear, and they were tearing through a wall of blackness as fast as the dogs could spring into it. This blackness was almost sticky, so nearly did it take on the seeming of substance.

Smoke felt the sled heel up on one runner as it rounded an invisible curve, and from ahead came the snarl of beasts and the oaths of men. This was known afterward as the Barnes-Slocum Jam. It was the teams of these two men which first collided, and into it, at full career, piled Smoke's seven big fighters. Scarcely more than semi-domesticated wolves, the excitement of that night on Mono Creek had sent every dog fighting-mad. The Klondike dogs, driven without reins, cannot be stopped except by voice, so that there was no stopping this glut of struggle that heaped itself between the narrow rims of the creek. From behind, sled after sled hurled into the turmoil. Men who had their teams nearly extricated were overwhelmed by fresh avalanches of dogs—each animal well-fed, well-rested, and ripe for battle.

'It's knock down an' drag out an' plough through!' Shorty yelled in his partner's ear. 'An' watch out for your knuckles! You drag out an' let me do the punchin'!'

What happened in the next half-hour Smoke never distinctly remembered. At the end he emerged exhausted, sobbing for breath, his jaw sore from a fist blow, his shoulder aching from the bruise of a club, the blood running warmly down one leg from the rip of a dog's fangs, and both sleeves of his *parka* torn to shreds. As in a dream, while the battle still raged behind, he helped Shorty reharness the dogs. One, dying, they cut from the traces, and in the darkness they felt their way to the repair of the disrupted harnesses.

'Now you lie down an' get your wind back,' Shorty commanded.

And through the darkness the dogs sped, with unabated breath, down Mono Creek, across the long cut-off, and to the Yukon. Here, at the junction with the main river-trail, somebody had lighted a fire, and here Shorty said good-bye. By the light of the fire, as the sled leaped behind the flying dogs, Smoke caught another of the unforgettable pictures of the North Land. It was of Shorty, swaying and sinking down limply in the snow, yelling his parting encouragement, one eye blackened and closed, knuckles bruised and broken, and one arm, ripped and fang-torn, gushing forth a steady stream of blood.

## V

'How many ahead?' Smoke asked, as he dropped his tired Hudson Bays and sprang on the waiting sled at the first relay station.

'I counted eleven,' the man called after him, for he was already away behind the leaping dogs.

Fifteen miles they were to carry him on the next stage, which would fetch him to the mouth of White River. There were nine of them, but they composed his weakest team. The twenty-five miles between White River and Sixty Mile he had broken into two stages because of ice-jams, and here two of his heaviest, toughest teams were stationed.

He lay on the sled at full length, face-down, holding on with both hands. Whenever the dogs slackened from topmost speed he rose to his knees, and, yelling and urging, clinging precariously with one hand, threw his whip into them. Poor team that it was, he passed two sleds before White River was reached. Here, at the freeze-up, a jam had piled a barrier allowing the open water, that formed for half a mile below, to freeze smoothly. This smooth stretch enabled the racers to make flying exchanges of sleds, and down all the course they had placed their relays below the jams.

Over the jam and out on to the smooth, Smoke tore along, calling loudly, 'Billy! Billy!'

Billy heard and answered, and by the light of the many

fires on the ice, Smoke saw a sled swing in from the side
and come abreast. Its dogs were fresh and overhauled his.
As the sleds swerved toward each other he leaped across
and Billy promptly rolled off.

'Where's Big Olaf?' Smoke cried.

'Leading!' Billy's voice answered; and the fires were left
behind and Smoke was again flying through the wall of
blackness.

In the jams of that relay, where the way led across a
chaos of up-ended ice-cakes, and where Smoke slipped off
the forward end of the sled and with a haul-rope toiled
behind the wheel-dog, he passed three sleds. Accidents had
happened, and he could hear the men cutting out dogs and
mending harnesses.

Among the jams of the next short relay into Sixty Mile,
he passed two more teams. And that he might know ade-
quately what had happened to them, one of his own dogs
wrenched a shoulder, was unable to keep up, and was
dragged in the harness. Its team-mates, angered, fell upon
it with their fangs, and Smoke was forced to club them off
with the heavy butt of his whip. As he cut the injured
animal out, he heard the whining cries of dogs behind him
and the voice of a man that was familiar. It was Von
Schroeder. Smoke called a warning to prevent a rear-end
collision, and the Baron, hawing his animals and swinging
on the gee-pole, went by a dozen feet to the side. Yet so
impenetrable was the blackness that Smoke heard him
pass but never saw him.

On the smooth stretch of ice beside the trading post at
Sixty Mile, Smoke overtook two more sleds. All had just
changed teams, and for five minutes they ran abreast, each
man on his knees and pouring whip and voice into the
maddened dogs. But Smoke had studied out that portion
of the trail, and now marked the tall pine on the bank that
showed faintly in the light of the many fires. Below that
pine was not merely darkness, but an abrupt cessation of
the smooth stretch. There the trail, he knew, narrowed to a
single sled-width. Leaning out ahead, he caught the haul-
rope and drew his leaping sled up to the wheel-dog. He

caught the animal by the hind-legs and threw it. With a snarl of rage it tried to slash him with its fangs, but was dragged on by the rest of the team. Its body proved an efficient brake, and the two other teams, still abreast, dashed ahead into the darkness for the narrow way.

Smoke heard the crash and uproar of their collision, released his wheeler, sprang to the gee-pole, and urged his team to the right into the soft snow where the straining animals wallowed to their necks. It was exhausting work, but he won by the tangled teams and gained the hard-packed trail beyond.

## VI

On the relay out of Sixty Mile, Smoke had next to his poorest team, and though the going was good, he had set it a short fifteen miles. Two more teams would bring him in to Dawson and to the Gold-Recorder's office, and Smoke had selected his best animals for the last two stretches. Sitka Charley himself waited with the eight Malemutes that would jerk Smoke along for twenty miles, and for the finish, with a fifteen-mile run, was his own team—the team he had had all winter and which had been with him in the search for Surprise Lake.

The two men he had left entangled at Sixty Mile failed to overtake him, and, on the other hand, his team failed to overtake any of the three that still led. His animals were willing, though they lacked stamina and speed, and little urging was needed to keep them jumping into it at their best. There was nothing for Smoke to do but to lie face-downward and hold on. Now and again he would plunge out of the darkness into the circle of light about a blazing fire, catch a glimpse of furred men standing by harnessed and waiting dogs, and plunge into the darkness again. Mile after mile, with only the grind and jar of the runners in his ears, he sped on. Almost automatically he kept his place as the sled bumped ahead or half-tilted and heeled on the swings and swerves of the bends. First one, and then another, without apparent rhyme or reason, three faces limned themselves on his consciousness: Joy Gastell's, laughing and audacious; Shorty's, battered and exhausted by the struggle down Mono Creek; and John Bellew's, seamed and rigid, as if cast in iron, so unrelenting was its severity. And sometimes Smoke wanted to shout aloud, to chant a pæan of savage exultation, as he remembered the office of the *Billow* and the serial story of San Francisco which he had left unfinished, along with the other fripperies of those empty days.

The grey twilight of morning was breaking as he exchanged his weary dogs for the eight fresh Malemutes. Lighter animals than Hudson Bays, they were capable of greater speed, and they ran with the supple tiredlessness of true wolves. Sitka Charley called out the order of the teams ahead. Big Olaf led, Arizona Bill was second, and Von Schroeder third. These were the three best men in the country. In fact, ere Smoke left Dawson, the popular betting had placed them in that order. While they were racing for a million, at least half a million had been staked by others on the outcome of the race. No one had bet on Smoke, who, despite his several known exploits, was still accounted a *chechaquo* with much to learn.

As daylight strengthened, Smoke caught sight of a sled ahead, and, in half an hour, his own lead-dog was leaping at its tail. Not until the man turned his head to exchange greetings, did Smoke recognize him as Arizona Bill. Von Schroeder had evidently passed him. The trail, hard packed, ran too narrowly through the soft snow, and for another half-hour Smoke was forced to stay in the rear. Then they topped an ice-jam and struck a smooth stretch below, where were a number of relay camps and where the snow was packed widely. On his knees, swinging his whip and yelling, Smoke drew abreast. He noted that Arizona Bill's right arm hung dead at his side, and that he was compelled to pour leather with his left hand. Awkward as it was, he had no hand left with which to hold on, and frequently he had to cease from the whip and clutch to save himself from falling off. Smoke remembered the scrimmage in the creek

9*

bed at Three Below Discovery, and understood. Shorty's advice had been sound.

'What happened?' Smoke asked, as he began to pull ahead.

'I don't know,' Arizona Bill answered. 'I think I threw my shoulder out in the scrapping.'

He dropped behind very slowly, though when the last relay station was in sight he was fully half a mile in the rear. Ahead, bunched together, Smoke could see Big Olaf and Von Schroeder. Again Smoke arose to his knees, and he lifted his jaded dogs into a burst of speed such as a man only can who has the proper instinct for dog-driving. He drew up close to the tail of Von Schroeder's sled, and in this order the three sleds dashed out on the smooth going, below a jam, where many men and many dogs waited. Dawson was fifteen miles away.

Von Schroeder, with his ten-mile relays, had changed five miles back and would change five miles ahead. So he held on, keeping his dogs at full leap. Big Olaf and Smoke made flying changes, and their fresh teams immediately regained what had been lost to the baron. Big Olaf led past, and Smoke followed into the narrow trail beyond.

'Still good, but not so good,' Smoke paraphrased Spencer to himself.

Of Von Schroeder, now behind, he had no fear; but ahead was the greatest dog-driver in the country. To pass him seemed impossible. Again and again, many times, Smoke forced his leader to the other's sled-trail, and each time Big Olaf let out another link and drew away. Smoke contented himself with taking the pace, and hung on grimly. The race was not lost until one or the other won, and in fifteen miles many things could happen.

Three miles from Dawson something did happen. To Smoke's surprise, Big Olaf rose up and with oaths and leather proceeded to fetch out the last ounce of effort in his animals. It was a spurt that should have been reserved for the last hundred yards instead of being begun three miles from the finish. Sheer dog-killing that it was, Smoke followed. His own team was superb. No dogs on the Yukon had had harder work or were in better condition. Besides, Smoke had toiled with them, and eaten and bedded with them, and he knew each dog as an individual, and how best to win in to the animal's intelligence and extract its last shred of willingness.

They topped a small jam and struck the smooth-going below. Big Olaf was barely fifty feet ahead. A sled shot out from the side and drew in toward him, and Smoke understood Big Olaf's terrific spurt. He had tried to gain a lead for the change. This fresh team that waited to jerk him down the home stretch had been a private surprise of his. Even the men who had backed him to win had had no knowledge of it.

Smoke strove desperately to pass during the exchange of sleds. Lifting his dogs to the effort, he ate up the intervening fifty feet. With urging and pouring of leather, he went to the side and on until his lead-dog was jumping abreast of Big Olaf's wheeler. On the other side, abreast, was the relay sled. At the speed they were going, Big Olaf did not dare the flying leap. If he missed and fell off, Smoke would be in the lead and the race would be lost.

Big Olaf tried to spurt ahead, and he lifted his dogs magnificently, but Smoke's leader still continued to jump beside Big Olaf's wheeler. For half a mile the three sleds tore and bounced along side by side. The smooth stretch was nearing its end when Big Olaf took the chance. As the flying sleds swerved towards each other, he leaped, and the instant he struck he was on his knees, with whip and voice spurting the fresh team. The smooth pinched out into the narrow trail, and he jumped his dogs ahead and into it with a lead of barely a yard.

A man was not beaten until he was beaten, was Smoke's conclusion, and drive no matter how, Big Olaf failed to shake him off. No team Smoke had driven that night could have stood such a killing pace and kept up with fresh dogs —no team save this one. Nevertheless, the pace *was* killing it, and as they began to round the bluff at Klondike City, he could feel the pitch of strength going out of his animals.

Almost imperceptibly they lagged, and foot by foot Big Olaf drew away until he led by a score of yards.

A great cheer went up from the population of Klondike City assembled on the ice. Here the Klondike entered the Yukon, and half a mile away, across the Klondike, on the north bank, stood Dawson. An outburst of madder cheering arose, and Smoke caught a glimpse of a sled shooting out to him. He recognized the splendid animals that drew it. They were Joy Gastell's. And Joy Gastell drove them. The hood of her squirrel-skin *parka* was tossed back, revealing the cameo-like oval of her face outlined against her heavily-massed hair. Mittens had been discarded, and with bare hands she clung to whip and sled.

'Jump!' she cried, as her leader snarled at Smoke's.

Smoke struck the sled behind her. It rocked violently from the impact of his body, but she was full up on her knees and swinging the whip.

'Hi! You! Mush on! Chook! Chook!' she was crying, and the dogs whined and yelped in eagerness of desire and effort to overtake Big Olaf.

And then, as the lead-dog caught the tail of Big Olaf's sled, and yard by yard drew up abreast, the great crowd on the Dawson bank went mad. It *was* a great crowd, for the men had dropped their tools on all the creeks and come down to see the outcome of the race, and a dead heat at the end of a hundred and ten miles justified any madness.

'When you're in the lead I'm going to drop off!' Joy cried out over her shoulder.

Smoke tried to protest.

'And watch out for the dip curve half way up the bank,' she warned.

Dog by dog, separated by half a dozen feet, the two teams were running abreast. Big Olaf, with whip and voice, held his own for a minute. Then, slowly, an inch at a time, Joy's leader began to forge past.

'Get ready!' she cried to Smoke. 'I'm going to leave you in a minute. Get the whip.'

And as he shifted his hand to clutch the whip, they heard Big Olaf roar a warning, but too late. His lead-dog, incensed at being passed, swerved in to the attack. His fangs struck Joy's leader on the flank. The rival teams flew at one another's throats. The sleds overran the fighting brutes and capsized. Smoke struggled to his feet and tried to lift Joy up. But she thrust him from her, crying:

'Go!'

On foot, already fifty feet in advance, was Big Olaf, still intent on finishing the race. Smoke obeyed, and when the two men reached the foot of the Dawson bank, he was at the other's heels. But up the bank Big Olaf lifted his body hugely, regaining a dozen feet.

Five blocks down the main street was the Gold-Recorder's office. The street was packed as for the witnessing of a parade. Not so easily this time did Smoke gain to his giant rival, and when he did he was unable to pass. Side by side they ran along the narrow aisle between the solid walls of fur-clad, cheering men. Now one, now the other, with great convulsive jerks, gained an inch or so only to lose it immediately after.

If the pace had been a killing one for their dogs, the one they now set themselves was no less so. But they were racing for a million dollars and great honour in Yukon Country. The only outside impression that came to Smoke on that last mad stretch was one of astonishment that there should be so many people in the Klondike. He had never seen them all at once before.

He felt himself involuntarily lag, and Big Olaf sprang a full stride in the lead. To Smoke it seemed that his heart would burst, while he had lost all consciousness of his legs. He knew they were flying under him, but he did not know how he continued to make them fly, nor how he put even greater pressure of will upon them and compelled them again to carry him to his giant competitor's side.

The open door of the Recorder's office appeared ahead of them. Both men made a final, futile spurt. Neither could draw away from the other, and side by side they hit the doorway, collided violently, and fell headlong on the office door.

They sat up, but were too exhausted to rise. Big Olaf,

the sweat pouring from him, breathing with tremendous, painful gasps, pawed the air and vainly tried to speak. Then he reached out his hand with unmistakable meaning; Smoke extended his, and they shook.

'It's a dead heat,' Smoke could hear the Recorder saying, but it was as if in a dream, and the voice was very thin and very far away. 'And all I can say is that you both win. You'll have to divide the claim between you. You're partners.'

Their two arms pumped up and down as they ratified the decision. Big Olaf nodded his head with great emphasis, and spluttered. At last he got it out.

'You damn *chechaquo*,' was what he said, but in the saying of it was admiration. 'I don't know how you done it, but you did.'

Outside the great crowd was noisily massed, while the office was packing and jamming. Smoke and Big Olaf essayed to rise, and each helped the other to his feet. Smoke found his legs weak under him, and staggered drunkenly. Big Olaf tottered towards him.

'I'm sorry my dogs jumped yours.'

'It couldn't be helped,' Smoke panted back. 'I heard you yell.'

'Say,' Big Olaf went on with shining eyes. 'That girl—one damn fine girl, eh?'

'One damn fine girl,' Smoke agreed.

# THE SCORN OF WOMEN

## I

ONCE FREDA and Mrs Eppingwell clashed. Now Freda was a Greek girl and a dancer. At least she purported to be Greek; but this was doubted by many, for her classic face had over-much strength in it, and the tides of hell which rose in her eyes made at rare moments her ethnology the more dubious. To a few—men—this sight had been vouchsafed, and though long years may have passed, they have not forgotten, nor will they ever forget. She never talked of herself, so that it were well to let it go down that when in repose, expurgated, Greek she certainly was. Her furs were the most magnificent in all the country from Chilcoot to St Michael's, and her name was common on the lips of men. But Mrs Eppingwell was the wife of a captain; also a social constellation of the first magnitude, the path of her orbit marking the most select coterie in Dawson—a coterie captioned by the profane as the 'official clique'. Sitka Charley had travelled trail with her once, when famine drew tight and a man's life was less than a cup of flour, and his judgment placed her above all women. Sitka Charley was an Indian; his criteria were primitive; but his word was fiat, and his verdict a hall-mark in every camp under the circle.

These two women were man-conquering, man-subduing machines, each in her own way, and their ways were different. Mrs Eppingwell ruled in her own house, and at the Barracks, where were younger sons galore, to say nothing of the chiefs of the police, the executive, and the judiciary. Freda ruled down in the town; but the men she ruled were the same who functioned socially at the Barracks or were fed tea and canned preserves at the hand of Mrs Eppingwell in her hillside cabin of rough-hewn logs. Each knew the other existed; but their lives were apart as the Poles, and while they must have heard stray bits of news and were curious, they were never known to ask a question. And there would have been no trouble had not a free lance in the shape of the model-woman come into the land on the first ice, with a spanking dog-team and a cosmopolitan reputation. Loraine Lisznayi—alliterative, dramatic, and Hungarian—precipitated the strife, and because of her Mrs Eppingwell left her hillside and invaded Freda's domain, and Freda likewise went up from the town to spread confusion and embarrassment at the Governor's ball.

All of which may be ancient history so far as the Klondike is concerned, but very few, even in Dawson, know the inner truth of the matter; nor beyond those few are there any fit to measure the wife of the captain or the Greek dancer. And that all are now permitted to understand, let honour be accorded Sitka Charley. From his lips fell the main facts in the screed herewith presented. It ill befits that Freda herself should have waxed confidential to a mere scribbler of words, or that Mrs Eppingwell made mention of the things which happened. They may have spoken, but it is unlikely.

## II

Floyd Vanderlip was a strong man, apparently. Hard work and hard grub had no terrors for him, as his early history in the country attested. In danger he was a lion, and when he held in check half a thousand starving men, as he once did, it was remarked that no cooler eye ever took the glint of sunshine on a rifle-sight. He had but one weakness, and even that, rising from out his strength, was of a negative sort. His parts were strong, but they lacked co-ordination. Now it happened that while his centre of amativeness was pronounced, it had lain mute and passive during the years he lived on moose and salmon and chased glowing Eldorados over chill divides. But when he finally blazed the corner-post and centre-stakes on one of the richest Klondike claims, it began to quicken; and when he took his place in society, a full-fledged Bonanza King, it awoke and took charge of him. He suddenly recollected a girl in the States, and it came to him quite forcibly, not only that she might be waiting for him, but that a wife was a very pleasant acquisition for a man who lived some several degrees north of 53. So he wrote an appropriate note, enclosed a letter of credit generous enough to cover all expenses, including trousseau and chaperon, and addressed it to one Flossie. Flossie? One could imagine the rest. However, after that he built a comfortable cabin on his claim, bought another in Dawson, and broke the news to his friends.

And just here is where the lack of co-ordination came into play. The waiting was tedious, and having been long denied, the amative element could not brook further delay. Flossie was coming; but Loraine Lisznayi was here. And not only was Loraine Lisznayi here, but her cosmopolitan reputation was somewhat the worse for wear, and she was not exactly so young as when she posed in the studios of artist queens and received at her door the cards of cardinals and princes. Also, her finances were unhealthy. Having run the gamut in her time, she was now not averse to trying conclusions with a Bonanza King whose wealth was such that he could not guess it within six figures. Like a wise soldier casting about after years of service for a comfortable billet, she had come into the Northland to be married. So, one day, her eyes flashed up into Floyd Vanderlip's as he was buying table linen for Flossie in the P. C. Company's store, and the thing was settled out of hand.

When a man is free much may go unquestioned, which, should he be rash enough to cumber himself with domestic ties, society will instantly challenge. Thus it was with Floyd Vanderlip. Flossie was coming, and a low buzz went up when Loraine Lisznayi rode down the main street behind his wolf-dogs. She accompanied the lady reporter of the *Kansas City Star* when photographs were taken of his Bonanza properties, and watched the genesis of a six-column article. At that time they were dined royally in Flossie's cabin, on Flossie's table linen. Likewise there were comings and goings, and junketing, all perfectly proper, by the way, which caused the men to say sharp things and the women to be spiteful. Only Mrs Eppingwell did not hear. The distant hum of wagging tongues rose faintly, but she was prone to believe good of people and to close her ears to evil; so she paid no heed.

Not so with Freda. She had no cause to love men, but, by some strange alchemy of her nature, her heart went out to women—to women whom she had less cause to love. And her heart went out to Flossie, even then travelling the Long Trail and facing into the bitter North to meet a man who might not wait for her. A shrinking, clinging sort of a girl, Freda pictured her, with weak mouth and pretty pouting lips, blow-away sun-kissed hair, and eyes full of the merry shallows and the lesser joys of life. But she also pictured Flossie, face nose-strapped and frost-rimed, stumbling wearily behind the dogs. Wherefore she smiled, dancing one night, upon Floyd Vanderlip.

Few men are so constituted that they may receive the smile of Freda unmoved; nor among them can Floyd Vanderlip be accounted. The grace he had found with the model-woman had caused him to re-measure himself, and by the favour in which he now stood with the Greek dancer he felt himself doubly a man. There were unknown qualities and depths in him, evidently, which they perceived. He did not know exactly what those qualities and depths were, but he had a hazy idea that they were there somewhere, and of them was bred a great pride in himself. A man who could force two women such as these to look upon him a second time was certainly a most remarkable man. Some day, when he had the time, he would sit down and analyse his strength; but now, just now, he would take what the gods had given him. And a thin little thought began to lift itself, and he fell to wondering whatever under the sun he had seen in Flossie, and to regret exceedingly that he had sent for her. Of course, Freda was out of the running. His dumps were the richest on Bonanza Creek, and they were many, while he was a man of responsibility and position. But Loraine Lisznayi—she was just the woman. Her life had been large; she could do the honours of his establishment and give tone to his dollars.

But Freda smiled, and continued to smile, till he came to spend much time with her. When she, too, rode down the street behind his wolf-dogs, the model-woman found food for thought, and the next time they were together dazzled him with her princes and cardinals and personal little anecdotes of courts and kings. She also showed him dainty missives, superscribed, 'My dear Loraine', and ended 'Most affectionately yours', and signed by the given name of a real live queen on a throne. And he marvelled in his heart that the great woman should deign to waste so much as a moment upon him. But she played him cleverly, making flattering contrasts and comparisons between him and the noble phantoms she drew mainly from her fancy, till he went away dizzy with self-delight and sorrowing for the world which had been denied him so long. Freda was a more masterful woman. If she flattered, no one knew it. Should she stoop, the stoop were unobserved. If a man felt she thought well of him, so subtly was the feeling conveyed that he could not for the life of him say why or how. So she tightened her grip upon Floyd Vanderlip and rode daily behind his dogs.

And just here is where the mistake occurred. The buzz rose loudly and more definitely, coupled now with the name of the dancer, and Mrs Eppingwell heard. She, too, thought of Flossie lifting her moccasined feet through the endless hours, and Floyd Vanderlip was invited up the hillside to tea, and invited often. This quite took his breath away, and he became drunken with appreciation of himself. Never was man so maltreated. His soul had become a thing for which three women struggled, while a fourth was on the way to claim it. And three such women!

But Mrs Eppingwell and the mistake she made. She spoke of the affair, tentatively, to Sitka Charley, who had sold dogs to the Greek girl. But no names were mentioned. The nearest approach to it was when Mrs Eppingwell said, 'This—er—horrid woman,' and Sitka Charley, with the model-woman strong in his thoughts, had echoed, 'This—er—horrid woman.' And he agreed with her, that it was a wicked thing for a woman to come between a man and the girl he was to marry. 'A mere girl, Charley,' she said, 'I am sure she is. And she is coming into a strange country without a friend when she gets here. We must do something.' Sitka Charley promised his help, and went away thinking what a wicked woman this Loraine Lisznayi must be, also what noble women Mrs Eppingwell and Freda were to interest themselves in the welfare of the unknown Flossie.

Now Mrs Eppingwell was open as the day. To Sitka Charley, who took her once past the Hills of Silence, belongs the glory of having memorialized her clear-searching eyes, her clear-ringing voice, and her utter downright frankness. Her lips had a way of stiffening to command, and she was used to coming straight to the point. Having taken Floyd Vanderlip's measurement, she did not dare this with him; but she was not afraid to go down into the town to Freda. And down she went, in the bright light of day, to the house of the dancer. She was above silly tongues, as was her husband, the captain. She wished to see this woman and to speak with her, nor was she aware of any reason why she should not. So she stood in the snow at the Greek girl's door, with the frost at sixty below, and parleyed with the waiting-maid for a full five minutes. She had also the pleasure of being turned away from that door, and of going back up the hill, wroth at heart for the indignity which had been put upon her. 'Who was this woman that she should refuse to see her?' she asked herself. One would think it the other way around, and she herself but a dancing girl denied at the door of the wife of a captain. As it was, she knew, had Freda come up the hill to her—no matter what the errand—she would have made her welcome at her fire, and they would have sat there as two women, and talked, merely as two women. She had overstepped convention and lowered herself, but she had thought it different with the women down in the town. And she was ashamed that she had laid herself open to such dishonour, and her thoughts of Freda were unkind.

Not that Freda deserved this. Mrs Eppingwell had descended to meet her who was without caste, while she, strong in the traditions of her own earlier status, had not permitted it. She could worship such a woman, and she would have asked no greater joy than to have had her into the cabin and sat with her, just sat with her, for an hour. But her respect for Mrs Eppingwell, and her respect for herself, who was beyond respect, had prevented her doing that which she most desired. Though not quite recovered from the recent visit of Mrs McFee, the wife of the minister, who had descended upon her in a whirlwind of exhortation and brimstone, she could not imagine what had prompted the present visit. She was not aware of any particular wrong she had done, and surely this woman who waited at the door was not concerned with the welfare of her soul. Why had she come? For all the curiosity she could not help but feel, she steeled herself in the pride of those who are without pride, and trembled in the inner room like a maid on the first caress of a lover. If Mrs Eppingwell suffered going up the hill, she too suffered, lying face downward on the bed, dry-eyed, dry-mouthed, dumb.

Mrs Eppingwell's knowledge of human nature was great. She aimed at universality. She had found it easy to step from the civilized and contemplate things from the barbaric aspect. She could comprehend certain primal and analogous characteristics in a hungry wolf-dog or a starving man, and predicate lines of action to be pursued by either under like conditions. To her, a woman was a woman, whether garbed in purple or the rags of the gutter; Freda was a woman. She would not have been surprised had she been taken into the dancer's cabin and encountered on common ground; nor surprised had she been taken in and flaunted in prideless arrogance. But to be treated as she had been treated, was unexpected and disappointing. Ergo, she had not caught Freda's point of view. And this was good. There are some points of view which cannot be gained save through much travail and personal crucifixion, and it were well for the world that its Mrs Eppingwells should, in certain ways, fall short of universality. One cannot understand defilement without laying hands to pitch, which is very sticky, while there be plenty willing to undertake the experiment. All of which is of small concern, beyond the fact that it gave Mrs Eppingwell ground for grievance, and bred for her a greater love in the Greek girl's heart.

### III

And in this way things went along for a month—Mrs Eppingwell striving to withhold the man from the Greek dancer's blandishments against the time of Flossie's coming; Flossie lessening the miles each day on the dreary trail; Freda pitting her strength against the model-woman;

the model-woman straining every nerve to land the prize; and the man moving through it all like a flying shuttle, very proud of himself, whom he believed to be a second Don Juan.

It was nobody's fault except the man's that Loraine Lisznayi at last landed him. The way of a man with a maid may be too wonderful to know, but the way of a woman with a man passeth all conception; whence the prophet were indeed unwise who would dare forecast Floyd Vanderlip's course twenty-four hours in advance. Perhaps the model-woman's attraction lay in that to the eye she was a handsome animal; perhaps she fascinated him with her old-world talk of palaces and princes; leastwise she dazzled him whose life had been worked out in uncultured roughness, and he at last agreed to her suggestion of a run down the river and a marriage at Forty Mile. In token of his intention he bought dogs from Sitka Charley—more than one sled is necessary when a woman like Loraine Lisznayi takes to the trail—and then went up the creek to give orders for the superintendence of his Bonanza mines during his absence.

He had given it out, rather vaguely, that he needed the animals for sledding lumber from the mill to his sluices and right here is where Sitka Charley demonstrated his fitness. He agreed to furnish dogs on a given date, but no sooner had Floyd Vanderlip turned his toes up-creek, than Charley hied himself away in perturbation to Loraine Lisznayi. Did she know where Mr Vanderlip had gone? He had agreed to supply that gentleman with a big string of dogs by a certain time; but that shameless one, the German trader Meyers, had been buying up the brutes and skimped the market. It was very necessary he should see Mr Vanderlip, because of the shameless one he would be all of a week behindhand in filling the contract. She did know where he had gone? Up-creek? Good! He would strike out after him at once and inform him of the unhappy delay. Did he understand her to say that Mr Vanderlip needed the dogs on Friday night? that he must have them by that time? It was too bad, but it was the fault of the shameless one who had bid up the prices. They had jumped fifty dollars per head, and should he buy on the rising market he would lose by the contract. He wondered if Mr Van-derlip would be willing to meet the advance. She knew he would? Being Mr Vanderlip's friend, she would even meet the difference herself? And he was to say nothing about it? She was kind to so look to his interests. Friday night, did she say? Good! The dogs would be on hand.

An hour later, Freda knew the elopement was to be pulled off on Friday night; also, that Floyd Vanderlip had gone up-creek, and her hands were tied. On Friday morn-ing, Devereaux, the official courier, bearing despatches from the Governor, arrived over the ice. Besides the des-patches, he brought news of Flossie. He had passed her camp at Sixty Mile; humans and dogs were in good condi-tion; and she would doubtless be in on the morrow. Mrs Eppingwell experienced a great relief on hearing this; Floyd Vanderlip was safe up-creek, and ere the Greek girl could again lay hands upon him, his bride would be on the ground. But that afternoon her big St Bernard, valiantly defending her front stoop, was downed by a foraging party of trail-starved Malemutes. He was buried beneath the hirsute mass for about thirty seconds, when rescued by a couple of axes and as many stout men. Had he remained down two minutes, the chances were large that he would have been roughly apportioned and carried away in the respective bellies of the attacking party; but as it was, it was a mere case of neat and expeditious mangling. Sitka Charley came to repair the damages, especially a right fore-paw which had inadvertently been left a fraction of a second too long in some other dog's mouth. As he put on his mittens to go, the talk turned upon Flossie and in natural sequence passed on to the—'er horrid woman'. Sitka Charley remarked incidentally that she intended jumping out down river that night with Floyd Vanderlip, and further ventured the information that accidents were very likely at that time of year.

So Mrs Eppingwell's thoughts of Freda were unkinder than ever. She wrote a note, addressed it to the man in question, and intrusted it to a messenger who lay in wait at the mouth of Bonanza Creek. Another man, bearing a note from Freda, also waited at that strategic point. So it happened that Floyd Vanderlip, riding his sled merrily down with the last daylight, received the notes together. He tore Freda's across. No, he would not go to see her. There were greater things afoot that night. Besides, she was out of the running. But Mrs Eppingwell! He would observe her last wish—or rather, the last wish it would be possible for him to observe—and meet her at the Governor's ball to hear what she had to say. From the tone of the writing it was evidently important; perhaps— He smiled fondly, but failed to shape the thought. Confound it all, what a lucky fellow he was with the women anyway! Scattering her letter to the frost, he *mushed* the dogs into a swinging lope and headed for his cabin. It was to be a masquerade, and he had to dig up the costume used at the Opera House a couple of months before. Also, he had to shave and to eat. Thus it was that he, alone of all interested, was unaware of Flossie's proximity.

'Have them down to the water-hole off the hospital, at midnight, sharp. Don't fail me,' he said to Sitka Charley, who dropped in with the advice that only one dog was lacking to fill the bill, and that that one would be forthcoming in an hour or so. 'Here's the sack. There's the scales. Weigh out your own dust and don't bother me. I've got to get ready for the ball.'

Sitka Charley weighed out his pay and departed, carrying with him a letter to Loraine Lisznayi, the contents of which he correctly imagined to refer to a meeting at the water-hole off the hospital, at midnight, sharp.

IV

Twice Freda sent messengers up to the Barracks, where the dance was in full swing, and as often they came back without answers. Then she did what only Freda could do— put on her furs, masked her face, and went up herself to the Governor's ball. Now there happened to be a custom— not an original one by any means—to which the official clique had long since become addicted. It was a very wise custom, for it furnished protection to the womankind of the officials and gave greater selectness to their revels. Whenever a masquerade was given, a committee was chosen, the sole function of which was to stand by the door and peep beneath each and every mask. Most men did not clamour to be placed upon this committee, while the very ones who least desired the honour were the ones whose services were most required. The chaplain was not well enough acquainted with the faces and places of the townspeople to know whom to admit and whom to turn away. In like condition were the several other worthy gentlemen who would have asked nothing better than to serve. To fill the coveted place, Mrs McFee would have risked her chance of salvation, and did, one night, when a certain trio passed in under her guns and muddled things considerably before their identity was discovered. Thereafter only the fit were chosen, and very ungracefully did they respond.

On this particular night Prince was at the door. Pressure had been brought to bear, and he had not yet recovered from amaze at his having consented to undertake a task which bid fair to lose him half his friends, merely for the sake of pleasing the other half. Three or four of the men he had refused were men whom he had known on creek and trail—good comrades, but not exactly eligible for so select an affair. He was canvassing the expediency of resigning the post there and then, when a woman tripped in under the light. Freda! He could swear it by the furs, did he not know that poise of head so well. The last one to expect in all the world. He had given her better judgment than to thus venture the ignominy of refusal, or, if she passed, the scorn of women. He shook his head, without scrutiny; he knew her too well to be mistaken. But she pressed closer. She lifted the black silk ribbon and as quickly lowered it again. For one flashing, eternal second he looked upon her face. It was not for nothing, the saying which had arisen in the country, that Freda played with men as a child with bubbles. Not a word was spoken. Prince stepped aside, and a few moments later might have been seen resigning, with warm incoherence, the post to which he had been unfaithful.

A woman, flexible of form, slender, yet rhythmic of strength in every moment, now pausing with this group, now scanning that, urged a restless and devious course among the revellers. Men recognized the furs, and marvelled—men who should have served upon the door committee; but they were not prone to speech. Not so with the women. They had better eyes for the lines of figure and tricks of carriage, and they knew this form to be one with which they were unfamiliar; likewise the furs. Mrs McFee, emerging from the supper-room where all was in readiness, caught one flash of the blazing, questing eyes through the silken mask-slits, and received a start. She tried to recollect where she had seen the like, and a vivid picture was recalled of a certain proud and rebellious sinner whom she had once encountered on a fruitless errand for the Lord.

So it was that the good woman took the trail in hot and righteous wrath, a trail which brought her ultimately into the company of Mrs Eppingwell and Floyd Vanderlip. Mrs Eppingwell had just found the opportunity to talk with the man. She had determined, now that Flossie was so near at hand, to proceed directly to the point, and an incisive little ethical discourse was titillating on the end of her tongue, when the couple became three. She noted, and pleasurably, the faintly foreign accent of the 'Beg pardon' with which the furred woman prefaced her immediate appropriation of Floyd Vanderlip; and she courteously bowed her permission for them to draw a little apart.

Then it was that Mrs McFee's righteous hand descended, and accompanying it in its descent was a black mask torn from a startled woman. A wonderful face and brilliant eyes were exposed to the quiet curiosity of those who looked that way, and they were everybody. Floyd Vanderlip was rather confused. The situation demanded instant action on the part of a man who was not beyond his depth, while *he* hardly knew where he was. He stared helplessly about him. Mrs Eppingwell was perplexed. She could not comprehend.

An explanation was forthcoming, somewhere, and Mrs McFee was equal to it.

'Mrs Eppingwell,' and her Celtic voice rose shrilly, 'it is with great pleasure I make you acquainted with Freda Moloof, *Miss* Freda Moloof, as I understand.'

Freda involuntarily turned. With her own face bared, she felt as in a dream, naked, upon her turned the clothed features and gleaming eyes of the masked circle. It seemed, almost, as though a hungry wolf-pack girdled her, ready to drag her down. It might chance that some felt pity for her, she thought, and at the thought, hardened. She would by far prefer their scorn. Strong of heart was she, this woman, and though she had hunted the prey into the midst of the pack, Mrs Eppingwell or no Mrs Eppingwell, she could not forgo the kill.

But here Mrs Eppingwell did a strange thing. So this, at last, was Freda, she mused, the dancer and the destroyer of men; the woman from whose door she had been turned. And she, too, felt the imperious creature's nakedness as though it were her own. Perhaps it was this, her Saxon disinclination to meet a disadvantaged foe, perhaps, forsooth, that it might give her greater strength in the struggle for the man, and it might have been a little of both; but be that as it may, she did do this strange thing. When Mrs McFee's thin voice, vibrant with malice, had raised, and Freda turned involuntarily, Mrs Eppingwell also turned, removed her mask, and inclined her head in acknowledgment.

It was another flashing, eternal second, during which these two women regarded each other. The one, eyes blazing, meteoric; at bay, aggressive; suffering in advance and resenting in advance the scorn and ridicule and insult she had thrown herself open to; a beautiful, burning, bubbling lava cone of flesh and spirit. And the other, calm-eyed, cool-browed, serene; strong in her own integrity, with faith in herself, thoroughly at ease; dispassionate, imperturbable; a figure chiselled from some cold marble quarry. Whatever gulf there might exist, she recognised it not. No bridging, no descending; her attitude was that of perfect equality.

She stood tranquilly on the ground of their common womanhood. And this maddened Freda. Not so, had she been of lesser breed; but her soul's plummet knew not the bottomless, and she could follow the other into the deeps of her deepest depths and read her aright. 'Why do you not draw back your garment's hem?' she was fain to cry out, all in that flashing, dazzling second. 'Spit upon me, revile me, and it were greater mercy than this!' She trembled. Her nostrils distended and quivered. But she drew herself in check, returned the inclination of head, and turned to the man.

'Come with me, Floyd,' she said simply. 'I want you now.'

'What the——' he began explosively, and quit as suddenly, discreet enough to not round it off. Where the deuce had his wits gone, anyway? Was ever a man more foolishly placed? He gurgled deep down in his throat and high up in the roof of his mouth, heaved as one his big shoulders and his indecision, and glared appealingly at the two women.

'I beg pardon, just a moment, but may I speak first with Mr Vanderlip?' Mrs Eppingwell's voice, though flute-like and low, predicated will in its every cadence.

The man looked his gratitude. He, at least, was willing enough.

'I am very sorry,' from Freda. 'There isn't time. He must come at once.' The conventional phrases dropped easily from her lips, but she could not forbear to smile inwardly at their inadequacy and weakness. She would much rather have shrieked.

'But, Miss Moloof, who are you that you may possess yourself of Mr Vanderlip and command his actions?'

Whereupon relief brightened his face, and the man beamed his approval. Trust Mrs Eppingwell to drag him clear. Fred had met her match this time.

'I—I——' Freda hesitated, and then her feminine mind putting on its harness—'and who are you to ask this question?'

'I? I am Mrs Eppingwell, and——'

'There!' the other broke in sharply. 'You are the wife of a captain, who is therefore your husband. I am only a dancing girl. What do you with this man?'

'Such unprecedented behaviour!' Mrs McFee ruffled herself and cleared for action, but Mrs Eppingwell shut her mouth with a look and developed a new attack.

'Since Miss Moloof appears to hold claim upon you, Mr Vanderlip, and is in too great haste to grant me a few seconds of your time, I am forced to appeal directly to you. May I speak with you, alone, and now?'

Mrs McFee's jaws brought together with a snap. That settled the disgraceful situation.

'Why, er—that is, certainly,' the man stammered. 'Of course, of course,' growing more effusive at the prospect of deliverance.

Men are only gregarious vertebrates, domesticated and evolved, and the chances are large that it was because the Greek girl had in her time dealt with wilder masculine beasts of the human sort; for she turned upon the man with hell's tides aflood in her blazing eyes, much as a bespangled lady upon a lion which has suddenly imbibed the pernicious theory that he is a free agent. The beast in him fawned to the lash.

'That is to say, ah, afterward. To-morrow, Mrs. Eppingwell; yes, to-morrow. That is what I meant.' He solaced himself with the fact, should he remain, that more embarrassment awaited. Also, he had an engagement which he must keep shortly, down by the water-hole off the hospital. Ye gods! he had never given Freda credit! Wasn't she magnificent!

'I'll thank you for my mask, Mrs McFee.'

That lady, for the nonce speechless, turned over the article in question.

'Good-night, Miss Moloof.' Mrs Eppingwell was royal even in defeat.

Freda reciprocated, though barely downing the impulse to clasp the other's knees and beg forgiveness—no, not forgiveness, but something, she knew not what, but which she none the less greatly desired.

The man was for her taking his arm; but she had made her kill in the midst of the pack, and that which led kings to drag their vanquished at the chariot-tail led her toward the door alone, Floyd Vanderlip close at heel and striving to re-establish his mental equilibrium.

V

It was bitter cold. As the trail wound, a quarter of a mile brought them to the dancer's cabin, by which time her moist breath had coated her face frostily, while his had massed his heavy moustache till conversation was painful. By the greenish light of the aurora borealis, the quicksilver showed itself frozen hard in the bulb of the thermometer which hung outside the door. A thousand dogs, in pitiful chorus, wailed their ancient wrongs and claimed mercy from the unheeding stars. Not a breath of air was moving. For them there was no shelter from the cold, no shrewd crawling to leeward in snug nooks. The frost was every-where, and they lay in the open, ever and anon stretching their trail-stiffened muscles, and lifting the long wolf-howl.

They did not talk at first, the man and the woman. While the maid helped Freda off with her wraps, Floyd Vanderlip replenished the fire; and by the time the maid had with-drawn to an inner room, his head over the stove, he was busily thawing out his burdened upper lip. After that he rolled a cigarette and watched her lazily through the fra-grant eddies. She stole a glance at the clock. It lacked half an hour of midnight. How was she to hold him? Was he angry for that which she had done? What was his mood? What mood of hers could meet his best? Not that she doubted herself. No, no. Hold him she could, if need be at pistol point, till Sitka Charley's work was done, and Devereaux's too.

There were many ways, and with her knowledge of this her contempt for the man increased. As she leaned her head on her hand, a fleeting vision of her own girlhood, with its mournful climacteric and tragic ebb, was vouchsafed her, and for the moment she was minded to read him a lesson from it. God! it must be less than human brute who could not be held by such a tale, told as she could tell it, but—bah! He was not worth it, nor worth the pain to her. The candle was positioned just right, and even as she thought of these things sacredly shameful to her, he was pleasuring in the transparent pinkiness of her ear. She noted his eye, took the cue, and turned her head till the clean profile of the face was presented. Not the least was that profile among her virtues. She could not help the lines upon which she had been builded, and they were very good; but she had long since learned those lines, and though little they needed, was not above advantaging them to the best of her ability. The candle began to flicker. She could not do anything ungracefully, but that did not prevent her improving upon nature a bit, when she reached forth and deftly snuffed the red wick from the midst of the yellow flame. Again she rested head on hand, this time regarding the man thoughtfully, and any man is pleased when thus regarded by a pretty woman.

She was in little haste to begin. If dalliance were to his liking, it was to hers. To him it was very comfortable, soothing his lungs with nicotine and gazing upon her. It was snug and warm here, while down by the water-hole began a trail which he would soon be hitting through the chilly hours. He felt he ought to be angry with Freda for the scene she had created, but somehow he didn't feel a bit wrathful. Like as not there wouldn't have been any scene if it hadn't been for that McFee woman. If he were the Governor, he would put a poll tax of a hundred ounces a quarter upon her and her kind and all gospel sharks and sky pilots. And certainly Freda had behaved very ladylike —held her own with Mrs Eppingwell besides. Never gave the girl credit for the grit. He looked lingeringly over her, coming back now and again to the eyes, behind the deep earnestness of which he could not guess lay concealed a deeper sneer. And, Jove, wasn't she well put up! Wonder why she looked at him so? Did she want to marry him, too? Like as not; but she wasn't the only one. Her looks were in her favour, weren't they? And young—younger than Loraine Lisznayi. She couldn't be more than twenty-three or four, twenty-five at most. And she'd never get stout. Anybody could guess that the first time. He couldn't say it of Loraine, though. *She* certainly had put on flesh since the day she served as model. Huh! once he got her on trail he'd take it off. Put her on the snowshoes to break ahead of the dogs. Never knew it to fail, yet. But his thought leaped ahead to the palace under the lazy Mediterranean sky—and how would it be with Loraine then? No frost, no trail, no famine now and again to cheer the monotony, and she getting older and piling it on with every sunrise. While this girl Freda—he sighed his unconscious regret that he had missed being born under the flag of the Turk, and came back to Alaska.

'Well?' Both hands of the clock pointed perpendicularly to midnight, and it was high time he was getting down to the water-hole.

'Oh!' Freda started, and she did it prettily, delighting him as his fellows have ever been delighted by their womenkind. When a man is made to believe that a woman, looking up on him thoughtfully, has lost herself in meditation over him, that man needs be an extremely cold-blooded individual in order to trim his sheets, set a lookout, and steer clear.

'I was just wondering what you wanted to see me about,' he explained, drawing his chair up to hers by the table.

'Floyd,' she looked him steadily in the eyes, 'I am tired of the whole business. I want to go away. I can't live it out here till the river breaks. If I try, I'll die. I am sure of it. I want to quit it all and go away, and I want to do it at once.'

She laid her hand in mute appeal upon the back of his, which turned over and became a prison. Another one, he thought, just throwing herself at him. Guess it wouldn't hurt Loraine to cool her feet by the water-hole a little longer.

'Well?' This time from Freda, but softly and anxiously.

'I don't know what to say,' he hastened to answer, adding to himself that it was coming along quicker than he had expected. 'Nothing I'd like better, Freda. You know that well enough.' He pressed her hand, palm to palm.

She nodded. Could she wonder that she despised the breed?

'But you see, I—I'm engaged. Of course you know that. And the girl's coming into the country to marry me. Don't know what was up with me when I asked her, but it was a long while back, and I was all-fired young.'

'I want to go away, out of the land, anywhere,' she went on, disregarding the obstacle he had reared up and apologized for. 'I have been running over the men I know and reached the conclusion that—that——'

'I was the likeliest of the lot?'

She smiled her gratitude for his having saved her the embarrassment of confession. He drew her head against his shoulder with the free hand, and somehow the scent of her hair got into his nostrils. Then he discovered that a common pulse throbbed, throbbed, throbbed, where their palms were in contact. This phenomenon is easily comprehensible from a physiological standpoint, but to the man who makes the discovery for the first time, it is a most wonderful thing. Floyd Vanderlip had caressed more shovel-handles than women's hands in his time, so this was an experience quite new and delightfully strange. And when Freda turned her head against his shoulder, her hair brushing his cheek till his eyes met hers, full and at close range, luminously soft, ay, and tender—why, whose fault was it that he lost his grip utterly? False to Flossie, why not to Loraine? Even if the women did keep bothering him, that was no reason he should make up his mind in a hurry. Why, he had slathers of money, and Freda was just the girl to grace it. A wife she'd make him for other men to envy. But go slow. He must be cautious.

'You don't happen to care for palaces, do you?' he asked. She shook her head.

'Well, I had a hankering after them myself, till I got to thinking, a while back, and I've about sized it up that one'd get fat living in palaces, and soft and lazy.'

10—J.L. IV

'Yes, it's nice for a time, but you soon grow tired of it, I imagine,' she hastened to reassure him. 'The world is good, but life should be many-sided. Rough and knock about for a while, and then rest up somewhere. Off to the South Seas on a yacht, then a nibble of Paris; a winter in South America and a summer in Norway; a few months in England——'

'Good society?'

'Most certainly—the best; and then, heigho! for the dogs and sleds and the Hudson Bay Country. Change, you know. A strong man like you, full of vitality and go, could not possibly stand a palace for a year. It is all very well for effeminate men, but you weren't made for such a life. You are masculine, intensely masculine.'

'Think so?'

'It does not require thinking. I know. Have you ever noticed that it was easy to make women care for you?'

His dubious innocence was superb.

'It is very easy. And why? Because you are masculine. You strike the deepest chords of a woman's heart. You are something to cling to—big-muscled, strong, and brave. In short, because you *are* a man.'

She shot a glance at the clock. It was half after the hour. She had given a margin of thirty minutes to Sitka Charley; and it did not matter, now, when Devereaux arrived. Her work was done. She lifted her head, laughed her genuine mirth, slipped her hand clear, and rising to her feet called the maid.

'Alice, help Mr Vanderlip on with his *parka*. His mittens are on the sill by the stove.'

The man could not understand.

'Let me thank you for your kindness, Floyd. Your time was invaluable to me, and it was indeed good of you. The turning to the left, as you leave the cabin, leads the quickest to the water-hole. Good-night. I am going to bed.'

Floyd Vanderlip employed strong words to express his perplexity and disappointment. Alice did not like to hear men swear, so dropped his *parka* on the floor and tossed his mittens on top of it. Then he made a break for Freda, and she ruined her retreat to the inner room by tripping over the *parka*. He brought her up standing with a rude grip on the wrist. But she only laughed. She was not afraid of men. Had they not wrought their worst with her, and did she not still endure?

'Don't be rough,' she said finally. 'On second thought,' here she looked at his detaining hand, 'I've decided not to go to bed yet a while. Do sit down and be comfortable instead of ridiculous. Any questions?'

'Yes, my lady, and reckoning, too.' He still kept his hold. 'What do you know about the water-hole? What did you mean by—no, never mind. One question at a time.'

'Oh, nothing much. Sitka Charley had an appointment there with somebody you may know, and not being anxious for a man of your known charm to be present, fell back upon me to kindly help him. That's all. They're off now, and a good half hour ago.'

'Where? Down river and without me? And he an Indian!'

'There's no accounting for taste, you know, especially in a woman.'

'But how do I stand in this deal? I've lost four thousand dollars' worth of dogs and a tidy bit of a woman, and nothing to show for it. Except you,' he added as an afterthought, 'and cheap you are at the price.'

Freda shrugged her shoulders.

'You might as well get ready. I'm going out to borrow a couple of teams of dogs, and we'll start in as many hours.'

'I am very sorry, but I'm going to bed.'

'You'll pack if you know what's good for you. Go to bed, or not, when I get my dogs outside, so help me, onto the sled you go. Mebbe you fooled with me, but I'll just see your bluff and take you in earnest. Hear me?'

He closed on her wrist till it hurt, but on her lips a smile was growing, and she seemed to listen intently to some outside sound. There was a jingle of dog bells, and a man's voice crying 'Haw!' as a sled took the turning and drew up at the cabin.

'*Now* will you let me go to bed?'

As Freda spoke she threw open the door. Into the warm room rushed the frost, and on the threshhold, garbed in trail-worn furs, knee-deep in the swirling vapour, against a background of flaming borealis, a woman hesitated. She removed her nose-trap and stood blinking blindly in the white candlelight. Floyd Vanderlip stumbled forward.

'Floyd!' she cried, relieved and glad, and met him with a tired bound.

What could he but kiss the armful of furs? And a pretty armful it was, nestling against him wearily, but happy.

'It was good of you,' spoke the armful, 'to send Mr Devereaux with fresh dogs after me, else I would not have been in till to-morrow.'

The man looked blankly across at Freda, then the light breaking in upon him, 'And wasn't it good of Devereaux to go?'

'Couldn't wait a bit longer, could you, dear?' Flossie snuggled closer.

'Well, I was getting sort of impatient,' he confessed glibly, at the same time drawing her up till her feet left the floor, and getting outside the door.

That same night an inexplicable thing happened to the Reverend James Brown, missionary, who lived among the natives several miles down the Yukon and saw to it that the trails they trod led to the white man's paradise. He was roused from his sleep by a strange Indian, who gave into his charge not only the soul but the body of a woman, and having done this drove quickly away. This woman was heavy, and handsome, and angry, and in her wrath unclean words fell from her mouth. This shocked the worthy man, but he was yet young and her presence would have been pernicious (in the simple eyes of his flock), had she not struck out on foot for Dawson with the first grey of dawn.

The shock to Dawson came many days later, when the summer had come and the population honoured a certain royal lady at Windsor by lining the Yukon's bank and watching Sitka Charley rise up with flashing paddle and drive the first canoe across the line. On this day of the races, Mrs Eppingwell, who had learned and unlearned numerous things, saw Freda for the first time since the night of the ball. 'Publicly, mind you,' as Mrs McFee expressed it, 'without regard or respect for the morals of the community,' she went up to the dancer and held out her hand. At first, it is remembered by those who saw, the girl shrank back, then words passed between the two, and Freda, great Freda, broke down and wept on the shoulder of the captain's wife. It was not given to Dawson to know why Mrs Eppingwell should crave forgiveness of a Greek dancing girl, but she did it publicly, and it was unseemly.

It were well not to forget Mrs McFee. She took a cabin passage on the first steamer going out. She also took with her a theory which she had achieved in the silent watches of the long dark nights; and it is her conviction that the Northland is unregenerate because it is so cold there. Fear of hell-fire cannot be bred in an ice-box. This may appear dogmatic, but it is Mrs McFee's theory.

# LOVE OF LIFE

This out of all will remain—
    They have lived and have tossed:
So much of the game will be gain,
    Though the gold of the dice has been lost.

THEY LIMPED painfully down the bank, and once the foremost of the two men staggered among the rough-strewn rocks. They were tired and weak, and their faces had the drawn expression of patience which comes of hardship long endured. They were heavily burdened with blanket packs which were strapped to their shoulders. Head straps, passing across the forehead, helped support these packs. Each man carried a rifle. They walked in a stooped posture, the shoulders well forward, the head still farther forward, the eyes bent upon the ground.

'I wish we had just about two of them cartridges that's layin' in that cache of ourn,' said the second man.

His voice was utterly and drearily expressionless. He spoke without enthusiasm; and the first man, limping into the milky stream that foamed over the rocks, vouchsafed no reply.

The other man followed at his heels. They did not remove their footgear, though the water was icy cold—so cold that their ankles ached and their feet went numb. In places the water dashed against their knees, and both men staggered for footing.

The man who followed slipped on a smooth boulder, nearly fell, but recovered himself with a violent effort, at the same time uttering a sharp exclamation of pain. He seemed faint and dizzy and put out his free hand while he reeled, as though seeking support against the air. When he had steadied himself he stepped forward, but reeled again and nearly fell. Then he stood still and looked at the other man, who had never turned his head.

The man stood still for fully a minute, as though debating with himself. Then he called out:

'I say, Bill, I've sprained my ankle.'

Bill staggered on through the milky water. He did not look around. The man watched him go, and though his face was expressionless as ever, his eyes were like the eyes of a wounded deer.

The other man limped up the farther bank and continued straight on without looking back. The man in the stream watched him. His lips trembled a little, so that the rough thatch of brown hair which covered them was visibly agitated. His tongue even strayed out to moisten them.

'Bill!' he cried out.

It was the pleading cry of a strong man in distress, but Bill's head did not turn. The man watched him go, limping grotesquely and lurching forward with stammering gait up the slow slope toward the soft sky-line of the low-lying hill. He watched him go till he passed over the crest and disappeared. Then he turned his gaze and slowly took in the circle of the world that remained to him now that Bill was gone.

Near the horizon the sun was smouldering dimly, almost obscured by formless mists and vapours, which gave an impression of mass and density without outline or tangibility. The man pulled out his watch, the while resting his weight on one leg. It was four o'clock, and as the season was near the last of July or first of August—he did not know the precise date within a week or two—he knew that the sun roughly marked the northwest. He looked to the south and knew that somewhere beyond those bleak hills lay the Great Bear Lake; also, he knew that in that direction the Arctic Circle cut its forbidding way across the Canadian Barrens. This stream in which he stood was a feeder to the Coppermine River, which in turn flowed north and emptied into Coronation Gulf and the Arctic Ocean. He had never been there, but he had seen it, once, on a Hudson's Bay Company chart.

Again his gaze completed the circle of the world about him. It was not a heartening spectacle. Everywhere was soft sky line. The hills were all low-lying. There were no trees, no shrubs, no grasses—naught but a tremendous and terrible desolation that sent fear swiftly dawning into his eyes.

'Bill!' he whispered, once and twice; 'Bill!'

He cowered in the midst of the milky water, as though the vastness were pressing in upon him with overwhelming force, brutally crushing him with its complacent awfulness. He began to shake as with an ague fit, till the gun fell from his hand with a splash. This served to rouse him. He fought with his fear and pulled himself together, groping in the water and recovering the weapon. He hitched his pack farther over on his left shoulder, so as to take a portion of its weight from off the injured ankle. Then he proceeded, slowly and carefully, wincing with pain, to the bank.

He did not stop. With a desperation that was madness, unmindful of the pain, he hurried up the slope to the crest of the hill over which his comrade had disappeared—more grotesque and comical by far than that limping, jerking comrade. But at the crest he saw a shallow valley, empty of life. He fought with his fear again, overcame it, hitched the pack still farther over on his left shoulder, and lurched on down the slope.

The bottom of the valley was soggy with water, which the thick moss held, spongelike, close to the surface. This water squirted out from under his feet at every step, and each time he lifted a foot the action culminated in a sucking sound as the wet moss reluctantly released its grip. He picked his way from muskeg to muskeg, and followed the other man's footsteps along and across the rocky ledges which thrust like islets through the sea of moss.

Though alone, he was not lost. Farther on, he knew, he would come to where dead spruce and fir, very small and wizened, bordered the shore of a little lake, the *titchin-nichilie*, in the tongue of the country, the 'land of little sticks'. And into that lake flowed a small stream, the water of which was not milky. There was rush grass on that stream—this he remembered well—but no timber, and he would follow it till its first trickle ceased at a divide. He would cross this divide to the first trickle of another stream, flowing to the west, which he would follow until it emptied into the river Dease, and here he would find a cache under an upturned canoe and piled over with many rocks. And in this cache would be ammunition for his empty gun, fish-hooks and lines, a small net—all the utilities for the killing and snaring of food. Also he would find flour—not much—a piece of bacon, and some beans.

Bill would be waiting for him there, and they would paddle away south down the Dease to the Great Bear Lake. And south across the lake they would go, ever south, till they gained the Mackenzie. And south, still south, they would go, while the winter raced vainly after them, and the ice formed in the eddies, and the days grew chill and crisp, south to some warm Hudson's Bay Company post, where timber grew tall and generous and there was grub without end.

These were the thoughts of the man as he strove onward. But hard as he strove with his body, he strove equally hard with his mind, trying to think that Bill had not deserted him, that Bill would surely wait for him at the cache. He was compelled to think this thought, or else there would not be any use to strive, and he would have lain down and died. And as the dim ball of the sun sank slowly into the northwest he covered every inch—and many times—of his and Bill's flight south before the down-coming winter. And he conned the grub of the cache and the grub of the Hudson's Bay Company post over and over again. He had not eaten for two days; for a far longer time he had not had all he wanted to eat. Often he stooped and picked pale muskeg berries, put them into his mouth, and chewed and swallowed them. A muskeg berry is a bit of seed enclosed in a bit of water. In the mouth the water melts away and the seed chews sharp and bitter. The man knew there was no nourishment in the berries, but he chewed them patiently with a hope greater than knowledge and defying experience.

At nine o'clock he stubbed his toe on a rocky ledge, and from sheer weariness and weakness staggered and fell. He lay for some time, without movement, on his side. Then he slipped out of his pack straps and clumsily dragged himself into a sitting posture. It was not yet dark, and in the lingering twilight he groped about among the rocks for shreds of dry moss. When he had gathered a heap he built a fire— a smouldering, smudgy fire—and put a tin pot of water on to boil.

He unwrapped his pack and the first thing he did was to count his matches. There were sixty-seven. He counted them three times to make sure. He divided them into several portions, wrapping them in oil paper, disposing of one bunch in his empty tobacco pouch, of another bunch in the inside band of his battered hat, of a third bunch under his shirt on the chest. This accomplished, a panic came upon him, and he unwrapped them all and counted them again. There were still sixty-seven.

He dried his wet footgear by the fire. The moccasins were in soggy shreds. The blanket socks were worn through in places, and his feet were raw and bleeding. His ankle was throbbing, and he gave it an examination. It had swol-

len to the size of his knee. He tore a long strip from one of
his two blankets and bound the ankle tightly. He tore other
strips and bound them about his feet to serve for both
moccasins and socks. Then he drank the pot of water,
steaming hot, wound his watch, and crawled between his
blankets.

He slept like a dead man. The brief darkness around
midnight came and went. The sun arose in the northeast
—at least the day dawned in that quarter, for the sun was
hidden by grey clouds.

At six o'clock he awoke, quietly lying on his back. He
gazed straight up into the grey sky and knew that he was
hungry. As he rolled over on his elbow he was startled by
a loud snort, and saw a bull caribou regarding him with
alert curiosity. The animal was not more than fifty feet
away, and instantly into the man's mind leaped the vision
and the savour of a caribou steak sizzling and frying over
a fire. Mechanically he reached for the empty gun, drew a
bead, and pulled the trigger. The bull snorted and leaped
away, his hoofs rattling and clattering as he fled across the
ledges.

The man cursed and flung the empty gun from him. He
groaned aloud as he started to drag himself to his feet. It
was a slow and arduous task. His joints were like rusty
hinges. They worked harshly in their sockets, with much
friction, and each bending and unbending was accomplished only through a sheer exertion of will. When he
finally gained his feet, another minute or so was consumed
in straightening up, so that he could stand erect as a man
should stand.

He crawled up a small knoll and surveyed the prospect.
There were no trees, no bushes, nothing but a grey sea of
moss scarcely diversified by grey rocks, grey lakelets, and
grey streamlets. The sky was grey. There was no sun nor
hint of sun. He had no idea of north, and he had forgotten
the way he had come to this spot the night before. But he
was not lost. He knew that. Soon he would come to the
land of the little sticks. He felt that it lay off to the left
somewhere, not far—possibly just over the next low hill.

He went back to put his pack into shape for travelling.
He assured himself of the existence of his three separate
parcels of matches, though he did not stop to count them.
But he did linger, debating, over a squat moose-hide sack.
It was not large. He could hide it under his two hands. He
knew that it weighed fifteen pounds—as much as all the
rest of the pack—and it worried him. He finally set it to
one side and proceeded to roll the pack. He paused to gaze
at the squat moose-hide sack. He picked it up hastily with
a defiant glance about him, as though the desolation were
trying to rob him of it; and when he rose to his feet to
stagger on into the day, it was included in the pack on his
back.

He bore away to the left, stopping now and again to eat
muskeg berries. His ankle had stiffened, his limp was more
pronounced, but the pain of it was as nothing compared
with the pain of his stomach. The hunger pangs were sharp.
They gnawed and gnawed until he could not keep his mind
steady on the course he must pursue to gain the land of
little sticks. The muskeg berries did not allay this gnawing,
while they made his tongue and the roof of his mouth sore
with their irritating bite.

He came upon a valley where rock ptarmigan rose on
whirring wings from the ledges and muskegs. 'Ker—ker—
ker' was the cry they made. He threw stones at them, but
could not hit them. He placed his pack on the ground and
stalked them as a cat stalks a sparrow. The sharp rocks cut
through his pants' legs till his knees left a trail of blood; but
the hurt was lost in the hurt of his hunger. He squirmed
over the wet moss, saturating his clothes and chilling his
body; but he was not aware of it, so great was his fever for
food. And always the ptarmigan rose, whirring, before him,
till their 'ker—ker—ker' became a mock to him, and he
cursed them and cried aloud at them with their own cry.

Once he crawled upon one that must have been asleep.
He did not see it till it shot up in his face from its rocky
nook. He made a clutch as startled as was the rise of the
ptarmigan, and there remained in his hand three tail
feathers. As he watched its flight he hated it, as though it

had done him some terrible wrong. Then he returned and shouldered his pack.

As the day wore along he came into valleys or swales where game was more plentiful. A band of caribou passed by, twenty and odd animals, tantalizingly within rifle range. He felt a wild desire to run after them, a certitude that he could run them down. A black fox came toward him, carrying a ptarmigan in his mouth. The man shouted. It was a fearful cry, but the fox, leaping away in fright, did not drop the ptarmigan.

Late in the afternoon he followed a stream, milky with lime, which ran through sparse patches of rush grass. Grasping these rushes firmly near the root, he pulled up what resembled a young onion sprout no larger than a shingle nail. It was tender, and his teeth sank into it with a crunch that promised deliciously of food. But its fibres were tough. It was composed of stringy filaments saturated with water, like the berries, and devoid of nourishment. He threw off his pack and went into the rush grass on hands and knees, crunching and munching, like some bovine creature.

He was very weary and often wished to rest—to lie down and sleep; but he was continually driven on—not so much by his desire to gain the land of little sticks as by his hunger. He searched little ponds for frogs and dug up the earth with his nails for worms, though he knew in spite that neither frogs nor worms existed so far north.

He looked into every pool of water vainly, until, as the long twilight came on, he discovered a solitary fish, the size of a minnow, in such a pool. He plunged his arm in up to the shoulder, but it eluded him. He reached for it with both hands and stired up the milky mud at the bottom. In his excitement he fell in, wetting himself to the waist. Then the water was too muddy to admit of his seeing the fish, and he was compelled to wait until the sediment had settled.

The pursuit was renewed, till the water was again muddied. But he could not wait. He unstrapped the tin bucket and began to bail the pool. He bailed wildly at first, splash-

ing himself and flinging the water so short a distance that
it ran back into the pool. He worked more carefully, striving to be cool, though his heart was pounding against his
chest and his hands were trembling. At the end of half an
hour the pool was nearly dry. Not a cupful of water remained. And there was no fish. He found a hidden crevice
among the stones through which it had escaped to the
adjoining and larger pool—a pool which he could not
empty in a night and a day. Had he known of the crevice,
he could have closed it with a rock at the beginning and
the fish would have been his.

Thus he thought, and crumpled up and sank down upon
the wet earth. At first he cried softly to himself, then he
cried loudly to the pitiless desolation that ringed him
around, and for a long time after he was shaken by great
dry sobs.

He built a fire and warmed himself by drinking quarts
of hot water, and made camp on a rocky ledge in the same
fashion he had the night before. The last thing he did was
to see that his matches were dry and to wind his watch. The
blankets were wet and clammy. His ankle pulsed with pain.
But he knew only that he was hungry, and through his
restless sleep he dreamed of feasts and banquets and of food
served and spread in all imaginable ways.

He awoke chilled and sick. There was no sun. The grey
of earth and sky had become deeper, more profound. A raw
wind was blowing, and the first flurries of snow were
whitening the hilltops. The air about him thickened and
grew white while he made a fire and boiled more water. It
was wet snow, half rain, and the flakes were large and
soggy. At first they melted as soon as they came in contact
with the earth, but ever more fell, covering the ground,
putting out the fire, spoiling his supply of moss fuel.

This was a signal for him to strap on his pack and
stumble onward, he knew not where. He was not concerned
with the land of little sticks, nor with Bill and the cache
under the upturned canoe by the river Dease. He was
mastered by the verb 'to eat'. He was hunger-mad. He took
no heed of the course he pursued, so long as that course

led him through the swale bottoms. He felt his way through the wet snow to the watery muskeg berries, and went by feel as he pulled up the rush grass by the roots. But it was tasteless stuff and did not satisfy. He found a weed that tasted sour and he ate all he could find of it, which was not much, for it was a creeping growth, easily hidden under the several inches of snow.

He had no fire that night, nor hot water, and crawled under his blanket to sleep the broken hunger sleep. The snow turned into a cold rain. He awakened many times to feel it falling on his upturned face. Day came—a grey day and no sun. It had ceased raining. The keenness of his hunger had departed. Sensibility, as far as concerned the yearning for food, had been exhausted. There was a dull, heavy ache in his stomach, but it did not bother him so much. He was more rational, and once more he was chiefly interested in the land of little sticks and the cache by the river Dease.

He ripped the remnant of one of his blankets into strips and bound his bleeding feet. Also he recinched the injured ankle and prepared himself for a day of travel. When he came to his pack he paused long over the squat moose-hide sack, but in the end it went with him.

The snow had melted under the rain, and only the hilltops showed white. The sun came out, and he succeeded in locating the points of the compass, though he knew now that he was lost. Perhaps, in his previous days' wanderings, he had edged away too far to the left. He now bore off to the right to counteract the possible deviation from his true course.

Though the hunger pangs were no longer so exquisite, he realized that he was weak. He was compelled to pause for frequent rests, when he attacked the muskeg berries and rush-grass patches. His tongue felt dry and large, as though covered with a fine hairy growth, and it tasted bitter in his mouth. His heart gave him a great deal of trouble. When he had travelled a few minutes it would begin a remorseless thump, thump, thump, and then leap up and away in a painful flutter of beats that choked him and made him go faint and dizzy.

In the middle of the day he found two minnows in a large pool. It was impossible to bail it, but he was calmer now and managed to catch them in his tin bucket. They were no longer than his little finger, but he was not particularly hungry. The dull ache in his stomach had been growing duller and fainter. It seemed almost that his stomach was dozing. He ate the fish raw, masticating with painstaking care, for the eating was an act of pure reason. While he had no desire to eat, he knew that he must eat to live.

In the evening he caught three more minnows, eating two and saving the third for breakfast. The sun had dried stray shreds of moss, and he was able to warm himself with hot water. He had not covered more than ten miles that day; and the next day, travelling whenever his heart permitted him, he covered no more than five miles. But his stomach did not give him the slightest uneasiness. It had gone to sleep. He was in a strange country, too, and the caribou were growing more plentiful, also the wolves. Often their yelps drifted across the desolation, and once he saw three of them slinking away before his path.

Another night; and in the morning, being more rational, he untied the leather string that fastened the squat moosehide sack. From its open mouth poured a yellow stream of coarse gold dust and nuggets. He roughly divided the gold in halves, caching one half on a prominent ledge, wrapped in a piece of blanket, and returning the other half to the sack. He also began to use strips of the one remaining blanket for his feet. He still clung to his gun, for there were cartridges in that cache by the river Dease.

This was a day of fog, and this day hunger awoke in him again. He was very weak and was afflicted with a giddiness which at times blinded him. It was no uncommon thing now for him to stumble and fall; and stumbling once, he fell squarely into a ptarmigan nest. There were four newly hatched chicks, a day old—little specks of pulsating life no more than a mouthful; and he ate them ravenously, thrusting them alive into his mouth and crunching them like eggshells between his teeth. The mother ptarmigan beat about him with great outcry. He used his gun as a club with which to knock her over, but she dodged out of reach. He threw stones at her and with one chance shot broke a wing. Then she fluttered away, running, trailing the broken wing, with him in pursuit.

The little chicks had no more than whetted his appetite. He hopped and bobbed clumsily along on his injured ankle, throwing stones and screaming hoarsely at times; at other times hopping and bobbing silently along, picking himself up grimly and patiently when he fell, or rubbing his eyes with his hand when the giddiness threatened to overpower him.

The chase led him across swampy ground in the bottom of the valley, and he came upon footprints in the soggy moss. They were not his own—he could see that. They must be Bill's. But he could not stop, for the mother ptarmigan was running on. He would catch her first, then he would return and investigate.

He exhausted the mother ptarmigan; but he exhausted himself. She lay panting on her side. He lay panting on his side, a dozen feet away, unable to crawl to her. And as he recovered she recovered, fluttering out of reach as his hungry hand went out to her. The chase was resumed. Night settled down and she escaped. He stumbled from weakness and pitched head foremost on his face, cutting his cheek, his pack upon his back. He did not move for a long while; then he rolled over on his side, wound his watch, and lay there until morning.

Another day of fog. Half of his last blanket had gone into foot-wrappings. He failed to pick up Bill's trail. It did not matter. His hunger was driving him too compellingly —only—only he wondered if Bill, too, were lost. By mid-day the irk of his pack became too oppressive. Again he divided the gold, this time merely spilling half of it on the ground. In the afternoon he threw the rest of it away, there remaining to him only the half blanket, the tin bucket, and the rifle.

A hallucination began to trouble him. He felt confident that one cartridge remained to him. It was in the chamber

of the rifle and he had overlooked it. On the other hand,
he knew all the time that the chamber was empty. But the
hallucination persisted. He fought it off for hours, then
threw his rifle open and was confronted with emptiness.
The disappointment was as bitter as though he had really
expected to find the cartridge.

He plodded on for half an hour, when the hallucination
arose again. Again he fought it, and still it persisted, till
for very relief he opened his rifle to unconvince himself.
At times his mind wandered farther afield, and he plodded
on, a mere automaton, strange conceits and whimsicalities
gnawing at his brain like worms. But these excursions out
of the real were of brief duration, for ever the pangs of the
hunger bite called him back. He was jerked back abruptly
once from such an excursion by a sight that caused him
nearly to faint. He reeled and swayed, doddering like a
drunken man to keep from falling. Before him stood a
horse. A horse! He could not believe his eyes. A thick mist
was in them, intershot with sparkling points of light. He
rubbed his eyes savagely to clear his vision, and beheld
not a horse but a great brown bear. The animal was studying him with bellicose curiosity.

The man had brought his gun halfway to his shoulder
before he realized. He lowered it and drew his hunting
knife from its beaded sheath at his hip. Before him was
meat and life. He ran his thumb along the edge of his knife.
It was sharp. The point was sharp. He would fling himself
upon the bear and kill it. But his heart began its warning
thump, thump, thump. Then followed the wild upward leap
and tattoo of flutters, the pressing as of an iron band about
his forehead, the creeping of the dizziness into his brain.

His desperate courage was evicted by a great surge of
fear. In his weakness, what if the animal attacked him? He
drew himself up to his most imposing stature, gripping the
knife and staring hard at the bear. The bear advanced
clumsily a couple of steps, reared up, and gave vent to a
tentative growl. If the man ran, he would run after him;
but the man did not run. He was animated now with the
courage of fear. He, too, growled, savagely, terribly, voic-

ing the fear that is to life germane and that lies twisted about life's deepest roots.

The bear edged away to one side, growling menacingly, himself appalled by this mysterious creature that appeared upright and unafraid. But the man did not move. He stood like a statue till the danger was past, when he yielded to a fit of trembling and sank down into the wet moss.

He pulled himself together and went on, afraid now in a new way. It was not the fear that he should die passively from lack of food, but that he should be destroyed violently before starvation had exhausted the last particle of the endeavour in him that made toward surviving. There were the wolves. Back and forth across the desolation drifted their howls, weaving the very air into a fabric of menace that was so tangible that he found himself, arms in the air, pressing it back from him as it might be the walls of a wind-blown tent.

Now and again the wolves, in packs of two and three, crossed his path. But they sheered clear of him. They were not in sufficient numbers, and besides, they were hunting the caribou, which did not battle, while this strange creature that walked erect might scratch and bite.

In the late afternoon he came upon scattered bones where the wolves had made a kill. The debris had been a caribou calf an hour before, squawking and running and very much alive. He contemplated the bones, clean-picked and polished, pink with the cell life in them which had not yet died. Could it possibly be that he might be that ere the day was done! Such was life, eh? A vain and fleeting thing. It was only life that pained. There was no hurt in death. To die was to sleep. It meant cessation, rest. Then why was he not content to die?

But he did not moralize long. He was squatting in the moss, a bone in his mouth, sucking at the shreds of life that still dyed it faintly pink. The sweet meaty taste, thin and elusive, almost as a memory, maddened him. He closed his jaws on the bones and crunched. Sometimes it was the bone that broke sometimes his teeth. Then he crushed the bones between rocks, pounded them to a pulp, and swallowed them. He pounded his fingers, too, in his haste, and yet found a moment in which to feel surprise at the fact that his fingers did not hurt much when caught under the descending rock.

Came frightful days of snow and rain. He did not know when he made camp, when he broke camp. He travelled in the night as much as in the day. He rested wherever he fell, crawled on whenever the dying life in him flickered up and burned less dimly. He, as a man, no longer strove. It was the life in him, unwilling to die, that drove him on. He did not suffer. His nerves had become blunted, numb, while his mind was filled with weird visions and delicious dreams.

But ever he sucked and chewed on the crushed bones of the caribou calf, the least remnants of which he had gathered up and carried with him. He crossed no more hills or divides, but automatically followed a large stream which flowed through a wide and shallow valley. He did not see this stream nor this valley. He saw nothing save visions. Soul and body walked or crawled side by side, yet apart, so slender was the thread that bound them.

He awoke in his right mind, lying on his back on a rocky ledge. The sun was shining bright and warm. Afar off he heard the squawking of caribou calves. He was aware of vague memories of rain and wind and snow, but whether he had been beaten by the storm for two days or two weeks he did not know.

For some time he lay without movement, the genial sunshine pouring upon him and saturating his miserable body with its warmth. A fine day, he thought. Perhaps he could manage to locate himself. By a painful effort he rolled over on his side. Below him flowed a wide and sluggish river. Its unfamiliarity puzzled him. Slowly he followed it with his eyes, winding in wide sweeps among the bleak, bare hills, bleaker and barer and lower-lying than any hills he had yet encountered. Slowly, deliberately, without excitement or more than the most casual interest, he followed the course of the strange stream toward the sky line and saw it emptying into a bright and shining sea. He was still unexcited. Most unusual, he thought, a vision or a mirage

—more likely a vision, a trick of his disordered mind. He was confirmed in this by sight of a ship lying at anchor in the midst of the shining sea. He closed his eyes for a while, then opened them. Strange how the vision persisted! Yet not strange. He knew there were no seas or ships in the heart of the barren lands, just as he had known there was no cartridge in the empty rifle.

He heard a snuffle behind him—a half-choking gasp or cough. Very slowly, because of his exceeding weakness and stiffness, he rolled over on his other side. He could see nothing near at hand, but he waited patiently. Again came the snuffle and cough, and outlined between two jagged rocks not a score of feet away he made out the grey head of a wolf. The sharp ears were not pricked so sharply as he had seen them on other wolves; the eyes were bleared and bloodshot, the head seemed to droop limply and forlornly. The animal blinked continually in the sunshine. It seemed sick. As he looked it snuffed and coughed again.

This, at least, was real, he thought, and turned on the other side so that he might see the reality of the world which had been veiled from him before by the vision. But the sea still shone in the distance and the ship was plainly discernible. Was it reality after all? He closed his eyes for a long while and thought, and then it came to him. He had been making north by east, away from the Dease Divide and into the Coppermine Valley. This wide and sluggish river was the Coppermine. That shining sea was the Arctic Ocean. That ship was a whaler, strayed east, far east, from the mouth of the Mackenzie, and it was lying at anchor in Coronation Gulf. He remembered the Hudson's Bay Company chart he had seen long ago, and it was all clear and reasonable to him.

He sat up and turned his attention to immediate affairs. He had worn through the blanket wrappings, and his feet were shapeless lumps of raw meat. His last blanket was gone. Rifle and knife were both missing. He had lost his hat somewhere, with the bunch of matches in the band, but the matches against his chest were safe and dry inside the tobacco pouch and oil paper. He looked at his watch. It marked eleven o'clock and was still running. Evidently he had kept it wound.

He was calm and collected. Though extremely weak, he had no sensation of pain. He was not hungry. The thought of food was not even pleasant to him, and whatever he did was done by his reason alone. He ripped off his pants' legs to the knees and bound them about his feet. Somehow he had succeeded in retaining the tin bucket. He would have some hot water before he began what he foresaw was to be a terrible journey to the ship.

His movements were slow. He shook as with a palsy. When he started to collect dry moss he found he could not rise to his feet. He tried again and again, then contented himself with crawling about on hands and knees. Once he crawled near to the sick wolf. The animal dragged itself reluctantly out of his way, licking its chops with a tongue which seemed hardly to have the strength to curl. The man noticed that the tongue was not the customary healthful red. It was a yellowish brown and seemed coated with a rough and half-dry mucus.

After he had drunk a quart of hot water the man found he was able to stand, and even walk as well as a dying man might be supposed to walk. Every minute or so he was compelled to rest. His steps were feeble and uncertain, just as the wolf's that trailed him were feeble and uncertain; and that night, when the shining sea was blotted out by blackness, he knew he was nearer to it by no more than four miles.

Throughout the night he heard the cough of the sick wolf, and now and then the squawking of the caribou calves. There was life all around him, but it was strong life, very much alive and well, and he knew the sick wolf clung to the sick man's trail in the hope that the man would die first. In the morning, on opening his eyes, he beheld it regarding him with a wistful and hungry stare. It stood crouched, with tail between its legs, like a miserable and woebegone dog. It shivered in the chill morning wind and grinned dispiritedly when the man spoke to it in a voice that achieved no more than a hoarse whisper.

The sun rose brightly, and all morning the man tottered and fell toward the ship on the shining sea. The weather was perfect. It was the brief Indian summer of the high latitudes. It might last a week. Tomorrow or next day it might be gone.

In the afternoon the man came upon a trail. It was of another man, who did not walk, but who dragged himself on all fours. The man thought it might be Bill, but he thought in a dull, uninterested way. He had no curiosity. In fact sensation and emotion had left him. He was no longer susceptible to pain. Stomach and nerves had gone to sleep. Yet the life that was in him drove him on. He was very weary, but it refused to die. It was because it refused to die that he still ate muskeg berries and minnows, drank his hot water, and kept a wary eye on the sick wolf.

He followed the trail of the other man who dragged himself along, and soon came to the end of it—a few fresh-picked bones where the soggy moss was marked by the foot pads of many wolves. He saw a squat moose-hide sack, mate to his own, which had been torn by sharp teeth. He picked it up, though its weight was almost too much for his feeble fingers. Bill had carried it to the last. Ha-ha! He would have the laugh on Bill. He would survive and carry it to the ship in the shining sea. His mirth was hoarse and ghastly, like a raven's croak, and the sick wolf joined him, howling lugubriously. The man ceased suddenly. How could he have the laugh on Bill if that were Bill; if those bones, so pinky-white and clean, were Bill?

He turned away. Well, Bill had deserted him; but he would not take the gold, nor would he suck Bill's bones. Bill would have, though, had it been the other way round, he mused as he staggered on.

He came to a pool of water. Stooping over in quest of minnows, he jerked his head back as though he had been stung. He had caught sight of his reflected face. So horrible was it that sensibility awoke long enough to be shocked. There were three minnows in the pool, which was too large to drain; and after several ineffectual attempts to catch them in the tin bucket he forbore. He was afraid, because of his great weakness, that he might fall in and drown. It was for this reason that he did not trust himself to the river astride one of the many drift logs which lined its sandpits.

That day he decreased the distance between him and the ship by three miles; the next day by two—for he was crawling now as Bill had crawled; and the end of the fifth day found the ship still seven miles away and him unable to make even a mile a day. Still the Indian summer held on, and he continued to crawl and faint, turn and turn about; and ever the sick wolf coughed and wheezed at his heels. His knees had become raw meat like his feet, and though he padded them with the shirt from his back it was a red track he left behind him on the moss and stones. Once, glancing back, he saw the wolf licking hungrily his bleeding trail, and he saw sharply what his own end might be— unless—unless he could get the wolf. Then began as grim a tragedy of existence as was ever played—a sick man that crawled, a sick wolf that limped, two creatures dragging their dying carcasses across the desolation and hunting each other's lives.

Had it been a well wolf, it would not have mattered so much to the man; but the thought of going to feed the maw of that loathsome and all but dead thing was repugnant to him. He was finicky. His mind had begun to wander again and to be perplexed by hallucinations, while his lucid intervals grew rarer and shorter.

He was awakened once from a faint by a wheeze close in his ear. The wolf leaped lamely back, losing its footing and falling in its weakness. It was ludicrous, but he was not amused. Nor was he even afraid. He was too far gone for that. But his mind was for the moment clear, and he lay and considered. The ship was no more than four miles away. He could see it quite distinctly when he rubbed the mists out of his eyes, and he could see the white sail of a small boat cutting the water of the shining sea. But he could never crawl those four miles. He knew that, and was very calm in the knowledge. He knew that he could not crawl half a mile. And yet he wanted to live. It was unreasonable that he should die after all he had undergone.

Fate asked too much of him. And, dying, he declined to die. It was stark madness, perhaps, but in the very grip of death he defied death and refused to die.

He closed his eyes and composed himself with infinite precaution. He steeled himself to keep above the suffocating languor that lapped like a rising tide through all the wells of his being. It was very like a sea, this deadly languor that rose and rose and drowned his consciousness bit by bit. Sometimes he was all but submerged, swimming through oblivion with a faltering stroke; and again, by some strange alchemy of soul, he would find another shred of will and strike out more strongly.

Without movement he lay on his back, and he could hear, slowly drawing nearer and nearer, the wheezing intake and output of the sick wolf's breath. It drew closer, ever closer, through an infinitude of time, and he did not move. It was at his ear. The harsh dry tongue grated like sandpaper against his cheek. His hand shot out—or at least he willed them to shoot out. The fingers were curved like talons, but they closed on empty air. Swiftness and certitude require strength, and the man had not this strength.

The patience of the wolf was terrible. The man's patience was no less terrible. For half a day he lay motionless, fighting off unconsciousness and waiting for the thing that was to feed upon him and upon which he wished to feed. Sometimes the languid sea rose over him and he dreamed long dreams; but ever through it all, waking and dreaming, he waited for the wheezing breath and the harsh caress of the tongue.

He did not hear the breath, and he slipped slowly from some dream to the feel of the tongue along his hand. He waited. The fangs pressed softly; the pressure increased; the wolf was exerting its last strength in an effort to sink teeth in the food for which it had waited so long. But the man had waited long, and the lacerated hand closed on the jaw. Slowly, while the wolf struggled feebly and the hand clutched feebly, the other hand crept across to a grip. Five minutes later the whole weight of the man's body was on top of the wolf. The hands had not sufficient strength to choke the wolf, but the face of the man was pressed close to the throat of the wolf and the mouth of the man was full of hair. At the end of half an hour the man was aware of a warm trickle in his throat. It was not pleasant. It was like molten lead being forced into his stomach, and it was forced by his will alone. Later on the man rolled over on his back and slept.

There were some members of a scientific expedition on the whaleship *Bedford*. From the deck they remarked a strange object on the shore. It was moving down the beach toward the water. They were unable to classify it, and, being scientific men, they climbed into the whaleboat alongside and went ashore to see. And they saw something that was alive but which could hardly be called a man. It was blind, unconscious. It squirmed along the ground like some monstrous worm. Most of its efforts were ineffectual, but it was persistent, and it writhed and twisted and went ahead perhaps a score of feet an hour.

Three weeks afterward the man lay in a bunk on the whaleship *Bedford*, and with tears streaming down his wasted cheeks told who he was and what he had undergone. He also babbled incoherently of his mother, of sunny southern California, and a home among the orange groves and flowers.

The days were not many after that when he sat at table with the scientific men and ship's officers. He gloated over the spectacle of so much food, watching it anxiously as it went into the mouths of others. With the disappearance of each mouthful an expression of deep regret came into his eyes. He was quite sane, yet he hated those men at mealtime. He was haunted by a fear that the food would not last. He inquired of the cook, the cabin boy, the captain, concerning the food stores. They reassured him countless times; but he could not believe them, and pried cunningly about the lazaret to see with his own eyes.

II*

It was noticed that the man was getting fat. He grew stouter with each day. The scientific men shook their heads and theorized. They limited the man at his meals, but still his girth increased and he swelled prodigiously under his shirt.

The sailors grinned. They knew. And when the scientific men set a watch on the man they knew. They saw him slouch for'ard after breakfast, and, like a mendicant, with outstretched palm, accost a sailor. The sailor grinned and passed him a fragment of sea biscuit. He clutched it avariciously, looked at it as a miser looks at gold, and thrust it into his shirt bosom. Similar were the donations from other grinning sailors.

The scientific men were discreet. They let him alone. But they privily examined his bunk. It was lined with hardtack; the mattress was stuffed with hardtack; every nook and cranny was filled with hardtack. Yet he was sane. He was taking precautions against another possible famine—that was all. He would recover from it, the scientific men said; and he did, ere the *Bedford*'s anchor rumbled down in San Francisco Bay.

# THE UNEXPECTED

IT IS a simple matter to see the obvious, to do the expected. The tendency of the individual life is to be static rather than dynamic, and this tendency is made into a propulsion by civilization, where the obvious only is seen, and the unexpected rarely happens. When the unexpected does happen, however, and when it is of sufficiently grave import, the unfit perish. They do not see what is not obvious, are unable to do the unexpected, are incapable of adjusting their well-grooved lives to other and strange grooves. In short, when they come to the end of their own groove, they die.

On the other hand, there are those that make toward
survival, the fit individuals who escape from the rule of the
obvious and the expected and adjust their lives to no matter what strange grooves they may stray into, or into which
they may be forced. Such an individual was Edith Whittlesey. She was born in a rural district of England, where
life proceeds by rule-of-thumb and the unexpected is so
very unexpected that when it happens it is looked upon as
an immorality. She went into service early, and while yet a
young woman, by rule-of-thumb progression, she became
a lady's maid.

The effect of civilization is to impose human law upon
environment until it becomes machine-like in its regularity.
The objectionable is eliminated, the inevitable is foreseen.
One is not even made wet by the rain nor cold by the frost;
while death, instead of stalking about gruesome and acci-
dental, becomes a pre-arranged pageant, moving along a
well-oiled groove to the family vault, where the hinges are
kept from rusting and the dust from the air is swept continually away.

Such was the environment of Edith Whittlesey. Nothing
happened. It could scarcely be called a happening, when,
at the age of twenty-five, she accompanied her mistress on
a bit of travel to the United States. The groove merely
changed its direction. It was still the same groove and well
oiled. It was a groove that bridged the Atlantic with un-
eventfulness, so that the ship was not a ship in the midst
of the sea, but a capacious, many-corridored hotel that
moved swiftly and placidly, crushing the waves into sub-
mission with its colossal bulk until the sea was a millpond,
monotonous with quietude. And at the other side the
groove continued on over the land—a well-disposed, respectable groove that supplied hotels at every stopping-
place, and hotels on wheels between the stopping-places.

In Chicago, while her mistress saw one side of social life,
Edith Whittlesey saw another side; and when she left her
lady's service and became Edith Nelson, she betrayed, perhaps faintly, her ability to grapple with the unexpected and
to master it. Hans Nelson, immigrant, Swede by birth and

carpenter by occupation, had in him that Teutonic unrest that drives the race ever westward on its great adventure. He was a large-muscled, stolid sort of a man, in whom little imagination was coupled with immense initiative, and who possessed, withal, loyalty and affection as sturdy as his own strength.

'When I have worked hard and saved me some money, I will go to Colorado,' he had told Edith on the day after their wedding. A year later they were in Colorado, where Hans Nelson saw his first mining and caught the mining fever himself. His prospecting led him through the Dakotas, Idaho, and eastern Oregon, and on into the mountains of British Columbia. In camp and on trail, Edith Nelson was always with him, sharing his luck, his hardship, and his toil. The short step of the house-reared woman she exchanged for the long stride of the mountaineer. She learned to look upon danger clear-eyed and with understanding, losing for ever that panic fear which is bred of ignorance and which afflicts the city-reared, making them as silly as silly horses, so that they await fate in frozen horror instead of grappling with it, or stampede in blind self-destroying terror which clutters the way with their crushed carcasses.

Edith Nelson met the unexpected at every turn of the trail, and she trained her vision so that she saw in the landscape, not the obvious, but the concealed. She, who had never cooked in her life, learned to make bread without the mediation of hops, yeast, or baking-powder, and to bake bread, top and bottom, in a fry-pan before an open fire. And when the last cup of flour was gone and the last rind of bacon, she was able to rise to the occasion, and of moccasins and the softer-tanned bits of leather in the outfit to make a grub-stake substitute that somehow held a man's soul in his body and enabled him to stagger on. She learned to pack a horse as well as a man—a task to break the heart and the pride of any city-dweller—and she knew how to throw the hitch best suited for any particular kind of pack. Also she could build a fire of wet wood in a downpour of rain and not lose her temper. In short, in all its guises she mastered the unexpected. But the Great Unexpected was yet to come into her life and put its test upon her.

The gold-seeking tide was flooding northward into Alaska, and it was inevitable that Hans Nelson and his wife should be caught up by the stream and swept toward the Klondike. The fall of 1897 found them at Dyea, but without the money to carry an oufit across Chilcoot Pass and float it down to Dawson. So Hans Nelson worked at his trade that winter and helped rear the mushroom outfitting-town of Skaguay.

He was on the edge of things, and throughout the winter he heard all Alaska calling to him. Latuya Bay called loudest, so that summer of 1898 found him and his wife threading the mazes of the broken coastline in seventy-foot Siwash canoes. With them were Indians, also three other men. The Indians landed them and their supplies in a lonely bight of land a hundred miles or so beyond Latuya Bay, and returned to Skaguay; but the three other men remained, for they were members of the organized party. Each had put an equal share of capital into the outfitting, and the profits were to be divided equally. In that Edith Nelson undertook to cook for the outfit, a man's share was to be her portion.

First, spruce trees were cut down and a three-room cabin constructed. To keep this cabin was Edith Nelson's task. The task of the men was to search for gold, which they did; and to find gold, which they likewise did. It was not a startling find, merely a low-pay placer where long hours of severe toil earned each man between fifteen and twenty dollars a day. The brief Alaskan summer protracted itself beyond its usual length, and they took advantage of the opportunity, delaying their return to Skaguay to the last moment. And then it was too late. Arrangements had been made to accompany the several dozen local Indians on their fall trading trip down the coast. The Siwashes had waited on the white people until the eleventh hour, and then departed. There was no course left the party but to wait for chance transportation. In the meantime the claim was cleaned up and firewood stocked in.

The Indian summer had dreamed on and on, and then, suddenly, with the sharpness of bugles, winter came. It came in a single night, and the miners awoke to howling wind, driving snow, and freezing water. Storm followed storm, and between the storms there was the silence, broken only by the boom of the surf on the desolate shore, where the salt spray rimmed the beach with frozen white.

All went well in the cabin. Their gold-dust had weighed up something like eight thousand dollars, and they could not but be contented. The men made snowshoes, hunted fresh meat for the larder, and in the long evenings played endless games of whist and pedro. Now that the mining had ceased, Edith Nelson turned over the fire-building and the dish-washing to the men, while she darned their socks and mended their clothes.

There was no grumbling, no bickering, nor petty quarrelling in the little cabin, and they often congratulated one another on the general happiness of the party. Hans Nelson was stolid and easy-going, while Edith had long before won his unbounded admiration by her capacity for getting on with people. Harkey, a long, lank Texan, was unusually friendly for one with a saturnine disposition, and, as long as his theory that gold grew was not challenged, was quite companionable. The fourth member of the party, Michael Dennin, contributed his Irish wit to the gaiety of the cabin. He was a large, powerful man, prone to sudden rushes of anger over little things, and of unfailing good-humour under the stress and strain of big things. The fifth and last member, Dutchy, was the willing butt of the party. He even went out of his way to raise a laugh at his own expense in order to keep things cheerful. His deliberate aim in life seemed to be that of a maker of laughter. No serious quarrel had ever vexed the serenity of the party; and, now that each had sixteen hundred dollars to show for a short summer's work, there reigned the well-fed, contented spirit of prosperity.

And then the unexpected happened. They had just sat down to the breakfast table. Though it was already eight o'clock (late breakfasts had followed naturally upon cessation of the steady work at mining) a candle in the neck of a bottle lighted the meal. Edith and Hans sat at each end of the table. On one side, with their backs to the door, sat Harkey and Dutchy. The place on the other side was vacant. Dennin had not yet come in.

Hans Nelson looked at the empty chair, shook his head slowly, and, with a ponderous attempt at humour, said: 'Always is he first at the grub. It is very strange. Maybe he is sick.'

'Where is Michael?' Edith asked.

'Got up a little ahead of us and went outside,' Harkey answered.

Dutchy's face beamed mischievously. He pretended knowledge of Dennin's absence, and affected a mysterious air, while they clamoured for information. Edith, after a peep into the men's bunk-room, returned to the table. Hans looked at her, and she shook her head.

'He was never late at meal-time before,' she remarked.

'I cannot understand,' said Hans. 'Always had he the great appetite like the horse.'

'It is too bad,' Dutchy said with a sad shake of his head.

They were beginning to make merry over their comrade's absence.

'It is a great pity!' Dutchy volunteered.

'What?' they demanded in chorus.

'Poor Michael,' was the mournful reply.

'Well, what's wrong with Michael?' Harkey asked.

'He is not hungry no more,' wailed Dutchy. 'He has lost der appetite. He does not like der grub.'

'Not from the way he pitches into it up to his ears,' remarked Harkey.

'He does dot shust to be politeful to Mrs Nelson,' was Dutchy's quick retort. 'I know, I know, and it is too pad. Why is he not here? Pecause he haf gone out. Why haf he gone out? For der development of der appetite. How does he develop der appetite? He walks barefoots in der snow. Ach! don't I know. It is der way der rich people chases after der appetite when it is no more and is running away. Michael haf sixteen hundred dollars. He is rich peoples.

He haf no appetite. Derefore, pecause, he is chasing der appetite. Shust you open der door und you will see his barefoots in der snow. No, you will not see der appetite. Dot is shust his trouble. When he sees der appetite he will catch it und come to preakfast.'

They burst into loud laughter at Dutchy's nonsense. The sound had scarcely died away when the door opened and Dennin came in. All turned to look at him. He was carrying a shot-gun. Even as they looked, he lifted it to his shoulder and fired twice. At the first shot Dutchy sank upon the table overturning his mug of coffee, his yellow mop of hair dabbling in his plate of mush. His forehead, which pressed upon the near edge of the plate, tilted the plate up against his hair at an angle of forty-five degrees. Harkey was in the air, in his spring to his feet, at the second shot, and he pitched face down upon the floor, his 'My God!' gurgling and dying in his throat.

It was the unexpected. Hans and Edith were stunned. They sat at the table with bodies tense, their eyes fixed in a fascinated gaze upon the murderer. Dimly they saw him through the smoke of the powder, and in the silence nothing was to be heard save the drip-drip of Dutchy's spilled coffee on the floor. Dennin threw open the breech of the shot-gun, ejecting the empty shells. Holding the gun with one hand, he reached with the other into his pocket for fresh shells.

He was thrusting the shells into the gun when Edith Nelson was aroused to action. It was patent that he intended to kill Hans and her. For a space of possibly three seconds of time she had been dazed and paralysed by the horrible and inconceivable form in which the unexpected had made its appearance. Then she rose to it and grappled with it. She grappled with it concretely, making a cat-like leap for the murderer and gripping his neck-cloth with both her hands. The impact of her body sent him stumbling backward several steps. He tried to shake her loose and still retain his hold on the gun. This was awkward, for her firm-fleshed body had become a cat's. She threw herself to one side, and with her grip at his throat nearly jerked him to the floor. He straightened himself and whirled swiftly. Still faithful to her hold, her body followed the circle of his whirl so that her feet left the floor, and she swung through the air fastened to his throat by her hands. The whirl culminated in a collision with a chair, and the man and woman crashed to the floor in a wild struggling fall that extended itself across half the length of the room.

Hans Nelson was a half second behind his wife in rising to the unexpected. His nerve processes and mental processes were slower than hers. His was the grosser organism, and it had taken him half a second longer to perceive, and to determine, and proceed to do. She had already flown at Dennin and gripped his throat, when Hans sprang to his feet. But her coolness was not his. He was in a blind fury, a Berserker rage. At the instant he sprang from his chair his mouth opened and there issued forth a sound that was half roar, half bellow. The whirl of the two bodies had already started, and still roaring, or bellowing, he pursued this whirl down the room, overtaking it when it fell to the floor.

Hans hurled himself upon the prostrate man, striking madly with his fists. They were sledge-like blows, and when Edith felt Dennin's body relax she loosed her grip and rolled clear. She lay on the floor panting and watching. The fury of blows continued to rain down. Dennin did not seem to mind the blows. He did not even move. Then it dawned upon her that he was unconscious. She cried out to Hans to stop. She cried out again. But he paid no heed to her voice. She caught him by the arm, but her clinging to it merely impeded his effort.

It was no reasoned impulse that stirred her to do what she then did. Nor was it a sense of pity, nor obedience to the 'Thou shalt not' of religion. Rather was it some sense of law, an ethic of her race and early environment, that compelled her to interpose her body between her husband and the helpless murderer. It was not until Hans knew he was striking his wife that he ceased. He allowed himself to be shoved away by her in much the same way that a ferocious but obedient dog allows itself to be shoved away by its master. The analogy even went farther. Deep in his throat, in an animal-like way, Hans's rage still rumbled, and several times he made as though to spring back upon his prey and was only prevented by the woman's swiftly interposed body.

Back and farther back Edith shoved her husband. She had never seen him in such a condition, and she was more frightened of him than she had been of Dennin in the thick of the struggle. She could not believe that this raging beast was her Hans, and with a shock she became suddenly aware of a shrinking, instinctive fear that he might snap her hand in his teeth like any wild animal. For some seconds, unwilling to hurt her, yet dogged in his desire to return to the attack, Hans dodged back and forth. But she resolutely dodged him, until the first glimmerings of reason returned and he gave over.

Both crawled to their feet. Hans staggered back against the wall, where he leaned, his face working, in his throat the deep and continuous rumble that died away with the seconds and at last ceased. The time for the reaction had come. Edith stood in the middle of the floor, wringing her hands, panting and gasping, her whole body trembling violently.

Hans looked at nothing, but Edith's eyes wandered wildly from detail to detail of what had taken place. Dennin lay without movement. The overturned chair, hurled onward in the mad whirl, lay near him. Partly under him lay the shot-gun, still broken open at the breech. Spilling out of his right hand were the two cartridges which he had failed to put into the gun and which he had clutched until consciousness left him. Harkey lay on the floor, face downward, where he had fallen; while Dutchy rested forward on the table, his yellow mop of hair buried in his mush-plate, the plate itself still tilted at an angle of forty-five degrees. This tilted plate fascinated her. Why did it not fall down? It was ridiculous. It was not in the nature of things for a mush-plate to up-end itself on the table, even if a man or so had been killed.

She glanced back at Dennin, but her eyes returned to the tilted plate. It was so ridiculous! She felt an hysterical impulse to laugh. Then she noticed the silence, and forgot the plate in a desire for something to happen. The monotonous drip of the coffee from the table to the floor merely emphasized the silence. Why did not Hans do something? say something? She looked at him and was about to speak, when she discovered that her tongue refused its wonted duty. There was a peculiar ache in her throat, and her mouth was dry and furry. She could only look at Hans, who, in turn, looked at her.

Suddenly the silence was broken by a sharp, metallic clang. She screamed, jerking her eyes back to the table. The plate had fallen down. Hans sighed as though awakening from sleep. The clang of the plate had aroused them to life in a new world. The cabin epitomized the new world in which they must thenceforth live and move. The old cabin was gone for ever. The horizon of life was totally new and unfamiliar. The unexpected had swept its wizardry over the face of things, changing the perspective, juggling values, and shuffling the real and the unreal into perplexing confusion.

'My God, Hans!' was Edith's first speech.

He did not answer, but stared at her with horror. Slowly his eyes wandered over the room, for the first time taking in its details. Then he put up his cap and started for the door.

'Where are you going?' Edith demanded, in an agony of apprehension.

His hand was on the door-knob, and he half turned as he answered, 'To dig some graves.'

'Don't leave me, Hans, with——' her eyes swept the room—'with this.'

'The graves must be dug some time,' he said.

'But you do not know how many,' she objected desperately. She noted his indecision, and added, 'Besides, I'll go with you and help.'

Hans stepped back to the table and mechanically snuffed the candle. Then between them they made the examination. Both Harkey and Dutchy were dead—frightfully dead, because of the close range of the shot-gun. Hans refused to go near Dennin, and Edith was forced to conduct this portion of the investigation by herself.

'He isn't dead,' she called to Hans.

He walked over and looked down at the murderer.

'What did you say?' Edith demanded, having caught the rumble of inarticulate speech in her husband's throat.

'I said it was a damn shame that he isn't dead,' came the reply.

Edith was bending over the body.

'Leave him alone,' Hans commanded harshly, in a strange voice.

She looked at him in sudden alarm. He had picked up the shot-gun dropped by Dennin and was thrusting in the shells.

'What are you going to do?' she cried, rising swiftly from her bending position.

Hans did not answer, but she saw the shot-gun going to his shoulder. She grasped the muzzle with her hand and threw it up.

'Leave me alone!' he cried hoarsely.

He tried to jerk the weapon away from her, but she came closer and clung to him.

'Hans! Hans! Wake up!' she cried. 'Don't be crazy!'

'He killed Dutchy and Harkey!' was her husband's reply; 'and I am going to kill him.'

'But that is wrong,' she objected. 'There is the law.'

He sneered his incredulity of the law's potency in such a region, but he merely iterated, dispassionately, doggedly, 'He killed Dutchy and Harkey.'

Long she argued it with him, but the argument was one-sided, for he contented himself with repeating again and again. 'He killed Dutchy and Harkey.' But she could not escape from her childhood training, nor from the blood that was in her. The heritage of law was hers, and right conduct, to her, was the fulfilment of the law. She could see no other righteous course to pursue. Hans's taking the law in his own hands was no more justifiable than Dennin's deed.

Two wrongs did not make a right, she contended, and there was only one way to punish Dennin, and that was the legal way arranged by society. At last Hans gave in to her.

'All right,' he said. 'Have it your own way. And to-morrow or next day look to see him kill you and me.'

She shook her head and held out her hand for the shotgun. He started to hand it to her, then hesitated.

'Better let me shoot him,' he pleaded.

Again she shook her head, and again he started to pass her the gun, when the door opened, and an Indian, without knocking, came in. A blast of wind and flurry of snow came in with him. They turned and faced him, Hans still holding the shot-gun. The intruder took in the scene without a quiver. His eyes embraced the dead and wounded in a sweeping glance. No surprise showed in his face, not even curiosity. Harkey lay at his feet, but he took no notice of him. So far as he was concerned, Harkey's body did not exist.

'Much wind,' the Indian remarked by way of salutation. 'All well? Very well?'

Hans, still grasping the gun, felt sure that the Indian attributed to him the mangled corpses. He glanced appealingly at his wife.

'Good morning, Negook,' she said, her voice betraying her effort. 'No, not very well. Much trouble.'

'Good-bye, I go now, much hurry,' the Indian said and without semblance of haste, with great deliberation stepping clear of a red pool on the floor, he opened the door and went out.

The man and woman looked at each other.

'He thinks we did it,' Hans gasped, 'that I did it.'

Edith was silent for a space. Then she said, briefly, in a businesslike way—

'Never mind what he thinks. That will come after. At present we have two graves to dig. But first of all, we've got to tie up Dennin so he can't escape.'

Hans refused to touch Dennin, but Edith lashed him securely, hand and foot. Then she and Hans went out into the snow. The ground was frozen. It was impervious to a blow of the pick. They first gathered wood, then scraped the snow away and on the frozen surface built a fire. When the fire had burned for an hour, several inches of dirt had thawed. This they shovelled out, and then built a fresh fire. Their descent into the earth progressed at the rate of two or three inches an hour.

It was hard and bitter work. The flurrying snow did not permit the fire to burn any too well, while the wind cut through their clothes and chilled their bodies. They held but little conversation. The wind interfered with speech. Beyond wondering at what could have been Dennin's motive, they remained silent, oppressed by the horror of the tragedy. At one o'clock, looking toward the cabin, Hans announced that he was hungry.

'No, not now, Hans,' Edith answered. 'I couldn't go back alone into that cabin the way it is, and cook a meal.'

At two o'clock Hans volunteered to go with her; but she held him to his work, and four o'clock found the two graves completed. They were shallow, not more than two feet deep, but they would serve the purpose. Night had fallen. Hans got the sled, and the two dead men were dragged through the darkness and storm to their frozen sepulchre. The funeral procession was anything but a pageant. The sled sank deep into the drifted snow and pulled hard. The man and the woman had eaten nothing since the previous day, and were weak from hunger and exhaustion. They had not the strength to resist the wind, and at times its buffets hurled them off their feet. On several occasions the sled was overturned, and they were compelled to reload it with its sombre freight. The last hundred feet to the graves was up a steep slope, and this they took on all fours, like sled-dogs, making legs of their arms and thrusting their hands into the snow. Even so, they were twice dragged backward by the weight of the sled, and slid and fell down the hill, the living and the dead, the haul-ropes and the sled, in ghastly entanglement.

'To-morrow I will put up head-boards with their names,' Hans said, when the graves were filled in.

Edith was sobbing. A few broken sentences had been all

she was capable of in the way of a funeral service, and now her husband was compelled to half carry her back to the cabin.

Dennin was conscious. He had rolled over and over on the floor in vain efforts to free himself. He watched Hans and Edith with glittering eyes, but made no attempt to speak. Hans still refused to touch the murderer, and sullenly watched Edith drag him across the floor to the men's bunk-room. But try as she would, she could not lift him from the floor into his bunk.

'Better let me shoot him, and we'll have no more trouble,' Hans said in final appeal.

Edith shook her head and bent again to her task. To her surprise the body rose easily, and she knew Hans had relented and was helping her. Then came the cleansing of the kitchen. But the floor still shrieked the tragedy, until Hans planed the surface of the stained wood away and with the shavings made a fire in the stove.

The days came and went. There was much of darkness and silence, broken only by the storms and the thunder on the beach of the freezing surf. Hans was obedient to Edith's slightest order. All his splendid initiative had vanished. She had elected to deal with Dennin in her way, and so he left the whole matter in her hands.

The murderer was a constant menace. At all times there was the chance that he might free himself from his bonds, and they were compelled to guard him day and night. The man or the woman sat always beside him, holding the loaded shot-gun. At first, Edith tried eight-hour watches, but the continuous strain was too great, and afterwards she and Hans relieved each other every four hours. As they had to sleep, and as the watches extended through the night, their whole waking time was expended in guarding Dennin. They had barely time left over for the preparation of meals and the getting of firewood.

Since Negook's inopportune visit, the Indians had avoided the cabin. Edith sent Hans to their cabins to get them to take Dennin down the coast in a canoe to the nearest white settlement or trading post, but the errand was fruitless. Then Edith went herself and interviewed Negook. He was head man of the little village, keenly aware of his responsibility, and he elucidated his policy thoroughly in few words.

'It is white man's trouble,' he said, 'not Siwash trouble. My people help you, then will it be Siwash trouble, too. When white man's trouble and Siwash trouble come together and make a trouble, it is a great trouble, beyond understanding and without end. Trouble no good. My people do no wrong. What for they help you and have trouble?'

So Edith Nelson went back to the terrible cabin with its endless alternating four-hour watches. Sometimes, when it was her turn and she sat by the prisoner, the loaded shotgun in her lap, her eyes would close and she would doze. Always she aroused with a start, snatching up the gun and swiftly looking at him. These were distinct nervous shocks and their effect was not good on her. Such was her fear of the man that, even though she were wide awake, if he moved under the bed-clothes, she could not repress the start and the quick reach for the gun.

She was preparing herself for a nervous breakdown, and she knew it. First came a fluttering of the eye-balls, so that she was compelled to close her eyes for relief. A little later the eyelids were afflicted by a nervous twitching that she could not control. To add to the strain, she could not forget the tragedy. She remained as close to the horror as on the first morning when the unexpected stalked into the cabin and took possession. In her daily ministrations upon the prisoner she was forced to grit her teeth and steel herself, body and spirit.

Hans was affected differently. He became obsessed by the idea that it was his duty to kill Dennin; and whenever he waited upon the bound man or watched by him, Edith was troubled by the fear that Hans would add another red entry to the cabin's record. Always he cursed Dennin savagely and handled him roughly. Hans tried to conceal his homicidal mania, and he would say to his wife, 'By and by you will want me to kill him, and then I will not kill him. It would make me sick.' But more than once, stealing into the room when it was her watch off, she would catch the two men glaring ferociously at each other, wild animals the pair of them, in Hans's face the lust to kill, in Dennin's the fierceness and savagery of the cornered rat. 'Hans!' she would cry, 'wake up!' and he would come to a recollection of himself, startled and shamefaced and unrepentant.

So Hans became another factor in the problem the unexpected had given Edith Nelson to solve. At first it had been merely a question of right conduct in dealing with Dennin, and right conduct, as she conceived it, lay in keeping him a prisoner until he could be turned over for trial before a proper tribunal. But now entered Hans, and she saw that his sanity and his salvation were involved. Nor was she long in discovering that her own strength and endurance had become part of the problem. She was breaking down under the strain. Her left arm had developed involuntary jerkings and twitchings. She spilled her food from her spoon, and could place no reliance in her afflicted arms. She judged it to be a form of St Vitus' dance, and she feared the extent to which its ravages might go. What if she broke down? And the vision she had of the possible future, when the cabin might contain only Dennin and Hans, was an added horror.

After the third day, Dennin had begun to talk. His first question had been, 'What are you going to do with me?' And this question he repeated daily and many times a day. And always Edith replied that he would assuredly be dealt with according to law. In turn, she put a daily question to him: 'Why did you do it?' To this he never replied. Also, he received the question with outbursts of anger, raging and straining at the rawhide that bound him and threatening her with what he would do when he got loose, which he said he was sure to do sooner or later. At such times she cocked both triggers of the gun, prepared to meet him with leaden death if he should burst loose, herself trembling and palpitating and dizzy from the tension and shock.

But in time Dennin grew more tractable. It seemed to her that he was growing weary of his unchanging recumbent position. He began to beg and plead to be released. He made wild promises. He would do them no harm. He would himself go down the coast and give himself up to the officers of the law. He would give them his share of the gold. He would go away into the heart of the wilderness, and never again appear in civilization. He would take his own life if she would only free him. His pleadings usually culminated in involuntary raving, until it seemed to her that he was passing into a fit; but always she shook her head and denied him the freedom for which he worked himself into a passion.

But the weeks went by, and he continued to grow more tractable. And through it all the weariness was asserting itself more and more. 'I am so tired, so tired,' he would murmur, rolling his head back and forth on the pillow like a peevish child. At a little later period he began to make impassioned pleas for death, to beg her to kill him, to beg Hans to put him out of his misery so that he might at least rest comfortably.

The situation was fast becoming impossible. Edith's nervousness was increasing, and she knew her breakdown might come any time. She could not even get her proper rest, for she was haunted by the fear that Hans would yield to his mania and kill Dennin while she slept. Though January had already come, months would have to elapse before any trading schooner was even likely to put into the bay. Also, they had not expected to winter in the cabin, and the food was running low; nor could Hans add to the supply by hunting. They were chained to the cabin by the necessity of guarding their prisoner.

Something must be done, and she knew it. She forced herself to go back into a reconsideration of the problem. She could not shake off the legacy of her race, the law that was of her blood and that had been trained into her. She knew that whatever she did she must do according to the law, and in the long hours of watching, the shot-gun on her knees, the murderer restless beside her, and the storms thundering without, she made original sociological researches and worked out for herself the evolution of the law. It came to her that the law was nothing more than the judgment and the will of any group of people. It mattered not how large was the group of people. There were little groups, she reasoned, like Switzerland, and there were big groups like the United States. Also, she reasoned, it did not matter how small was the group of people. There might be only ten thousand people in a country, yet their collective judgment and will would be the law of that country. Why, then, could not one thousand people constitute such a group? she asked herself. And if one thousand, why not one hundred? Why not fifty? Why not five? Why not— two?

She was frightened at her own conclusions, and she talked it over with Hans. At first he could not comprehend, and then, when he did, he added convincing evidence. He spoke of miners' meetings, where all the men of the locality came together and made the law and executed the law. There might be only ten or fifteen men altogether, he said, but the will of the majority became the law for the whole ten or fifteen, and whoever violated that will was punished.

Edith saw her way clear at last. Dennin must hang. Hans agreed with her. Between them they constituted the majority of this particular group. It was the group-will that Dennin should be hanged. In the execution of this will Edith strove earnestly to observe the customary forms, but the group was so small that Hans and she had to serve as witnesses, as jury, and as judges—also as executioners. She formally charged Michael Dennin with the murder of Dutchy and Harkey, and the prisoner lay in his bunk and listened to the testimony, first of Hans, and then of Edith. He refused to plead guilty or not guilty, and remained silent when she asked him if he had anything to say in his own defence. She and Hans, without leaving their seats, brought in the jury's verdict of guilty. Then, as judge, she imposed the sentence. Her voice shook, her eyelids twitched, her left arm jerked, but she carried it out.

'Michael Dennin, in three days' time you are to be hanged by the neck until you are dead.'

Such was the sentence. The man breathed an unconscious sigh of relief, then laughed defiantly, and said, 'Thin' I'm thinkin' the damn bunk won't be achin' me back anny more, an' that's a consolation.'

With the passing of the sentence a feeling of relief seemed to communicate itself to all of them. Especially was it noticeable in Dennin. All sullenness and defiance disappeared, and he talked sociably with his captors, and even with flashes of his old-time wit. Also, he found great satisfaction in Edith's reading to him from the Bible. She read from the New Testament, and he took keen interest in the prodigal son and the thief on the cross.

On the day preceding that set for the execution, when Edith asked her usual question, 'Why did you do it?' Dennin answered, ' 'Tis very simple. I was thinkin'——'

But she hushed him abruptly, asked him to wait, and hurried to Hans's bedside. It was his watch off, and he came out of his sleep, rubbing his eyes and grumbling.

'Go,' she told him, 'and bring up Negook and one other Indian. Michael's going to confess. Make them come. Take the rifle along and bring them up at the point of it if you have to.'

Half an hour later Negook and his uncle, Hadikwan, were ushered into the death-chamber. They came unwillingly, Hans with his rifle herding them along.

'Negook,' Edith said, 'there is to be no trouble for you and your people. Only is it for you to sit and do nothing but listen and understand.'

Thus did Michael Dennin, under sentence of death, make public confession of his crime. As he talked, Edith wrote his story down, while the Indians listened, and Hans guarded the door for fear the witnesses might bolt.

He had not been home to the old country for fifteen years, Dennin explained, and it had always been his intention to return with plenty of money and make his old mother comfortable for the rest of her days.

'An' how was I to be doin' it on sixteen hundred?' he demanded. 'What I was after wantin' was all the goold, the whole eight thousan'. Thin I cud go back in style. What ud be aisier, thinks I to myself, than to kill all iv yez, report

it at Skaguay for an Indian killin', an' thin pull out for
Ireland? An' so I started in to kill all iv yez, but, as Harkey
was fond of sayin', I cut out too large a chunk an' fell down
on the swallowin' iv it. An' that's me confession. I did me
duty to the devil, an' now, God willin', I'll do me duty to
God.'

'Negook and Hadikwan, you have heard the white man's
words,' Edith said to the Indians. 'His words are here on
this paper, and it is for you to make a sign, thus, on the
paper, so that white men to come after will know that you
have heard.'

The two Siwashes put crosses opposite their signatures,
received a summons to appear on the morrow with all their
tribe for a further witnessing of things, and were allowed
to go.

Dennin's hands were released long enough for him to
sign the document. Then a silence fell in the room. Hans
was restless, and Edith felt uncomfortable. Dennin lay on
his back, staring straight up at the moss-chinked roof.

'An' now I'll do me duty to God,' he murmured. He
turned his head toward Edith. 'Read to me,' he said, 'from
the book', then added, with a glint of playfulness, 'mayhap
'twill help me to forget the bunk.'

The day of the execution broke clear and cold. The thermometer was down to twenty-five below zero, and a chill
wind was blowing which drove the frost through clothes
and flesh to the bones. For the first time in many weeks
Dennin stood upon his feet. His muscles had remained in-
active so long, and he was so out of practice in maintaining
an erect position, that he could scarcely stand. He reeled
back and forth, staggered, and clutched hold of Edith with
his bound hands for support.

'Sure, an' it's dizzy I am,' he laughed weakly.

A moment later he said, 'An' it's glad I am that it's over
with. That damn bunk would iv been the death iv me, I
know.'

When Edith put his fur cap on his head and proceeded
to pull the flaps down over his ears, he laughed and said—

'What are you doin' that for?'

'It's freezing cold outside,' she answered.

'An' in tin minutes' time what'll matter a frozen ear or so to poor Michael Dennin?' he asked.

She had nerved herself for the last culminating ordeal, and his remark was like a blow to her self-possession. So far, everything had seemed phantom-like, as in a dream, but the brutal truth of what he had said shocked her eyes wide open to the reality of what was taking place. Nor was her distress unnoticed by the Irishman.

'I'm sorry to be troublin' you with me foolish spache,' he said regretfully. 'I mint nothin' by it. 'Tis a great day for Michael Dennin, an' he's as gay as a lark.'

He broke out in a merry whistle, which quickly became lugubrious and ceased.

'I'm wishin' there was a priest,' he said wistfully, then added swiftly, 'But Michael Dennin's too old a campaigner to miss the luxuries when he hits the trail.'

He was so very weak and unused to walking that when the door opened and he passed outside, the wind nearly carried him off his feet. Edith and Hans walked on either side of him and supported him, the while he cracked jokes and tried to keep them cheerful, breaking off, once, long enough to arrange the forwarding of his share of the gold to his mother in Ireland.

They climbed a slight hill and came out into an open space among the trees. Here, circled solemnly about a barrel that stood on end in the snow, were Negook and Hadikwan, and all the Siwashes down to the babies and the dogs, come to see the way of the white man's law. Near by was an open grave which Hans had burned into the frozen earth.

Dennin cast a practical eye over the preparations, noting the grave, the barrel, the thickness of the rope, and the diameter of the limb over which the rope was passed.

'Sure, an' I couldn't iv done better myself, Hans, if it'd been for you.'

He laughed loudly at his own sally, but Hans's face was frozen into a sullen ghastliness that nothing less than a trump of doom could have broken. Also, Hans was feeling very sick. He had not realized the enormousness of the task of putting a fellow-man out of the world. Edith, on the other hand, had realized; but the realization did not make the task any easier. She was filled with doubt as to whether she could hold herself together long enough to finish it. She felt incessant impulses to scream, to shriek, to collapse into the snow, to put her hands over her eyes and turn and run blindly away, into the forest, anywhere, away. It was only by a supreme effort of soul that she was able to keep upright and go on and do what she had to do. And in the midst of it all she was grateful to Dennin for the way he helped her.

'Lind me a hand," he said to Hans, with whose assistance he managed to mount the barrel.

He bent over so that Edith could adjust the rope about his neck. Then he stood upright while Hans drew the rope taught across the overhead branch.

'Michael Dennin, have you anything to say?' Edith asked in a clear voice that shook in spite of her.

Dennin shuffled his feet on the barrel, looked down bashfully like a man making his maiden speech, and cleared his throat.

'I'm glad it's over with,' he said. 'You've treated me like a Christian, an' I'm thankin' you hearty for your kindness.'

'Then may God receive you, a repentant sinner,' she said.

'Ay,' he answered, his deep voice as a response to her thin one, 'may God receive me, a repintant sinner.'

'Good-bye, Michael,' she cried, and her voice sounded desperate.

She threw her weight against the barrel, but it did not overturn.

'Hans! Quick! Help me!' she cried faintly.

She could feel her last strength going, and the barrel resisted her. Hans hurried to her, and the barrel went out from under Michael Dennin.

She turned her back, thrusting her fingers into her ears. Then she began to laugh, harshly, sharply, metallically; and Hans was shocked as he had not been shocked through the whole tragedy. Edith Nelson's breakdown had come. Even in her hysteria she knew it, and she was glad that she had been able to hold up under the strain until everything had been accomplished. She reeled towards Hans.

'Take me to the cabin, Hans,' she managed to articulate.

'And let me rest,' she added. 'Just let me rest, and rest, and rest.'

With Hans's arms around her, supporting her weight and directing her helpless steps, she went off across the snow. But the Indians remained solemnly to watch the working of the white man's law that compelled a man to dance upon the air.